John Shirley was bo
novels in the past de
He has also played
Nation. He lives in Po

By the same author

Transmaniacon
Dracula in Love
Three-Ring Psychus
City Come A-Walkin'
Cellars
The Brigade
A Song Called Youth
A Splendid Chaos
Eclipse
Eclipse Penumbra
Heatseeker

JOHN SHIRLEY

In Darkness Waiting

GRAFTON BOOKS
A Division of the Collins Publishing Group

LONDON GLASGOW
TORONTO SYDNEY AUCKLAND

Grafton Books
A Division of the Collins Publishing Group
8 Grafton Street, London W1X 3LA

A Grafton UK Paperback Original 1991

Copyright © John Shirley 1988

ISBN 0-586-21010-5

Printed and bound in Great Britain by
Collins, Glasgow

Set in Times

All rights reserved. No part of this publication may
be reproduced, stored in a retrieval system, or
transmitted, in any form, or by any means, electronic,
mechanical, photocopying, recording or otherwise,
without the prior permission of the publishers.

This book is sold subject to the condition that it
shall not, by way of trade or otherwise, be lent,
re-sold, hired out or otherwise circulated
without the publisher's prior consent in any
form of binding or cover other than that in
which it is published and without a similar
condition including this condition being imposed
on the subsequent purchaser.

For Mike Shirley
who perhaps remembers
the Odd-shaped Rocks

1

It was a broken-down, sunbaked little town, but Perry was glad to see it. They'd changed buses twice, with layovers in dreary, steamy bus stations catered by Post House. Aunt June called the food tasteless. Perry only wished it were.

They'd flown from San Diego to Portland, then ridden the bus from the moist green of western Oregon to the arid volcanic waste of central Oregon, twelve hours telescoped out into one seamless continuum of jouncing metal, grimy vinyl seats, bellyaching children, yowling babies, all of it steeped in the reek of the chemical toilet.

Grey Line for sure, Perry thought.

Aunt June bore it stoically, but about the ninth hour she'd muttered, 'If Jasper were civilized, we could have taken a train in.'

If you weren't so cheap, old girl, Perry thought, we could have rented a car.

Now, they stood at the bus stop in the headaching heat of the desert plateau's late afternoon, looking at the irregular row of shop fronts: *Fishing Tackle and Bait*; Western souvenir shops, most of them gone out of business and gutted, padlocked; a couple of kids playing sun-faded video-arcade games just inside the open door of Kerney's Roadside Market. And a service station across the street, with brand-new digital pumps; the old ones, cylindrical with rust-streaked numbers in their gauge windows, uprooted and leaning against the chain-link fence out back. But beside the station was a red cooler . . .

Perry gazed longingly at the old red Coca-Cola cooler. The oval, chrome-segmented station – with its peeling, time-drabbed 1950s notion of futurism – was antique; so was the Coke cooler. The cooler would be filled with ice water and dewy bottles of toy-colored strawberry Nehi and Coca-Cola, like when he was a kid; you just reached in and fished out a bottle and paid the man when you got around to it . . .

Perry put down the baggage, crossed the street, and ran to the cooler. He opened it, and his heart sank.

It was dusty, bone-dry, cobwebby, like Jasper; empty except for a couple of old bottle caps. They didn't trust you anymore, anywhere. He went to the station's office and bought two cans of lime-flavored soda from the vending machine – he had to put in his seventy-five cents first – and returned to Aunt June, who was waiting with amused impatience on the sidewalk.

'You know I don't take anything with sugar in it,' she said, turning a shoulder to the soft drink as if recoiling from it. 'White death.'

'You kidding? Hot as it is?'

'Maybe this once.' She snatched the drink from his hand and quickly drank it off. Perry drank his, and then they set out again, Perry carrying most of the luggage, sweating in the hot July afternoon.

Okay, Perry thought, so the cooler's junk. Garvey's Saloon, at least, across the street, looked like an old-fashioned saloon – down to the batwing doors and the hitching post out front. Western-boomtown-style false fronts and rustic lettering decorated every building on Main Street, and a tattered ANNUAL JASPER RODEO & ROUNDUP JULY 4–7 banner sagged over the street.

'Oh, too bad,' Perry said, 'the rodeo was last weekend.'

'Uh-huh . . .' Aunt June was squinting at a sheet of notebook paper. She took her blue-tint prescription sunglasses from her purse, put them on, and read, 'Five Second Street.'

'This is Fourth,' Perry said. 'Come on.'

'I thought she'd meet us,' she said. 'Maybe more problems with Tetty.'

Perry glanced at Aunt June, wondering when she was going to finally give him the whole story on Tetty. All he knew was what he'd overheard, when Aunt June had spoke to Sandra on the phone, back in San Diego. *'What did you say, dear, it's a crackly connection – she's what? Worse? . . . Yes, I'll come. I don't mind. I'm still on sabbatical, I was getting bored, thinking of coming to Oregon anyway.'* And she'd gone on with more polite, kindly untruths: *'Oh no, it's not an inconvenience. No, you keep your money, dear, I'm happy to come if you think I can help. And I haven't seen you in so long, it's really unforgivable . . . Anyway, I was thinking about writing a paper on Tetty's condition for the APA convention – what? No, of course I wouldn't mention her by name – did I tell you I had an assistant? My nephew, Perry. He's my assistant for the summer. The college pays his salary. Well, no, he's not a psych student, he's a music-theory student, but he needs the – oh, you're quite right, I'm running up your bill. July ninth, all right? Okay if I bring Perry?'*

They turned right on to the blessedly shadier Second Street. Pines lined the street on both sides. Perry and Aunt June crunched along the gravel road to Sandra Cummings's house, number 5, just at the corner of Pine – oh, naturally, Pine – and Second. The house was a mottled gray white; once it had been painted white, with thick, cheap enamel, and the hot sun of the plateau had cracked the paint, the dry winds had clawed at it, and now it was peeling away, flaking so badly the house looked like a fat gray hen, molting. There was a beaklike gable over the little front porch and the windows of the room at the front of the second floor – Tetty's room – were the hen's mindless eyes.

Gratefully, Perry toted the baggage to the shade of the front porch. Aunt June rang the bell. They waited a surprisingly long time; Perry could hear people moving about in the house. What were they doing? Aunt June rang the bell a second time; it was the loud, abrasive sort of bell that sounded like a miniature burglar alarm. Sandra couldn't help but hear it. Was she straightening the house at the last moment? But she'd known Aunt June and Perry were coming . . .

Perry shrugged and glanced at his aunt. She insisted he call her simply June, but he could think of her only as his aunt. She was forty-eight to his twenty, tall and long-necked, hollow-cheeked, a little stooped; her brown hair, clipped short and parted on the side, was slivered with silver. She wore her awfulest green doubleknit polyester pants suit, and in that moment Perry regarded her with undiluted affection.

The door opened, and Sandra stood there, blurred by the screen between them, her large, downturned eyes moist, her lipstick a sloppy scrawl around her thin lips.

'Hullo, June. And this must be Perry. Well, glad you're here.' A tired voice. She fumbled with the hook latch on the screen door in a way that told Perry she was drunk. She swore at the latch, smiling at them between each breathless profanity, then at last popped the latch free and pushed the creaking door open.

Perry lifted the baggage – and dropped it, flailing at his

face. Something dark – many somethings – were flying at his eyes, shrieking out an ear-splitting *buzzzzzzzz*. A sound you could feel in your throat. He felt a dirty caress across his Adam's apple at the same moment – he wasn't quite sure what made it dirty – and then the buzzing, black things were gone. And it was very quiet.

Sandra and June were staring at him.

'What – ' he began, looking around. 'What, uh – was that?'

'Was what?' Aunt June asked.

'Didn't you see something fly out of the house when she opened the door? At my eyes?' Perry asked. Telling himself, Pick up the bags, don't be a dork . . . He picked them up.

'No,' Aunt June said. 'Flies?'

'Flies,' said Sandra, nodding to herself. 'Flies. We have a little problem with them here. A few too many, sometimes. It's this part of the country . . .'

Flies, Perry thought. What a jerk. Freak out from some flies.

Moving like an automaton, he carried the bags into the living room and set them in the middle of the dusty gray rug.

'Well, take a load off,' Sandra said. 'I'll ferret out some lemonade – or perhaps you'd prefer a beer, Perry?'

'Lemonade's fine,' said Perry. He'd rather have beer.

He watched Sandra go into the kitchen. She was British, though she'd lived for so many years in the US she had very little accent. She was one of those compact little English women – the arms seemed a touch short, the head a pinch too big for the body. She was pale, and her pageboy cut was white with a blonde rinse. She wore a tentlike blue housedress printed with lavender hibiscus blossoms. At forty-six she was young for white hair. And for all the lines on her face. And her shaking hands . . .

'Oh June,' she called from the kitchen, 'what will you have, dear?'

'What did you used to make me in college?'

'A panache? Lemonade and beer! Sure!'

Perry looked at Aunt June in mild surprise. She smiled and said, 'The alcohol is so diluted it's hardly even there.'

'Yeah, but lemonade and *beer*? I mean, yuck . . . I'll have one too.'

Sandra returned with the drinks on a wooden tray. A dead bluebottle fly lay in one corner of the tray. She didn't seem to notice it. She put the drinks on a tumbler-marked wooden coffee table that stood beside the great brown lump of the couch like a calf beside a cow. Sitting across from them in a wicker rocking chair, Sandra drank what was probably a martini in a highball glass. Perry and June sat on the musty brown imitation-velvet couch; it creaked whenever they moved. There were no paintings, no decorations at all on the dull yellow plaster walls, except for a shelf of knick-knacks under the plastic-covered front window. Flies droned near the ceiling, ice cubes clinked in the glasses. Perry found himself listening for Tetty. Was she upstairs? Or at some local hospital? Somehow he felt sure she was upstairs. And listening.

Sandra downed a third of her drink, took a deep breath, and launched into a series of complaints about Jasper. There was no cultural life, and not even a movie theater. The nearest 'big town' newspaper came from Bend – hardly a big town – and it was hopelessly provincial. Jasper had two bars, and women were not encouraged to frequent either of them. They were served, but grudgingly . . . The ladies' bridge club she described as 'a nightmare of tedium. In a trailer park. A *trailer* park, I *ask* you!'

'How about the rodeo?' Aunt June asked. 'That sounds like fun.'

'If you like baking in the hot sun and watching a lot of macho dilettantes wrestling cows,' Sandra said. Her syllables were slurring together.

'Dilettantes?' Perry asked.

'The Jasper rodeo is a piddly little thing, attracts mostly amateurs. They're as likely to lasso themselves as the bloody calves. Anyway the whole thing is barbaric. Cowboys! You see them hanging around the bars, cocky in their Stetsons and boots, hand-rolling Top tobacco and getting drunk. Their idea of country recreation is to run their jeeps all over the hills chasing the antelope, run them down with their damn snowmobiles in the winter, ruining the scenery . . . Bunch of idiots.'

'But don't they work on ranches?' Perry asked, feeling silly when he realized he was disappointed.

'A few do. Mostly the Indians. The Indians are all right, when they're sober. The rest of the so-called cowboys work at the feed mill, or at the slaughterhouse, or – or at the strip mines ripping out bauxite, boron, things like that. A little gold and silver. Not miners, really – just twits who work all day clearing away gravel with machinery and all night – ' She shrugged. 'All night working up their courage to go into Bend to chase the fillies.' She took a deep breath and said, 'The saloon contains two WCs with signs on them that say, on my word of honor, Pointers and Setters.' She stood to make another drink.

When she returned from the kitchen and sat staring into the middle distance – into the little negative galaxy of droning flies near the ceiling – Perry asked, 'Well, it's none of my business but after all that I can't help asking – '

'Why I stay in this benighted place?' Sandra interrupted, smiling bitterly. She exhaled a sigh that was also a name: 'Tetty.'

'She can't travel?' Aunt June suggested.

'No. No, she cannot. And even if it was wise to move her, I'd have to have her taken out in some kind of ambulance. Complications, complications. Anyway – ' Sandra hesitated, glancing at the stairway, to the right of the couch, leading to a second-floor landing. 'Anyway, I have some hopes. There is . . .' She lowered her voice again. 'A gentleman.'

Aunt June smiled. 'I'm pleased to see that you haven't entirely changed.'

Sandra looked at her with a blankness that was also a warning. 'Entirely? You mean I have, *mostly*? How?'

'Well.' Aunt June swallowed. 'My God, how many years has it been? Fifteen? We've both changed. But you're really the same person, in essence . . .'

Sandra snorted. Smiling crookedly, she glanced again at the shadowy stairway. 'Now then, as to this gentleman: he is my ray of sunshine. He is just a very sickly little ray of sunshine so far, but I have my hopes. He lives at the Chemeka Village. He owns a bit of it too – quite a bit. It's one of those condominium housing projects, with lots of trees and an artificial lake, thirty or so houses. Some retired people, all so charming petite bourgeoisie, with their seascapes from Sears, come down for the summer. And some bachelors who come for the fishing season. And I have gained admittance to that charmed circle. I have joined their nightmarishly tedious bridge club. That's where I met Mr Finch and Professor Nearing and . . .'

Her voice trailed off when the call came from upstairs. 'Mama.' Just one word, the two syllables so compressed they were almost indistinguishable. A childish voice, though Perry knew that Tetty was seventeen. To Perry's surprise, Sandra picked up where she'd left off, but more loudly. As if in defiance. '. . . I was just thinking about graduation, how disappointed I was when you said you were going to stay and take your master's, June. I was all jazzed up to take you to Manhattan. But I wish I'd stayed, to be honest . . .'

They talked about their days as roommates, and the ensuing years, so that, in bits and pieces, Perry caught the general outline of Sandra's life. Sandra had majored in art and political science, June in psychology. They saw one another on holidays for years after school, even touring Europe together. Sandra's parents worked in a New York branch of Lloyd's of London. Sandra had planned it all out: American citizenship, law school, volunteer work for the ACLU, commissioner of something-or-other, some sort of bureaucratic underdog-advocacy niche.

But just after graduation, she'd met Roy Cummings, a mining engineer. They'd married six weeks later, and spent their twenty years of marriage 'lurching around the country' with Roy's transfers.

Two years ago he'd died in a boating accident on the artificial lake . . . and Sandra had stayed in Jasper, because Tetty's problem had started almost immediately after Roy's death.

'*Mama.*' More insistently now, and with a touch of fear in it. Sandra, June, and Perry glanced at the ceiling.

'I wonder,' said Sandra abstractedly, 'if she's slipped her restraints again . . .'

Perry felt a chill. Restraints.

'Perry dear,' said Sandra abruptly, smiling at him sunnily, 'I wonder if you'd think I was too much of a sot if I sent you to the liquor store for me? I'm just out of gin. I know you're tired, but if you'll do that I'll fix dinner for you while you're out.'

'I don't mind at all,' Perry said. 'But I'm only twenty.'

She gave him a five-dollar bill from a haggard alligator handbag and said, 'Just a pint, I think, please. You can't miss it, the state liquor store, down the road on the left. And don't worry about your age. That place doesn't much care about selling booze to minors.'

'Down the road?'

'Main Street.'

He smiled awkwardly, tucked the bill in a shirt pocket, and said, 'Be right back.'

He was relieved to go. There was a quiet but insistent pressure in the house now.

He went out through the squawking screen door; the afternoon sunlight fell like something molten on the back of his neck. He stuck his hands into the pockets of his khaki trousers. It was too hot to keep his hands there, but he always put his hands in his pockets when he felt like he was under scrutiny. And he imagined he felt someone watching him . . . from the bedroom window above the porch.

He moved quickly to the shade of the pines and, slipping a little on the layer of fallen pine needles, trudged to Main Street. He turned left at Main, walked by a deserted souvenir shop called *The Hitchin' Post*, past the *Jasper Bar and Grill*, over a culvert channeling an anemic creek haunted by mud daubers, and up to the clusters of wood and imitation-stucco concrete buildings. He was glad to see that the shadows from the telephone poles were long; evening, and escape from the heat, was on its way. He could smell the sun-heated tar bubbled on the telephone poles and in the softer spots on the asphalt road. Ahead, pasted to the side of a leaning wooden building next to a vacant lot, a poster said, INDIAN RIGHTS RALLY AT BROKEN TREATY ROCK, CHEMEKA RESERVATION. AUGUST 7. Over the poster someone had spray-painted a swastika in red – they'd got the swastika backward – and the word *White Power*.

The defacing swastika annoyed Perry. So when he noticed four rawboned men staring at him from the jeep parked across the street, he did something he wouldn't normally do: he stared back at them.

Three teenagers, he amended, and one man. Permanently sunburned. All four wearing nearly identical sunglasses. He almost said, *You guys just come from a 3-D movie?* but thought better of it . . . The older man wore a straw cowboy hat and no shirt: gray-black hairs bristled from his chest and down the red flab of his belly. The others were hatless. They sat in the shade of the jeep's canopy, drinking Olympia from bottles and staring at him.

What do they think when they look at me? Perry wondered. A tall, skinny young man? Would they call him 'Stretch'? Or maybe 'Slim'? Did they think his sandals and khaki trousers and powder-yellow short-sleeve shirt were out of place? At least, he had a darker tan than theirs. And he'd opted for short hair this year – around here that should make him less conspicuous.

He imagined saying, *How do you do, I'm Perry Strandman; I'm an utterly normal, Regular Sort of Guy. See? My glossy black hair brings out my dark blue eyes; I'm thin, yes, but I'm in pretty good shape and I mind spit in public. My nose is big, by some standards, but in a handsome way, and no I'm not Jewish, you racist bastards.*

But he hurried silently past the jeep to the liquor store.

The liquor store wore the Oregon state seal, painted in gold on the window. He was about to go in when someone hissed at him from the corner of the building, to the left. A girl blinked at him there, half hidden by the building's edge. She crooked a finger to say, *Come here!* and smiled.

Perry didn't hesitate. The girl was a knock-out.

'Hi,' he said, as casually as he could manage, stepping into the dusty vacant lot with her. The liquor store hid them from the jeep half a block down the street.

She's a golden girl, he thought.

She had blonde-brown hair – the colour of dark honey – and a tan that, so far as he could see, was perfectly uniform. She had large gold-flecked brown eyes, dimples that were too good to be true, and long, wide, resilient lips. She wore no makeup; there was a jade stud in each earlobe. She wore a white blouse, sleeveless and low cut, showing the golden swell of small, widely spaced breasts. Her long legs were emphasized by her white short-shorts, and she was almost as tall as Perry. Her narrow feet, in worn-out blue thongs, were tipped with pink nail-polish, a shade he associated with young girls. He guessed her to be about eighteen. She shaded her eyes with a flattened hand, squinting at him in a way he found endearingly kidlike. At that moment, she could have spat messily on his shoe and he'd have found it endearing.

'Could you kindly do me a favor?' she asked, smiling softly. Pronouncing kindly *kandly*. Her accent was native central Oregonian.

He kept himself, with an effort, from saying *Anything!* and said, 'And what would that be – ma'am?'

Her smile widened. Her voice became conspiratorial. 'Now, me and some friends are going to have us a lake party tonight. And to do that, we need to get us some of the necessary party juice, you see. Now the gentleman who runs this liquor store knows my guardian – my Uncle Marv is my guardian – and he won't sell me liquor. And anyway Uncle Marv is down the street, waitin' for me, and he's got his eye on this store, because he knows I'm trying to get a party going and he knows we need the juice and he don't allow me none.' Something about her – maybe the humorous way she phrased her sentences – convinced him that she could speak with perfectly standard English if she chose.

'Now then,' she went on, 'I have this bag here – ' She patted a large white canvas bag jammed with books and candy wrappers and unidentifiable odds and ends. 'And if you would be so kind as to take this money and purchase for me a fifth of Jack Daniel's, I would be most obliged, and then I can hide the bottle in my bag here, you see, and trouble you no more.'

This, Perry told himself, is a rare opportunity. A golden opportunity. For once, untie your tongue and get to know her.

'Sure,' Perry said, 'on one condition. You tell me your name, and how old you are, and if you live around here.'

She tilted her head to one side and this time compressed her lips to keep from smiling. 'Oh, an operator, hey? Big-city wiles, huh? I *saw* you come in on the bus.'

He said, 'Hey. I'm harmless.' He hoped his smile was disarming.

'You are? I'll tell you my name anyway. Lois Rutherford. I'm nineteen, I live at Chemeka Lake since last April – we lived on the reservation before then, because my uncle was director of the reservation. But then the government fired him. That enough?'

'My name's Perry. Perry Strandman.' They shook hands. Hers was soft, surprisingly dry.

'Perry?' She dropped his hand. 'No kidding? Because my name's Lois and I know a guy named Jim Olsen. So if we meet Clark Kent, I start watching the skies.'

He laughed, a little too much.

'Hey,' she said, with mock asperity, 'it's hot. I was supposed to meet my girlfriend Judy here and give her the money, but she didn't show up – and I've been standing in this hot place for an hour . . .'

'Really? You've really got, uh, endurance.' He took the ten she handed him and went into the liquor store, an air-conditioned enclave of coolness and stately bottles.

He bought a pint of gin and the Jack Daniel's from the sour-faced man behind the counter, and returned, hastily, to the vacant lot. She bounced a little on the soles of her feet with pleasure, seeing the brown-paper sack. 'Oh great!' She hid the bottle at the bottom of her bag and stood, the canvas straps looped over one arm. She looked at him quietly, expectantly.

It's now or never, he told himself.

'Um, which way you walking?' he asked.

'Back the way you came,' she said . . . *the way yew caium*. Her countrified accent sounded deliberately heavy, too, and he hoped she was putting it on to charm him. Was there such a thing as a *western* belle?

They walked along the gravel alley behind the liquor store, up between a barber shop and a service station, and to the sidewalk. To his relief, she continued with him towards Second Street. They were on the side of the road the jeep sat on, walking along the sidewalk toward it. Four pairs of dark glasses watched them approach.

Perry pictured the men in the jeep jumping out to impose themselves on Lois; he pictured them jumping up and down on his back in their cowboy boots when he protested.

He glanced at the books in her canvas bag. There was one by Thomas Pynchon and one that said, *The Autobiography of W. B. Yeats*: Western belle. Right.

'How long you here for?' she asked, as if she were only asking to be polite.

'Anywhere from a month to . . . maybe till October. It depends on how long my aunt wants to stay. She's a doctor. We're here to, um, help out a friend of hers. Sandra Cummings.'

'Over on Second Street?'

'That's her. You know her?'

'Know of her. In a town like this, everybody at least knows of everybody else. More'n they want to know, most the time. Your aunt's a doctor, huh? I 'spect you're helping out with that girl of Sandra's?'

'I'm, uh, doing a kind of secretarial thing for my aunt.'

'Hey, now I like the sound of that: doing a kind of secretarial thing. That sounds real Southern California. That's it, right?'

'You got it. San Diego.'

'I always wanted to go to Southern California, I hear it's really grotesque. Your aunt's a psychiatrist? For that my Aunt's girl with the Problem? What's her name – Betty?'

'Tetty. Yeah, my aunt's a psychiatrist. You go to school with Tetty?'

'Why sure. Didn't really get to know her much. She seemed okay, but after her Dad died she got real pushy, I heard – ' She hesitated.

'Go ahead, I'd like to get the story on her.'

'I don't know much of it. Just that she got kind of weird after she went to Doctor Rofocale.' She said it *Roffo-calley*.

'Who's Dr Rofo – ?'

'Dr Rofocale, he's not a doctor really, he's one of those self-made therapist guys playing doctor because he's got a Ph.D. Writing those self-help books about how to find your real identity, how to keep from being intimidated and all that. I met him. Lordy, what a creep-o. You ever been to Portland?'

'Sure. I've got friends there.'

'I'm going to Portland State in the fall.'

'Maybe I'll see you there – I visit my friends sometimes. You said something about a lake party . . . what, uh, happens at a lake party?'

'Why don't you come on out tonight and find out? You're invited 'cause you got the Jack. We play the radio. Drinkin' and dancin' and that sort of adolescent ritual.' She grinned, then whispered out of the side of her mouth, 'Shh, this is my Uncle Marv, don't say anything about the party . . .'

They'd walked up to the jeep, and to his horror, she stopped beside it and said, 'This is my Uncle Marv. Marv, this young furrener is named Perry Something.'

'Strandman,' Perry said, swallowing.

The older man in the jeep was Uncle Marv.

To Perry's astonishment, he said, 'Well, how do you do!' His accent was softly western. His smile was something more urbane.

'Find out who did it?' Lois asked her uncle.

'The damn swastika? No, nobody's talkin'. When I find out, I'll wring the bastard's neck.'

She turned to Perry. 'Don't listen to that macho talk, he couldn't wring anybody's neck. But he's pissed off because he put up that poster himself – he's one of the guys behind that Indians rights rally – and the next damn day somebody – '

'You?' Perry blurted, turning to blink confusedly at Uncle Marv.

'Correct you are, boy, I put it up myself. You had me pegged differently?'

22

The three boys with him – they turned out to be Marv's sons, Lois's cousins – cawed with laughter while Perry reddened.

'I could tell,' said the oldest boy, wearing a T-shirt, a pack of Marlboros rolled into one sleeve. 'I could tell when he looked at us, it was written all over him, he thought we were some rednecks out of *Easy Rider*.'

Embarrassed and a little ashamed, Perry pretended to laugh too. 'I guess I did, sort of.'

'You need a ride, chief?' Marv asked, chuckling, starting the engine of the jeep.

'No – I'm just going a block more. Thanks. Nice meeting you. Bye, Lois.'

She got into the jeep, between two cousins, and nodded austerely. But, soundlessly, she mouthed, *Lake party*.

He nodded. The jeep U-turned from the curb, rumbled grudgingly a half block up the highway, then swung on to a gravel road and took off as if somebody had counted down from ten to blastoff. He watched Lois's hair flutter in the wind. The jeep raised a plume of dust. After it was gone, the street seemed dead. The only motion was the dun-colored cloud of dust settling where the gravel road began.

Never would have believed it, he thought. If someone had told me I'd be glad I came here.

But how would he find the lake party? Probably just walk around the shore of the lake, watch for a bonfire . . .

Swinging the gin bottle at the end of his arm, humming, he returned to Sandra's.

Perry hesitated on the front porch. Someone had broken the screen door; one hinge was ripped from the jamb. He pushed it aside and went in.

The living room was the aftermath of some sort of

human eruption. There was broken glass on the floor – the shattered drinking glasses. The wicker armchair was overturned. One of the pillows of the couch had been ripped – or slashed – open. The coffee table was overturned and one of its legs freshly broken off.

Aunt June was in the doorway to the kitchen, a sponge in her hand. Her blouse was torn, and there were scratches on her cheeks.

'It's okay,' she said, seeing the look on his face. 'She's quieted down now. Sandra's with her.'

'What happened?'

She shrugged. 'Tetty got loose.'

2

'There are a lot of things I don't understand,' Perry said, attempting to eat the gooey 'insta-filling' blueberry pie Sandra had insisted he take, 'but mostly I don't understand how she could have got loose. The way you describe the restraints – I've seen leather restraints like that. They look foolproof.' He forced himself to swallow a bite of the glutinous pie, wondering how it qualified as blueberry – there were no detectable berries in it.

He cleared his throat with a long drink of milk as Sandra said, 'Do I detect a note of accusation in your nephew's voice, June?' More amused than offended.

Aunt June smiled. Perry noted resentfully that her blueberry pie lay untouched on her plate. 'He's just protective of me.'

'I don't like to see my aunt clawed up,' Perry said.

'It's all part of the job, I guess,' Aunt June said, glancing at the ceiling. 'It seems worse to you than it was, Perry. And I've dealt with worse. It wasn't so bad – she gave in pretty quick, let us put her back in her room again.'

They were sitting at the Formica-topped kitchen table, finishing dinner. They'd eaten enchilada TV dinners, mealy and suspect, like Post House food. Sandra had eaten two; Perry and Aunt June had made only token forays into theirs.

The kitchen was long and narrow, with a blue painted wooden floor that sagged near the back porch; an ancient Frigidaire groaned beside a gas range that might have done well at an antiques auction. The walls were orange-speckled yellow tile. Over the stove hung one of the few decorations in the house, a ten-year-old calendar topped by a photo of the Space Needle in Seattle; the heat from the stove had gradually warped the photo so the Space Needle looked shriveled. Flies whipped in eccentric orbits around the dusty, spherical overhead light fixture set in the center of the cracked blue ceiling.

They sat with their elbows on the table – Sandra gazing out the back window – between the refrigerator and the door to the porch. The back porch, where Perry was to sleep, was a recently built annex made of unpainted two-by-fours; it was a small room itself, with two glassless windows protected by screens, and an army cot. Thinking about the cot, Perry sighed. Well, the porch would be cool.

'So, then, right-ho,' Sandra said abruptly, 'our charming lad would like to know how Tetty got loose.'

It was at that moment, nettled by Sandra's tone, that Perry decided definitively that he didn't like her. He smiled coldly at her as she went on, 'Well, I'd jolly well like to know how she got loose myself, Perry. It's not the first time. She won't say, except to make filthy remarks about Houdini. It's as if someone helps her. But the windows upstairs are all nailed shut. And I never find anyone hiding in her room – and never see anyone go in or out just before she gets out. Now, I suspect that June is speculating . . .' She paused and looked with mock suspicion and narrowed eyes at Aunt June. 'Speculating about me.'

June laughed lightly. 'Am I that obvious? I was wondering if you might be helping her. Yes – maybe doing it without consciously knowing it. "Forgetting" to lock the restraints . . .'

Sandra shook her head firmly. 'Not on your life.' She smirked at Perry. 'Tetty won't tell me how she does it. But maybe she'll tell our handsome young Perry here.'

June looked at him and nodded. 'It's time he met her.'

Perry looked from June to Sandra and back to Aunt June. 'Me? Now?'

Aunt June shrugged. 'You don't have to if you don't want to. But we agreed, I thought, that you were going to help me.'

'Yes, well, excuse me if it seems cowardly, but that was before you told me she was violent.'

'She has peaks,' Sandra said, blowing smoke at the ceiling. 'Peaks of agitation or something. Finding things to scream about, to hate everyone for, how she's all put upon and we're all preying on her and the like. And after she has a big demonstration and made a big fuss, she's quiet and harmless for a few days. Might seem almost normal. And lucid. And let me tell you something: she's more clever now than she was, before she started having the fits. She's – she's become precocious, marvelously verbal. Articulate. Making little extemporaneous speeches about things. Never used to be able.'

'Not uncommon in certain disorders,' June murmured. 'In some ways schizophrenia hones the mind.'

'Anyway, Perry my child, she's harmless now.'

Perry took a deep breath and then stood; the chair grated too loudly on the floor as he pushed it aside to stand. He glanced at the windows, saw the evening's darkness had thickened outside. It made the light bulb seem to glare. 'I'll get it over with,' he said softly.

'Won't you finish your pie?' Sandra asked, suddenly playing the cheery hostess.

'No.' That was one good thing to come of this. 'I want to go while I've got the nerve up.'

June chuckled. 'Oh, it's not as bad as all that. She doesn't twist her head around backward or spit up pea soup.'

Perry shrugged, trying to appear resolved and unafraid. 'Should I take a pen and notebook?'

'No,' Aunt June said, 'not this time. That would make her self-conscious. And – if you mention what happened tonight, what she did . . . well, don't make a big deal about it. Be casual. Don't try to figure her out. Just be yourself getting to know a stranger. As if you were sitting by her on a train.'

'Okay.'

He turned and left the kitchen, walked through the living room, and climbed the shadowy stairs. 'Hi!' he called, reaching the second floor. He wanted to give her warning. Best not to startle her.

'Come in!' A high, affectedly lilting voice. Artificial sweetness, but nothing sinister. He relaxed a little. He pushed open the door to her bedroom and looked around. The room was an almost perfect square. At the front side were the two high green-curtained windows. It was almost sauna hot, but the windows were indeed nailed shut.

Her bed was on the left. Next to it was a low robin's-egg-blue bureau with matching mirror frame, from which the mirror was missing. Atop the bureau were two yellowed doilies and a china doll old enough to be a relic from Sandra's childhood. The walls were covered in light green wallpaper, a fading pattern of a boy and a girl climbing a hill together, carrying a pail and holding hands; in the alternating pattern they were tumbling down the hill, laughing. Jack and Jill. Here and there, long irregular swatches of Jack and Jill had been ripped away. Overhead was a rose-glass light fixture shaped like an inverted blossom.

'Do you like my room?' Tetty asked. There was something unnervingly similar in the artificial sweetness of her tone and Sandra's sarcastic hostess's cheeriness.

He nodded, smiling. She was, to his relief, not at all 'mad' looking, or even mussed. It was a round, soft face, without makeup. Pale, dark eyelashes, dark eyebrows, sulky pink lips, the suggestion of a double chin. Her forehead was unlined. The look on her face was complacent, with a touch of I-know-a-secret in it. Her hair was brown, and very long, wavy, curling around her full breasts. She wore a pale blue, modestly cut nightgown; in her small ears dangled blue turquoise earrings. He was sure she'd just put the earrings on, hearing him come up the stairs. She reclined, halfway sitting in the bed, under a sheet, pillows bunched behind her neck and shoulders. She had her legs tucked under the blue sheet – and her wrists. So he wouldn't see the leather restraints at her wrists and ankles. Probably a loop about the wrist too, all of it connected to the metal bed frame that was bolted to the gray wooden floor.

'I guess you like blue, huh?' he said, sitting in the creaking, straight-backed wooden chair just out of reach of her hands (out of reach, if she should sit up rigidly, and make a grab for him . . .).

'You noticed! Absolutely! And you've got blue eyes.'

He squirmed in his chair a little. He waited for her to say something crazy, but she didn't.

'Oh, I've embarrassed you!' she said, as if saddened. 'I'm sorry, truly I am.'

'Hey, no problem. More girls should notice my eyes.'

'Right!' She beamed at him. 'Your name's Perry?'

'Uh-huh.' He was staring at a small bruise on her right cheek. It looked fresh. Had Sandra walloped her? Probably had to. 'And you're Tetty.'

'Some call me that. Mom claims it's a British variation of Elizabeth, but I don't see how. Anyway, I don't like to be called Elizabeth. It's too formal sounding.'

He noticed other things, now. Her bed was under the roof slant; the wall slanted towards him at a forty-five-degree angle. It made him nervous: it was as if she were in a sort of cave looking out at him. And in the stifling heat, the claustrophobic closeness of the room, he almost choked on the room's scents: perspiration, the sour of a sheet not changed often enough, a hint of menstruation, all wrapped up in the cloying odor of an aerosol room deodorizer. And the chains at the corners of the bed, and the way she kept her hands very, very still so the shackles wouldn't make a clanking sound when she moved, made his own brow bead with a sudden oily sweat.

'You need a fan or something up here.' Perry said. It seemed cruel to leave her up here in this pocket of heat. 'An air conditioner.'

'Oh, no. I don't want a fan. I don't like drafts and . . .' She watched her fingers tugging a thread from the sheet, and then shot him a sidelong smile. 'You came to help your aunt?' *To help your aunt psychoanalyze me*.

'I came to be, um, kind of a secretary. But mostly I'm a musician. This is a temporary job.'

'Really? Did you bring an instrument?'

'A mandolin. Easy to carry on a long trip. Usually I play guitar.'

'Will you play the mandolin for me sometime soon? Tonight? I get awfully bored and lonely. I broke my tape deck.'

'Sure, absolutely. I'd like that.'

'I'll bet you're wondering about me.' She fixed her pale green eyes on him, unblinking, waiting for his answer.

'Um – ' It would be useless to lie. 'Oh, naturally.

Maybe – ' He swallowed. 'Maybe you oughta, you know, tell me your side of it before they tell me theirs. They haven't really told me anything. Except that you – well, the downstairs is, um – '

'I don't think I'll tell you, really, my version. You wouldn't believe me.' She smiled thinly. 'And if you tell me that you might believe me, I wouldn't believe *you*.'

She was right. He probably wouldn't believe anything she said. He shrugged.

'They're going to tell you,' she went on, twisting a lock of hair with a finger, looking more abstractedly at him now, 'that I tried to kill a boy because he snubbed me. And some stories about my playing with a knife, and some other things. Lots of other little things.' She said it dismissively, sounding utterly sane. 'And it's peculiar: but the truth is in between. They're right and then they're not.'

'Things are like that a lot.'

'They'll pretend it started with Dr Rofocale. My mom thinks I don't know she's getting up a big lawsuit against him. She's hoping she'll clean up on that one. But it *didn't* start with Dr Rofocale. It started two years before and that's why he picked me out. Because he had another patient who knew me before and told him something about me that made him interested. Something that told him I was just born with the Genetic Sub-B3 in me. Maybe he let it go free, though. But that's his job, really.'

'Let what go free?'

She didn't reply immediately. She seemed to sag back in the bed, and Perry had the uneasy impression that the slanted wall, an attic ceiling actually, was somehow taking on greater weight and presence, threatening to fall in on them. He shook himself, and the feeling passed, only to be replaced by another strange feeling: something buzzing, flying past his head – though there was clearly nothing there at all. Like remembering a fly.

'What's the matter?' she said. 'You look funny.'

'Oh – felt a little weird for a moment. It's gone.'

She nodded, slowly. And then made a soft snorting sound. 'Okay, you asked me about Dr Rofocale. He had a best-selling book. It was to, you know, teach you to resist intimidation, to assert yourself, find your true feelings and act them out. Sort of like est or Lifespring but more . . . more intelligent, I think. And a little more specialized. A lot of people were turned off by the follow-up book. It opened up a whole new frontier. It's called *Ego Truth*. Took Ayn Rand five steps farther. Really gutsy stuff, you know. He had guts to publish that last chapter. I don't know if you – '

'Haven't read it.'

'You sure you didn't see a review, even? They tended to harp on the bits about "genetic destiny" and the, um, "Inner Superman"?'

'Not even a review, sorry. I read, but not book reviews.'

'Yeah, the book reviewers picked those phrases out, and made it sound as if he was racist.' She laughed softly. 'Racist! Rofocale has exactly the same attitude toward all people, regardless of their race, creed, or religion: they all belong to him.'

Startled, Perry said, 'Oh . . . yeah?'

'I don't mean he believes in ruling the world or something – he simply believes in Guidance . . . a kind of benign domination – dominating as many people as possible, as thoroughly as possible, in order to establish a Growth-oriented Social Context. And he believes that there is an Inner Superman in everyone, see, and some men are *genetically destined* to realize that Inner Superman. Regardless of race – that's very important. It's transracial. Or super-racial. He's found black people and Spanish people with active Sub-B3s in them. The external race doesn't matter.' She reeled all this off with a kind of patronizing boredom. No fanatic's excitement. 'Basically, you can draw out that inner person with a kind of meditation on the ego. You can liberate it, see. And it will do more than change your personality and make you stronger and smarter. It makes other changes too.'

On an impulse, Perry asked abruptly, 'It makes changes – like making you violent? So that you break things and claw my aunt?'

He expected her to react angrily, to become shrill. But she only shook her head sadly. 'That's just what happens when you interfere with the Pilot's development. If they didn't try to stop her, there'd be no violent reaction. It has its own infancy and it takes it awhile to learn how to push the right buttons in the world.' She laughed softly at herself, shaking her head. 'I know, some of what I said sounds like delirium.' She looked at him earnestly. 'But it's only because I'm using jargon you don't know. Rofocale's. When I say *her*, I'm not speaking of a split personality, even if I'm talking about another part of myself. I'm thinking about my *true* self. The ego truth.'

Perry stood up, stretched, trying to look receptive. Trying to look like he wasn't unnerved. 'Well, frankly, it sounds like the usual cultism to me. Like the Moonies or Dianetics but with different terms. And Rofocale sounds like a megalomaniac.'

'He doesn't seem that way when you meet him. He's charming and genteel.' She shrugged. 'Well, you'll meet him, soon.'

'Yeah? Maybe he'll give me a different, uh, perspective on it. Anyway, I've got to go.'

'Hey.'

A subtle tension in her voice made him turn back to her. 'Something . . . something I can get you?'

'Yeah. You can come back a little later and play for me.'

'It's pretty late. But tomorrow, for sure.'

'Oh, if you play for me tomorrow, I won't hear you. See, I'll be dead.' She looked at him blankly; she'd said it like *I'll be on a plane out of town*.

'What?'

She toyed with an earring, her expression bland. 'I'll be dead, tomorrow.'

He smiled, and then couldn't keep the smile up any longer. 'Look, if you're afraid you might want to – '

She fluttered a hand dismissively. 'I don't mean suicide. I'll just – I'll be dead. That's all. Nothing tragic. But you can play for the pilot. For *her*. She'll make you play for her.'

Well, there it is, he thought. Just when you're convinced she's not crazy after all. And she hits you with that.

He wanted to go downstairs, and she was playing games with him. He couldn't completely keep the anger down. 'Look, hey – you're not going to be dead. And this "she'll make you play for her" stuff . . .' He shrugged. 'I think you're trying freak me out. Forget it. Won't work. I don't believe in possession.'

'Possession? It's not possession. I'm not possessed. I'm not *real*, is what it is. *She's* real. What you see now, what you're talking to, that's all a lot of . . . a kind of . . . What do they call those mechanical arms they put on people who – '

'Prosthesis. I think.'

'Yeah. Personality is a prosthesis for the crippled true self. But people who have the Sub-B3 aren't crippled. Not when it comes out, asserts itself. Not possession. Emergence.'

He forced a smile. 'Okay. Well, I can't absorb all this at once. I got to go. But I will play for you, tomorrow. Promise.'

'Anything you say.' She stared at him with eyes like green stones, and went on quickly, before he could leave. 'You notice there's no decorations downstairs?'

'Yeah. I saw a picture of you, a couple of little statuettes of some kind.'

'But they're not up on the wall. I won't stand for things up on the wall, see. Images on the wall I mean. It imposes on my identity field.'

'Uh-huh.' *Out of here.*

'You think that's selfish? It is. You think it's compulsive? It's not.'

'No?' *Out of here!*

'But listen: once I was sitting, meditating on some things that Dr Rofocale gave me to meditate on. Not East Indian meditation, you know – more like just deep thinking about a thing, and picturing it. And then, at the end of the exercise, I made my mind clear, and empty, and receptive. That's what he wants you to do – like you make your mind into a blank blackboard waiting for someone to write. Or make it like a sky, waiting for something to fly through it. That's closer. And after that, the Sub-B3 woke. You should try it, see if you have it too.'

He nodded, just as if he understood. He looked at the window, then forced himself to look back at her. Sandra's tacky kitchen downstairs was a paradise. He yearned for it. He was suddenly aware that it was now very, very dark outside, and that beyond the buildings around the house were the pine woods and the desert. The desert and the artificial lake. A stark, rocky desert of broken black stone from ancient volcanos, sere but itchy with cold-blooded life. And he wondered how he'd come to this hot, musty room, caught in a social eddy with this broken girl . . . and trying to ignore the something he could never quite see, buzzing – subsonically, never completely audible – around his head, like one of those big, impudent summer flies. Probably it was dizziness from fatigue, from heat . . .

'You make your mind like an empty sky,' she went on, her eyes closed, 'like there's no limits to you, no skin or bone to define where you are and where the things around me are, but you're not trying to merge into the world, like a Buddhist – you're trying to make *it* merge *into you*.' Her eyes snapped open, flicked toward him. She seemed uncertain for a moment. 'Only, you, uh . . .' Her voice trailed off. She stared into the middle distance, her eyes going out of focus.

'I'll play for you tomorrow,' he said, to break the awful silence.

Blinking, she came back to him. 'You said that before,' she said teasingly, once more smiling and casual. 'I hope it's true.'

'See you later.' He hurried through the door and down the stairs; hurrying, but careful not to run.

'Even when she said those things at the end,' Perry said quietly, almost whispering, 'she didn't sound really – well, anyway her tone wasn't crazy.'

'What she said about her death,' Aunt June said, 'is not

part of the pattern I projected. I don't understand where it fits.'

'Suicide, I guess.'

'I doubt it. More like some kind of hysterical bid for sympathy from you. She's smart enough to make it more real seeming by being very cool about it. All the same, I'll keep an eye on her. Check up on her now and then.'

They were sitting on the cot, on the back porch. A breeze so gentle it was hardly there ghosted in through the screened windows, bringing the perfume of pine and roses from the backyard. Moths ticked at the naked light bulb burning in the slanted ceiling overhead. The light spilled yellow from the house on to the withered back lawn, and made it look like beach grass.

'Looks like Sandra doesn't water the lawn much,' Perry remarked.

Aunt June said, 'Umm. She's let the whole place fall apart. And the food she eats – she used to cook. She really ought to make some kind of effort. Sandra's changed. Maybe it's what happened to her daughter. But it's more fundamental than that. She seems to have no faith at all. Except in money and men. And only the most cynical sort of faith in those things.'

'Do psychiatrists usually talk about faith as if it's a good thing?' Perry asked.

'Oh, don't be so damned smart for your age.'

'Hey, you going to tell me what happened to Tetty?' Perry asked, a burr of impatience in his voice. 'Or not?'

Aunt June exhaled long and windily through her nose. She stretched her arms out in front of her, fingers laced together, cracked her knuckles, and shrugged. 'I don't know yet exactly what happened. It seems to have been triggered by the *Ego Truth* therapy; she was quite normal except she was painfully shy, and someone gave her

Rofocale's first book, and then she met one of his – his patients. Or whatever he calls them.' Her voice was dry with irony. She rubbed her eyes, looking suddenly bent and weary. 'And, uh, the "patient" took her to meet Rofocale and in a remarkably short time after she started the therapy – he's got some kind of clinic out in the desert, near here – her personality changed. Or, rather, she seemed to have turned it inside out. Everything that was on the inside bubbled up to the outside. She started saying anything that came to her mind at all. And I mean anything. If anyone annoyed her in the slightest, she hit them with a barrage of obscene language like you wouldn't believe. But it wasn't like an uncontrolled outburst, Sandra claims. And it wasn't like she was testing people. Sandra says it was sheer arrogance. What it really was, I don't know yet. Then Tetty seduced one of the teachers at the high school, and blackmailed him for two months before it came out. She was expelled from school and he was fired. There was also some teenage boy she tried to seduce – apparently with no subtlety at all. She developed an obsession with him. Had to have him or it was the end of everything. He rejected her, and she poisoned him. He lived through it, and talked his parents out of prosecuting.'

'Poisoned him? And she gets out all the time? Hey, I'm eating at the cafe after this.'

'It might be wise to do just that. Especially after' – she lowered her voice – 'sampling Sandra's cooking. Tetty couldn't make it much worse even with coyote poison.'

'*Coyote* poison?'

'Coyotes are a real problem for the ranchers around here. That's what she used on the kid: coyote poison. Anyway, the boy's little sister found out – I don't know how – it was Tetty who poisoned her brother, and she confronted Tetty . . . and Tetty cut her a little with a knife, trying to scare her so she wouldn't tell. But that terrified the girl so much she had to tell everything. The sheriff came around, and Tetty shot him in the leg, and shot out his car windows, with Sandra's handgun. Sandra got the gun away from her and they committed Tetty to the state hospital, for a while. But Sandra thought they were just sedating her and not doing anything else for her, "turning her into a thorazine vegetable," *so* . . .' She took an exaggeratedly deep breath. 'So Sandra managed to get Tetty remanded to her custody. Anyway the sheriff didn't see any point in prosecuting either, because it was clear that Tetty was "crazy" and she was already in an asylum at the time. And the court would just make it official. Also I don't think he wanted the details made public.' She smiled. 'How he hid under his car after the shooting started and shouted for help. It was a minor wound and the gun was only a twenty-two, you see.'

'And when was all this?'

'A few months back. She got out of the hospital about six weeks ago. She's been in restraints ever since. Sandra had a nurse for awhile, helping take care of her part-time, but she quit. She didn't say why, she just walked out, called in to say she was resigning, and hung up.'

'Jesus.' He shook his head in amazement. 'That baby-faced girl upstairs did all that? But then, after we talked awhile . . . she didn't get violent, but the way she talked was . . . even her voice actually changed. Not a whole lot, not like a "Sybil." But it was there.'

'Uh-huh. I should warn you that Sandra wants to sue Rofocale, and she may want you to testify about what Tetty said to you today.'

'Tell you the truth, I don't think I mind. I have the

definite impression this guy Rofocale is responsible for what happened to Tetty.'

To his surprise, Aunt June shook her head. 'I don't think so, except that he may have triggered it. It would have come anyway, I think. She's got it naturally.'

'Got what? Sub-B3?'

She blinked. 'What's Sub-B3?'

'I don't know. Something she said was part of her. Was always part of her . . . What's she got naturally?'

'Tell you' – she stood, yawning – 'tomorrow. It's too much to go into now. I'm going to go and hit my couch. No jokes about psychiatrists condemned to their own couches.'

'Okay. Uh, Aunt June . . . Suppose Tetty decides to go roaming again tonight – '

'No way. I locked her in myself this time. I still think Sandra was "forgetting" to really lock her restraints.'

'Oh. Good. Great. Well hey – good night.'

''Night.'

Perry stretched out on the cot, and just lay there, as if he'd decided to sleep in his clothes. He lay impatiently, listening until – not quite twenty minutes later – he heard the regular susurration of Aunt June's breathing from the living room. He swung off the cot, grabbed his mandolin by the neck, turned out the back porch light, and went out the rear screen door, wincing at its creak. The darkness had shed its Halloween masks; now, it was simply the silky mantle of a warm summer night. Somewhere, wrapped in that mantle, was a girl all of gold.

Crickets sang and dogs barked in the distance; the highway hummed with the occasional car. He strode confidently out between the houses and along Second Street to Pine. Just before Sandra had gone to bed he'd quizzed her with studied nonchalance about the route to the artificial lake and the little housing project on its shores. Pretending he was going to go there on some dull afternoon.

Why, he wondered now, had he been so secretive about going to the lake party?

Sandra. She would have made some acid comment about it.

'The hell with her,' he muttered. And then, louder, shouting it to the trees and the silent, darkened houses, 'The hell with her!' He smiled, listening to the echo.

He turned on to a dirt road that wound between two stone posts and through a stand of Joshua trees and mounds of volcanic rock. The only light, now, came from the waxy half-moon and the fiercely white stars. And a few lost flickers of light from one of Jasper's taverns fingered red between houses and tree trunks.

He walked on, listening to the rasp of his tennis shoes, enjoying the solitude and the coolness . . . and feeling only a fraction uneasy, when the last of the light from Jasper was completely swallowed by the trees and the boulders crowding more and more thickly about the road.

Gradually he became aware that there were rustlings in the clumps of yucca and sage and that something in a bristling group of cacti was making a low funereal clicking sound. It occurred to him that he might have misunderstood the directions. He might be getting himself lost. Spend the night in the desert, with the rattlers and scorpions. Stumble around the next day dehydrating.

He was carrying his mandolin by the neck, holding it like a towncrier's bell. He switched hands with it and began to pluck out a tune. It was a tune made from pieces of the night around him, weaving all the mystery and uneasiness in the desert darkness into an orderly, harmonious pattern. Out of uncertainty, the certainty of musical structure. Reassurance.

He stopped playing when he came to a fork in the road. He looked from one branch of the fork to the other, chewing his lower lip, trying to remember. 'She said bear left, didn't she?' he muttered.

'*Play again*,' came a soft voice from the trees. Soft, but somehow infinitely piercing, that voice. A voice that travels up the spine before reaching the ears. It sounded almost like –

'Tetty?' he called tentatively, peering through the darkness into the trees.

He saw no one, heard nothing more.

He decided that he had misheard some night-calling bird . . . and then he saw the bird.

It was, maybe, a horned owl, gray, but a trick of the light made it seem translucent as it flew from one pine tree to the next, high up in the branches, losing itself in the shadow. He'd had just a glimpse against the stars: a flurry of gray, an impression of a small pallid face. Maybe one of those owls with the white faces . . .

He heard, then, the buzzing noise, that unseen fly dive bombing his head. There, and – gone. Mosquitoes . . .

He hurried on, taking the left-hand path, and was relieved to see, two minutes later, a light flickering between the evergreen boughs. The road narrowed, then switched off to the right, and abruptly he had broken from the trees on to the bank of the reservoir.

The lake was oval, a mile long and a quarter mile wide at the middle. It was glassily motionless tonight, reflecting the stars and the half-moon; the trees along the shore looked like smoke in the night-shuttered reflection. To the left, about a hundred yards along the shore, just around the high arc of the oval, was the yellow-red flutter of a bonfire. Across the lake, opposite, were the geometrical lights of the housing project, rows of streetlights, muted glows in rectangular picture windows and floodlights on front doors.

Perry took a deep breath and walked toward the bonfire.

Suppose Lois was sitting with a group of her friends, deep in conversation? Should he interrupt them and sit beside her? No, he couldn't. He pictured her looking up at him and smiling politely, a little regret in her face telling him she had invited him impulsively and was sorry he had come.

This sort of anxiety making his fingers tight on the mandolin so the strings nearly cut into his skin, he walked into the circle of light around the fire.

Dammit, he thought, I should have brought some beer or something.

There were eight teenagers, and one woman in her middle twenties cradling a sleeping infant in her arms. Four boys, including one of the boys from the jeep. A Styrofoam cooler held ice water and a few cans of Olympia and Bud Lite. The group sat in a circle around the bonfire, yawning, talking softly, nudging, laughing softly when the logs spat sparks at someone, making him lurch back.

A couple of them looked Perry over carefully, then shrugged, and murmured a noncommittal 'Howdy.' Perry said, 'Hi.'

He was surprised at hearing no music, until he noticed a girl scowling over a tape recorder, fumbling with the batteries. Two girls sitting beside Lois passed her a bottle of Jack Daniel's and after waving at Perry, she took a long swig. She gasped and winced; she wasn't used to hard liquor after all. The two younger girls wore 501 jeans and Fiorucci sweat shirts. They pretended not to see him but kept watch on him with sidelong glances, chiefly looking to see if he were looking back at them. Both were about fifteen, bleached blonde, heavily made up; they smoked long thin Virginia Slims ostentatiously, holding them high between trembling fingers. Probably they were even less used to smoking than Lois was to drinking. Perry managed not to laugh, and felt himself put at ease by their naïveté.

Lois stood, just a little shakily, and walked over to him. He plucked absently at his mandolin, pretending to gaze thoughtfully into the leaping yellow bonfire. The fire was built on a concrete rim that – for reasons to do with the reservoir, he supposed – completely enclosed the lake's bank for some quarter of its circumference.

'*Mis*-ter Perry Strand,' Lois said, standing near him, fighting for balance. 'I'm glad you've brought your mandolin. Our radio's busted.' She offered him the Jack Daniel's.

Pleased that she'd recollected three-fourths of his name, at least, Perry took the Jack Daniel's and downed what must have been at least three neat shots. His stomach wanted to howl in outrage. But the night shifted subtly around him, and he was a man of wax melting in the heat of the bonfire. 'Whoa,' he said, in a comically high voice. He handed the bottle back to her as she laughed.

He looked at the Styrofoam cooler. 'Bud Lite. I thought it'd be, uh, Malt liquor, Mickey's Big Mouth – '

'God, you really do think we're rednecks out here. Well, we drink what's cheapest. Except for the bourbon. Can't stint on the bourbon.'

He smiled, trying to think of something to say. But the

firelight was dancing on her hair. Her smile quivered like a moth on a blossom.

She said, 'You got a funny look on your face. That stuff make you feel sick?'

'No, uh-uh. Just thinking I'm glad I met you.' And then he winced, thinking, Real Smart, you're going way too fast for her.

But her smile widened. 'Boy, you don't waste any time – but that's okay with me. I had a feeling about you.' She flushed herself – he saw it distinctly – and looked at his mandolin, to change the subject. 'I wish you'd play that thing.'

'You may wish I hadn't, pretty soon. But here goes.' He shifted the mandolin in his grip, began to trip out a tune. The Stones' 'Lady Jane.' He'd found that girls responded to it. And Lois hummed along with it, swaying slightly. He watched her as he played. She looked more golden than ever in the firelight. He could see its uppermost flames reflected in her deep amber eyes. And beyond her it made a bright leaping like a shamanistic dancer in the dark mirror of the lake water. He played other tunes, sixties things she knew the choruses to, and she sang clumsily but unself-consciously along, and there was something sexy about that, about singing badly without caring.

The music and the golden girl beside him and the sparks burning out in the air over the crackling pine logs and the perfumes of wood sap and sage and even the scent of the bourbon . . . all of it whirled into one harmony of the senses, turning ponderously to create a hurricane's eye between them, a partial vacuum, so that he had to follow the path of least resistance, had to move closer to her . . . until he brought 'Pretty Woman' from art to life: he bent and kissed her, just as the last notes of the tune faded.

She kissed him back.

After that – he was never afterward sure how the transition came about – they were sitting on her sleeping bag, on the bank a little ways off from the fire, lazily slapping at mosquitoes and talking in alternating bursts, first he and then she, about their lives. She wanted to study anthropology, maybe teach one day. She was interested in Indian culture.

They sat with their hips touching, holding hands; occasionally she leaned her head on his shoulder. They hadn't yet kissed a second time. Now, she stopped talking and leaned against him, turned her face up toward him, and parted her lips. He wasted no time.

And there was another bourbon-drowned, silky transition, with a little fumbling, and the sounds of zippers coming undone; there were caresses, and the joining, moving sweetly together on the sleeping bag. They lay on their sides, she with one leg looped over his, copulating so gently – at first – he could almost imagine it wasn't really outright sex. But it was. And she guided his fingers . . . and for the first time in Perry's life he held off his ejaculation . . . until he felt her undulating in orgasm. It was his first really satisfying lovemaking.

She astonished him when, as they lay slack in each other's arms, wrapped in the sleeping bag, half asleep, she murmured, 'Man, you're all right, Perry. You're better than all right.'

'Me?'

'Is anyone else here?'

'If I'm good, it's the first time. So it must be your fault.'

'I hope so. Oh Jeez, my creep-o cousins are gonna come and drag me away unless you let me go.'

'Okay.' He kissed her once more, then sat up and began tugging his pants back on. 'Ugh, my head's going around. I hate that; means a hangover tomorrow. To be honest, I'm not very good at – well I don't drink much, you know, hard liquor.'

'Me neither. To be honest.' She shrugged. 'Hey, Perry,' she said suddenly, while trying to appear deeply interested in tying her tennis shoes, 'do you – I know this sounds like a typical girl – but do you think I'm, um, too easy, now?'

He laughed. 'I think you're just goddamn great in every way I can see. Look, I'm about as macho as Peewee Herman, but if I heard someone say you were "easy" like that, I'd punch him in the mouth. After which he'd beat the hell out of me.'

She made a sound halfway between a sigh and a chuckle and kissed him. 'Come on, Peewee, I'll walk you home. My place is too far for you to walk me. My cousins'll give me a ride later.'

She left the sleeping bag and the half-finished bourbon, and they tottered through the trees to the road, groaning now and then and making small jokes about hangovers.

Too soon he was at Sandra's back door. They kissed a last time – his lips were a little sore from all this unaccustomed kissing – and then she said, 'My uncle knows Sandra's number – very suspicious – because I saw it in his address book today. So I'll call you.'

'I'm counting on that.'

'Oh, don't worry. I'll call. Bye.' She squeezed his hand and turned away, and he watched her until the darkness swallowed her up.

Then he opened the screen door – and was surprised to see the kitchen light come on. Aunt June looked out at him from the door into the kitchen.

'Where've you been?' She seemed only distantly interested.

'Uh, a walk to the lake. Couldn't sleep. You okay?'

Her eyes were red, and her hair mussed. Her voice was cracked. He heard someone sobbing in the living room.

'Is that Sandra crying?' he whispered.

'Yes. That's Sandra.'

'Well – what, uh – '

'It's Tetty. She's dead.'

3

Perry and Aunt June sat together on the couch in the living room, saying nothing. Perry had turned his face away from her; he was a little embarrassed to have come home drunk, and he didn't want her to smell it: his drunkenness seemed disrespectful after Tetty's death.

He hadn't been merely drunk, he'd been elated. Thinking, embarrassingly enough, he might be in love. And now he was thinking about the corpse upstairs.

Sandra sat on the front porch, waiting for the ambulance. It would take a while; it had to come from a larger town. Between racking sobs, Sandra talked to herself. Perry couldn't make out what she was saying. He didn't want to, anyway.

All the lights in the house were on, and Perry pictured Sandra going about turning them all on, one by one, after finding Tetty's body. As if General Electric sixty-watt bulbs could disperse the shadow of death.

Aunt June had propped an elbow on the arm of the sagging couch, her head tilted to rest in her open hand, fingertips massaging her temples. Glancing at her, Perry could see the veins in her temples throbbing.

'Oh shit,' Perry muttered. 'Tough time for you to get a migraine.'

'Uh-huh,' Aunt June said. They said nothing more for several minutes, until Perry broke the silence.

'I guess you're sure she's dead. I mean, there's no hope of using, I don't know, CPR or something.'

'For God's sake, Perry,' Aunt June snapped, 'didn't anybody ever tell you a psychiatrist has to be an MD?'

'Oh, yeah. Sorry. You said she bled to death?'

'I think that's what happened.' She spoke in a monotone. 'She's gouged somewhere on the face. I didn't look close, and there's blood on her neck. From the broken glass, I guess.' She hesitated. 'I'm waving my MD in your face, but actually I didn't try any CPR, or – ' She winced. 'I guess I was – ' She stood. 'Come on. It's too late, it was just a couple of minutes before you came in that I found her and she was still warm. I know it's too late. But I guess I have to. Let's go.'

Perry swallowed. 'Uh, I'm no medical expert. I won't be much help.'

'Look, I can't go up there alone. Okay?' She stood and stretched. 'Oh, damn my headache.'

Perry was a little relieved to realize that Aunt June was afraid to go to Tetty's room alone. There's comfort in shared fear.

Why should we be afraid? he wondered, standing. Sickened he could understand. Saddened, definitely. But what was there to be afraid of? Who could be more harmless than the dead?

He followed Aunt June and climbed the stairs just behind her. His hand made a protesting squeak on the banister.

It's not like Aunt June to be scared, he thought. She was a Red Cross volunteer in the Vietnamese refugee camps in Thailand a few years ago. She saw the Vietnamese army raiding the camp, butchering men and women and children at random. She's seen worse things than this could be.

What wasn't she telling him?

Aunt June paused at the top of the stairs. Turning

hesitantly to Perry, she said, 'Just before we found her, I had a dream. And it had to do with broken glass.' She shook her head. 'I guess I'd better tell you later. Come on.'

Aunt June opened the door, and they went in. Perry closed the door as quietly as possible behind him and then wondered why. He wouldn't wake Tetty with its noise.

Tetty was lying on her back, atop the blue sheet; the bedclothes had been kicked to the floor, an almost organic-looking heap at the foot of the bed. The overhead light was on, the rose-glass fixture tinging the scene faintly pink. 'Was her leg drawn up like that before?' Perry asked softly.

Aunt June nodded.

Tetty's right leg was cocked, just as if she were lying casually on the bed, awake but resting, her knee pointing at the ceiling, her foot flat on the sheet. Her right arm was thrown over her face. Perry thought he saw her chest move with breathing – but he always thought he saw that on corpses at funerals.

Her right leg was bare; it looked like ivory. And then he noticed the shackle at her ankle, the strap over her waist, the leather cuffs, chained to the metal bed frame, at her wrists. The blood on her cheeks. The blood on her throat.

The blood was not completely dry. His stomach gave a lurch when he realized that, congealed, the blood looked like blueberry pie filling.

He followed Aunt June to the bedside. She reached out, took Tetty's limp left wrist, and felt for a pulse. 'I don't feel a pulse.' He noticed that she kept her eyes averted from Tetty's face. 'And she doesn't look like she's breathing. She's still a little warm, though. Not – not stiff.' She let out a long breath. 'Perry, you're stronger than I am; you'll have to do it.'

'Do what?'

'Try to restart her breathing. Press her chest. You have to do it fairly violently.'

Perry was afraid she'd ask him to give Tetty artificial respiration. He couldn't. There was blood on Tetty's lips. Her mouth was filled with congealed blood. He couldn't. He leaned over, put his hands out – and drew them back. 'It's a waste of time. You can see she's dead.'

'I know. But Sandra will never forgive us if we don't try.'

'She should do it herself,' he blurted, and then realized he was being insensitive. He took a deep breath. 'Okay. Sorry. Here goes.' He placed his hands flat against her chest, on the sternum, between her breasts; he pressed, hard. Tetty jounced on the bed; there was a faint crackling noise from within her; a lifeless sigh from the nose: the last of the air trapped in her lungs rushing out. He pressed again, and again, the bed creaking with his efforts. There was no response from Tetty. He was unpleasantly aware that her breasts were pressing against the outside of his hands. He could smell, faintly, the rot of congealing blood, and the smell of urine and feces.

He took his hands away and straightened. The room reeled around him with the motion, and he remembered he'd had a good deal to drink. His stomach contracted warningly.

He knew there was something he was putting out of his mind: the necessity of moving her right arm from her face, looking to see what had caused the blood flow. He glanced at Aunt June, was surprised to see she wasn't looking at Tetty at all. She was staring at the windows.

The left window was broken, its lower pane smashed

through, a hole a little bigger than a basketball, jagged crack lines running outward from the hole like a strange negative radiance around a black sun.

'The window's broken, you know,' Aunt June murmured. 'I saw that when I was up here before. And you know something, Perry? It's broken from the inside, out on to the porch roof. Glass all over that roof. None inside. But she's chained down. I tested the chains. She couldn't have broken that window, unless she'd got a key to the restraint locks hidden somewhere. But Sandra insists there's only one key, and she's got it.' She shrugged.

That's part of what is scaring her, Perry realized. The window, broken from the inside. So Sandra must be responsible somehow. Had Sandra really done this to Tetty? As much as he disliked Sandra, he couldn't believe that.

Aunt June turned back to Tetty, said firmly, 'Once more, and we go downstairs.'

Perry sighed, bent over Tetty's body again, placed his hands close together flat on her chest – expecting her to sit up, her face a mask of blood, slap his hands away, screech at him: *What's the big idea?* After which she'd throw back her head and laugh like a sadistic child. But she didn't move. His palms were pressed half against the soft cloth of her blue cotton nightgown, fingertips against the flesh beneath her collarbone. Her skin had only the slightest trace of warmth, like riverbank clay at twilight; and it was almost claylike pliable. There was no thud under his hands, where her heartbeat should have been; he imagined he could feel her heart like a cold, motionless stone under the flesh.

Oh, if you play for me tomorrow, I won't hear you. See: I'll be dead.

She'd said it lying on this same bed.

He thought: Once more, and then the hell with it. He pressed hard, violently, down on her chest. Her body jerked on the bed, and the arm that had been covering the upper part of her face fell away, revealing the eyes.

Her right eye was missing.

It looked as if it had been pressed from the socket, from within; broken, exploded outward – like the bedroom window – and its remains lay spattered in ragged scarlet shreds on her round, ivory cheek. The blood from the socket had run down the cheek, on to the throat. There were no marks such as broken glass would make. Her head was tilted away from him. When he straightened, removing the pressure from her chest, the bedsprings bounced a little, and her head lolled on its neck with the motion of the bed and seemed to turn its bloody socket to glare wetly at him. Now, for the first time, he saw that rigor mortis had begun to draw her face into rigidity, pulling her mouth into a taut, clown's-mask smile. The wet red eye socket; the smile . . . Perry gagged, bolted for the door, yanked it open – and saw Tetty standing on the landing, outside the door, staring at him, that same death-rotten, collapsed face.

He stood frozen, a squeaking sound in his throat, his stomach wrenching. And then he realized that it wasn't Tetty. It was Sandra. Her face wasn't collapsed – just older, and worn by alcoholism. He hadn't seen the family resemblance so much before . . .

'The ambulance is – ' Sandra began. Perry shook his head violently, pushed past her, wondering if he'd make it to the toilet, seeing that childlike round face, that bloody eye socket hanging in his mind's eye like the afterimage of a bright red light . . .

* * *

He found himself in the bathroom, draped over the toilet bowl, staring into the multicolored whorl of his own vomit turning slowly in the water. His stomach contracted again, he groaned, dry-heaved, swore with the pain. And again. The heaving quieted, and he gasped for air. When Aunt June tapped on the bathroom door and said, 'Hey, you okay, Perry?' he managed to say, 'Yuh. Okay, I guess.' He stood and began to wash out his mouth, feeling a little better as he spat bitterness into the bathroom sink. Over the shushing of water in the sink, he heard male voices from the living room. 'She musta put out her eye when she shoved her head through the window – bled to death, I guess. Not that much blood, though. I guess she picks the locks on those chains, huh?'

Jeez, Perry thought. What a clod. Sandra doesn't want to hear him talking about Tetty bleeding to death just now, for God's sake.

Picked the locks? He washed his face, flushed the toilet, thinking. The guy thinks she picked the locks, went to the window, smashed her head through in some kind of fit, returned to the bed, and, half blinded, in agony, relocked the restraints. Bullshit. But how had she done it? Perry shrugged. His head hurt; thinking was painful right now.

He dried his face, replaced the damp, mould-odorous towel, and returned to the living room. The ambulance attendants were carrying her out. The one who'd spoken was backing down the steps, lifting his end of the gurney, talking too loudly to the cop on the front porch. A sheriff, Perry guessed. He fit the country sheriff stereotype: red-faced, overweight. But his expression didn't belong to the stereotype. It was sad, almost like a little boy whose feelings had been hurt.

Perry went to the kitchen and sat at the table, his head on his arms. He dozed, vaguely aware that Sandra and

Aunt June were talking to the sheriff on the front porch. He couldn't hear most of what they were saying. He pictured Lois, standing in the starlight, nude, her hair mussed. He almost smiled. He sat up with a jerk, feeling a touch on his shoulder. It was Aunt June, looking sympathetic. 'You okay now?'

'I guess so.' Better come clean. 'I went out. Met some people by the lake. Drank too much. I'm not much help to you this way. Sorry.'

'That's okay. I feel a little sick myself.'

'The sheriff gone?'

'Uh-huh. Sandra too. She went with the ambulance. You want a cup of tea? Or do you think you could sleep?'

'I – ' He could sleep, but he didn't want to. He didn't want to dream. 'Yeah, I'll have some tea if you're having some.' He listened to the water hissing in the pan as it came to a boil, watched the steam rising, and tried not to visualize that bloody eye socket swiveling to glare at him. Aunt June made a pot of strong black tea, then put a bottle of Tylenol on the table next to his cup. Perry stared at the bottle as he sipped his tea, and made no move to open it.

'You don't want to take something for your headache?' she asked, sitting across from him. She hunched wearily over the table, her elbows planted on either side of her cup, listlessly stirring the tea with a butter knife – she couldn't find a clean spoon and she was too tired to wash any. The thing was crouching under the table, between them: Tetty's death. It wasn't possible not to talk about it, but they kept it abstract, to make it easier to deal with. And it began indirectly, with her question about the headache medicine.

'Looking at the Tylenol, I remember reading about that guy about a couple of years ago who put arsenic or cyanide or something into a whole lot of bottles of Tylenol. And then another guy, inspired by the fine example of the first one, put some kind of caustic acid in eyewash.' He shook his head. 'I'm still amazed by that. The people that died, and were blinded. And those guys did it for fun.'

'There's something particularly intriguing to me about the Tylenol murders,' Aunt June said. 'The victims were faceless, to the killer. He never saw them. They were just part of the milling mass of humanity. Because he made them part of that lump, not really feeling individuals, it was easier for him to have no empathy for them. He could enjoy the thought of the random violence – like a little kid kicking at an anthill – but he never had to feel guilty for it. Because those people weren't real for him. Or at least, they weren't human the way people around him are. The key to the whole thing was his tendency to dehumanize people. Maybe it came about because of some pathological pressure – or maybe it happened because he had a spell of ESS.'

'I've forgotten at least a hundred bunches of initials for things. What's ESS?'

'Something you never heard about, probably. Something I thought Tetty suffered from. That's why I'm thinking about it. But suicide doesn't fit for ESS.'

'Well what *is* – '

'Uh-uh,' she interrupted, raising a hand palm outward. 'Forget it. Not tonight. I'm too tired to go into it.'

'Okay. One thing: you're pretty sure it *was* suicide?'

'No. But how else? I just don't think it's possible Sandra killed her. Even if it's possible she secretly hated Tetty, she needed her testimony for that lawsuit. She was counting on the money from the lawsuit. Look, I'll tell you what happened, as far as I know it . . .'

* * *

Sandra and Aunt June had been asleep downstairs, Sandra in her bedroom, Aunt June on the couch. Aunt June was awakened by the sound of glass breaking. She'd sat up, listening, and heard nothing more. Decided that some drunk had broken a bottle on the curb outside the house. She glanced through the half-open bedroom door, saw Sandra asleep on the bed; she could see her clearly in the light from the reading lamp Sandra had left on beside the bed.

And then Aunt June had gone back to sleep. She was awakened a second time by a nightmare. The kind that's so awful you force yourself to wake, hitting some panic button hidden deep in the unconscious so you don't have to face it. She'd dreamed of a huge, slick-skinned insect – mottled gray – trying to force its tongue into her mouth. The insect was something like an oversized housefly, but it was as big as a half-grown cat. It gripped her face with small, almost human hands and tried to sting her on the throat with a barb extruding from the bristly tip of its shivering abdomen. She'd clawed it away from her, and it buzzed angrily – and then she woke. She'd sat up on the couch and, blearily, thought she'd seen something fluttering in the air over the couch, a big gray thing, half seen.

'It must have been a carryover hallucination from the dream,' she told Perry. 'Hypnogogic imagery. That happens to people. But I was scared, and covered my eyes. I thought I heard it buzzing. God, I must have been still half asleep – and then I knew it was gone. I just sensed it. I uncovered my eyes, and sure enough, the hallucination was gone. It really shook me up. I got up, then; I wanted to get some air. And I saw the front door was open. I don't know how that happened; I should have asked Sandra, maybe she got up and went out first, for some reason. I went out on the front porch, and I saw the broken glass on the lawn. I went into the yard and looked up, and Tetty's window was broken. I got Sandra up and we ran upstairs. The door was still locked from the outside; that padlock, she puts it on – to keep her in if she breaks loose. She unlocked it and we found Tetty. And the windows were still locked.'

'Christ.' He tapped the rim of his cup until he could see from the look on Aunt June's face that it annoyed her. He stopped, said, 'I'll bet Tetty managed it herself, somehow. I figure she wanted to shake everyone up. Especially Sandra. Maybe she threw something through the window from the bed. Okay, you didn't find anything on the porch or the lawn, but someone might have picked it up. You might have missed it. And then she gouged her eye out with something, in a fit of – you know. Rage.'

'I don't know. Maybe. It's a pretty good theory but – ' She broke off and looked at the ceiling. 'Did you hear a buzzing sound just now?'

Perry stiffened. 'What?'

'It was behind my head.' She turned in her seat, looked toward the kitchen sink. Perry heard it now. And it got louder. Louder than a fly. And the sound seemed to travel, coming from first one end of the room, then another, like the balance shifting on stereo speakers. But they could see nothing flying past.

'Must be something in the walls,' Perry said. Not believing it. The buzzing circled once more – and then it was gone. To be replaced by another noise: a rattling at the living-room windows. Perry stood, wincing; the room spun a little; his headache throbbed. He walked stiffly into the living room. There was a piece of dusty, transparent plastic stretched over the living-room window on the outside, probably left over from the previous winter;

a feeble attempt at insulation. The dawn light made the window a vertical rectangle of ashen gray – except for the blot of black in the upper right corner. Something vaguely oval, like a cat with its legs tucked under it seen from beneath. Probably just a patch of some kind. So why was he staring at it? It moved, just a little. The plastic creased under the oval blot, as if it were gripping the surface more tightly. He heard the buzzing again, from the windowsill. He stared at the sill, which held a photograph of Tetty with her mother, and the small ceramic figures of Prince Charles and Lady Diana posing together in wedding regalia. Only, Sandra had stuck a little skirt in tinfoil on Prince Charles, to make fun. The figures began to move . . .

. . . to shiver, rattling, moving across the sill on the ceramic base, as if dancing together; moving faster, and faster, sliding toward the photograph. The framed photo began to slide, too; the photo and the ceramics clapped together with a crunch; the figures shattered, Lady Diana's head falling to one side, Charles's head to the other, rolling away like marbles. The glass over the photo was cracked; it lay on its back. The buzzing had accompanied this sliding, cracking; it had taken two seconds. Now the buzzing receded . . . Gone. The blot against the corner of the window was gone, too. 'I'm drunk,' Perry said to himself, aloud, and then again, with less conviction, 'I am. I'm drunk.' He was aware that Aunt June had come up behind him. She was staring at the window. 'So,' he began, swallowing. 'Did you see it? The things breaking?'

'No. I heard it, though. The semitrucks.'

'What?'

'Big semitrucks. They barrel through here, Sandra told me. Right in front of the house, one or two a night. Some kind of shortcut some of them take. Makes vibrations that rattle things around. Must've made these things fall.'

The sound of a car pulling up in front of the house. They both looked toward the front door. A car door slammed with a hollow metallic sound. Boot steps on the walk. A creaking as someone moved the broken screen door so he could bang on the inner one. Aunt June, moving slowly, opened the door.

It was the big, red-faced, sad-eyed sheriff, framed against the blue-gray dawn light. ''Morning,' he said, sounding western.

'No, it isn't really,' said Aunt June. 'Not a good one.'

'I didn't say *good* morning,' he said, without a trace of humour. 'We have us another little problem.'

'What's that?' Perry asked, standing just behind Aunt June. The sheriff glanced at him.

'Now who's this?'

'My nephew Perry.'

'I'll want to talk to him, later. What happened, your nephew asks me. Well, a little girl has been drowned in Chemeka Lake. Just a few hours ago, we think. Marks on her make us think someone drowned her. Held her under. Thing is, her brother claims he saw Tetty talking to her, at the back door, though what that little girl – just a first-grader – what she'd be doing up at that hour . . .' Perry wasn't listening, now. He was staring at the front window, at the plastic over the window, where he'd thought he'd seen something clinging, a few minutes before. An outline had been impressed into the plastic there. As if someone had pressed their face against it, until the plastic took the impression of their features. It was a doll-sized face, and blurred. But recognizable.

4

Wendy Marsteller, shivering a little in the morning chill, stepped off the condo's porch and walked across the unfinished lawn to the new white sidewalk, wearing her bathrobe over a slip and barefeet. She held her two-month-old baby, Billy, tightly against her small chest to keep him warm and to stifle his yowlings. He'd awakened her a few minutes before, at six-thirty, yelling for his bottle. He began, now, to demand it once more, with an amazingly loud cry for such a small creature, and his howling mingled in something like harmony with the siren of the ambulance, pulling away from the curb down the street. The ambulance's approach had brought Wendy to the sidewalk; nothing much happened in the Chemeka Village housing project, and Wendy was grateful for any break in the monotony.

Two blocks down, the cluster of people at the lake's edge began to break up; two of them stood together on a concrete abutment looking at the lake. Now and then they gestured toward the cold, knife-blue expanse of water. The lake was glassy still that morning; the far bank sparkled where the sunlight reached through the thinner strands of pine. Nearer, the lake was still in shadow. A fish eagle wheeled over the lake's middle, about five hundred yards away. The pines and Joshua trees around the housing project looked more blue than green in the morning light. Wendy could see the blackened lump on the far bank where they'd had their lake party the night before.

Evan had been angry when she'd come home a little tipsy; he'd said it was stupid to take Billy outdoors, late at night. But he'd gone to visit his brother after dinner – and they'd probably got wrecked on his brother Danny's homegrown pot – and she'd been left all alone. And a person gets tired of TV. She smiled, thinking that it was more entertaining watching Lois throw herself at that new guy Perry than watching fake romance on TV. 'Lois is a bad girl, Billy, don't you think so?' she asked the baby absently as she started back to the house. The baby had ceased crying and responded by making that funny piggish sound he sometimes made, making her think of the piglet baby in *Alice in Wonderland*. 'My little piglet,' she said, glancing once more at the place where the ambulance had been.

She stopped, staring. Now that the crowd was gone, she could see Mr and Mrs Stiggins on their front lawn; she knew it was them because Mr Stiggins was so tall, and long-necked, and his wife so short and round. At first she thought they were arguing, then she saw him take her in his arms, and Wendy realized he was comforting her. Mrs Stiggins sagged; she seemed to have lost the strength of her legs.

'It must have been one of her kids got drowned in the lake, in that ambulance, Billy,' Wendy murmured. 'I wonder, was it that boy Conway, or maybe his little sister Ella. Gee, that's awful – they had that problem with Conway getting poisoned by what's-her-name a few months ago and now this. What do you think of that, Billy?' He began to whimper. 'Okay, okay, I'll get your bottle.'

She was glad to get into the warmth of the house; it was cold outside in just a bathrobe and slip. 'But it's going to be too damn hot everywhere later today, Billy. Oh, your bottle's nice and warm now.' She yawned, felt a pang of weariness, the throb of an oncoming headache. Her drinking catching up to her. 'Stayed up too late, Billy. And then you wake me at six-thirty. Why can't babies eat three square meals a day like everyone else?' The baby coughed at the same time he drank, and some of the milk found its way into his lungs. He began to sputter, to yowl and gag. In an outburst of irritability she shook him, harder than she should have, making his head wobble on his neck; he looked shocked for a moment, then began to howl twice as loud as before. 'Oh dammit, I'm sorry, Billy.' She hugged him, patting his back until he quieted. 'Mommy's got what they call premenstrual tension. I read about it in *Woman's Day*. I'm not myself. You forgive me?' She kissed him and was rewarded with a gurgle. 'Here, finish your bottle, my little piglet.' She was hungry herself, and wished he'd finish so she could eat. He took his damn time about it, until her arm ached from holding the bottle. At last, she got him fed and back to sleep in his plastic bed basket.

'*I'll* never get back to sleep now,' she told herself. In some ways, Evan had it a little harder; he had to be out of the house by six to get to work on time, commuting an hour to get to the lumber processing site. But then, she reflected, making herself a bowl of Malt-o-Meal, he uses that as an excuse to give me hell for everything. How hard he works, how he didn't want the job. Well, he didn't have to take it. It was simply a matter of exchange; her dad had offered to arrange the condo for them in exchange for Evan's taking on the forest maintenance engineer apprenticeship. Evan had wanted to study architecture. He should have thought of that before he got me pregnant, Wendy thought. Saying he was sure it would be safe, talking her into it, and then refusing to consider an abortion. Wendy had just turned eighteen three months before. She'd had to leave school. Both sets of parents had insisted they get married. 'Too young,' Wendy muttered, turning on the radio. She sang falsetto on the choruses of an *A-ha!* song till she glanced at the clock, realized it was time for an early morning talk show. She turned off the radio, turned on the TV, and melted into the programming. It was two hours before she came up for air: someone was knocking on the back door. She hoped it was Lois.

It was. 'Hi, kiddo,' Lois said, a little breathlessly. She'd just come to the end of a morning jog; she wore jogging shorts and a Nike ski equipment T-shirt. 'You like my new jogging shoes? That's leather, on the side.'

'How can you get up and jog after drinking so much last night and staying out until four with that guy?' Wendy asked, pouring Lois a glass of Tang.

'That's one reason I'm jogging. Makes me feel better. Sweats out the hangover. I am tired, though . . . and you know what?' She scratched a nipple through the Nike shirt. 'I got a mosquito bite on a nipple and it itches like a bitch.'

Wendy giggled. 'I can't be-*lieve* you! Mosquito bites on your *ni*-pples!'

Lois cracked up, then covered her eyes, pretending shame. 'I know. It's terrible.'

'You should be ashamed. For having fun when I can't.'

Lois looked up. 'Hey, did I leave my purse over here the other day? Not the big canvas one, the little black plastic one.'

'Yeah, here it is. Watch, you'll forget it again.' They sat on the brown vinyl living-room couch; out of habit they kept their eyes on the TV's perpetual dance of brightly coloured banalities, never taking it in consciously.

'I couldn't sleep very well,' Lois confided. 'I kept thinking about Perry.'

'He's really cute,' Wendy said obligingly, knowing it was an exaggeration. 'And he plays that thing – what is it?'

'Mandolin.'

'I like the way he plays.'

'So do I,' Lois said. 'He plays *real* nice.'

'*Lo*-is you're *ter*-rible!'

They laughed, and then Wendy lowered her voice to ask, 'No, seriously, did you guys really make it?' Lois nodded. 'Was it good for real?'

'*Yeah*. And not because he studied the *Kama Sutra* or something. Because we really like each other and he's a tender guy. Only I know I shouldn't have practically dragged him into the sleeping bag like that. It was our first date, for God's sake, where is Modern Woman's sense of decorum? But, uh – no seriously – I knew he might leave town soon and I knew after I talked to him for five minutes we were going to, eventually, so I figured –'

'Say no more! All is understood! I hear your confession and give you ten thousand Hail Marys. Oh God, I've got to take some aspirin or something. You want some?'

'Yeah, okay.' After Wendy returned from the kitchen with the aspirin and more Tang, Lois went on, 'I'm scared he's going to go back to San Diego and forget about me. But he says he has friends in Portland, and I'm going to go to school there, so maybe – I don't know – I wonder how I can feel so strongly about a guy I hardly know. But I do.'

'It happens that way.' Wendy suddenly felt sad, thinking that she'd never really felt anything that strong about Evan. Lois's new romance made her feel a little envious.

She changed the subject. 'What happened down the street at the Stigginses' place, do you know? I saw an ambulance and –'

'You didn't hear?' Lois lowered her voice. 'That little girl Ella was drowned. Or strangled and thrown in the water. They think she was murdered, I heard. And her big brother says he saw – oh God. I guess I'm blurry in the head today. I just realized that it's that girl Perry's aunt is taking care of or analyzing or something. She's supposed to be the one who killed Ella. God, it must be weird for Perry. And that'll probably mean he leaves sooner . . .'

'That girl Tetty? Yeah, she's crazy. I never knew her much.'

'She never seemed crazy to me. Just shy. But – she shot the sheriff.' Both girls grinned at that. 'Oh shit, what are we smiling about! That poor little girl.' Dutifully, Lois and Wendy dropped their smiles, gazed sadly at the TV, looking at the flow of images the way people used to watch the clouds pass or a stream rush. The baby began to mewl, then gave out great gulping wet howls.

'Oh God,' Wendy said, getting up. 'He needs to be changed.' After a few minutes she returned from the extra bedroom they used as a nursery, carrying Billy, who was raptly ogling the wallpaper, the floor, everything but what moved, his pale blue eyes always slightly crossed. She held him on her lap, bouncing him a little to keep him occupied, and sighed.

'You look fed up or something,' Lois said.

'Oh God, it's nothing new. I just keep thinking, What am I doing here, with Evan and a baby and nothing to make me feel like I'm – I don't know how to explain. I mean, I love Billy.' She kissed the baby as if to confirm this. 'But you've got to have something for yourself in your life. And I'm just eighteen and everyone else is going to go to college or making a career somewhere – '

'Having a baby doesn't end everything. It's just a setback. Lots of career women have children.'

'Yeah but . . .' Wendy was not in the mood to be consoled. 'But then there's Evan. I don't think he'd ever let me do anything else. He feels so martyred all the time. Like I talked him into getting married.' She covered Billy's ears to whisper, 'I wanted an abortion. Evan acts like it's my fault he had to work and study forest maintenance and lumber processing because it was my dad who owns the housing project and who got him the apprenticeship. I mean, if you ask me, that's not a bad deal, a house and a job just like that. Most people would be grateful. And lately he won't even help me take care of the baby.'

'No kidding?'

'No kidding. He claims that working all day and then having to study forest maintenance, he's too tired to do it. But he doesn't study much. He gets stoned with his brother and their friends and plays video games at that stupid bar. And then I'm alone and bored all night. I bet you're sorry you asked why I looked depressed.'

Wendy had forgotten that Lois hadn't actually asked. 'No, Wendy, hey come on, I'm your friend. Listen, I think you should stand up to Evan and make him take care of the baby. You do lots of work too, around the house. You should go to the community college part-time this fall. You can get a baby-sitter.'

'Maybe. I doubt if he'd – ' She shrugged.

'Hey, lighten up. I got to go take a shower, I smell like the girl's locker room at the Moscow Olympics. I'll call you later. You think about what I said.'

'Bye.' Wendy remained sitting, gazing blankly at the TV, as Lois left. Gradually she began to get caught up in the soap opera dialogue as Billy went to sleep on her lap. The last soap finished at eleven-thirty. She roused herself, blinking, looking around. She spotted Lois's black plastic purse on a kitchen chair. Wendy chuckled. 'She's so absentminded. Forgot it again.'

Rather than spend the rest of the afternoon alone except for Billy – and the TV – she decided to take the purse over to Lois's. That was a mile away, too far to carry the baby in her arms, so she'd need the backpack frame with its baby carrier harness. She stood, stretched. Where was the damn thing? Oh. The basement. She made a face. She didn't like going down in basements. Evan insisted on storing the harness there because 'it's always underfoot when it's upstairs.' As if the harness crawled by itself just to get in his way.

She put the baby in his bed, grimacing when he began to whimper. 'Goddammit,' she muttered, 'don't start in on mama now, Billy.' Just as if he'd heard her and taken pity, he fell silent, closed his eyes. She looked around the nursery, shaking her head. Bottles with a film of souring milk in them, wet diapers, and pacifiers lay about on the rug. She'd have to clean up, not just here but the whole house, before Evan got home. He was such a stickler about cleanliness. Anal retentive or something. They were always arguing about that. But the more he called her a slob, the less she felt like accommodating him by cleaning up. Better do it anyway, she thought, heading for the kitchen, because I can't take another fight today. One too many fights.

At the back of the kitchen was the basement door. Over Evan's protests, she kept it open, with the light always on in the basement. He couldn't understand why it scared her to have the door closed. She could feel the darkness behind the door almost like a palpable pressure against it.

She descended the basement steps, careful because they were steep and their concrete was slick. She stepped on to the basement floor. Where was the baby carrier? She couldn't see it.

The light came from a small, yellowish bulb dangling near the wooden underpinnings of the ground floor above her and from the little basement window, through which she could see the dying rosebush she'd planted. She noted with annoyance that someone had broken a pane on the little hinged window. Neighborhood kids with their Frisbees probably. The basement was narrow, with paint cans in one corner and odds and ends of junky furniture taking up most of the remaining storage space. The room was dim and smelled of damp concrete and mildewed cardboard. Every corner, every rafter, sheltered a shadow; and she was sure that every shadow sheltered a spider. The squat black hairy kind.

The baby carrier. 'Where the hell did he put the silly thing?' There it was, in the far right-hand corner. Under the window, where it was in a damn shadow . . .

She stepped over a box of kitchen implements, leaned forward, balanced on one foot, reaching down behind the folding chairs, gingerly feeling for the carrier.

Something buzzed, abrasively, suddenly, behind her.

She felt a weird spongy slap at the inside of her knee; the knee of the leg she stood on. She fell forward, making a whimpering sound, a sound like Billy would make. There was a stab of weird, fizzling pain in her right elbow as she struck her funny bone on the corner of an aluminum chair frame. And then she was lying across the box, against the chairs, her left hand entangled in the netting of a folded Ping-Pong table.

She jerked at the netting, trying to get loose, imagining a thousand bugs crawling on her – and hearing again that buzzing, just overhead. It stopped. There was another noise now: a clicking, scratching coming from the ceiling. Wendy froze, then, slowly, looked up toward the sound. There was something clinging to one of the two-by-fours; it clung to the support beam, hanging upside down, reminding her of those ugly wasp nests you sometimes found in attics. She couldn't see it very clearly; but now, when it started to move, she knew it was no wasp's nest. It began to crawl along the beam toward the space directly over her head.

It looked at first like an immense gray-black spider with wings. But she saw it was more like an enormous housefly, big as an owl. Creeping upside-down to emerge from a band of shadow, twisting its head impossibly backward to gaze down at her with a face that – it leapt from the rafter, fluttering, its wings a blur like a hummingbird's wings, dropping directly at her head. The basement swallowed her scream as she ripped free of the netting and twisted around to lurch toward the stairway, falling over the clattering box of pans, feeling her skin contract tightly on her, her hands go cold and clumsy; but all the time the gray insect thing was buzzing, flying around her head. She kicked the box aside, stood, shouting without words, covering her head with her arms, thinking, *Where is it? Where is it now? I can't see it.*

A feathery touch on the back of her neck. It was there.

It clung to the back of her neck. She wanted to claw it away but her arms felt heavy, the heaviness spreading out through her from the stinging between her shoulder blades. And she fell. Fell against the stairs, not feeling them.

All the rest of her thoughts were swept up in the roaring

that filled her, a feeling like four days of the flu going through her in one second. Going through and then gone, leaving numbness. And then she slumped against the steps, numb, forgetting about the thing on the back of her neck, the rustling sound it made as it nosed into her hair . . .

She slid into a warm, gray ooze. A great pit of living glutinosity: she'd fallen into herself. And she kept falling, beyond self, into sleep.

Perry knew he was dreaming. But it was no use to him, knowing it was a dream, because he was powerless to change the dream's course. He was dreaming he was in the bathroom, lathering shaving cream over his jaw. The mirror was not flat against the medicine cabinet. He reached up, shut the mirror door of the cabinet – doing so, the image reflected in the mirror swung, shifted to catch a different corner of the bathroom: the window.

Something oval, gray-black, blurred, clung to the windowpane from the outside. Then the window shattered, blasted inward, the glass shards flying toward him in slow motion while at the same instant, as he stared at his face in the mirror, he saw his right eye begin to bulge, then explode outward, spattering the mirror with –

He sat up in bed, his hand clasped over his right eye. He wasn't quite awake yet, though he sat up with his eyes open. He removed his hand from his eye, stared at the palm. Nothing. No blood. He relaxed, smiled at himself. 'Jerk.'

He stretched. The dream, he supposed, had been suggested to his unconscious by seeing Tetty with her eye missing, and the thing – probably a tired fruit bat – clinging to the window plastic. Making the mark he'd thought looked like Tetty's face in miniature. Looking at it closer, later, the resemblance had seemed less obvious. He'd probably superimposed her face over the mark because she'd been on his mind. A projection, right out of Psych 101.

He swung his legs off the cot, peering out through the screened glassless window at the backyard. The shadows of the trees fringing the yard were long. It was nearly evening. He'd taken a nap in the afternoon, after helping Aunt June get rid of the reporter from the Bend newspaper. He felt groggy and hungry, and there was a taut, soundless whining somewhere inside him: the residue of disorientation and anxiety from having seen Tetty dead. Dead and disfigured.

Don't think about it, he told himself, and the feeling will go away.

The smell of food cooking lured him to the kitchen. Aunt June was setting the table with two plates, forks, and knives. Apparently Sandra hadn't come back yet. 'How you feeling?' she asked, spooning a steaming vegetarian casserole on to his plate. She looked hollow-eyed; he guessed she hadn't slept yet. 'Oh, I'm okay, I guess,' he said.

'You look tired.'

'Uh-huh.' He sat down and, blowing on the hot food to cool it, began to eat. She'd made it herself from fresh ingredients; after Sandra's meals, it was a revelation. 'Hey, this is good.'

'Naturally.' She smirked to pretend smugness. 'Sandra called, said she'd spend the night in Bend. She'll be back tomorrow. She begged me to stay awhile. I know it's depressing but – do you mind?'

'Staying?' He thought about Lois. 'No. I don't mind.'

'Have some milk. Slow down, you'll choke. So tell me what – ' She was interrupted by the telephone, ringing from the living room. 'I'll get it.' She spoke to someone for about ten minutes, then returned, sat down, looking distracted. She made no move to finish her dinner.

'So?' Perry said.

'Hm? Oh, that was the sheriff. Dawson, I think his name is. Real western sheriff sort of name. He said that apparently Tetty wasn't the one who killed the little girl; according to the coroner, she died after we'd already called the ambulance for Tetty – after Tetty was dead. I think that story about the girl's brother seeing Tetty luring her out into the night is baloney. I think the sheriff knows that too. But he seems to think that two deaths in one night are too coincidental. Especially in light of the fact that the two people who died had some connection with one another.' She broke off, staring at the remains of her casserole, as if reading a divination in it. 'And the sheriff wants to talk to us. I got him to put it off until tomorrow evening, when Sandra's back. He wants us to come to the office. "Routine questioning." You, me, Sandra, and that Stiggins boy.'

Perry shrugged. 'Okay. Sounds like a pointless pain in the ass but I guess we have to.'

'I suppose he's connecting the two deaths in the obvious way.'

'That boy hated Tetty because of the poisoning, and the other harassment, maybe didn't want to prosecute because he was afraid of her, and – '

'Yeah, and killed her. I guess he could have come in by the window. Via the roof. Then maybe she saw him at the window, threw something at him. That broke the window and he reached in and opened the window latch, pulled the window open, climbed in and killed her with a knife or something – through the eye. Then went out through the window, locked it behind him. Why he'd lock the window again I don't know.'

'But – ' Perry felt queasy, now. 'Why didn't she shout when she saw him up there, when he came in? A scream or something.'

She shrugged. 'I don't know. I don't think he was ever there, anyway.'

'What? Why not?'

'I think the coroner's report will tell us something else. I've wired a friend, asked him to send me something express. It's a book, contains a paper by a Dr Horescu. Rumanian scientist, died years ago. The paper was written in 1906, and no one took it seriously. In fact, it got him certified as a crank in scientific circles. I read it when I was doing research on ESS. It's related to that.'

'Are you going to tell me what ESS – '

'No I'm not. Later. Anyway, there was something in it about a village in which everyone disappeared. Three hundred people, gone. They only found about a dozen bodies. And all of them were missing the right eye – '

'Aunt June.'

' – and a close examination of the bodies revealed that the brains were underweight by – '

'*Aunt June.*'

She stared at him. 'Ye-es?'

'Tell me. I insist. ESS. What is it? I'm a poor lost soul and I want to know. What is it and what's it got to do with Tetty?'

'You want a logical explanation.' She shrugged. 'It won't be that. But Empathy Suppression Syndrome is the biological mechanism for dehumanization. Well – ' She spread her hands self-deprecatingly. 'Anyway, that's my theory. Dehumanization is at work in any form of brutality. From treating people in heavy traffic like they're just obstacles and not people, to genocide. Okay, the classic example, Hitler. How did he persuade thousands of people to, uh, facilitate the Holocaust? Germans aren't inherently evil people.'

'Um . . . sheer charisma? Mass hypnosis? Propaganda?'

'Those things helped him set up the right conditions, but there was another force at work. Something Hitler liberated. The same thing that made it possible for the so-called Christian Phalangists to massacre the women and children in a refugee camp in Beirut. You ever hear those stories about concentration camp guards in World War II taking pity on hungry pigeons and tossing them bits of bread on the snow while hundreds of people died of starvation in the camps behind them? It wasn't only racism; they'd suppressed their empathy for anyone human they didn't identify with. How did they do it so thoroughly? How do people achieve that pinnacle of ruthlessness? People who kiss their wives and children. It happened in Vietnam, with our side and theirs. It's not racial.'

'I know what you mean. It's like a switch is thrown in 'em, and their eyes glaze over, and – '

'Perry?'

'Huh?'

'The professor is lecturing here. Don't interrupt the professor.'

'Sorry, professor. Go on.'

'Anyway, I think it's a biological mechanism, genetically programmed into all of us. Nature errs on the side of excess.'

Perry raised his hand. 'Oh, professor!'

Aunt June rolled her eyes. 'What is it?'

'How can you call that a survival trait? It makes people

aggressive, right? So they lose all interest in cooperating. And that's not great for survival.'

'Not now it isn't, not in our society. But it was once. It was created for primitive humanity, and we still retain it. When primitive men felt threatened, and if all the other conditions were right, the brain referred to the genetic programming that triggers the functioning of a gland I haven't yet proven exists. This gland produces a hormone that instantly alters the character. Suppresses certain inhibitions. Most of all, removes all ability to identify with or sympathize with potential victims. This way primitive man could react without hesitation to defend himself.'

'So what's the connection with Tetty?'

'She was a sociopath. I think sociopaths suffer from sporadic bursts in the production of this hormone. It's a kind of neurological appendicitis.'

'But you said it was tied in with self-interest. Survival. And if she committed suicide . . .'

'I know. That's the problem. I thought –'

Perry jumped a little, startled by a knock on the front door. Ashamed of his edginess, he said, 'I'll see who it is.' He stood, went into the living room, opened the door.

The man standing in the thickening dusk on the porch was very ordinary looking. He had a round face, the long sideburns of middle-aged men who hope to look younger that way, and an obvious hair transplant; friendly brown eyes, brown hair, a brown sports coat. Until he began to talk, he was nearly identical to a million contemporary middle-aged men; right down to the aviator glasses and digital watch. When he spoke, Perry was mildly surprised by his middle European accent. And something intense in his voice.

'Good evening, my friend,' said the man at the door. 'I wonder if I could please speak to Sandra Cummings. You might tell her that Dr Arthur Rofocale is here.'

5

Wendy Marsteller woke in the early evening. And then again, she didn't wake at all.

She found herself coming into a sort of self-awareness, though, as she was climbing the stairs. There was nothing wrong with that, with waking up to find herself standing, climbing the stairs. Nothing weird about it. She climbed the stairs to the kitchen, walked through the kitchen to the living room – and stopped.

She stood in the center of the living room, between the sofa with its sickeningly geometrical throw pillows and the portable colour TV. She stood there waiting. She knew that things were happening inside her. She was waiting for those happenings to come to their conclusion. For the next step. She was aware of a strange objectivity, as if she were watching a movie of herself and not experiencing things directly. The way a person feels in a dream, yes – and yet she was awake, and aware. All her physical sensations were very sharp. But mentally she was . . . distanced.

She was aware of another sensation. A kind of inner seething, like a pot of water on its way to a boil. The sensation wasn't part of her yet but it was coming at her from somewhere inside, like a truck on a freeway at night, the headlights growing as it bore down, and when it hit her – *there*. A flood of warmth as it hit her. The feeling of distance was gone, completely replaced by the heat of that boiling. And it had radiated its heat glow on to everything around her. All that she saw – her canary-yellow kitchen, her olive-green living room – was now tinted burning red or throbbing rose, like one of those pictures taken with infrared film. The clock's ticking sounded like a hammer pounding. The neighbor's dog started to bark, just then. That damn German shepherd who snarled at her from his chain when she walked by, who woke her at night with his howls. She pictured wrapping him in barbed wire and then leaving him to dangle, alive and gouged, from the top of a telephone pole, somewhere far away where his yelps wouldn't disturb her. She wanted quiet now. So she could think coolly and make plans.

But her ears, her nerves, were ripped by an explosive sound from another room. The nursery. A quintessentially human sound: a baby crying at the top of its lungs. The way she felt just then, the baby's yowl for attention was as terrible, as loud, as a supersonic jet's takeoff. It was the sound of the engine that had hijacked her life. And there was pure, uncut *demand* in it. *I want now, I want NOW*.

How *dare* he make such demands of her? She knew, at that moment, that the boiling sensation was anger. It had seemed like a new sensation because she'd never felt it unadulterated, untempered before. This was anger at its purest and most absolute. Anger at its most satisfying. Anger like the best cognac in the world.

Drink deeply, Wendy, all you want. It's all yours now. Everything is yours!

A voice. Whose?

Just a friend, Wendy.

'Where are you?' she asked, looking around. Not at all afraid, or surprised. She had sensed this other one too, she realized. It was a sort of living background she'd taken for granted. It belonged there.

Lots of places, the voice said. *Look at the basement stairs. That's one place you'll see me.*

She looked. Just shadow down there, edging the stairs. But as she watched, the ordinary shadows, where the light was blocked, began to thicken, and then to shift. Becoming like smoke whorled into just the hint of a bestial face.

I helped you become a Higher person, Wendy. I sent the liberator, the flying thing you saw.

She felt a surge of suspicion. 'You think that means I work for you?'

What put that idea in your head? Not at all. I just like to see people get free. I was bound up with guilt once too. Now I'm free from everything. Wendy, that kid is yelling again. How can you stand it?

The baby yowling. The walls vibrating with it. Selfish little pig. It did make her angry. The anger like a silky liquor . . .

It was funny about the anger, though. One part of her felt it profoundly. The other part – the part that used to make decisions for her, but which was now in the backseat – experienced the anger only impartially, dreamily. But the new side of her, the new Wendy, the one who had sat in the back and who now had taken the driver's seat, that part of Wendy let the heat propel her along like a hot current from the living room, down the hall, into the nursery. And dimly she remembered the flying thing in the basement. She wondered what it was she'd been so scared of. The flying thing had been simply one step, one stage in the process. The process of liberation. Of becoming Higher.

Smiling like a mannequin, she strode with calm deliberation into the nursery. The anger was still growing, and as it grew, the redness drained out of the walls, as if she'd soaked it up to help power the anger.

And then she saw the child. Child? The . . . organism. The pink, veined, maggot-squirming thing that had grown in her like a parasite. Like a tapeworm. It had been a long, painful pregnancy. Sick every day for four months, and then the headaches, and then a new set of aches in her back, her legs. And then a ten-hour labour. The child. That was what had forced her to marry Evan. And she realized with a sense of revelation that she'd never loved Evan, not at all.

That she fucking hated Evan's guts.

The child, this organism – not something she would ever refer to as *he* ever again – had forced her to live with Evan's constant bitterness, his complaining, his prissy neatness. She looked at it. Its mouth was wide open, its face contorted with its bellowing. Spittle dribbled from its lips.

She should have realized before that it was just a *thing* that had used her to grow in. Like a tick fattening on your blood. And the things it had done to her, things babies did to all women in the nine-month course of pregnancy: nausea, vaginal discharge all day every day, making her underwear into a sewer . . . lower abdominal aches . . . constipation, heartburn, indigestion, flatulence, bloating . . . headaches, dizziness, fainting . . . nasal congestion, that constant drip in her nose, nosebleeds . . . leg cramps, backache, varicose veins, hemorrhoids, difficulty sleeping, clumsiness . . . periods of pointless anxiety, irritability, depression . . .

All of it from pregnancy, like the symptoms of a disease. A disease! Why hadn't she seen it before?

And the creature itself . . . At this stage it wasn't much more, she knew, than the fetus that people so casually abort. It's just a monkeylike lower organism really, not yet much aware or intelligent. And why had she been adoring it and taking care of it so conscientiously? It could only have been instinct. They taught you what instincts were in high school now: DNA programming, that's all. A gimmick for the survival of the species. Just a lot of glandular button pushing on behalf of the Master Molecule. Instincts were a kind of tyranny. She saw that now. The Master Molecule was the tyrant. To hell with the Master Molecule. To hell with instincts.

When Wendy didn't answer her knock, Lois decided to go inside anyway, to pick up her purse. There was a book in it she wanted to show Perry. She wanted him to see that she had more depth to her than she'd shown him in the sleeping bag.

She tried the door; it was unlocked. She opened it, stepped into the kitchen, calling softly, 'Wendy? You here?' No answer. She could hear the baby whimpering from the bedroom. That was strange; Wendy should be here, or a baby-sitter, if the baby were here. Maybe Wendy was down in the basement. Or maybe Evan was here.

'Evan!' Lois called. But then she realized that Evan probably wasn't home. His van hadn't been out front.

Lois went to the living room, half expecting to find Wendy asleep on the couch. She found only the TV droning moronically to itself: a Chuck Barris quiz show. She found her purse on the couch, half under a dingy throw pillow. She drew the strap over her shoulder, then headed for the back door.

She stopped in the kitchen, listening. The baby was no longer whimpering. It was shrieking. It wasn't the ordinary baby's howl for attention. It was a squeal of pure terror.

She ran down the hall and threw open the bedroom door. In the far corner of the almost barren room, beneath a bedroom window framed by yellow curtains printed with bright blue dancing bears, surrounded by a haphazard array of brightly colored baby toys and baby bottles, Wendy was setting her son afire.

She crouched by the small blue plastic basket bed, holding a flaming cigarette lighter to one corner of the baby's blankets near Billy's feet. The other corner was already burning; the baby was recoiling from the flames, squealing, lying on his back, trying to see what was burning him, unable to lift his head far enough. The small yellow flames looked almost toylike. But in a few seconds more, they would fill the bed basket.

Lois broke from her paralysis of amazement and ran across the room. She slapped the lighter out of Wendy's hand, grabbed the baby under the armpits, and swung him away from the flames. And almost in the same motion, she began to back away from Wendy.

Lois expected to see Wendy's face contorted with madness – she had to be crazy to be doing a thing like that – and she was confused when she saw Wendy's face was calm, almost blank. A little bemused, perhaps, like a person watching a movie that interests but doesn't move them deeply. Somehow, this placidity scared Lois more than a look of rage.

Lois backed out of the bedroom door, then turned and ran into the bathroom. The baby kicked and screamed against her chest. She held him in the crook of one arm, using her free hand to lock the bathroom door behind her – and just as she locked it she heard Wendy trying the knob. She carried the baby to the sink and cooed at him as she bathed his burns. They weren't bad. If she'd come five seconds later, they would have been.

She realized, then, that she was sobbing. She made herself stop and dried her eyes. Then she rubbed an analgesic gel on the baby's burns. She held him against her; he wailed, pausing now and then to take a long, wet, rattling breath. She looked at the door. She's outside the door, Lois thought. Lois started convulsively when she heard the tapping on the door. And Wendy's voice.

'Lois? Open the door, kid, huh?'

'I can't right now,' Lois called. She was afraid to. Although Wendy didn't seem overtly violent, now. Her voice sounded normal. But then, she'd had that cool, collected look on her face when she'd been setting the baby's bedclothes afire. Fire! 'Wendy, you'd better put out that fire before it gets bigger, or the whole house'll go. There's a fire extinguisher your dad left in the garage.'

'Yes, I think you're right,' Wendy said. And then she said something more softly that Lois couldn't be sure of, but it sounded like, 'The house could be useful.' Minutes later, Lois heard the sound of the fire extinguisher swishing from the nursery.

'She's sane enough to do that, anyway,' Lois murmured. The baby quieted, whimpering a little, every so often his face twisting as if he were about to cry. But he was tired; probably hoarse from crying.

Another tapping at the door. 'It was a weird kind of accident, Lois. Come on out and I'll explain.'

An accident? Had she misunderstood what Wendy was doing with the lighter? Maybe she just happened to have it in her hand and –

She shook her head. 'Bullshit, Wendy. You've been taking drugs. PCP or something. You should call a doctor for you and the ba – ' She broke off, staring.

Staring at the shiny chrome blade of a screwdriver thrust between the door and the jamb.

Wendy was trying to force the door.

What would she do, Lois wondered, once she'd got the door open?

'You don't think Sandra will be back within say' – Rofocale looked at his watch – 'an hour?'

'No. I doubt it,' Aunt June said. She and Perry sat on the couch, across from Rofocale, who was perched a little awkwardly on a threadbare footstool.

Perry glanced at Aunt June, wondering what she was up to. Why had she invited Rofocale in? From what she'd said about him, she clearly detested him. Maybe she wanted to pump him for information about Tetty. Rofocale had spent more time with Tetty than anyone except Sandra in the past six months.

'I'm curious about your therapeutic center, doctor,' Aunt June said evenly. 'I'd like to come out for a visit sometime.' Aunt June had introduced herself; Rofocale knew her work.

'Naturally, of course you must,' Rofocale said, with all the enthusiasm of sawdust.

'Now as I understand it,' Aunt June began, 'your therapy – '

'My therapy,' Rofocale interrupted, something mischievous in his voice, 'has entered a new phase. A whole new direction. And I owe that partly to you, doctor.'

'Me?' Aunt June looked startled.

Rofocale smiled. 'Yes indeed. Your paper on the self-interest gene. A gene that controls the manufacture of, I believe, Empathy Suppression hormone . . .'

Aunt June blurted, 'But that paper was never published! There wasn't enough substantiation!'

He looked at her blandly. 'Never published? I had assumed it was published somewhere. One of your friends

85

was kind enough to show it to me. He was one of my clients. A Mr Berman.'

'Berman? He was a student, a graduate student in my – damn! He must have photocopied it, the bastard. I only left him with it for an hour.'

He shrugged. 'It was really just a kind of springboard for me, frankly. You stopped short of the truth. But you mentioned Dr Horescu's work in Rumania. And I followed up on that.'

'How does ESS apply to – therapy? Is this something you used to treat Tetty?' There was only the faintest edge of anger in Aunt June's tone. But Perry could see by the clenching of her jaw muscles that she was furious. She hated the idea of Rofocale misusing her work.

'Naturally my work with Tetty is confidential. You understand. At any rate Tetty was not a part of my current methodology. She was not a part of the New Direction.'

The son of a bitch is lying, Perry thought. He's too damn smooth.

Rofocale glanced at his watch, then flashed a wide, brilliant smile at them. It was like he'd thrown a switch, to make something shine out of him.

'I really wanted to talk to Sandra. I'm sure we could work things out.' Meaning the lawsuit, Perry thought. 'I can't afford a settlement but my new process will involve instructional videotapes and as Tetty was involved in my research, I willingly confess to owing her family a little something – only for that involvement, not for any subsequent problems, you understand – and, ah, I can offer Sandra a percentage of the videotape sales.'

'If she drops the lawsuit? That's rather speculative,' Aunt June said.

'So is a lawsuit, doctor,' Rofocale said, standing.

He beamed at Perry and actually winked – and then went to the door, where he turned toward Aunt June. He took a pen from an inside pocket of his coat, found a small notebook in another pocket, and wrote an address and phone number on it. Briskly, he tore the sheet from the notebook and handed it to Aunt June. 'Give a call before you come to the therapy center, doctor.' He looked around the room, seemed to be listening. He was suddenly distant. 'And may I say – ' He never said it. He cut himself off, turned to look at the back door, visible through the length of the kitchen.

Perry had already stood and started for the kitchen. He'd heard the same thing Rofocale had. A woman crying.

Lois stood in the open back door, sobbing softly. Her hair was disheveled. There was blood on her blouse, and blood dripped from a cut on her forehead over her right eye.

6

'No, no thanks, I don't need an ambulance, nothing like that,' Lois said finally. She was sitting at the kitchen table. Aunt June had gone for a first-aid kit. 'It's just a little cut, and a couple of bruises. I'm just sort of all shook up. And I've got a headache. Thanks.'

She swallowed the two aspirin Perry gave her, drinking half a beer to chase it. Aunt June bustled back into the kitchen, opened the small plastic kit, and laid out Band-Aids, iodine, alcohol.

'Hey, that's okay, just a Band-Aid,' Lois said, trying to smile. 'No major surgery.' She winced when Aunt June dabbed the iodine on her cut forehead.

Perry couldn't hold back any longer. 'Lois – '

'Wendy hit me,' Lois said. Her eyes got shiny, but she didn't let the tears go. 'She – ' She shook her head in disbelief. 'She jabbed a screwdriver at my head. It didn't hit straight on, just kind of glanced off me. But I really think she wanted to put it through my head. And she was kicking me and – ' She hesitated, looking up at Perry. 'You're not going to believe this. You wouldn't if you knew her.'

'Try me.'

'She bit me. Bad.' She tugged her sleeve up to show the white-edged toothmarks on her forearm. The bite had broken the skin in three places.

Aunt June splashed alcohol over it and bandaged it. 'You keep your eye on that. Bites from people are dangerous. Your name is Lois?'

'Yeah – you're Perry's Aunt June, right? Hi. I'm sorry to meet you in such a weird, uh, situation.'

'Wendy is that girl with the little kid?' Perry asked, pulled a chair up beside Lois. He took her right hand, held it between his.

'Her baby, Billy – that's the worst part.' She looked at Aunt June. 'You're a psychiatrist, right? Well, how do you explain this: she loved that baby, but *she was trying to set him on fire*. She put a cigarette lighter to his bed and the blankets caught fire and she kept spreading fire around. With this sort of dreamy smile on her face. So I took the baby away and locked myself in the bathroom with it and she broke in and – and slashed me, and bit me. And then her husband Evan came home with these guys and, uh, she saw them coming and she ran out the back. She didn't seem, you know, manic. I think she was humming a little tune all the time. She didn't seem even worried – or angry.'

'Lots of times people don't seem angry when they're brimming over with it,' Aunt June said. 'But I can't really explain what happened until I know more about her. Maybe not even then. Is the baby okay?'

'He's all right, I guess. Just first-degree burns, looked like. He's out at Evan's parents house. Damn, I'm worried about Wendy. She was carrying that screwdriver when she left.'

'Excuse me,' said Rofocale, stepping into the room, 'but perhaps it is best if you tell us how long ago this happened.' He glanced apologetically at Perry. 'I could not help overhearing. I'm concerned.'

'Was this girl Wendy your patient?' Perry asked him.

He shook his head. 'We have no one named Wendy.'

Lois stared at Rofocale. She'd recognized him. 'Why

do you want to know how long ago it happened?' She didn't try to conceal her suspicion.

'I think we should notify the police, tell them when it happened, what direction she went in. She's clearly dangerous. For her protection and everyone else's we'd better find her,' Rofocale said.

'Have you called the police, Lois?' Aunt June asked.

She shook her head, made a face as if she'd bitten something sour. 'No, I was afraid they'd hurt her, the cops around here are trigger-happy. I mean, she's just flipped, that's all, but she'll come out of it. She used to take acid sometimes, before they got married. Maybe she got bored and took some acid and it was too much for her. Or it was bad acid or something.'

'Acid?' Aunt June said, surprised. 'People still take LSD?'

Perry nodded thoughtfully. 'Some do. It's coming back into fashion. Underground chemists are whipping it up again. She might've got some in Portland.'

Aunt June said, 'That could be it, I suppose.' But she didn't sound as if she believed it. 'Has Wendy been upset lately about anything?'

'Sure,' Lois said. 'Not happy in her marriage. Feeling trapped.'

'Then it would be a dangerous time for her to take LSD. She could well have gone off the deep end; sometimes it flings depressed people into a kind of temporary psychosis.'

'Yeah,' Perry said, relieved at having found a logical explanation. But he thought: First Tetty. Then the little girl drowns. Now this. In twenty-four hours. But aloud he said, 'Yeah, she probably flipped out on acid. Or PCP.'

'In which direction did she go?' Rofocale asked again, gently.

Lois answered distantly. 'Oh, northeast through the woods back of the housing project. She lives on Lakeshore, Twenty-seven Lakeshore, right at the end of the road, and there's woods just behind their garage, with a lot of paths in it. Goes into a campsite eventually. She took off into that about a half hour ago. Evan's at home, hoping she'll come back.'

Perry turned to Rofocale – and was a little startled to see that he'd gone. He hadn't stopped to use the phone.

Aunt June stared at the open front door. Then, slowly, she went to the telephone and dialed the sheriff's office. 'Sheriff Dawson, please. No, it's urgent. Sheriff, this is – that's right. I'm all right, thanks. Listen, a friend of my nephew has had some kind of hysterical fit. Tried to set her house on fire, attacked someone, and then wandered off into the woods. Now, I'm going to let you talk to a friend of hers who'll give you her description and all we know about it, but I wanted to ask you, first, to deputize some civilians to find her – men without guns, you see – and ask them to try not to hurt her. She might be dangerous but she hasn't got a gun. What? Yes, it might be drugs. All right.' She put the receiver down on the table and called, 'Lois? Could you talk to the sheriff, please?'

'Now what the hell,' said Suze Bergstrom, finding her husband asleep in his workshop. It was Harry's day off, and she'd suggested that he spend it resting – he was overworked, the doctor said, and he was pushing sixty-five – but he'd refused to consider it. Said he had to replace the broken leg of that old coffee table so he could give the table to his sister. Big job, just *had* to do it, no putting it off. 'So then you fall asleep in a pile of wood shavings, for God's sake,' Suze muttered with affectionate disgust. 'Boy, you're a case, Harry, you're really a case.'

Harry was sitting on his wooden bench, slumped over the scarred, paint-spattered oak table, his arms on either side of the wood shavings, his head on the mealy yellow heap as if it were a pillow. It was sawdust spilled from the mini-lathe, just in front of him. The sawdust was left over from the last project. He hadn't touched the chunk of wood he'd picked for the new table leg; it was still suspended in the lathe. Harry hadn't even selected a tool to shape it with; they were all in their racks on the wall – a perforated wooden wall patched with the tops of old tin cans. To one side was a rack of wrenches, screwdrivers, hammers, small saws and blades, everything still coated with fine sawdust left over from the kitchen chair he'd made for her two weeks ago. A film of dust seemed to cover even Harry. He usually wore a mouth mask to keep from breathing the dust, and here he was sleeping on the stuff. The mask hung on its nail to the left. Maybe –

Some kind of attack. Stroke. Heart attack. Her stomach constricted at the thought. She bit her lip, bending over him, trying to keep calm.

'Harry?' He was breathing, anyway; she could see tiny flecks of sawdust jumping with each breath, just under his nostrils. She studied him for a moment, looking for signs of some kind of attack. His face was florid – but it always was. He'd been that way since he'd started his second tour in the navy as a chief bosun's mate, years before. She studied his thick, large-pored nose and saw no blood. There was no blood on his heavy brown mustache. His wide forehead was wrinkled but otherwise unmarked.

She shook him, said in his ear, 'Harry? You okay?' He didn't react. She ran her fingers through his thinning brown-gray hair, wondering if she should call an ambulance. She felt a slight breeze on her cheek and looked up.

The breeze was coming through a broken pane in a small, precisely square window. The sawdusty spiderwebs around the frame trembled in the slight air flow from a round break in the glass. Looked like the sort of hole a baseball made. But there was no baseball on the floor. Some hooligan had heaved a rock, then. Some roughneck from the campsite. She returned to Harry.

'He's just fallen asleep,' she told herself.

But he never took naps in the daytime. And then she noticed the blister on the back of his neck. Like a beesting swelling. Funny place to get a blister. Something bit him. Black widow, maybe? She shook him more vigorously. 'Harry? Harry!'

She stopped breathing, until he stirred and sleepily raised his head. 'Whuh? Whuh?' he said.

She laughed in relief. 'You were just asleep!' She reached out to brush the fine sawdust from his cheek.

He slapped her hand away. Suddenly he was completely awake. He was sitting rigidly on the bench, staring at her, smiling in a way that was new to her. Had he slapped her hand playfully? She reached for him again. 'You act like a kid, sometimes, Harry.'

This time he shoved her away, straight-arming her in the left shoulder so she staggered backward.

She gaped at him. Twenty-seven years of marriage and he'd never laid a hand on her before. 'Boy, you sure woke up grumpy,' she murmured. 'You okay, Harry?'

'Okay? How can a failure be okay?' he asked, his voice smooth. She'd never heard a tone like that from him.

'What failure is that, Harry?'

'A failure is never okay, Suze. Because it's always there

eating at him, somewhere in his mind, telling him, You're a failure. You could have been something and you're a foreman at a lumber mill.'

'You don't think that's something? Foreman? That's a high position there, Harry.'

'I could have been an NCO. An officer. But you talked me out of it. You talked me into leaving the navy. Another four years and I would've been an NCO for sure. I could have – '

'Christ Harry, that was ten years ago! You never mentioned being mad about it before! I wouldn't have minded so much, only you were gone half the time at sea. But if I'd known how much you wanted to be – '

'Oh you knew. You knew. You knew. You knew.'

'Harry, stop talking like that.'

'You knew. You knew. You knew. You knew. You – '

'Harry – '

' – knew.'

'Harry.'

Something rebellious in Harry, something that was deeply loyal to Suze, struggled, and broke through the membrane of emotional distance. It was like waking up, though you were already awake; a second level of waking. A vision had helped him break out – a picture of Suze, but Suze in miniature, in his head, shaking him awake again the way she'd wakened his outer self in the workshop. And so, briefly, the old Harry woke and took control – but with an effort that almost split him in two – and looked around. He was in his workshop. He'd had a dream about a flying thing breaking the window and then he'd dreamed he'd got mad at Suze about something, and then he dreamed he'd taken her in his hands –

He couldn't remember what happened after that. Until he saw it.

Suze's severed head, staring up at him from the workbench. And he had the bloody-edged saw still gripped in his right hand. Harry screamed, until the other part of him took control again.

And then he smiled.

'Look, you don't know the local cops,' Lois was saying. 'They're dorks. They're creep-os. Well, there's Albright, one of the deputies. He's okay. But that creep Lancer; he was a senior when I was a freshman at school. God, he's such a yokel. He's so proud of his gun and his badge. Just to show you what kind of dork he is, I heard he's a Klansman.'

'You've got KKK around here?' Perry asked.

'Sure. Oregon's a hotbed of it. Anyway, Dawson's deputies are the nervous type, like they say in the movies. If they see Wendy come at them with something sharp, they'll probably start shooting.'

'Maybe. I'm wondering about Rofocale, too. He acted like he was going to call the cops. But he didn't. So why did he want to know where Wendy went?' They sat on the back porch, on the cot, leaning against the rear wall of the house. They needed a porch swing, Perry thought.

'Yeah,' Lois was saying, 'Rofocale's a – well, when he came to our school to talk to my psych class at the community college – the teacher was high on him then – I thought when I first saw him he was a creep-o.'

Perry smiled. 'You think he's a mad scientist?'

'No, not a mad scientist – a mad salesman. The guy is a salesman type, through and through. A manipulator. He lets people think he's a medical doctor, but he's just a Ph.D. And he always swings the talk back to himself. The guy is a megalomaniac. It isn't real obvious but it's there. It's the real him.' The back door opened with a squeaking that Perry found pleasantly homey, and Aunt June came to sit beside them.

'Well,' she said, not looking at them, 'I know, Perry, you will be really deeply disappointed to learn I have to go somewhere and leave you alone with your beautiful young friend. Sheriff Dawson wants me to help him look for Wendy. The poor guy has his hands full. He seems to think the certified "psychiatric authority" will be able to second-guess her, figure out where she's gone. I doubt it, but I'll have a look at his maps and give it a shot. Nice meeting you, Lois.' She stood. 'I'm going to walk over and see Dawson.'

'Thanks for helping to find Wendy,' Lois said. 'I guess I should help too, but the whole thing shook me up so much – '

'I understand, sure. No, it's best you take it easy. See you guys later.' She went into the kitchen, and they heard her walk out the front door. The sheriff's office was only a quarter mile away.

'Your aunt's pretty nice.'

'Yeah. But sometimes she's just a touch megalomaniacal herself. I think it's second nature for doctors.' Perry wondered why he felt so nervous about putting his arm around Lois. They'd been nearly as intimate as two people can get, but somehow, now, he felt it would be an intrusion to so much as take her hand. So he was startled when, as soon as it was clear that Aunt June was gone, she turned and slid her arms around him, pressing him against the wall with a long, slow kiss.

Then she put her head against his chest, snuggled into his arms, murmuring, 'I needed that. After Wendy tried to kill me, I need to feel like someone likes me for real. I mean, I thought she was my best friend, and we were devoted to each other. And she changed just like that. I can understand her getting mad and yelling. But it made me feel for a minute that there was nothing real anymore, nothing you could depend on. No one you could trust.'

'Hey. Trust me.'

She smiled up at him.

'Yeah? I can?' She made a face that was a comic exaggeration of doubtfulness. 'Nah. You're a Ramblin' Man, right? Just passin' through, ma'am. Like to stay and work your ranch for you but I gotta have the wind at my back.'

He laughed. 'Hey gimme a break.'

'I'm serious; you're gonna go back to San Diego.'

'No, I'm not,' he said, deciding then and there.

She sat up and looked directly in his eyes. 'You mean it?'

'I won't go back unless you come too.'

'I can't. I got to go to Portland State.'

'I wouldn't mind living in Portland. I've got some friends who offered me a gig in their band there if I ever . . .' He shrugged. 'What the hell.'

'Well, then, where is it?' She looked around, even peering under the cot. 'Where is it?'

'Where's what?'

'The goddamn champagne, cheapskate!'

'Oh! Uh, beer.'

'Well that's what I mean. That's what we use around here for champagne: Miller's, the Champagne of Bottled Beer.'

'Miller's has a crummy aftertaste.'

'Then cough up for the good stuff!'

'You're getting Olympia, the Pisswater of Bottled Beer.'

Perry went to get the beer. 'Listen,' he said, coming back and handing her a can, 'I think Wendy's probably peaked on whatever drug it was by now. She's probably saying to herself, A parking lot outside a trailer camp! How'd I get to a parking lot for a trailer camp? And asking directions to get back home.'

'Yeah.' Her voice was suddenly distant. She stared at her shoes, tapping them together like Dorothy in *The Wizard of Oz*. There's no place like home, there's no place like home. 'Yeah. You got a radio? Sometimes in the evening there's an FM station in Bend that plays some old stuff. Sixties.'

Perry got a portable radio out of his baggage, and they sorted through various country music stations and ranchers' weather reports until they found an FM deejay playing The Doors' 'Riders on the Storm.'

> There's a killer on the road
> His brain is squirming like a toad . . .

But Perry and Lois weren't listening to the lyrics. They stretched out on the cot. The radio rocked from the floor beneath. The first crickets of the evening began to chirrup. These sounds were joined by the regular gasps from Lois as Perry worked his hand between her legs, under her skirt, as their tongues intertwined, as she ground her breasts against his pectorals. Lois rolled on her side so she could reach between them to unbutton her blouse, then unzip Perry's jeans. And they managed to forget the toad, the gray and unnamed thing they both sensed squirming in the shadows outside their small, frail pool of light.

Perry walked through the kitchen to the living room, tugging his jeans up over his hips as he went. He buttoned them, then reached for the phone, annoyed with its loud jangling and the cold stickiness dripping down the inside of his thigh. 'Hello. Yes. Oh, Aunt June? Did you – '

'No.' Aunt June sounded far away. A bad connection. 'We didn't find her yet. Listen, I'm going to be back late, I just wanted to tell you don't stay up late yourself tonight; first thing in the morning we've got a long drive over to Fallen Pine Creek.'

'What's at Fallen Pine Creek?'

'Rofocale's Center for Renewed Selfhood. We're going to "observe." Unless Wendy turns up and I'm busy with her.'

Perry sighed. 'Okay.'

'So tell her to get dressed and go home so you can get some rest.'

'Hey for God's sake.'

Aunt June laughed and hung up.

It wasn't an attic, really. It was just a crawl space.

Crawl space, Rofocale thought, as, flashlight in hand, he climbed on to the little aluminum stepladder and pushed the door in the ceiling aside. The paint was smudged from his fingerprints, from many times before. Crawl space. You crawl through this space. You crawl. Like a bug. You must crawl. For the Lord of Dark Corners.

Hatred and resentment swirled together and curdled in him. But he went on with it, because he knew what would happen if he didn't.

The trapdoor fell back on to the fiberglass insulation with a soft crunch. He thrust his head up into the shadows and felt the sweat begin to trickle down his ribs; he felt the hot flashes, the pins and needles in his hands. The flashlight growing slippery in his grip.

He spread his elbows on to the frame of the crawl hole and pulled himself up, grunting. And as always it felt as if the darkness were a solid thing, something damp and furry that gave when you pushed up into it – but gave reluctantly.

He found a cross-rafter and gripped it with his free hand, pulled himself up on to the planks running between the big cotton-candyish swatches of insulation.

He was in darkness. Dust scraped at his sinuses, and he felt a pressure on his ears as if he were diving deep underwater.

He fumbled at the flashlight, and flicked it on.

Why have you brought that electrical light in here?

Its voice was soft, gentle – but repugnant. Like the breath of a diseased infant. It was a sound with halitosis. It came from the far end of the crawl space, in the darkest place under the roof peak. It was always the same. Its equanimity frightened him. The psychopathic sweetness of its voice. The alien tilt of its peculiar, archaic phrasing. *Electrical light*, it had said.

'I can't bear it without a light, not anymore,' Rofocale said. Knowing he was whining, unable to keep from it. Not sure if he were speaking his native tongue or English. 'Just to have a little light with me. Not to point it at anything. I almost screamed last time. If I scream, it could scare away the patients. We need them.'

You are wheedling. You attempt to negotiate.

'Forgive me. I must.'

Then keep it pointed downward. Now approach me.

Rofocale's mouth went dry. Carefully keeping the light down, he crawled toward the Lord of Dark Corners. The planks were raw; he felt splinters work their way into his knees, the meat of his palms.

It hurts. Its voice was smiling.

'Yes,' Rofocale said. Hoarsely.

In the flashlight's glow he could see the rafters angling up to meet overhead. As always he thought of ribs, the painting he'd seen of Jonah in the belly of the whale. But it was a much worse place than the belly of a whale. He imagined things dropping down his collar, crawling up his sleeves. Small black things that were much worse than spiders and bugs. Perhaps he wasn't imagining them. The Lord of Dark Corners could make them come true.

He reached the end of the plank and stared down into the comforting glow of the flashlight, trying to put off the moment.

Look up at me.

Heart hammering, panting, Rofocale made himself look up.

There was only darkness up there. But it was a coalesced darkness, as if this was a place where shadows became liquid; as if the attic darkness was draining into that corner. He felt himself pulled; a lamprey had latched on to his eyesight and was sucking it. He felt an internal plunge, a fall into absolute zero. The Lord of Dark Corners crumbled the graven image of his self-worth, his sense of justified being. The attic was his own skull: he had crawled into his own skull and found, inside, a pocket of living darkness nesting in the corner like a web satchel of spider eggs on a dusty ceiling.

Why did you allow the breeder to escape?

Rofocale's lips seemed fused. He pulled them apart with a painful rasp as he spoke. 'I didn't know how to do the extraction properly. I'm trying but . . . it's working in . . .' He didn't want to say working in the dark. 'It's experimental, it's working blind. If you would let the others break out, the others who were changed . . . if you'd let them go, Lord . . .'

No. Once they have emerged I cannot control them. When they are inside I can influence them. I can spread the darling gospel. But their emergence is a turning inward to their own appetites and away from mine. No. I will make more such with the breeder, from our Wendy, once you have her. Wendy, our little whiner who is just the same sort of little girl our sweet little Rofocale is.

'I'm not a – '

Oh yes.

'Don't!'

Why not? It is what I do. And you wanted me. You sought me. You were looking for the part of the mind that connects with the big world. The big world had many corners in it, and the corners are dark, and did you think you could enter the corners without calling on the Lord? Did you not call out my name?

'It wasn't like that! It was an experiment to see if there was a subconscious significance to those names.' Rofocale babbled, his voice breaking. 'Some kind of subverbal significance.'

And that is why you killed the little animals?

'That was to trigger the release of atavistic imagery . . . another link to the subconscious, you see, uh, you see. Don't. Don't.'

But the Lord already had. Rofocale was a little boy, and his father was dressing him in his mother's lingerie, and he was reaching under the silk with his greased thumb and saying, 'Bad little girl. Bad little girl.'

Downstairs, the patients heard the screaming and the bumping, and Rofocale's voice, dim and far away, shouting, 'I promise I promise, take it away, I promise!'

It didn't frighten the center's patients away. It made them feel better to hear it. They assumed he was taking some of his own therapy.

* * *

There was a white van belonging to the center parked out front of the condo, next to a dusty truck; behind the truck was a yellow VW Cabriolet with its top down and Rofocale's silver Mercedes. Aunt June parked the rented Toyota in the gravel margin behind the Mercedes.

It was a two-unit condo, and Rofocale had bought both units. They were harmless looking and a pale blue, the outer walls rimmed near the ground with red dust; the ground around the center was red clay, tufted with fiddlehead ferns and white-blossomed trilliums. The center's condo was the end building of eight other nearly identical condos in the development along Fallen Pine Creek, a good one hundred feet apart; the only difference between Rofocale's and the other condos was the color: the others were a burnt sienna chosen to blend with the clay and to look rustic. Rofocale had repainted his blue.

The place was symmetrically split, the right half the mirror image of the left. The Center for Renewed Selfhood sign hung over the right-hand porch. Perry and Aunt June went up to that door.

It was a fresh, central Oregon morning. The creek rushed and gurgled behind the buildings; the unhurried breeze, aromatic of pines and the wet yeastiness of creek life, nudged the tree trunks so they murmured and squeaked. The pines and Douglas firs gave a stained-glass tint of soft green to the shafts of sunlight streaming through their branches. 'The hell with Rofocale,' Aunt June said wistfully, pausing on the porch to look around, 'let's stay out here.'

'That's cool with me,' Perry said.

'"Cool with me?" You been watching reruns of *The Mod Squad* again? Come on, let's go in and get it over with.'

They rang the bell, and a moment later they heard a

buzz. Aunt June pushed on the door – a split second after the buzzing stopped and the door relocked. 'Dammit,' she muttered, pressing the bell again. This time the door opened.

Inside, they were standing on a brown rug, flecked at the edges by sloppy painting – Rofocale had had the inside repainted light blue too. They looked at the strange parity of the condo's interior. The wall had been knocked down between the two condos, on this floor, and the right-side room was a living room with a kitchenette recessed at the back, a curtained picture window on the right wall, and a stairway against the back wall, halfway to the left-side room; the left-side room was exactly the same, but mirror reversed. Around the room was a circle of chairs. There was nothing else, except an oval mirror standing on the floor.

'Now we can see how condos reproduce,' Aunt June muttered. 'By mitosis. Just splitting like amoebas.'

A woman came down the right-hand stairs and crossed to them, smiling. She was small-boned, with a heart-shaped face and dyed auburn hair, a loose bun; she wore white shorts, a dove-colored blouse, sandals, and a Greek symbol Perry couldn't interpret on an oversized gold chain around her neck. She had silver-flecked blue eyes set off by peacock-blue eye shadow. Her movements were a study in warmhearted body language and she struck Perry as one of those women people would refer to as perky.

'Hi! I'm glad to see you got in okay!' Her voice had a cartoonlike lilt. She reached out both her hands and pressed Aunt June's right hand between them, in lieu of a handshake, looking her in the eye as she said, 'I'm Lola Turnette, Dr Rofocale's assistant.'

Aunt June muttered her own name and title, and Lola

repeated the greeting with Perry. Her hands were tiny, warm, and a little stubby; Perry noticed she wore artificial fingernails. Lavender, and absurdly long, cookie-cutter perfect.

She let go of his hand and gestured toward the stairs, but continued to maintain eye contact as she spoke, alternating between Perry and Aunt June. 'This morning we have some first-stage SOTs, and a few second-stagers who'll be part of the session for guidance – they'll be down in a moment, they're doing their video warm-ups.'

'What are SOTs?' Aunt June asked. 'And video warm-ups?'

'SOT stands for Students of Themselves. It just means anyone who comes here for help. Video warm-ups are . . . well, basically they have a talk with a counselor – we have two counselors besides Dr Rofocale – and then they watch it all back on videotape, and the counselor points out their Self-Defeats.'

'I get the general idea.'

'I don't,' Perry said. 'But here they come.'

People were trickling down both stairs, one and two at a time. They filtered into the room and, glancing without curiosity at Aunt June and Perry, who remained standing by the door, took seats around the circle. There were about thirty of them, a few more women than men, ages ranging from midtwenties to middle-aged. They seemed mostly middle class. There were two blacks – one of them perhaps mulatto – and a young Japanese.

Lola carried two light plastic chairs from the kitchen and set them down outside the circle. 'Have a seat.' She motioned to Aunt June and Perry. 'Would you like some coffee or tea or Diet Coke?'

They both said no thanks and sat down as Rofocale came down the stairs. He was wearing a powder-blue

105

leisure suit and a broad, self-satisfied smile. He carried a clipboard and extended his hand to them as he came round the circle of chairs. Perry and June shook hands with him; his was large and clammy.

'Please feel welcome here,' Rofocale said. But at the same time he handed Aunt June the clipboard and a pen. On the clipboard was a statement about the confidentiality a physician owes his patients, whatever the signer witnesses will not be divulged in any public forum, print or otherwise, without obtaining permission from the . . . et cetera.

Aunt June hesitated, and then signed. Perry too.

Rofocale took the clipboard and sat in the only seat left in the circle, the one with its back to the white-curtained window. He laid the mirror flat on to the rug beside him so it reflected the ceiling and part of a fake chandelier, continuing the symmetry motif. Lola sat beside him, smiling . . . perkily.

Rofocale said, 'Our guests today are visiting from the San Diego State University Medical Center. They have signed a contract in which they agree, ah, to complete confidentiality. This is, in a way, a test: if you can't overcome Self-Defeats with strangers here, you'll never be able to. Now then, we're starting today with . . . Joanie.' A rustling of the students as they turned to look at an odd-looking woman of about twenty-three; she had thin brown hair – in fact, Perry saw, it was patchy in spots, some sort of scalp disease – thick dark eyebrows, and a weak chin. She wore soft pink overalls and tennis shoes with pink laces. She sat with her knees pressed tightly together, her hands making washing motions in her lap. Joanie.

Joanie cleared her throat. Looking at the floor, she said, 'I was going to call my mother this morning but I didn't because I was afraid to because I knew she'd be mad at me about the therapy because she doesn't like me taking this.' She took a deep breath and went on. 'So I didn't call her just because I was scared and then –'

'Joanie!' Rofocale's voice was a bark, but somehow friendly. Joanie's narrow shoulders twitched. 'Joanie, look at me, look at us when you're Reclaiming Self.'

She looked up . . . and then looked back down. In a small voice she said, 'That's the hardest thing for me to do.'

'Joanie,' Rofocale said.

'Joanie,' Lola said.

Other people in the circle took it up, till everyone was chanting, '*Joanie Joanie Joanie Joanie!*'

Perry and Aunt June looked at one another.

Joanie bit her lip and stared at Rofocale. The chanting ceased. She sat rigid with the effort of looking him in the eye. The room was quiet till she went on. 'I should have confronted my mother. I was suppressing Self.'

Rofocale nodded. 'Now tell your Self.'

Lola reached down and tipped the mirror up. Rofocale took it in his hands and held it up. Moving like an automaton, Joanie walked across the room and stared into the mirror.

She looked away.

'Joanie!' Lola said sharply. A sound like a falcon's cry.

Joanie snapped her eyes back to the mirror. She cleared her throat, said, in a barely audible voice, 'I should have confronted my mother – I should have told her . . .'

'What, Joanie? What should you have told her?' Rofocale asked; his voice came from behind the mirror. It was as if the mirror was asking it. 'Reach down for the gut truth. Remember we talked about the gut truth? What would you say that's got the anger attached to it? Tell us!'

'I'd say, um . . .'

'What do you mean 'um? And *louder*!'

She took a deep breath and tried to yell, but it came out haltingly. 'I . . . should have told her: *Go to hell*, Mom!'

'Tell *yourself*, Joanie,' Lola said, when she saw the girl's eyes were wandering from the mirror.

Joanie looked at herself and winced. 'I don't like to look at myself.'

'Why, Joanie?' Rofocale asked.

'Because . . . I don't like the way I look.'

'Can you be someone else?'

'No.' In a very small voice.

'Then what else is there to do?'

'Be myself . . . be happy with myself.'

'That's not enough! You've got to reach for the gut truth! You've got to be yourself *with a vengeance*. You've got to believe the face you see is the best damn face you ever saw – and it *will be*!'

'I . . .' She shook her head.

'Joanie, I want you to say: *It's the best damn face I ever saw and anybody that doesn't like it can go to hell!*'

'It's the best damn face I ever saw and, um, anybody who doesn't like it can, um, go to hell.'

There were titters around the circle. Joanie cringed.

'Joanie, that's not making it! Joanie! Joanie! Joanie!'

And the others took it up. '*Joanie Joanie Joanie!*'

The room resounded with her name as she shouted, 'It's the best damn face I ever saw – '

'*Louder!*' Rofocale shouted. 'Drown out everybody else! Be louder!'

Rofocale nodded at Lola, who began to chant, '*Joanie's ugly Joanie's ugly Joanie's ugly!*'

And Joanie bent over, as if shivering up into herself.

'Come on now, Joanie! What do you say to that?'

She took a deep breath and – to get the whole thing over, Perry supposed – she shouted, *'It's the best damn face I ever saw and anybody doesn't like it can go to hell!'*

'Louder! Say it like you believe it and drown them out!'
Joanie's ugly Joanie's ugly Joanie's ugly . . .
'IT'S THE BEST DAMN FACE I EVER SAW – '
Joanie's ugly Joanie's ugly . . .
'AND ANYBODY WHO DOESN'T LIKE IT – '
'JOANIE'S UGLY!'
'CAN GO TO HELL!'
'Scream it into the mirror, Joanie, tell the mirror!' Rofocale shouted.

She went on, shouting over the chanting till she was hoarse. Perry felt the hair rise on the back of his neck; he felt an undefined pressure in the room squeezing him toward the door. A great pressure of embarrassment and empathy. He found himself picturing Wendy Marsteller clawing at Lois's face, and he wondered if that clawing had started here somehow.

And then Joanie was done. She went upstairs, moving like a ghost, to talk into the videotape machine. A chair was empty.

Next up was the Japanese, Tommy. As a boy in school, he said, he'd done poorly in mathematics and other practical skills; he'd done well only in the arts. In Japan, he explained, the college you get into is even more important than in America in determining one's career. Your success in school slants your whole life. Parents exert a constant pressure on students to learn in Japan – from the age of three. The demands are relentless, and when Tommy failed a course, he was made to feel subhuman. So, as a large number of Japanese youth do, he opted for suicide. 'You even failed in that,' his father said, in the hospital. He sent Tommy to live in America with the American in-law they'd named him after. But even here Tommy couldn't rid himself of the feeling that he was tainted, inferior, worthless.

'Failure!' Lola chanted as Tommy looked into the mirror. And the others took it up. *'FAILURE FAILURE FAILURE!'*

Tommy began to gasp. He shook his head convulsively.

'Come on, Tommy!' Rofocale boomed. 'Shout it: *I am better than the rest of you!*'

Tommy shook his head again, a spasmodic movement, and as he stared into the mirror his chest rose and fell, rose and fell.

'He's hyperventilating,' Aunt June muttered.

Perry glanced at her, realizing it was hard for her to keep silence here.

'Failure failure failure!'

Tommy nodded. His lips moved soundlessly. Perry read: 'Yes.'

Tommy turned and ran. He sprinted for the door, shouting in Japanese, clawed at the knob. Rofocale jumped up, dropping the mirror. It rolled, spinning the room in its reflection.

Tommy got the door open and ran outside. Perry turned to Aunt June, and then saw she was gone from her chair; she was up, moving behind him, and then out the door. Perry jumped up and ran after her.

Outside, it took a moment for his eyes to adjust to the light and perspective. Then, the dappled distances shifted into focus, and he saw Aunt June running stiffly after Tommy, who was heading for the creek.

Perry ran down the steps, but Rofocale had burst out the door behind him, took the steps in two leaps, perhaps visualizing another lawsuit.

Panting, Perry caught up with them on the rocky, lichen-painted rocks edging the creek. Aunt June and Rofocale were struggling with the boy, who was shouting in Japanese and trying to throw himself in the water.

Christ, Perry thought. It'd be funny if it weren't so sad.

'It wasn't just today,' Aunt June said as Perry drove them home in the Toyota. 'They'd been playing with the boy's head for a couple of weeks. But it had to happen, in Tommy's case. They were toying with a foreign, volatile cultural conditioning, without really knowing what they were doing. The whole thing is incredibly simple-minded.'

'Seems to me like they're using sledgehammers to fix everybody's china cups,' Perry said.

'That's a good way to put it. Of course, Rofocale said it was our fault.'

'What!'

'Yes. We were there, so we disrupted the normal "flow to Selfhood." It's bullshit, of course. But you know what really bothers me? What we saw had to be their mildest stuff; they wouldn't show us anything *really* dangerous. And I definitely have a feeling there's a lot they're not showing us. Look, I want to have a word with the sheriff about this attempted suicide and, uh, I'll just drop you off at home and take the car. Okay?'

Perry didn't like being in Sandra's house alone.

He was sitting on the back porch, feeling the presence of the house behind him. Imagining Tetty upstairs, seeing her with a piece of window glass in her hand.

He shook himself, and wandered into the backyard.

It was almost noon, and the heat fell on him as soon as he stepped out of the shade of the back porch. He stood in the yellow grass, blinking in the sunlight. But it smelled of pines out there, and not the musty introversion of the house. He listened to the trill of a bird, and tried to find it, peering up at the trees. The trilling ceased, replaced with a buzzing. Something whipping unseen around his head; buzzing, flying closer, buzzing louder. He took a step backward. Something –

'Hey, sailor!'

Lois was coming up the path into the backyard, one hand raised to shade her eyes. The buzzing was gone.

She was wearing a yellow bikini, a straw sun hat, and trim little Reebok jogging shoes. She walked up to him and stopped to look at him with her head cocked, smiling. 'You stand out here looking at the trees like you never saw any before.'

He clasped his hands under his chin and batted his eyes, singing, '"I never saw them at ah-all, till there was – "'

'Oh *gawd*, spare me, boy!' She laughed, and came into his arms. 'I mean, I like romance, but please, make it something closer to my generation.'

'How about "Let's Get Physical"?'

'That was years ago.'

'How about "Sexual Healing"?'

'Still too old.'

'The hell with it, let's write our own.'

They went indoors.

Her name was Ellen Marple and she was seven years old.

She was lying in bed, waiting for Gramma to come and draw pictures for her. Gramma was taking care of her tonight while her mom and dad went to that party.

Gramma, as Ellen never tired of telling her friends in the second grade, was an artist, a real artist who sold pictures. She made oil paintings of the desert and the ocean and sometimes of people with white faces and a single tear coming down from one eye. Sometimes she'd draw pictures on Ellen's back with her finger and ask Ellen to guess what it was just from feeling the outline – simple things, sailboats and dogs and Christmas trees. It helped Ellen go to sleep. Ellen had trouble going to sleep because she had nightmares. She heard Gramma tell her mother once that the nightmares were because Mom and Dad argued and had separations and that scared her.

Some nights, Gramma brought her sketchbook with her and made up stories and drew pictures from the stories in the sketchbook with coloured pencils. And then she let Ellen keep the drawings.

It was going to be like that tonight. Gramma had come to the front door, carrying one of the big brown sketchbooks. They'd had dinner, and then Mom and Dad had put Ellen to bed, and gone off to the party, and Ellen had lain there, with all her lights on, waiting for Gramma.

Gramma would come. She always did. Ellen nestled in the security Gramma's visits gave her, because the feeling was rare. She didn't feel warm and safe like that much because Mom and Dad yelled and threw things and sometimes Dad hit Mom. And sometimes after Dad hit Mom, Mom would come in and hit Ellen.

She was afraid of her parents, now. But she could trust Gramma. Gramma would never hurt her. It was taking Gramma a long time to come tonight.

Ellen decided to go and look. Clad in her nighty, her long curly honey-blonde hair falling around her shoulders, rubbing the big blue eyes that people always said 'Oh, aren't they pretty' about, she tiptoed out to the living room. She was tiptoeing because she wasn't supposed to be out of bed.

She found Gramma asleep on the living-room floor. Funny place for Gramma to sleep.

But she wasn't hurt or anything. She could see her breathing, stirring a little. Just asleep.

Ellen hunkered down and shook Gramma's shoulder. She stirred and mumbled something but didn't wake up. Ellen started to get a little scared. Maybe she *was* hurt. She shook Gramma again, and again, and once more.

Finally, Gramma's eyes snapped open. Just like that: snap, wide open. She sat up, real suddenly. Maybe she'd just been pretending to sleep because she sat up too suddenly for a person just waking up. Gramma looked around, then looked down at Ellen. Like somebody talking to herself, Gramma said, 'Ellen. Ellen is the child of my child. The child of *that* child.'

Ellen smiled at her, uncertainly.

Gramma went on, talking to Ellen now. 'Did you know that Grandpa died when your mommy said some bad things to him one day? He got upset and had a stroke.'

'Mommy is bad sometimes,' Ellen said gravely. 'Will you draw a story for me now?'

'Yes,' Gramma said. 'A story for a child of my child.'

She stood, then picked Ellen up and carried her into Ellen's bedroom, laid her on the bed. Smiling, Gramma tucked her in, then took up the drawing pad and pencils she'd left on the chair beside the bed. She sat on the edge of the bed, opened the pad, and selected a pencil. She began sketching. 'Once there was a little girl named Ellen who was all alone in the house with a woman named Betty.'

'Betty is your name!' Ellen said, proud of herself for remembering.

'That's right. And Betty knows that Ellen is very much afraid . . . of coyotes. Ellen had bad dreams about coyotes because another little girl was chewed up by them and Ellen heard about it at school.'

Gramma showed her the sketchpad. She'd done a kind of comic-book drawing of a little girl with golden hair sitting in bed staring at the window with big eyes. As Ellen watched, Gramma sketched something in at the window.

'And,' Gramma said, 'Ellen's mommy has told her that coyotes eat little girls who make messes and mommies will often throw little girls into ravines where there are hungry coyotes waiting.'

Gramma sketched in a coyote, seen through the little girl's window, silhouetted against the moon.

'I don't want a story about coyotes,' Ellen said.

'And Ellen is afraid that Betty might leave the door open and let the coyotes in. But that won't happen, because Betty is a magic woman and she can turn into a coyote so she won't leave the door open to let the other coyotes in because she wants Ellen all to herself because Betty has always had a secret dream about finding out what people taste like.'

Ellen stared at the picture forming on the second page of the sketchpad, at the dripping fangs and hungry eyes of Gramma's coyote, and then she said, close to tears, 'I don't like that picture!'

'Are you afraid, Ellen? Don't you trust your Gramma? You know if there's one person who won't hurt you, it's your Gramma. Right?'

The little girl nodded.

Gramma sketched something on the third page of the book, something Ellen couldn't see.

After a minute she stopped and looked at her with nothing in her face and said, 'Give Gramma a big hug.'

Ellen smiled, relieved, and opened her arms. Gramma hugged her, hugged her so hard she lifted her a little bit out of bed, and with the shifting of the bed, the sketchbook fell open and Ellen saw the third page, the picture Gramma hadn't shown her, a picture of Gramma biting a big hole in Ellen's throat with her teeth.

And Ellen felt Gramma's warm breath on her neck.

And again, the phone jangled between them. And again, it was Aunt June.

Perry stood in the living room, nude, hoping Sandra wasn't going to come home early, as he said, 'Hello?'

'Perry?' Aunt June. 'Has Lois heard from Wendy?'

'Nope. Maybe you should call Wendy's house. Maybe she came back there.'

'Well, there's no answer there, we just called. We've been in touch with her parents. Her dad's here, in fact. He got a call from some friends of his out at one of the campsites in some state park. Oh, Volcano Rock State Park. Some friends of his family saw Wendy walking barefoot through the park, carrying a screwdriver. They said she was smiling. They spoke to her and she looked at them and said something to herself they couldn't understand and walked past without saying anything else. So one of them was getting worried about her because there are rattlers in that area and she was barefoot – so he put his hand on her shoulder and *she* said something to him he said he wouldn't repeat to anyone. Something that obscene. And then she walked away and went out on to a dirt road near the campsite – about thirty yards away – and a yellow pickup truck drove up, out of the woods.'

She paused. Perry thought: She sounds shook up.

'This pickup truck,' she went on, 'uh, it pulled up in front of her, blocked her path like police cars do. Three men the witnesses didn't know got out, surrounded Wendy, and took the screwdriver from her. She fought them for a minute, and then calmed down, and she was smiling and chatting with them, it looked like, when she got into the truck. And then they drove away with her, crammed into the cab of the truck with them. They said she waved and laughed when the truck drove by. The damn thing didn't have any license plates; that worried them too. That's why they called Wendy's father.'

'These witnesses get a description of any of the men in the truck?'

'Only one with any distinctiveness. They said he had long red hair and a red beard and a tattoo on his forearm. They couldn't make out the tattoo. I thought maybe Lois might know who this guy was so I called to – '

'Right. Hold on.'

'What is it?' Lois asked. She came into the room wearing only a blouse.

'Uh, some guys in a yellow pickup found Wendy, drove off with her. Maybe they took her home. But they'd taken the license plate off the truck and – oh, one of them had red hair, long red hair, and a red beard and a tattoo on his forearm. Do you know him?'

'Not personally. I think it's Charlie Myers. He's one of Rofocale's people. I heard he got into a fight defending Rofocale when somebody called the guy a crook.'

Perry stared at her. 'This guy is close to Rofocale?'

'I've heard he just sort of works for him.'

'Aunt June,' Perry began, 'She said – '

'I heard, I think. The guy is one of Rofocale's assistants?'

'Yeah.'

'Huh. I spoke to Rofocale ten minutes ago. I called him because he seemed so interested in – '

'Well, what did he say?'

'He said he hadn't seen her. Didn't know who the guy with the red hair could be.'

'Are they going to – '

'Yeah, of course. Dawson's arranging a search warrant for Rofocale's therapy center. Does Lois know the name of the red-haired – '

'Charlie Myers.'

'Charlie Myers? Hold on.' He waited while she gave the name to Dawson. 'Perry? Dawson says that Myers was alleged to have moved out of the area a month ago. He's disappeared; they were looking for him in connection with a beating. Listen, there's something else. Two things. I don't know if you should tell Lois.'

'What things?'

'Another local was killed, not far from the campsite where Wendy was seen. A woman . . . someone cut off her head. Her husband's missing. He was a foreman at the lumber mill, fairly prominent local citizen. Dawson thinks Wendy did it.'

'Oh, I – I hardly knew her but I don't believe – '

'What?' Lois asked anxiously. 'What don't you believe?'

Perry raised his hand to signal wait. 'What's the other thing?'

'They found the pickup truck, in a dry wash. Smashed up, burned. Empty. No one around, no one in it.'

7

Usually, it was the light that woke Perry in the mornings, the first time. The dawn would slant into his room, and his eyes would flutter open for a moment, and he'd think, Morning. And then he'd put his head under a pillow and go back to sleep.

This morning, it was the darkness that woke him. He had a sense that something was out of place, and he opened his eyes and sat up on his cot to see what it was.

He glanced at his watch: 10:00 A.M. He looked out the back window; it was too dark for ten in the morning. That was what had awakened him; the light was wrong. It was like twilight.

He went to the windows. Low, dense gray-black clouds occupied the sky like the armored division of an encamped army. In the distance, the clouds bled streaks of black. A desert rainstorm was coming to Jasper. He saw a flicker of lightning but heard no thunder. He turned – and froze.

Sandra was standing in the door to the kitchen, staring at him. Perry wore only a pair of rather battered briefs. He could feel the damp breeze come through the screen behind him; the wet air raised goose bumps on his back. 'I guess – ' he began lamely, then broke off.

'You guess I came back last night while you were asleep, I'll wager,' she said. She obviously took pleasure in making him uncomfortable, staring at him when he was nearly nude. She stood with her arms crossed over her terrycloth bathrobe, her hair down and tousled, leaning against the door frame. Her eyes were red; he could smell last night's gin on her from two yards away.

As nonchalantly as possible, he went to the cot – aware that his testicles were swinging in his briefs with every step – and began to put on his trousers. She kept her eyes on him until he had the jeans snapped shut, then she yawned and went into the kitchen. He decided she'd stared at him because it suited her odd sense of humor, not because she had any sexual interest in him. He pulled on T-shirt, socks, and tennis shoes, thinking it was time he visited the local laundromat, and went into the kitchen.

There was a stranger sitting at the kitchen table. A cleric of some kind. He had the black shirt, the collar. But somehow it wasn't a Catholic priest's collar. He was a nut-brown little man, thin but intense, thirtyish, going bald. He toyed with an unlit cigarette – no, Perry saw, it wasn't a cigarette, it was one of those plastic, menthol-flavored pseudo-cigarettes people chew on when they're trying to give up smoking. Its filter end was badly mangled.

Sandra stood at the stove, a Silvathins, half-smoked, in her compressed lips, her face looking heavy, as if the heat from the burner had melted it a little. She was staring at a pot, waiting for it to boil.

'Watched pots don't you-know-what, Sandra,' said Aunt June, coming into the room. She wore the same green suit she'd arrived in; she'd washed it by hand and hung it up on the front porch to dry the night before. It was discolored, with stray dampness around the edges. Her glasses dangled on their gold chain, the lenses on her chest like an amulet. 'Hullo, Perry.' She smiled. Perry was glad to see her. 'Your friend still here?' Perry winced and glanced at Sandra. She made a half smile but said nothing.

Perry said, 'No, she went home last night.'

'So – so this is Perry,' said the dark-eyed cleric nervously as he stood to shake Perry's hand. His hand was warm and moist, like the storm-heavy air outside.

Not sure what was expected of him, Perry sat across from the minister, who seemed to have forgotten to introduce himself. The man put the plastic pseudo-cigarette in his lips, chewed on it for a moment, then took it out again and held it in his dark, hairy fingers, as if restraining it from making another try for his lips.

'This is Reverend Martindale,' Aunt June said. She set a bowl of cereal, milk, and sliced peaches in front of Perry. Sandra's staring had made Perry feel self-conscious. Now he was embarrassed to eat while the others watched. Oh, don't be an ass, he told himself, and poured milk over the cereal. He was hungry, thanks to Lois. He wished he were having breakfast with her and Aunt June, instead of with a stranger and a woman who was always vaguely hostile. Of course, now Sandra had an excuse to be hostile to the world: she'd lost her only child.

Sandra served instant coffee in three cracked china cups and a greasy red thermos top. Perry got the thermos top. Aunt June sat on Perry's left. Sandra took a sip of her coffee, grimaced, set it down on the table, and said, 'I think I'll just get dressed. Right back.'

When she'd gone, Perry asked, 'What did they find out about Tetty?' Reverend Martindale looked from Aunt June to Perry, back to Aunt June, trying to seem interested, supportive, but not intrusive.

Aunt June said softly, 'She died of some kind of brain lesion. Something exploded in her brain, they said. Did that to her eye.'

'Is Sandra going to try to connect Rofocale with it? Hit him with the suit even without Tetty's testimony?'

'Yes. I don't know how successful she'll be. That's one reason I sent for my paper. Rofocale said it had influenced him. Maybe he used something in it, something suggested by Dr Horescu – used it, I mean, when he was working with Tetty. But I don't see how any of it could apply. The paper came this morning. I've been telling Reverend Martindale about it.'

She glanced at him, and apparently feeling he had to say something then, he blurted, 'Ah, I have, you know, talked to Dr Rofocale, and your aunt gave me the general idea of what her paper was about, what Rofocale used – '

'Then she told you a hell of a lot more about it than she told me,' Perry groused.

Martindale paused, chuckled, then went on in what Perry learned was his characteristic gush of words. 'And I find it just really fascinating, the way this man – and your aunt – have tried to explain evil. Naturally that's a concern of mine.' A self-deprecatory smile. 'Well, your aunt hasn't told you about it? As I understand it, the basic concept is that there are indeed genes that control behaviour, to some extent. Not completely. But certain kinds of behavior. And, ah, your aunt believes that there are genes for complete selfishness – as opposed to self-preservation – and these genes are only activated under special conditions. And when they are, they completely suppress empathy. What was it?' He looked at Aunt June. 'Empathy Syndrome – uh – '

'Empathy Suppression Syndrome,' she said. She was turning a butter knife over and over in her vein-marbled fingers. In the leaden light, she looked very old.

'Yes! ESS. It suppresses empathy for other people – and other people means anyone they don't identify with. Someone outside the family, the party.'

'"Gooks,"' Perry said.

'It's fascinating,' Martindale went on, 'and sort of comforting. Because it *explains* things.'

Aunt June smiled, the patronizing smile of a scientist politely listening to a theologian. She knew what was coming.

'Perhaps, if you don't mind my suggesting it,' Martindale went on, 'this comfort is the real reason for the theory. It gives people an explanation that's easy to deal with. Easier than the belief in evil. When you believe evil behavior is dictated by a gene, you don't have any real responsibility for your behavior. And you don't have to fear God, or worry that the devil is gaining ground in the world.'

'My theory,' Aunt June said, looking at her reflection in the butter knife, 'really doesn't obviate choice. Not until after a certain point. I have it that people willingly – although not knowingly – create the conditions for the emergence of the ESS gene's control. When they continually perceive the world in an adversary way, choose to be continuously competitive, suspicious, they flood their systems with adrenaline and ACTH and other secretions, which, after a certain saturation level, trigger the activation of the ESS gene, for reasons of efficiency. The body has been fooled into thinking an emergency exists, a marauder is trying to steal one's children, say. If you stop to worry about the marauder, if you have empathy for him, you may be slow to crack him over the head with your club, and he'll win out. So you need total empathy suppression. It's supposed to be temporary, but we've created an atmosphere of social anxiety that in some people puts it permanently in control. Once it's taken over, they lose choice. But before it takes over, they can choose to prepare its way or not.' She shrugged. 'On some level, we know what choice we're making.'

'I think you have only sidestepped the issue of choice, doctor,' Martindale said. 'You've only said that you lose choice when it seems time to be profoundly evil instead of mildly evil!'

'Not exactly what I said. But I don't mind you misinterpreting me; Rofocale may have misinterpreted me in a more dangerous way. He may have interpreted the theory to accommodate some kind of twisted notion he has of social engineering. Something that boils down to might means right and the ends justify the means.'

'I'll tell you frankly,' Martindale said, shifting uneasily in his seat, 'I've been nervous about Dr Rofocale for a while. I think he's a man who has his own interests at heart, before the interests of the people who come to him for help.' Martindale said this gravely, and Perry could see that from the reverend's viewpoint, this was a deeply serious charge. Perry was puzzled at a faint thumping sound from beneath the table until, getting up to put his bowl in the sink, he saw that it was made by Martindale's foot. He was one of those people who perpetually jounce a knee or tap a foot, as if their motor's idling, always ready to take to the road.

Martindale caught Perry looking at him and said abruptly, 'Probably you're wondering what brings me here this morning.' He smiled, then decided the smile was inappropriate and dropped it.

Perry shrugged and sat down. 'Sort of.'

'I came to see Sandra. I assumed she was unhappy about the loss of her daughter. Well, of course she is, but –'

'But what?' Sandra asked, coming into the kitchen. She sat at the head of the table, on Perry's right. She laid a pack of cigarettes and a lighter down beside her left elbow, arranged them with her right hand as if the arrangement were meaningful to her.

Martindale had gone red. 'I only meant you didn't seem to need my help. You're a strong woman.'

'I came to his church once,' she said, to Perry, as if explaining all. 'He's hoping I'll come back.' The rain saved them from an awkward silence; it struck the house like a small tidal wave slapping down over the roof, and suddenly all the windows were dripping, the shingles rat-tatting.

'Whew!' Aunt June said. 'That's a relief. I've been waiting for it to hit all morning.'

'It'll be gone in an hour, and the place will steam like the devil,' Sandra said.

'Yes, it gets humid,' Martindale said, 'after a rain. But it smells nice.'

'Now isn't that just like the bloody clergy,' Sandra said. She hadn't so much interrupted him as bitten his sentence off. 'You say it's raining and he says, yes, but it smells nice after a rain. You say it's too hot and he says, yes, but the plants like the sunshine. You say it's too cold and he says but it does make us appreciate our nice cosy homes. Shit. What are you going to say,' she asked, bending a little toward him, pointing at him with the filter of an unlit cigarette she held in her hand like a wand, 'when they drop the hydrogen bomb on us? Or when the Moral Majority votes in a fascist who herds us into concentration camps?' She snorted, thrust the cigarette in her mouth, and lit it. 'You'll say, "Yes, it's awful but it'll be just that much better in the afterlife."'

Martindale had sat frozen through this verbal fusillade. When she paused to puff her cigarette, he said, 'I understand how you must feel.'

Perry was sorry to hear Martindale use this cliché. He

knew she would turn it back on him. So he broke in, 'Okay, so anyway, what would *you* say if they dropped the bomb and you were alive to comment on it, Sandra? Christ, whatever he'd say would be as good as anything else.'

'The best thing,' she said, staring at the ceiling, jetting smoke from her nostrils, 'is to say nothing, and to accept the shit when it comes down. And to try and stay under cover.'

The rain yammered on the roof in agreement. The rainfall came in waves; it would batter the roof in what seemed a fit of anger, then lapse for a while into a sulking sizzle; when they thought it had finished, it would begin its assault once more. Perry pictured the dry washes filling, flash-floods raging around corners, perhaps catching beery campers unaware and whirling them into mud-drenched chaos. The roadside ditches would be suddenly surging with water; in the woods there would be a pine-aromatic misting, like those mentholated steams for a chest-cold. Afterward, oddly shaped desert creatures he could only vaguely imagine – amphibian things, exotic insects – would climb up from their muddy lairs, awakened by the deluge, to perform some annual mating dance. And Lois would be sitting in her room at her uncle's ranch, listening to her tape deck, listening to the rain, looking out the window toward Jasper, thinking – he hoped – about him.

In a lull between waves of rainfall, Sandra said, abruptly, 'Do you know what Reverend Martindale's church is?'

After a moment, Perry realized she was talking to him. 'What church is it, Reverend?' Perry asked. He hoped Martindale wouldn't feel obliged to evangelize.

'The Church of Jesus the Nazarene,' he said softly,

tapping the tabletop with his plastic cigarette, tapping the floor with his toe.

Sandra chuckled. 'Did you ever hear of that church, Perry?'

'Um, no.'

'The church is – small,' Martindale admitted. 'There are only four congregations. One in Oregon, two in California, one in Chicago. I was a founding member. We are a certified church.' He shot Sandra a look of mild defiance.

'No doubt with a very useful tax-exempt status,' she replied.

'Really, Sandra,' Aunt June said, shaking her head sadly. 'Why don't you skip the blame-the-world stage? Why not just cry about it?'

Sandra shrugged. 'I've had the same attitude about the Church of Jesus the Nazarene all along. Before Tetty died. Only reason I didn't say anything was because when I went there, I went with my gentleman, Mr Markowitz, who was very interested in it for a while. Fortunately he's over that fad. I think he's into meditation now.'

Martindale cleared his throat. The color had gone out of his face. He sat very still for a moment, which was unnatural for him. Perry knew he was going to make a speech. 'Something is happening in Jasper,' Martindale said. He paused, and looked at them one at a time, making earnest eye contact. 'That's another reason I'm here. That's why I'm going to see some other people after I leave. Two deaths, and a young girl disappears, and then another death. Someone was decapitated and her husband is still missing. In just a few days, all this happened. And I felt it –'

'Here it comes,' Sandra said. 'I should warn you that the Reverend Martindale believes in demons and diabolic

127

influences, and worst of all, he wants us to believe he has some supernatural power himself. Clairvoyance. Exorcism – '

'Jesus gave his disciples authority over all unclean spirits, to cast them out and cleanse those they infested,' said Martindale simply, reasonable. He'd started tapping his foot again.

'I think, in a funny way, there may be something to the Bible's assertions about Satan,' Aunt June said, surprising everyone. 'I think there is a subsidiary personality in people that is distinct in itself, that we have to struggle with. I think it tempts us and leads us into a personal hell. It's a mechanism of the ESS gene. It's empowered to create its own nasty little personality around itself.'

'I can see what you mean,' said Martindale, shifting eagerly. 'Yes, but these instincts, these subpersonalities, I concede they exist, but just suppose – and how could you know otherwise for sure? – suppose they're Satan's tools, his biological method?'

'That's it,' Sandra snapped. 'I'll have no more of this crap in my house.' She stood, her chair clattering to the floor behind her. She went to the sink and, slamming pots and pans around, began to wash the dishes. 'Beat it, Martindale. Go. The rain is letting up.'

He sighed and stood, turning jerkily to catch the chair before it fell. He sighed again as he steadied the chair, then said, 'Perhaps I'd better.'

'Sandra,' Aunt June began wearily.

'It's my house, June.'

'But,' Perry said, 'it's raining out, still. It's starting up again.' Another sweep of rainfall had begun to rattle the windows.

'I don't mind the rain, really,' said Martindale with an empty smile. 'I have a hat.' He clapped a droopy khaki hat on his head – an anomaly with his clerical collar – and said, 'Good-bye.'

'I don't mind the rain,' Sandra mimicked. 'No doubt he thinks it's the tears of angels, shed for sinners. No, Martindale,' she went on, her back to him, 'you can sit quietly in the living room till the rain quits.'

'No, thank you, I have some other people to see.'

'Oh don't be a martyr!' She threw the sponge into the soapy water; the water splashed the sideboard. She turned furiously on him. 'But then it's your job to be a martyr, right?'

'Good-bye,' he said firmly, and went quickly into the living room, hastening to the front door. Perry followed, wondering why Sandra was so furious with him.

He opened the door for Martindale, and they stood for a moment on the front porch while the rain made a silvery curtain around them, dripping in sheets off the porch roof. 'I don't know why she's so upset,' Perry said.

'I think I do,' said Martindale. 'When she came to the service, about a month ago, she told me that there was something odd going on in her house. Buzzing sounds, and then things would move by themselves. I told her what I thought it was. I thought it was a diabolic influence. She wanted to hear a comforting story about it being a benevolent creature from the spirit world. Then she professed not to believe in the supernatural at all. I think she's very frightened of something – and it's something she's trying not to believe in.'

'What was it you started to tell us? Something you wanted to warn people about.'

His brow creased; he made a curious pout with his lips. 'I can't quite explain it to anyone's satisfaction. I had a series of dreams, of the sort that to me are clearly sendings from God. Warnings about something evil in Jasper. And now three people are dead in three days. One was killed almost ritually: that poor woman decapitated. There is something, I can feel it.'

Perry was about to tell him about the buzzing sounds, the independent movements of the ceramics, but Martindale turned away and lurched into the rain, shoulders hunched.

Aunt June came on to the porch. She and Perry stood together without speaking, watching the rain bow the branches of rosebushes in the neighbor's yard. Finally Perry said, 'I wonder if he cooked up this psychic warning thing just to attract people to his church.'

Aunt June shook her head. 'Reverend Martindale is a very, very serious man. He might be having some kind of, well, some kind of delusion. But he believes it, whatever it is. I'm sure of that.'

The rain stung Martindale's chin whenever he tilted his head back to examine the heavens. It sizzled on the wooden sidewalk and the asphalt street like hot grease on a grill. It slanted to Martindale's left, and he found this significant. When it began to let up, the bulky black clouds rushing on, he was almost disappointed. The rain had seemed to express his own feelings; it had made him feel better when it came crashing down around him, Wagnerian and dark. Yet when the clouds broke and the sun made half a dozen rainbows in the mists rising from the sodden ground, he felt almost cheerful.

Almost, but not quite. He was never quite happy.

The woman's anger proves there's something she's afraid of, he thought. I wish she'd let me perform the exorcism. That would be proof, there would surely be a manifestation at an exorcism.

The terrible truth was, Reverend Martindale was not

quite a believer himself. Not continuously. When he'd spoken to June about it, early that morning, he'd really believed. And when he spoke to the Reverend Earl Baldwin, in Chicago, his mentor, he believed. Baldwin inspired belief.

But the cold truth was that Martindale was basically a sceptic. But he was a sceptic who badly wanted to believe. Because if there was nothing to believe in, beyond the random growth and faltering that made up this world, then life seemed hollow to Martindale. Living for the moment wasn't enough. He couldn't bear the thought of there being no Great Plan to tie it all together. If there were any supernatural causative, Martindale reasoned, then there must be a God also. It was inconceivable that there could be a diabolical force without a divine one. In his way, Martindale sought God – by looking for proof of the Devil.

He'd been driven by this obsession since October 17, 1958, when his mother, his father, his older brother, and his younger sister had been burned to death in a fire set by an arsonist. The arsonist was never caught; his motive was never known.

Martindale, ten years old, had been away visiting his grandparents at the time; two people he heartily disliked. They were both stone-cold cynics, and atheists. His grandfather had been an army career officer, retired. The young Martindale had been as close to his parents and his brother and sister as he was alienated from his grandparents. He'd felt that the universe, in somehow arranging for his family to be burned to death, had struck him a terrible blow out of simple sadistic mischief. And a strong part of him wanted to believe there was no God, no purpose; that would be so much easier. You could do what you wanted, all the awful things you'd ever imagined, if there was no God to judge you for it.

But if there was a God, then there was a devil too. And it might be that the devil – in defiance of God – had arranged the death of his parents. It might be that the Lord was not all-powerful, not quite, that he was constantly fighting with the devil, and in the fight to save or destroy Martindale's family, the devil had won. If Martindale could prove that the devil existed, he could infer a rational cause for his family's death – a supernatural war.

That's why he was honestly and genuinely glad to see the devil waiting for him when he got home.

He didn't see it at first. He came into the little crackerbox cottage shivering, relieved to be somewhere dry. He hung his dripping coat up on a nail over the kitchen sink, tossed his hat on to the drainboard beside a stack of dirty dishes, and went into the bedroom – not much more than an elongated closet – to change his shirt. It was just after he had removed the damp clerical collar and black shirt that he felt the breeze. But he'd left the window shut. So what was the source of the misty wind he felt lapping at his spine? He looked around, saw the yellow satin curtains billowing a little.

He pressed the curtain aside – and let it drop. There was a hole in the upper window pane, a hole big as a fist. Just below the hole, clinging to the white-painted wooden window frame, was what looked like a translucent housefly with a human face – a fly at least eight inches long and four across its thorax. As he pushed the curtain aside, it swiveled its head to look at him. It was when he looked into its eyes that he knew: here is Evil. Its miniature human face could almost have been made of wax; its bright green eyes gleamed; its tiny, lipless mouth seemed to be smiling, but Martindale knew it was a cat's smile, an accident of its features, an illusion. The face was stylized, almost like an Egyptian death mask.

Heart hammering, Martindale thought: God has sent me both proof and a trial. This thing is no aberration of the insect world. This thing is not native to our world at all. This is truly a visitor from hell.

For two minutes, Martindale stood rooted, staring at the fly, thinking, It's his servant. Satan's servant, the Patron of Flies.

'Why – ' Martindale had to swallow hard, before he could speak in more than a croak. 'Why did you come here, Beelzebub?' The thing tilted its head a little more, then began to shift on its perch. It was turning to face him. So it could spring directly at him. 'Why did you come to this town, you and yours?' Martindale asked. 'I knew you were coming. I dreamed it. I command you, in Jesus Christ's name, by the power he bestowed on his disciples, tell me what you have come for.' It made no reply. It gave no reaction to the name of God's only Son. It gazed at him a little like a basilisk, and he wondered if he could move. He had to have proof. Otherwise he would never know for sure if he'd hallucinated it. A photo. Take a photo.

He forced himself to move, sliding to the cabinet in the headboard of the bed. Keeping his eyes on the demon, he slid the cabinet door open, reached in, felt for his camera. His fingers closed on the old Kodak. There was film in it. He raised the camera to his eye, his finger poised over the shutter button.

The camera was slapped from his hand. It smashed against the wall, sprang apart, exposing the film. The film unwound, by itself, then flew through the air and bounced off the opposite wall, fell on the bedspread in a tangled heap like a ribbon flower. And through all this, the air was filled by a sharp buzzing.

His skin tingling, mouth dry, Martindale stared at the shattered camera, the film. That's proof enough for me, he thought. It flew from my hands, all by itself. That thing reached out invisibly, magically, and knocked it away and broke it. I'm not strong enough to shatter it like that with one blow.

The fly-demon had remained unmoving on the window frame. Its expression had not changed. But it crouched now. Poised. Martindale shuddered – but not with horror. With a great relief. 'You're real,' he said as he fell to his knees. 'But I kneel for God, not you. To thank God for this sign. Thank you.'

He made a high, gulping noise as the thing flung itself at his head, its wings a blur, its small, black, human hands opening and closing spasmodically, its bristling tail quivering, extruding the yellow-oozing stinger. He flailed at it, lost sight of it, tried to shout Jesus' Name to command the thing, and managed only, 'Jes – ' The second part of the Holy Name blended into a warbling sob, a sound that spoke of the full horror of defilement.

The thing had found his neck, and driven its stinger into his spine, just under the skull. And the pain was another kind of revelation.

8

'The sheriff's department searched Rofocale's apartment, and the therapy center,' Aunt June said, coming into the room. She was carrying a thick sheaf of papers with both hands. Perry was sitting in the kitchen, trying to read *V* by Thomas Pynchon. Lois had given it to him, and he wondered if she'd really done better with it than he did. Aunt June went on, 'It was no go. No sign of Wendy. They still haven't found this guy Myers. But a deputy dropped this off while you were taking your afternoon nap. I've been reading it.' She slapped the sheaf of papers on to the table.

'What is it?'

'Tell you in a minute. After I get my brain back in gear.' She slumped into the chair across from him.

Perry glanced at the clock, wondering if 9:00 P.M. was too late to call Lois. The rain had moved on hours before. But Jasper steamed, even in the dark, with the summer heat and the rain damp. Perry wore a pair of cutoff jeans and a T-shirt. Aunt June wore a maroon shift. Sandra was in her bedroom, watching her portable TV, or asleep by now. She'd taken three Valiums.

Perry decided not to call Lois. She'd probably still be awake, but she'd worry all night if he told her the bad news about the search for Wendy. 'I just don't see what interest Rofocale would have in Wendy, anyway. Her husband says no way she could have even met Rofocale.'

Aunt June shrugged. 'He can't be sure what she does all day. It could be that Rofocale sold her the LSD or whatever it was. Ibogaine, maybe. Some so-called therapists use psychedelic drugs on their patients. And now he wants to keep her under wraps till she comes down.'

'So she doesn't blurt it out while she's stoned? Maybe. Maybe, if you think Rofocale is selling or donating drugs.'

Aunt June grinned, and wiped sweat from her upper lip with a handkerchief. 'You know me pretty well by now, it appears.'

'I know you don't believe that acid story. So what do you think?'

'I haven't made up my mind yet. Maybe after we talk to the sheriff tomorrow.'

'Oh, shit, but that was today, right? And we didn't go!'

'Delayed till tomorrow, because the Stiggins kid got a lawyer who says the boy ought not to be interrogated. Apparently he's "psychologically traumatized" by his sister's drowning. That's the phrase the attorney uses. There was some remark from his mother, Dawson said, about his not acting normally. Flying into a rage . . .'

Perry's eyes widened. 'You think? Like with Wendy?'

'We'll see.'

Perry yawned. 'God, I'm tired. This humidity wears me out. If you're going to explain something to me, do it now.'

She looked at the sheaf of papers, almost a ream of typewritten sheets, a few diagrams. 'Rofocale has dropped from sight. They raided his center; all they found of any interest were a few videotapes of him berating students. It showed some rather irresponsible stuff but nothing really actionable. And this.' She nodded toward the sheaf of papers. 'In a wall safe, hidden near the floor, behind a desk. This is a copy. He probably took the original with him and forgot about this one.'

'So what the hell *is* it?'

'It seems to be his magnum opus. And it's a report to his backers.'

'And who's that?'

'Worldkey Incorporated. You ever hear of them?'

'Nope.'

'Me neither. Maybe one of those dummy corporations, to cover up the real funding source.'

'Why would they use one of those?'

'Because of what's in the report.'

'You read that whole thing already?'

'Most of it was quite familiar. For one thing, there's a copy of my paper on ESS genes. But the last section . . .' She stared at a fly, looping lazily around the light bulb.

'You going to tell me?'

She took a deep breath. And then she told him.

Aunt June's conjecture on the nature of ESS 'stops just short of the truth,' Rofocale said in his report. 'Or perhaps several steps short.'

She had hypothesized the DNA-programmed glandular action that secretes mind-altering hormones. 'But the production of the hormone and our initial reaction to it is just the early stage of the process. It sets the stage for the awakening of the Waiting Ones. The Gray Pilots. The first level of the process is a sort of "gear" the brain shifts into for self-preservation. A low gear. The second level is, so to speak, the high gear. The second level, the preparation for the Gray Pilots, is only possible in certain people, unless they come into contact with a Breeder. And the Breeder infects them.'

'The Breeder? Some kind of microorganism?' Perry asked.

'No. Not a microorganism. It's a man, that doesn't look like a man, much. A man within a man. So Rofocale maintained. In its external form, it rather resembles an oversized insect. When it's inside a human being, preparing for "piloting" him or her, it's highly compact, composed of a subtle plasmalike stuff. Not blood plasma, but electrical plasma: ionized gas in a magnetic field. This intricate inner-patterned plasma acts as a nonmaterial outer body for the few material cells at the heart of it. It's not something that would show up on an X ray. Still, it's a kind of tissue, an unusual kind of tissue. It's highly permeable, and wispy, ethereal almost, till it's time to externalize.

'To emerge for breeding . . . If you're a Genetic Class Sub-B3, you have the potential to create a pilot that can become physically dense and organically self-sufficient. Once it's developed that far, it emerges from the host body – rips free from the brain, and flies away, to seek "vessels for insemination"'.

'They become flying insectlike things . . .'

'Hey, no, seriously, come on, he doesn't really say that, does he?' Perry said, sitting up straight in his chair, almost laughing. 'They, like, bust out of you and go cruising?'

Aunt June looked blank for a moment. Then she smiled, but it wasn't a real smile. 'Yeah. I know, it's hallucinatory. He cites the legends of "fairies," little people with wings who do mischief, legends of people turning into flying dryads and elementals, certain Indian legends, some paintings in the old Babylonian temple of Ba'al. But – ' She shrugged. 'It's about as believable as UFO contactees.'

'So what else does he say about these little buggers?'

'Very few of these hypothetical creatures develop to the point of breaking into Breeder mode. Or even to the point of influencing a person's behavior.'

'When they *do* influence a person's behavior, what do they do?'

'They utterly eliminate empathy, sympathy. They see to it that you identify with no one who is not immediately beneficial to you. And you're ruthless even with those. And then it leads you to more thorough indoctrination. Paranoia, rages, vindictive sadism. Murder.'

'He claims all murders are caused by these inner creatures?'

'No. Only the utterly brutal ones. Only the incredible ones, the serial killings, the genocides, the slow pleasure killings. But before the point where these things are brought about, there first has to be an extended incubation in the Empathy Suppression hormone. Something we saturate ourselves with when we insist on taking certain attitudes. Then the Gray Pilot begins to grow inside certain people. Painlessly and undetectably.

'When the Gray Pilot begins to grow inside someone, it locks its own neurosystem into the brain . . .'

'Rofocale expects people to believe in this, like, brain parasite?' Perry asked incredulously.

Aunt June shrugged. 'He insists it's not a parasite. He claims it gives more than it takes from the body. Remember, it's a creation of the body. It's the essence of certain kinds of human behavior. Sort of like the embodiment of self-interest, self-indulgence. It is the man or woman it inhabits. That man or woman deliberately – but unconsciously – grew the thing inside them. They set the stage for the takeover, but they're being taken over only by themselves. By another, secret level of themselves.'

'You talk as if you take him seriously.'

'I . . .' She got up, took the teapot to the sink, filled it, returned to the stove, lit the gas with a wooden match.

The gas went huh-*whoof!* into blue flame. She put some instant coffee in a cracked mug. 'You want some coffee?'

'Naw.'

She watched the greasy teapot, waiting for it to begin its shrilling. Finally she muttered, 'I don't know. Maybe I believe him in a metaphorical sense. Something about it . . .'

Perry hugged himself and waited. The teapot began to whimper, then to whine, then to shriek. She snatched it from the stove so it made a sound like a small girl crying in dismay and sloshed hot water in her cup. She couldn't find a clean spoon, so she used the handle of one rather than wash it. She sat down with her coffee, sipped it, grimaced, and said, 'He says it twice: *parasite* is the wrong word. The thing, this insect inside . . . it's the child, the demanding child who wants everything now, who cries and kicks when he can't have it. The sadistic child who pulls the legs off ants and torments smaller children. In a sense, the true self. Or what Rofocale thinks it is.'

'What's his evidence for this Breeder thing?'

Aunt June took another sip of her coffee, and then pushed it away. 'He's vague about that. He's circumspect about a lot of stuff. There's a Polaroid, paper-clipped to the last page, with no explanation. But, hell, it could be anything.'

She made no move to show it to Perry. But she didn't stop him when he lifted the sheaf of papers and found the photo. It was the old black-and-white sort. 'I didn't know they even made this kind of film anymore.' He looked at the picture and shrugged. It showed what looked like the corner of a ceiling. And there was a clump of something in the corner that might have been a motion-blurry image of a moth. But in relation to the lines of the wall, the thing was much too big to be a moth.

The image was murky. It might, indeed, be anything. It could be made of wool, some sort of stuffed animal hung in the shadows. But there was just the suggestion of a face, and Perry remembered the face pressed into the plastic over the window. 'What, uh, what you going to tell Dawson about this?'

'I don't know. I suppose the paper is about as useful as *Confessions of an Opium Eater*. Maybe Rofocale was on his own drug, if he's been giving drugs to people, when he wrote it. I don't know. I have to think about it.'

Perry yawned, and felt fatigue pull a gray wool blanket over his mind. 'I can't think about it anymore. This heat and the moisture, I'm so tired. I think I'm going to crash.'

'Me too. I guess I'll lie down.' Aunt June had been sleeping on the couch. Perry didn't ask her why she didn't take Tetty's old bed.

'So, is this kid Stiggins going to be at the sheriff's office when we are, or not?' Perry asked, getting up.

'Dawson says he'll be there, lawyer or no lawyer. 'Night.'

'Good night.' Perry went into the back-porch room, and sat on his cot, plucking idly at his mandolin. His mind wandered. He had a bad taste in his mind. It was the taste of many kinds of dull dread. He dreaded going to the sheriff's office, dreaded talking about Tetty, dreaded living any longer with Sandra.

He felt a twinge of rebelliousness – and his mood was reflected by brisker strumming as he thought, Why should I stay here? Lois and I could go somewhere else. Portland, for a while.

Did Aunt June really need him? Not as a secretary, now. But he knew she needed him to be there for 'moral support,' for comfort. She was scared too. And thinking this, his strumming became less strident, his chords softer.

But then – it wasn't his fault he couldn't stand Sandra. She was a pain in the ass. He'd like to see her tilted headfirst into a garbage can. He backed away from the thought. And as he recoiled from it, he knew that he'd recoiled from something more. There was a kind of hot-edged tightening in his mind, behind the anger at Sandra, behind the urge to desert Aunt June. It was like nothing he'd ever felt. It was dark, it was enticing, it was exciting – and he didn't know why. He'd thought angrily about people before, but never with that peculiar sensation – halfway between mental and physical – that somehow made him want to think that way again. It had the character of a sexual fantasy. Forbidden – but thinking about it brought a surge of pleasure.

Perry made a habit of trying to understand himself. This, he didn't understand. It was new. It had a weird quality of – of coming from outside. From outside himself.

Just an illusion, he told himself. It comes from your unconscious, and things in the unconscious sometimes seem like they're outside you. So Aunt June had told him once. But what the hell – why not experiment?

He sat on the edge of his cot, his bare feet flat on the wooden floor, his back itchy with sweat. The overhead light was out; the only light came from the kitchen, dividing the porch room with a diagonal yellow slash. His feet were in the slash of light, the rest of him in the shadow. The glassless screen window on his left was silvered by moonlight. He let his mind drift again, then gently guided it into the avenues of anger; his mandolin strumming went from folk to rock'n'roll. He visualized Sandra, sneering at him as Aunt June mentioned his rendezvous with Lois. She hadn't said anything, but he somehow read in her expression: *He's banging some slut in my house. The day after my daughter died here.*

He realized, then, that he'd felt guilty about that since he'd seen the look on her face. What right did she have to make him feel guilty for finding affection and consolation in someone he loved? And before he could stop himself, he visualized Sandra at the stove again – only now he saw himself behind her, pressing her face into a pan of boiling water.

He stopped strumming the mandolin. Christ, he thought, what's wrong with me?

He'd never thought anything like that before. Never visualized it consciously . . . But he'd felt something horribly delicious when he'd imagined forcing her into the boiling water.

Once more, just to be sure. To try and get the source of it . . . He pictured a 'Sōsh' he'd known in high school, three years before. A tall, brawny, flat-faced guy with eyes like chips of ice, immaculately cut longish brown hair, football jersey. Harminger, his name was. Harminger had had a gift for saying vicious things that seemed reasonably mild, on the surface. 'Here comes the sensitive artist,' he would say when Perry came down the hall. And with that one phrase he'd made Perry sound like a limp-wristed, self-important wimp. It was all in his tone. Everyone had laughed . . . Now, Perry pictured Harminger working on that big flashy red Trans-Am of his, his head under the hood. Perry saw himself slam the hood on Harminger's head, lock it down with wire. Harminger, alive, trapped with his head under the hood as Perry drove the car down the street into a brick wall. Perry forced the vision out of his mind. It took a major effort this time; it was like shouldering a man-high boulder to close a cave mouth, a cave that vomited verminous bats. He had to make a major mental effort to plug that dark cave.

Something was buzzing at the window. Perry looked, glimpsed an oval shadow against the silvered web of screen. It swooped up, out of sight.

A bird, he thought. But that buzzing sound. Gone, now. Silence. Even the crickets quiet.

Experimentally, watching the window, he pictured Harminger screaming under the hood, choking on gas fumes as the car picked up speed.

The buzzing resumed. The shadow at the window – something thumped against the screen, bouncing twice against it, then hovered, transparent wings shimmering in the moonlight. He saw only a silhouette of its body.

'Aunt June . . .' But it came out only a whisper. And he thought: Oh, no, I called that thing. Picturing those ugly things, I called it to me. I know I did.

He didn't know how he knew, but he was sure of it. It had heard him thinking. It had encouraged his line of thinking, transmitting the feelings of pleasure in return. It had encouraged him to prepare himself for it. To call it to him.

Stop picturing the things that attract it . . . But it was as if some floodgate had opened in his mind. He saw Harminger crushed against the wall, in slow motion, the car's bumper crunching into the brick, Harminger's blood spraying . . .

The buzzing at the window. Something clinging, now, to the window. *Stop thinking about Harminger. Stop dwelling on your anger. Stop –*

But now he saw it in sharp focus: Ellen Bachelor, Harminger's girlfriend. He'd always had the hots for her. Never mind that she had the IQ of a walnut, he'd always wanted her. Her with her strong, tanned thighs opening and closing as she did cheerleader jumping jacks at the games. Now he saw himself taking her, ripping the cheerleader's uniform in the backseat of Harminger's car, as the front of the car steamed, dripping Harminger's blood.

I'm not like this, Perry thought desperately.

Everyone is, said a soft, feminine voice in his head. *Everyone, Perry. You don't have to be ashamed. It's your true self.*

Every syllable rang in his head, soft though it seemed, and gave him a strange, whipping pain behind his temples. The thing clinging to the window screen was talking to him.

Leave me! Perry thought. I'm not sick, I'm not like that.

No, Perry, you're not. You're like everyone else. You've got some anger in you, all stored up, that has to come out.

No! I refuse it! Maybe everyone has it but there has to be a better way to deal with it!

No one would catch you, Perry . . .

He saw himself playing at a concert. Hundreds, thousands of people shouting his name, adoring him. But there, in the front row – Bob Potts. The guy who said he had no talent, way back in music class in the eighth grade. Here, at his concert, Potts was still mouthing it: 'You've got no talent, Strandman.' So Perry signaled his bodyguards, who grabbed Potts, carried him onstage, beat him to a pulp while the audience roared approval.

It's putting those things in my mind, he thought. Don't think about it.

But now he saw Potts impaled on a microphone stand.

The thing on the screen ripped through.

It buzzed around his head, then hovered for a moment, just above, caught in the moonlight. It was translucent, gray mottled with black, vitreous-skinned. Like plastic-bag material stretched over a frame. He could see its

internal organs pumping mercurial blood in its veins. It looked like a man, in its face and arms, small black miniatures of human hands on all six legs. But in the rest of it, it was insect. The man and insect parts were blended into a kind of hellish stylistic harmony. Its striated abdominal tail bristled with little hairs like shreds of fiberglass; it bent that tail toward him as it hovered, the motion forcing a stinger out, dripping. Its lipless mouth opened.
Perry . . .

It darted at him. He whirled aside, rolled on to the floor, feeling splinters dig into his forearms. He rolled on to his back. It hovered over him, darting back and forth every few seconds, like a wasp, looking for an opening.

Perry groped, his hand closed on something, and he threw it: a tennis shoe. The flying thing buzzed loudly, perhaps laughing, and the shoe was flung aside, as if it had hit an invisible wall. Perry tried to shout for help. His throat was frozen. He scrambled backward, to the wall, moving crablike. He reached up and switched on the light, hoping a sudden flash of light would frighten the thing away.

For one bright moment, the light burned; the room was lit golden with hope. And then the bulb shattered, broken by the buzzing, though the thing had flown nowhere near it, and darkness closed over the room.

But he could see the thing. It was clinging to the ceiling now, upside down, its head twisted backward on its neck so it could look unblinkingly down on him. He could see only its head clearly in the light from the kitchen. Then it was in the air again, the transition violently sudden; it flew through the kitchen door. He heard the buzzing. He heard a pop as the kitchen light shattered. The buzzing returned to the back porch, and now Perry was in a deeper darkness; there was a wan half-light, vaguely chrome, marking the left end of the cot, the window frame, the silhouettes of trees outside. I can't see it, he thought. Where is it? He tried to shout for Aunt June, but he could only croak. He felt a wispy touch against the back of his neck, a breath of air against his cheek.

He screamed silently and flung himself aside, twisting and covering his head with his arms, hearing the buzzing, feeling something soggy banging at his arms. It was hitting him with something. It felt like BBs in a plastic sack, swung like a blackjack. It hit him on the cheek, hard enough to bruise. Hit him with something that wasn't there. Instinctively, he took hold of the blanket with both hands, ripped it free of the cot, dragged it over his head. It was a thick army blanket; it might be thick enough to keep the thing's stinger out. His heart banged; he had to force himself to breathe because his chest was tight with tension. Holding the blanket over his head and shoulders, he lurched to his feet, staggered toward the kitchen door. He felt blindly with his hands, found the door frame, floundered through. He slammed the door behind him, heard a squealing sound. He turned, throwing off the blanket, hoping to see a flying thing caught in the door. But there was only the door and the glass window set in the upper panel. He couldn't see the thing. He forced himself to look through the glass. He saw it, a silhouette, hovering near the hole it had made in the screen, moving jerkily, angrily in the air.

As he watched, it passed out through the hole. It was gone. He was sure of it. Gone, for the moment.

Perry looked around at the dark kitchen. It was just a kitchen. He was numb, somehow. Not physically. But something in him, something had gone numb. And for the moment fear was locked in a refrigerator in a vacant lot, banging like a trapped child. Muffled.

Do something. Busy, keep busy.

Perry found the matches on the stove. Moving mechanically, breathing hard, he lit the top two burners of the gas stove. By the light of the stove burners, he found a dusty spare bulb in its cardboard carton atop the round-shouldered Frigidaire. After using a worn rubber dishwashing glove to take out the stub of the old bulb, he installed a new one and flicked the switch. He felt better, with the light back on. He peeled the glove off, threw it in the sink, and with the blanket draped over his shoulders like a cape, he went to the cupboard where Sandra kept her liquor.

He didn't realize how badly he'd been shaken until it came to him that he'd drunk three shots of straight gin, one after another, almost without noticing it.

He went to the bathroom, glancing uneasily at the dark square of the bathroom window, and looked at himself in the mirror.

There was a red-blue bruise on his right cheek. No dream did that, he thought. He turned sideways and, craning, looked at the back of his neck. It was unmarked. It hadn't stung him. It had wanted to sting him on the back of his neck, he was sure of that somehow. That stinger – big as a barbed-wire spur – would have left a mark. He'd have felt that.

That meant it hadn't achieved what it had come here for. It hadn't finished with him. It had spoken to him. It had called him by name. By his first name. He looked at the window once more and wondered if he should rouse the house and try to convince them to board the windows over. He could just picture Sandra's reaction. But the fly thing had said something about 'we.' There were others. How many? Where were they now? He glanced at the opaque window. Were they clinging to the sill just outside that glass? Were they on the roof, discussing him with their lipless mouths? Were they crawling, swarming over the shingles, looking for another way in?

But they could break in whenever they wanted. So they were waiting for something. For the right moment. And when that moment came, they'd do to him what they'd done to Tetty. Or worse.

He shook his head and went into the living room; he was reeling, half drunk. He passed by the couch, looked at the slack face of his aunt, and tried to imagine telling her what had happened to him. It was unimaginable.

But – the fly thing might come back.

He'd just have to stay awake, and on guard. He closed the kitchen door after him and rummaged in the cupboard. He made coffee and turned the radio on, softly. The announcer said it was 12:32.

'Good morning,' the announcer said, and played a record. Perry listened to a lady country singer tell him sadly that her daddy had wasted his life working in a coal mine. Maybe he should go and wake Aunt June, and tell her what had happened. But he couldn't. He told himself that the only reason he couldn't tell her was that he needed time to decide how he'd put it so she wouldn't think he was crazy.

He sat for hours at the kitchen table, alternating between gin and coffee, trying to think of a way to explain.

About three in the morning, the numbness melted away, and he began to feel deeply and overwhelmingly afraid. It hadn't really hit him until now. Now, the fear came in crashing waves like the summer rainstorms. He felt as if he were about to be washed away in it, as if his sanity was going to melt like a sand castle in a rush of dark waters. 'Oh, shit,' was all he said aloud. His hands balled into fists. He looked at the white, grease-streaked door of the gas oven. It was open just a crack, so he could see that it was dark inside it. He was, for a moment, utterly certain that if he opened that oven door, Tetty's head would be inside, staring out at him, grinning, one eye missing; the mouth would creak open, and an enormous, rat-sized fly would crawl out on her lolling tongue.

He forced himself to stand, to go to the oven, to throw it open. Of course, it was empty.

He went back to the table, feeling no better. Because he knew that outside the kitchen window, on the strip of grass at the side of the house, Tetty was standing, one eye gouting blood, and something gray-black and bristling was crawling over her face, pausing to dip its proboscis into the bloody socket. All he had to do was go to the window, bend over the sink, look out through the glass.

He forced himself to do it. And of course, there was nothing out there. Nothing you could see.

Perry returned to the table. He stood by the table, one hand on it, and looked around. He looked at the open oven; he looked at the cabinet under the sink (they could be in there, crawling on the pipe like oversized cockroaches, cockroaches who could call you by name); he looked at the refrigerator (anything could be in there); he looked at the kitchen door (they might be swarming over Aunt June as she slept, or they might have changed her already, and she could come out, and smile at him, and yawn, and offer him a piece of cake, and go to the drawer to get a knife to cut the cake, and then he'd realize that there wasn't any cake, just as she'd turn and, still smiling, she'd drive the knife deep into his belly, twisting it, smiling, letting his intestines slop on to the floor, smiling, smiling).

Get a goddamn hold on yourself, Strandman, he

thought. They like you scared. Don't think about violence, or death. That attracts them. Like flies to shit. Careful, careful what you think about.

He had to shake off the paranoia, or go mad. Face the fear, then. Look it in the eye and laugh.

He went to the refrigerator and jerked it open. Nothing but a half stick of butter on a plastic dish, flecks of bread stuck to the butter; a couple of rubbery carrots, a quart of milk, the grimy yellow refrigerator light making a halo against the plastic at the back. That was all. Oh, the freezer. That too, pal. He reached up and opened the freezer door.

Tetty's severed head was lying on its right ear, in the freezer's coat of frost. Her jaws moved, her blue cheeks quivered; fresh blood oozed from the ripped eye. The head began to edge itself along the shelf toward him, using its jaw to pull itself.

He slammed the freezer door and backed away, mouthing, 'Uh. Uh. Uh.'

He stood staring at the yellow-white refrigerator, rigid. Its motor started up, making a sound that, just then, was like mechanical laughter. Perry was afraid to look away from the refrigerator, afraid of what he might see somewhere else. Better not look at the window, the sink, the table. There might be anything.

And then he had a feeling he recognized: that sickly-sweet sensation in his nerves that had come when he'd found himself visualizing vengeance. He laughed, a laugh of nervous release. 'Oh,' he said aloud. 'I see. You've been putting things in my mind again.' He looked at the windows now.

'You hear me?' he asked softly. As if asking the night. 'It's because I know about you. Maybe you're hoping I'll flip out and get myself shot down by the local cops. No.

No, I know what you're doing. I know there's a part of me that – that conspires with you. Like a part of my mind is a traitor, that wants to sneak out and open the gates, to break the siege, right? Forget it. I won't let it happen.'

He went to the refrigerator. He gave it a vicious kick, only because it made him feel better. Then he reached out, opened the refrigerator door. His hand shook, just a little, as he stretched it out and opened the door to the freezer. The freezer was empty, except for a coat of blue-white ice, like a crystal cave. Rather pretty. He let out a long, relieved breath, closed the refrigerator, went to the stove. 'I refuse to consider the possibility,' he muttered, making coffee, 'that I am crazy. *Stay out of my mind.*'

He spent the next few hours sitting at the table, trying to think only about things that wouldn't attract them.

He thought about Lois. He thought about music.

At dawn, he rose stiffly and went to tell Aunt June what had happened. But when she sat up on the couch, rubbing sleep dust from her eyes, looking old, rumpled in her nightgown, he couldn't speak. He couldn't tell her about the thing that had torn the screen and bruised his cheek and tried to sting him. The flying, smiling insect with small perfect human hands.

He wanted to say, *It spoke to me, it called me by name. It wasn't human, but it was. And it put ugly seeds in my mind and came buzzing around to change me when those ugly seeds grew into ugly flowers.*

But he couldn't say a word about it. His jaw locked when he tried.

Aunt June looked up at him with narrowed eyes when he struggled to speak. Something inside him was blocking his ability to speak about it. Something deeper than taboo. A kind of instinct. He shook his head dumbly when she asked, 'There something you want to tell me, Perry?' He sat on the couch, his head cocked to one side, listening. Listening for the sound of its coming. Listening for the buzzing.

9

The Reverend Cyrus Martindale came to himself in the Grange Hall. Normally, the barnlike hall was used by ranchers for their agricultural club meetings; a big, echoing, dusty room with time-yellowed walls and open-air rafters. Martindale used it for a chapel, on Sundays.

Martindale stood on the foot-high stage at the far end from the door. He was leaning on the podium, gazing out over the empty room. He could see the diagonal floorboards in the patch of light given off by the fly-specked bulb above and behind him; he could just make out the folding, gray-painted metal chairs against the back wall, stacked three deep.

'So empty,' he said.

Every Sunday, the Grange Hall was turned over to Martindale. He would stand at the podium and preach his own peculiar mixture of theosophical occultism and Christianity. But he always emphasized the Christianity.

He leaned heavily on the podium. He was afraid that if he moved away from it, he might fall. He would fall into a spin like a World War I fighter plane, and he'd hit the floor and explode into flame.

Cyrus Martindale was stronger than Wendy Marsteller. So he was able to say to himself: 'Something's wrong.' He said it aloud. It sounded as if someone else had said it. He said it again, more loudly, so that it echoed a little. *Wrong-ong-ong*.

What was it that was wrong?

He realized: he couldn't remember how he had come there, to the Grange Hall.

He had been sleeping, somewhere. And then he had awakened here. And why was the room going red?

It was like looking through dark red sunglasses. Through the red he saw the room the way it was on Sunday. Two rows of chairs set up, seven or eight to a row. Never more than twelve people in those chairs, usually two empty. At least two. He didn't set up more chairs, though a church would normally have more, because it depressed him to see all the empty ones. Now, he could see his nine dependable church members. Mrs Green, seventy-seven, and her friends Mrs Goulter, seventy-six, and Miss Marmentia, eighty-one. And then the young set: Mr and Mrs Fairweather, in their sixties, old Dan Borrister, about sixty-seven, and two Indian women, in their fifties, who never spoke, and Lucy Angelino, about sixty.

'Old people,' he muttered. 'Lonely, desperate, bored, attracted by the wrong thing. Why don't the young come?'

But the youngest person he'd had in his congregation was Sandra Cummings. And she'd never come back.

Maybe he could have had some young people – if the regulars would bring their families. But they never brought anyone else. They made sheepish excuses when he asked them to. They were just parasites, really, leeching off him, soaking up a little reassurance from him because they were scared of dying and they could count on him to talk about life after death. Most of them probably had subscriptions to *Fate* magazine. They were sheep, really. And they all had one foot in the grave. He'd be doing them a favor, if he –

'What?' His voice echoed from the rafters. *What-at-at*. 'What was I thinking about? Jesus Lord.'

'What you were thinking about was only natural, Cyrus.' The man who had spoken was sitting in a chair a few feet in front of the podium. He hadn't been there a moment before. Neither had his chair. But he was there now, in the shadow, just outside the little pool of rose-coloured light. The shadow hid his face. He was in silhouette; and the silhouette showed something clinging to his shoulder. An insect big as a parrot.

'Why are you fighting yourself, Cyrus?' the man asked. His voice was soft, masculine, charismatic. 'Fighting a perfectly natural desire to assert your anger. Your Self.'

Martindale felt nauseated, and weak. He felt as if he were hanging on the edge of a cliff, with the weight of his body and the gravity of the whole earth pulling him; he was hanging by his fingers alone and he was going to fall.

'I'm fighting it,' Martindale said thickly, 'because it's evil.'

'Evil is relative, Cyrus. Don't you feel – tired? Weak? But if you stop fighting it, it will give you strength. You'll have all the strength you need.'

'Who are you?' Martindale demanded.

'A part of you. The proprietor of your dark corners, Cyrus.'

'You're not – not who I thought you were.'

'Beelzebub? The devil? Not exactly. But then again, yes. It depends on how you define these things. But I'm not the devil in the sense you mean. You know that, now; you're a perceptive man and you could only keep kidding yourself so long.'

'I won't do it: I won't kill them.'

'Do you know what happens if you fight us to a standstill?'

'Why do you say "us"? There's a group of you, working together?'

'I ask you again: do you know what will happen if you keep fighting us?'

Martindale wanted a drink of water. His throat was so dry. It hurt when he swallowed. Why was everything red? 'No,' he said, in a husky whisper. 'I don't know.'

'Simple: we kill you. From within. And you'll be a father, of sorts – because something you made in you, almost like a child, is going to break out of you. Can you imagine how it will feel, the actual sensation, when your living brain smashes out through your eye, and flies away?'

'Uh.' Cyrus Martindale lost his hold. He clawed at the imaginary cliffside, then fell away, and went spinning down and down.

When he came to himself, the second time, he was at the payphone at the back of the Grange Hall. He'd taken his address book from his back pocket. He had two dimes, four nickels, three quarters in his pockets. He could call seven of them and ask them to come to the Grange for an emergency meeting. He put in a quarter, referred to his pocket address book, and dialed.

'Hello? Good morning, Mr Fairweather. This is Reverend Martindale. I – really? Is it that early? Six-thirty? Sorry to wake you. But there's an emergency. A great emergency. Please get your wife and come to the Grange Hall. It's a matter of life and death.'

He hung up, and fumbled for another twenty-five cents. He felt better now. The redness had drained away. And everything was crystal clear.

Perry felt cold; cold and empty. But at the same time he seethed inside, with an insufferable tension.

He glanced at his watch, because checking the time made him feel more normal, more every day. It was

7:30 A.M. He listened to the clop-clop of his footsteps on the sun-washed wooden sidewalk. Here and there, small green shoots poked between the boards, rustling at the canvas of his shoes as he passed.

It was odd, feeling so cold inside when it was so sunny out. The day was already hot, but it was a heat he didn't feel. He passed a cafe; in the cafe's gravel parking lot, against the white-painted concrete sidewalls, were two garbage cans brimming with food scraps; flies wove a mindless filigree in the air over the garbage. He could hear them buzzing. He wrenched his eyes away and walked faster, to get well past the flies. He pictured them coming at him, in a voracious cloud. But he walked on, and the world ignored him. Two grade-school boys rattled past on Stingray bicycles, hooting at one another. Neither glanced at Perry.

The sky was cloudless and the kind of perfect blue that looked almost painted, the blue of a child's plastic toy. He walked across the asphalt parking lot of the Jasper Supermarket. The tarmac was patchy with gum wrappers and flattened beer cans. The store was well lit, but there was a wire padlock over the front doors' handles.

The place was closed. He looked at the schedule. It would open at eight-thirty. Almost an hour. He shrugged. It was all the same to him. Aunt June had sent him for eggs, bacon, bread for toast. But he couldn't eat eggs, or bacon, or toast that morning. He'd throw them up if he tried. He couldn't eat – he wouldn't – until he could tell Aunt June what had happened to him the night before. He'd tried three times. When he tried to talk about it, it was as if someone threw a switch in him, shutting off his voice box, paralyzing his fingers when he tried to write it down.

He wandered away from the supermarket – it was really

too small to merit that name – and shuffled across to the sidewalk. He walked down the highway, gazing vaguely at the shallow stream of water in the ditch. A few cars passed; he looked up once to watch a pickup truck pulling a horse trailer as it rounded a corner, creaking. Two chestnut-brown mustangs champed uneasily in the blue trailer. They looked scarred and shaggy, had probably been caught wild on some nearby plateau and now they were being taken to the slaughterhouse to be sold for horsemeat. He watched the trailer, saw its turn lights flashing as the truck swung on to the dirt road at the edge of town.

He saw an old woman pruning bushes in her front yard and wanted to shout it at her. *We're all going to the slaughterhouse!* But of course, he couldn't say a word.

He shook his head and stuck his hands in his back pockets. He was strolling in sunlight, and everyone was out on their errands, and yet he was still on that back porch, in the dead of night, flailing at something that was somehow as much human as it was insect and as much insect as it was human.

He couldn't get it out of his mind, and at the same time he couldn't say a word about it. That was an awful feeling. That felt bad.

He looked wistfully at the telephone booth, one of the town's two payphones, in front of the Jasper Bar and Grill. But it was too early to call Lois. And it would be useless to even try to feel comfortable with her, until he could talk about what had happened.

It spoke to me, he thought. It knew my name.

Next door to the bar was a storefront that jutted from the lower story of a two-story house. Across the window, someone had painted, by hand, in deliberately uneven lettering, JASPER OLD WEST MUSEUM. The front door opened, jangling a small brass bell, and a hunched, white-haired old man with a leathery face came out to sit on the wooden bench below the window. He squinted up at Perry, then down at his cigarette lighter, frowning when he saw it was almost empty. He lit a Camel, blew smoke at his Sears cowboy boots and said, 'You like to see the museum, it's open. One dollar.'

Perry had to smile. 'Kind of early in the day to open museums, isn't it?'

'Not if you want to look at it, it ain't too early. We don't get many customers any time of day.'

'Okay.' Perry gave the old man a dollar. He put it in the breast pocket of his overalls.

'Go ahead on in.'

Perry went in. The first thing he saw was a buffalo skull over a smudged glass case. Everything was labeled with a wooden slat on which the letters had been wood-burnt. Across from the skull, on a wooden shelf under the window, were rusted pieces of tooled iron that might have been anything. The placard said, CONESTOGA WAGON BOLTS. There were also an old-fashioned plow blade and a handful of Indian arrowheads. In the glass case were a broken Winchester rifle, pitted with rust, a steer's skull, the dried rattles of rattlesnakes, dead scorpions, and an entire shelf taken up by oddly shaped rocks. A wooden placard read, ODD-SHAPED ROCKS.

'Christ,' Perry muttered. 'A dollar for this.'

On the bottom shelf was a large, flat rock, propped up on a wooden chock. It was painted with what looked at first like cubistic designs. The placard read, INDIAN PETROGLYPHS. He studied the painting. He straightened, and backed away. The painting showed a man on his back, with something like a large, black insect squatting on his skull.

Feeling dizzy, and suddenly deeply tired, Perry turned and left the museum. He stood a moment outside, blinking in the sunlight.

He closed his eyes, remembering . . . remembering a dream he'd had when he was nine years old. A nightmare that had frightened him so much he'd never forgotten it. He'd dreamed he was sitting with his family, eating dinner. He sat at one end of a long, rectangular table, his parents and his younger sister at the other end. His sister sat directly across from him, his parents on either side of her. Behind them was a broad picture window looking on to a garden. He was eating oatmeal, a strange thing to eat at dinner time, and feeling vaguely uneasy. He looked up at the picture window – and saw something that made the oatmeal turn to wet concrete in his mouth. It was a huge, slavering ape: an overgrown mandrill with its bizarre red snout, at least twenty feet high, drooling, baring immense yellow teeth and wagging a knobby black erection big as a baseball bat; somehow the erection was as terrifying as the teeth. The mandrill was in the garden running toward the picture window, clearly intent on smashing through and tearing everyone to pieces. He had a vision of it squatting atop his sister's broken-doll body, thrusting its hideous erection in a wound it had made in her side. But the worst part of the nightmare was his paralysis: he'd been unable to say a thing about the ape, though all the time he knew that if he didn't shout a warning, and quickly, his family would be torn limb from limb.

The nightmare came back to him now, cast in black light and photonegatives. He thought: It was a premonition. It's come true now. I can't warn them.

The killing beast was coming, and he couldn't speak.

He turned to the old man, to try once more to warn

someone about the thing that had tried to drive its toxin-slick barb into his neck. But that wet concrete was once more in his mouth; it had hardened, gluing his jaws shut.

The old man was standing on the sidewalk, looking past Perry, down the street. Perry turned to see what he was looking at. A wavering column of blue-gray smoke rose from a hangar-shaped building across from the turn-off for the slaughterhouse. 'I'll be damned,' the old man said. 'I'll be damned.'

'What is it?' Perry asked. His mouth magically unglued when he talked about anything but the Gray Pilots. He knew, now, that was what they were. Rofocale was right, about some of it.

'That's the Grange Hall,' the old man said. 'Looks like it's on fire. There's the volunteer fire department, probably too late to do anything about it. Now how the hell did the Grange catch on fire at this hour of the morning? No kids going to be setting fires at this hour. No one in it to drop cigarette butts. Must be a tramp. Musta been a tramp broke in, left his cigarette smoldering, whatcha wanna bet?'

An old woman, remarkably identical to the old man except that her white hair was a little longer, leaned out an upstairs window and called, 'That the Grange burning, George?'

'Yeah, looks like.'

'Louella's onna phone, she says some nutcase went 'n' locked somebody in there and set a fire! She says he got caught in it. Her mother went down there and saw the fire; she said the guy called her this morning.'

'Stay off that phone, Birdie, I'm waiting for a call from that man about the acreage.'

Perry walked wearily home.

* * *

He was in a kind of stupor on the back-porch cot. Weary, but awake. He lay on his stomach, his chin on his crossed arms, staring at the unpainted plywood wall. He was trying not to think; when he thought, he got angry. He was angry about not being able to talk about what had happened. Vaguely, irrationally, he blamed his muteness on Sandra, and on Dr Rofocale. But he didn't dare think about it; he didn't dare let the anger color his mind. Because if he did, it might call the Gray Pilots. They came to bitterness like an obscene bee to a nightmare flower.

He tried to blot his thoughts, to fill his mind with rosy blur; he dozed, but he didn't let himself sleep, though he'd been too long without it. No telling what he might dream about.

He thought about Lois. She'd said her uncle kept her on a short leash. The guy seemed all right, but he had no authority, not reasonably, over a girl Lois's age. She wasn't a girl, really, she was a woman. How dare he –

Uh-uh. Stop it.

Stop it or they'll come. And then, anything. Anything, anything at all. They'd make you do it. And then they'd show you what you'd done, and wherever they were, they'd laugh about it as you screamed under the buzz saw of your own guilt.

Don't think about that either, he told himself.

He lay there, and knew that people in Jasper were buying groceries, and ice-cream bars, and gossiping, and bitching about prices, and telling racy jokes and talking about going to see a movie in Bend.

And the Gray Pilots were perched somewhere – maybe up in the trees, or in the shadows of eaves, watching.

Aunt June broke his concentration on the bare wooden wall by walking into his line of sight. He closed his eyes.

'How about a sandwich, Perry. Hm?'

Perry shook his head. He opened his eyes, but saw nothing.

'Perry, you want to tell me about it?'

'I can't. I'm sorry I didn't get to the grocery store. It sort of went out of my mind. It – ' He sat up, and shrugged.

'That's okay, I didn't mind going. It's nice out. Perry – ' She bit her lower lip and looked at him with a kind of inquiring blankness. 'Are you sure there isn't something? Uh, I mean, I know, I'm your aunt, but you know you can talk about anything to me, anything at all, I can be just as objective as you want me to be. Or as nonobjective. I mean – '

'I know what you mean.' He looked at her. He felt himself smile. He felt himself shrug and say, very convincingly, 'It's really nothing. Just homesick, I guess.'

He couldn't even hint with a look. He couldn't implore with his eyes, or beseech with a hand gesture, or sulk. Nothing that would communicate his fear to her, his knowingness.

And he could taste the frustration; he could smell it and feel it crawling on his skin. And the self-disgust. A feeling that he shouldn't even *want* to tell her. Because that would be telling on himself. Because, the feeling informed him, it was he who'd done all those things. Who'd cut off the woman's head, who'd drowned the kid. Who'd cut and strangled and burned. Who'd gleefully killed.

It wasn't me, he thought. It wasn't me at all.

It was all of us, the feeling said. It was you because it was the desire we all have, buried in us, the secret lust for mayhem. It was in someone else; it's in you too, and it's going to come out, and if you tell about them, you'll be telling on yourself.

All the time he was smiling, saying, *No problem, Aunt June!*

Showing nothing. Because she couldn't see the trickle of sweat down his back as he fought with the thing.

Really, I'm fine!

She didn't take his pulse, didn't know it was racing.

To be trapped behind *everything's fine*. To be locked up in *it's all okay*.

Picture being a man in a tuxedo at his wedding, smiling as he steps up to the altar with his lovely young bride. Under his clothes are fire ants, an army of them swarming over his skin, just out of sight of the guests, chewing. But the groom – feeling every bite, and no masochist – smiles and says, 'I do.' Picture him turning to find comfort in his bride. And she's lovely, she's sunny with femininity, she's all in white lace and blue silk; her eyes are sapphires and her lips are satin and she parts them and shows a long rubbery sucker-mouthed leech instead of a tongue. Picture him smiling when he wants to scream and kissing her and feeling the big stinking leech push into his mouth. But he can't do anything about it, he can't react, he can't show anyone.

Picture a pretty, newly painted little cottage, bordered in bright flowers, on a sunny day.

With a maggot-fertile corpse swelling in its bedroom.

The cottage was Perry.

'Everything's fine,' he said. 'It's all okay. Really.'

'Well, look.' She glanced at her watch. 'It's one o'clock. We'd better go to the sheriff's office.'

Perry went rigid. The thought of seeing the sheriff lashed him with panic. Cut it out, he told himself.

He took a deep breath and stood up. 'Okay. But I got to use the phone first.'

'Uh-huh. Go right ahead. I'll wait on the front porch, get a little fresh air.'

He went to the telephone, thumbed through his address book, looking for Lois's number. He smiled when he found it: she'd written it there herself, very decisively, in large blocky figures, and she'd underlined her name three times. Maybe she was still a young girl in some ways. That pleased him. He dialed, and waited. A brisk, masculine voice with a slight western twang said, 'Hello there.'

'Uh, hi. This is Perry Strandman. Could I talk to Lois?' Perry was nervous, knowing he was speaking to Lois's guardian. He expected to hear disapproval in the man's voice, or suspicion.

But her uncle's voice was even warmer when he replied, 'Why sure, chief, that'll make her happy. Lois!'

He heard the clack of a phone's earpiece set on a table, and then light footsteps approaching, a whisper that might have been, 'Privacy, if you don't mind.' And then: 'Perry?'

'Yeah, hi.'

'Hi, how you feeling, doll?'

'Oh, okay.' He suddenly felt vacant, mentally floundering for words.

'You okay?'

'Sure! Everything's fine!'

He seethed with fury. But he couldn't even say, *There's something I'm not allowed to say*.

'Huh. Me, I feel funny about all the weird shit. You hear about those three old people caught in the Grange fire? And that Reverend Whosis? He freaked out and got burned up himself.'

Perry felt a deep, deep chill. 'He's dead?'

'So I hear. You know him?'

'Met him yesterday. Lois, I know this is – look, what say – what say we leave town? The hell with uncles and aunts.'

'You mean run away?'

'Not exactly. We're old enough we don't have to run away. We just say, "We're going on a trip." And we can visit my friends in Portland.'

A crackling silence on the phone. 'I – that'd be great, but – okay, I could do it after the rally. The Indian rights rally. I'm helping my uncle prepare press releases and everything for it. He needs me for a lot of work connected with it, but as soon as it's over. Not long.'

'That's more than a week or so.'

'I know.'

He sighed. 'Okay. Listen. I'm pretty exhausted, didn't sleep last night, don't think I'll be able to come and see you today. Maybe tomorrow we could go swimming or something, somewhere. But for tonight – do me a favor, okay?'

'Think of you when I – '

'No, no, not – ' He laughed. 'No, just – it sounds dumb but promise me you'll keep your window locked, and put something over it. Does it have wooden shutters on the outside – for storms maybe?'

'Yeah.'

'Then keep the shutters closed. I know it'll look weird, and it's hot, but do it anyway. I can't explain . . . now.'

'Um – okay, if you say so.'

'I'm not crazy.'

'I didn't say you were. But what's going on?'

'I got to go. Look . . .' It was too corny. But he said it anyway. 'I think I'm falling for you.'

167

'Whatcha mean you think so? You're *definitely* falling for me!'

He laughed, and it hurt to laugh because of the fear tightening his chest. 'Bye, Lois.'

'Later.'

They'd walked almost a quarter mile along the highway before Perry realized that everyone was staring at them. Was it his imagination? The old woman looking out the window of her Winebago RV; the teenage girl, with her braids and freckles looking like something out of *Black Beauty*, staring at him from the saddle of her dust-powdered roan as her horse cantered by; the retired couple, both wearing billed fishing caps, sitting in their lawn chairs drinking iced tea, watching narrowly as Aunt June and Perry passed. 'Am I imagining it,' Perry began, 'or is everyone staring at us? And not like curiosity. Like, with suspicion.'

'I noticed it too. I guess it's – everyone's heard about Tetty's death; the little girl murdered; Reverend Martindale going crazy in the Grange Hall. Wendy's disappearance. And they're looking for causes. And we're new in town. Strangers come – and trouble starts.'

He snorted. 'That'd be funny, if it weren't for . . .' It wouldn't let him finish.

What wouldn't? What was it, exactly, that stopped him from talking about the Gray Pilots? Had the thing stung him after all – painlessly, somehow? No, he was sure he'd frustrated it. Then what was censoring him?

'Me,' he muttered.

'What?' Aunt June asked. She wore her tinted glasses; they caught the light and flashed as she turned to smile at him.

'Nothing.'

It's me, he thought. Some instinct, keeping me from talking about it. The Gray Pilots grow out of people organically, Rofocale said. So the potential for one is inside you. And you instinctively protect that potential by keeping quiet about them. A built-in cerebral failsafe to prevent their discovery. For people who've seen them in the flesh. But Rofocale seemed to know about them, and he was able to write a paper. So it must be possible to fight it, and win.

Perry began to struggle.

It wasn't a struggle that showed on him, except perhaps in a certain whiteness around his pursed lips, and in his clenched fists. It was an inner struggle. It came in waves. Now and then he rested, and then resumed the attack, thinking: I'll talk about what I damn please. I'm a free human being.

As he pursued his inner war, they walked on through the afternoon heat, on a dirt path beside the highway. There was a ditch between them and the gravel bordering the blacktop. The road hummed and rumbled as cars and trucks passed them; the wind of their passing brought a little relief from the heat. The water in the ditch had shrunk to a trickle.

They passed the turnoff for the slaughterhouse. Perry left off his inward struggle, resting awhile, and glanced at the slaughterhouse; he thought he heard, faintly, the frightened lowing of cattle. It was a one-story red brick building, sprawling in two wings, with a flat tarry roof and almost no windows.

Are they in there? he wondered. Were the Gray Pilots there, roosting in the shadows of the rafters, watching the slaughter, enjoying the death throes of the cattle?

He was hot, and thirsty, and tired, strung out between feeling hope and feeling beaten. And between these two he felt alone. 'How much farther to the sheriff's office?' he asked.

'It's just around the bend. You can see it through the trees – that little cinder-block building.'

Five minutes later they trudged up the gravel driveway, past a western-style wooden sign – its boards stained fo imitate redwood – declaring in sunken black letters:

CHEMEKA COUNTY SHERIFF'S DEPARTMENT
COUNTY ANIMAL CONTROL

Inside, after drinking from a water fountain, they told a reedy, scraggle-mustached deputy – the young one Lois had mentioned, probably – that they had an appointment with Sheriff Dawson.

'Come on back,' he said, unlatching the swinging wooden gate. He held the gate open and they passed into the back office. 'Down t' the right, folks,' said the deputy.

They passed down a gray, cool, cinder-block corridor, and through the open door of the sheriff's private office.

Dawson sat at his desk, wearing half glasses low on his nose. He tapped a pencil on the edge of his blotter and frowned over a sheaf of blue forms. He glanced up as they came in, his sad, hurt-child's eyes flicking from Perry to Aunt June; he nodded and muttered, 'Have a seat, right with you.'

Perry and his aunt sat in straight-backed wooden chairs across from the desk. In a chair backed against the wall, almost behind the door, sat a tall, knobby-kneed, long-necked boy of about seventeen; his stringy blond hair was raggedy long, its tips not quite reaching his shoulders, unpleasantly emphasizing his gangly neck. He had narrow but regular features, and the sort of perpetual blush on his cheeks that looks almost like rouge. He was gazing blankly at the floor, and smiling ever so slightly. He shifted in his seat, shrugging in his basketball player's jersey. He wore blue corduroys and high-top sneakers. This would be Conway Stiggins, Perry guessed.

Aunt June was looking around the office, at the elk's antlers on the wall over Dawson's head, the framed black-and-white photos of Dawson with various county officials, with the lieutenant governor, with a dead buck. Dawson on an Appaloosa horse, in fancy silver-wrought saddle gear and an Old West sheriff's outfit complete with white ten-gallon hat; he was leading the rodeo parade. Probably the only time of year he sat on a horse. There were two awards for public service from the Lions' Club and, on the sill of the blind-covered window, a bowling trophy.

Dawson dug an index finger into his right ear, twisted it as if dislodging a gnat, then used it to point at Perry and Aunt June. It was a gentle your-turn-now pointing. 'Let's have your story, again, please, for Conway's benefit. I've got it on file but I'd like him to hear it. Oh – this is Conway Stiggins; June and Perry Strandman.'

As Aunt June droned through the particulars of Tetty's death, Conway, sitting hunched over, his palms on his knees, elbows out, looked as if he were listening. He smiled politely, nodding now and then.

But all the time his eyes were on Perry.

Perry – still struggling to speak, to tell Dawson what he had seen the night before – looked hard into Conway's eyes. Perry wrestled with silence.

Oh Christ, Perry thought, gazing into those pale blue, blond-lashed eyes. Oh my God.

They were perfectly normal, human eyes. But somehow, at the same time, they were the eyes of an insect.

* * *

The hot sunlight glanced brilliantly off the chrome trim of the Holsteins' Travel-Size house trailer. It was parked on a yellow-clay fire-access road, about a quarter mile off the main highway, just above Willowah Creek. It was a large trailer – it had to be, as the Holsteins lived in it with their three children – but not so large as to be difficult to move. The Holsteins' four-wheel-drive Scout pulled it around the mountain curves with relative ease.

Hank Holstein and his wife Margaret sat at their portable, foldout aluminum picnic table, wearing tan safari shorts, matching shirts, and old-fashioned green sunglasses. Both were pasty-faced, sagging around the middle, waggling under the arms. They didn't mind; they were comfortable with one another. If Margaret saw her husband cheating at bridge – even if he was playing with another partner against her – she didn't breathe a word.

Margaret sipped a screwdriver through a long straw, her other hand patting down her band of copper-dyed hair. 'Those kids,' she said between sips, 'are just too much sometimes. What's wrong with 'em that makes 'em fall asleep in the middle of the day like that?'

Holstein looked across the road to the wall of red sandstone that rose abruptly out of the ferns; the rough sandstone outcropping was the base of a prow-shaped bluff. To either side of the prow, like the foam wake of a ship, sage and tumbleweed grew in wavy thickets. At the base of the 'prow' was the shallow cave the kids had been playing in that morning. Holstein had judged the cave safe, as it went back only ten feet or so, with no large crevices to hide rattlers or scorpions, and it seemed too solid-walled to collapse on anyone. A sort of natural playhouse. Last he knew, the nine-year-old triplets – Clement, Terry, and Louis – had been playing pirate there, just after lunch.

'You say they're asleep? I've seen 'em take naps in the day, after a big lunch. And if one does it, they all do.' He sighed. 'Christ, you know that.'

'I went and had a look at them when you were in the can. They looked fine. Sleeping like babies. Smiling. Almost looked cute to me again.'

'Anytime they're asleep, I like 'em,' Holstein said, snorting.

'Oh Billy, you're awful!' But she laughed that donkey-like laugh of hers. She let the laughter subside to a kind of grating spasm of hiccups and finished her drink. It was her third screwdriver, and her head wobbled when she spoke. 'I tell you what I think. I think th' little stinkers is drunk.'

'What! You think Clem got into that Oly that I – '

'Oly, hell. The vodka was about three fingers too low this morning. I think he snuck some out in a glass and they drank it after lunch. Put 'em right out.'

'Well I'll be damned.' Holstein didn't argue; he preferred his wife didn't know he'd drunk those three fingers before she'd risen that morning.

Holstein's eyes wandered to the cold ashes of the campfire, the three empty sleeping bags laid out, gaping wide beside it. 'Gonna get ants in 'em,' he muttered. Despite the boys' complaining of mosquitoes, Mr Holstein had insisted that they sleep outside the night before. 'Do you good,' he told them. 'Make you grown up.' He knew it had pissed them off. Holstein had hoped they'd sleep far enough from the trailer so Margaret would let him have a little, for once, despite the squeaking of the trailer springs when they got particularly gymnastic. But she wouldn't go for it. *'Dammit, Hank, don't, the kids'll hear.'* And one of the boys had awakened him at six in the morning, whining about bad dreams. Dreams about 'a bug' who told him 'bad things.' Holstein had said, 'Get the hell back in the sleeping bag and forget about it. Just a bad dream.' And then he'd had to drink all that vodka and take a couple Sominex to get back to sleep himself.

Vaguely, he wondered which of the triplets had woken him that morning. He couldn't tell them apart. He looked at the calendar window on his digital watch. Three days left of his vacation and then it was back to the car lot in Salem. It was his business and he could take longer off if he wanted to, but he didn't trust Barlett not to mess it up. Should never have left that dumb Okie in charge.

Margaret surprised him with, 'Well, Hank, maybe we shouldn't look the gift horse inna mouth. They being so stone asleep. I still got a little of that pot my sister give me.' She reached under the table and stroked his knee in a way that left no room for doubt: she wanted it. Grunting, he disengaged himself from the picnic table – damn thing was too small – and followed his wife into the trailer.

Presently, the springs began to squeak.

The Holstein triplets couldn't hear the squeaking. They were thirty yards away; they could see their parents go into the trailer, though, as it was downslope from them. They knew by the playful grabs Piggo made at Piggette that they were going to Do It. That was the boys' secret nickname for their parents: Piggo and Piggette.

Clement, Louis, and Terry had been awake for perhaps twenty minutes, concealed from their parents by the shade of the cave mouth as they stood together, barefoot on the clay floor, gazing out at the world.

The world looked different today. It was opening up from the mouth of the cave so wide, like a gift unwrapping itself for them. *I'm all yours*, the world was saying.

They'd awakened simultaneously, standing at the

mouth of the cave. It was a funny thing, waking up to find that you were already standing, looking around. So maybe there was more than one kind of sleep; they'd awakened from a new kind.

They felt very, very close, that day. They'd never felt so close before, though people said they acted as much alike as they looked. Today, something special made them closer than ever.

'Everything looks red out here,' Clement said when they stepped into the sunlight. He rubbed the swollen place on his neck. The other two nodded. They were pale, red-lipped, bird-eyed, slender boys, with ears that stuck out a little through soft brown hair. They wore denim shorts and three different colors – red, blue, green – of T-shirts and tennis shoes. Their parents had been advised by a pediatrician to dress them differently. They preferred to dress alike, even to the same colors.

'If a guy wanted to, he could do anything,' Louis said, smiling crookedly. 'If he was smart. I read in *Weekly Reader* that they solve less than twenty-seven percent of crimes.'

'What does that mean,' Terry asked, 'that twenty-seven percent?'

'It means, not very many. They don't catch 'em.'

Terry smiled the same crooked smile. 'You could do almost anything. You could – ' He looked out at the world and seemed to see it in flames. 'You could set the forest on fire.'

Clement nodded, in growing wonder; the world's potential was just dawning on him. 'You could – you could break into a hospital and steal babies and then cut off their faces with knives and put them back in their cribs for their mothers to find.'

The boys shrieked with laughter.

'You could – ' Louis broke in breathlessly, 'you could get even with creeps in school. You could put bombs in their lockers and watch them blow up.'

Terry, sober now, sneered at Louis's lack of imagination. 'A bomb? Big deal. You can watch bombs going off on TV. No, I think you should get that big guy, Bruce, who gives us shit and you could take him to that kiln they got in the art class for the pots and tie him up and put clay all over his head and bake it in a pot.'

The game went on for ten minutes more. Then the redness drained out of things, and they were ready.

They walked down the thin path towards the trailer, slipping on stones now and then, seething with new feelings. They stood beside the aluminum picnic table, looking at the trailer. It was quiet now. They were thinking about Piggo and Piggette. They were remembering that the Holsteins – on the pediatrician's advice, for fear of the boys' developing an excessive dependency on one another – wouldn't let them go to summer camp together. They'd had to go on separate weeks, and they hated to be apart for long. They were remembering that their parents told them they'd been 'a goddamn disaster' when they were born. 'Three kids at once, we couldn't afford two, let alone three. And what a pain in the ass to take care of three babies.' They were remembering that Piggo was planning to send Louis off to some kind of military school because he 'wouldn't behave.'

'Clement, Piggo showed you how to drive the car once. He let you drive on that dirt road. It's automatic,' Louis said slowly.

Clement nodded. They were tall for their ages; he could do it. Louis and Terry wired the door to the trailer shut from the outside, they used some pliers and heavy wire they found in the Scout.

Then Clement started the car. He had difficulty seeing out the front and pressing the accelerator too, till Louis came to help him, doing what Piggo had done before: he pressed the accelerator gently while Clement steered. They had some difficulty with the gears, but at last got the car rolling.

Terry sat in the backseat, tittering now and then when he heard his parents shouting from the front window of the trailer. 'Whudduh hell you think you're doing, you boys, you stop that car and – goddammit, take this shit off the door!' They could just barely hear their dear old Piggo shouting it, while Piggette tried to kick the door open. The trailer lurched off its chocks and came after the car, jouncing up the dirt road, creaking at the trailer hitch as they pulled on to the highway.

Even with power steering, they had some trouble getting the car turned the way they wanted it. But at last, they had the trailer sideways, at right angles to the white line, blocking both lanes, just this side of a hairpin curve. They'd seen a lot of 'big, hairy old logging trucks,' as Louis called them, on that road.

Sure enough a monstrous semitruck belching black smoke and blasting its horn came barreling around the corner only two minutes after the boys had got clear of the car. They had a glimpse of Piggo trying to squeeze out one of the trailer's windows – it was just too small for a piggo – and then they saw the surprise and horror on the face of the truck driver and then –

The crash was great, just too great. 'Wait'll we tell that show-off Sammy Bond about that, man he's gonna be impressed,' Louis said.

'He'd better be,' Clement said softly.

Louis and Terry laughed, then they fell quiet, watching with awe as the gas tank of the truck exploded, the flames consuming the wreckage, the trailer and truck all tangled up so you couldn't be sure which was which, the voice of Piggette screaming from the blackening metal trap.

Terry almost went back to the other place inside himself. He thought: Mom . . . Mom . . .

But then Louis and Clement took him by the arms, between them, and poked at his ears till he laughed and forgot it, and they turned away from the wreckage and began to walk toward that little town they'd seen, just before the lake, only a quarter mile down the road. 'What was that town called?' Clement asked.

'I think it was called Jasper,' Louis said.

'Jasper, huh,' Clement said.

'Okay, Jasper,' Terry said.

Maybe they could find something to do there.

'So you're saying,' the sheriff broke in, 'that you saw this girl Elizabeth Cummings, this Tetty, come to your house. When? Three in the morning?'

'Around there,' Conway answered evenly, shrugging.

Dawson nodded and paused to sip coffee from a Styrofoam cup. He had turned in his swivel chair toward the window blinds; bars of light and shadow fell across his face and chest.

Perry almost smiled, thinking he looked like an old-time prison convict.

Perry glanced over his shoulder; the skinny, hard-eyed deputy waited quietly in the doorway, arms crossed as he leaned on the jamb. The plastic name plate under his badge said, G. N. Lancer, Deputy Sheriff. His face was a mask of affected authority; it was a television caricature, to Perry, but he decided that there was nothing funny about such a man.

178

'Trouble is,' Dawson was saying, 'coroner says that girl was dead already, by the time you said you saw her.'

Perry glanced at Conway, who shifted in his seat, as if having difficulty arranging all that gangly length comfortably. But he seemed calm. His smile deepened a little, and he flicked his eyes toward Perry. Perry glimpsed again that nitrogen-cooled, dry-ice presence in Conway's eyes.

Perry shivered, and once more tried to speak. He could even visualize what he would do: he'd stand, bang on the desk with the flat of his hand, and say, *Listen, Dawson, there's something that's like an insect born out of a man, and it's been biting people and changing them. And one came to me last night and this kid Conway knows something about them, and maybe he's communicating with them.*

Oh, no. Even if he could speak, it would be a mistake to put it so bluntly. They'd naturally think he was crazy, and maybe assume it was he who'd strangled Conway's sister Ella and tossed her in the lake, and gouged out Tetty's eye, and cut off that woman's head, and –

But he had to tell them something.

Maybe just what had happened to him, from the beginning. If he could just begin to talk about it, he could find a way to make them believe he wasn't hallucinating.

He resumed the struggle, then shook his head, it was as if someone had shot xylocaine into his vocal cords.

'Trouble *is*,' Conway said, smiling, using Dawson's phrase in mild mockery, 'I couldn't be sure what time it was. I was asleep, and woke up all, you know, sleepy and bleary, and I just guessed what time it was.' He spread his hands. 'Guess I was wrong about the time I saw her. But I saw her.'

'And it was you who found your sister's body in the

lake in the morning. Now you say after you saw Tetty you didn't go back to sleep. You lay in bed for maybe hours, worrying about it, thinking the last time Tetty was around she poisoned you. Now, if it was me who had worries like that, well, I'd for sure just take a little walk down the hall and check on my sister. So why didn't you? You couldn't sleep anyway.'

Conway hesitated two beats before replying. 'Oh, my sister's kinda weird about that. You know little kids.'

'You mean your sister *was* weird about it. She ain't nothin' no more,' said Lancer abruptly, his voice a grating chirrup – high but with gravel deliberately worked into it to make it seem more masculine.

The sheriff sighed and gave the deputy a look of exasperation. 'Lancer, you are what back east they would call "insensitive." You know?' Lancer snickered at that, supposing the sheriff meant the sarcasm for Conway. Dawson cut the snickering off with, 'Go out and get me a goddamn fresh cuppa coffee, Lancer.'

Lancer looked startled, then peevish. He took a deep breath, which hardly showed on his thin chest, and turned to stride briskly down the hall, his keys, handcuffs, and belt buckle jangling as he went.

'Now, Conway,' Dawson went on, 'you say your sister was "weird" about – what?'

'About her door, at night. She kept her bedroom door locked. So I couldn't look in on her.'

'You could've knocked on the door. Seems to me the worry you had – considering you went to the hospital because of this Tetty Cummings – seems to me that was enough to get you to knock.'

Conway shook his head, once sharply. 'No, she was, uh, she'd start crying if I did that.'

Dawson swiveled to face Aunt June and Perry. He

pointed a finger at Aunt June. 'What do you think about that, Ms Strandman? You think that's normal for a child? I mean, from the viewpoint of a psychologist, you think it's normal the girl locking her door like that?'

'No,' Aunt June said. 'It would be unusual, for the average child. Well, many children develop irrational fears about doorways, closets, the dark places under beds. They don't usually carry it so far, though.'

'I wonder if that little girl had some kind of hunch,' Dawson said ruminatively, 'even if she was only six. I wonder if she was afraid of someone specific.'

Conway nodded. 'Could be you're right. Could be she heard my parents talking about Tetty, and she got real scared of her. My parents always talked about what a maniac Tetty was.'

'She was scared of Tetty Cummings? Maybe. But then how could Tetty have talked her into coming outside? You said you figured she tapped on Ella's window, got her to open it, and then talked her into going outside.'

'Maybe Tetty got hold of a gun and threatened to shoot her if she didn't.' Conway's smile flickered alive again. 'You remember Tetty had a gun, Sheriff; she shot you in the leg with it.'

The sheriff didn't react. Looking at Dawson, Perry suspected that the story about his having hidden under his car when Tetty shot at him was probably untrue. He suspected Dawson of deep-seated prejudice and narrow-mindedness, but not cowardice.

'So you think she got her to go outside with a gun. But it seems more likely if Tetty was at the window with a gun, the little girl wouldn't crawl out that window, she'd hide under a bed or behind a piece of furniture.'

'She wasn't too smart, Ella,' Conway said amiably.

'Conway' – the sheriff's tone had become sharper –

'don't you wonder now why I didn't ask your parents to be here? Of course, you have a right to have them here, and a lawyer, but your dad waived those rights because he didn't see you as under any suspicion. But your mother, well, she wanted to come, but I prevailed on your dad to get her to stay home, because I think she'd be kind of naturally protective of you. Even though she's a little worried about you, she – '

'What do you mean, worried?' Conway interrupted. He wasn't overtly angry or defensive, but there was an edge of aggression in his voice.

'Oh, she says you've been having some kind of fits lately. And she says she heard you talk to yourself for a long time when you were alone in your room. And she says you were tormenting Ella. So Ella was afraid of you. So maybe it was you Ella was locking the door against.'

'Why should I torment Ella?' All innocence, utterly convincing.

'Oh, gee, I tell you, I'm not quite sure – except that I heard you were real tight with your mom and dad before Ella came along. But Ella, far from being what you call "not too smart," was precocious. Real bright kid. And she was the pride of the home. So your parents started losing interest in what you accomplished in school sports. They were paying lots more attention to Ella than you.'

'That's the same with all kids, just ask her.' And he tossed his head toward Aunt June. 'When a new kid comes into the family, parents start, y'know, paying more attention to the young one. No big deal. That's something everybody knows about. So what. Not enough to make me torment her.'

'Well now, that might be true, but I think for different people, there's different reactions to a thing. Maybe you reacted too much. And God knows you could've had another reason to be mad at her.' Dawson broke off, scowling, as Lancer bustled into the room with a coffee-pot and a clean Styrofoam cup.

'Hot and black, Marvin, right?' Lancer asked, setting the pot and cup on the desk.

'No. Cream. Get me some of that diet creamer in the freezer. In the coffee room.' He was clearly annoyed at the interruption. And Lancer clenched his jaws at being sent off on another petty errand. But he jangled down the hall again, and the sheriff went on, 'Now what I'm wondering is, if maybe you were having some problems, the kind your mom was hinting about – and then maybe you had to find a kind of scapegoat for your problems, someone to blame, and you picked your sister, and decided if she was gone everything would be all right, and you justified that kind of thinking to yourself . . .' Dawson paused, turning to look directly at Conway, laying both hands flat on the desk as if about to push away from it – as if about to move toward Conway, maybe to put handcuffs on him. '. . . you justified that by telling yourself, hell, she saw Tetty putting that stuff in my drink – you told me that, right, that your sister saw Tetty put the poison in your shake? Forgetting your sister didn't know it was poison Tetty was putting in your drink, and then you – '

'Here you go, Sheriff!' The deputy interrupted, too loudly, as he came in with the little packet of creamer. He set it down next to the coffee cup on the sheriff's desk, then took a nervous step back, seeing the look on Dawson's face. 'Uh – '

Dawson had sagged back in his seat. 'Lancer, you go and stand in the door, and you wait there. And you be real quiet. Okay?'

'Yo, you got it, boss,' Lancer said, spreading his hands

in an exaggerated just-keep-calm gesture. He resumed his post in the door.

Conway stood. Everyone snapped about to look at him. He stretched. 'Hey – ' He seemed amused by the sudden tension. 'I ain't goin' nowhere. I gotta stretch a little, my leg's goin' to sleep.' He did a few quick knee bends. Perry could hear his joints cracking.

Lancer had gone rigid in the doorway, his right hand haunting the vicinity of his gun butt. Dawson had half risen. He sank back in his seat.

Lancer stuck his thumbs in his gunbelt and tried to look confident.

Perry's palms were sweating. Aunt June was watching Conway fixedly, her eyes following his slightest movement.

Languidly, Conway strolled toward the window. All eyes swung to follow him. He stood with one hand on his left hip; the other lifted a blind so he could look out the window.

Perry looked past him and saw there was a heavy iron mesh over the window, on the outside, the space between each interstice no bigger than a silver dollar. There was a jail cell in the building; apparently the mesh was there to keep prisoners from breaking out the window when they were in the office.

Conway dropped the blind and strolled past Perry, past Aunt June, pausing in front of Lancer.

He stood with his back to Lancer, gazing distantly at Dawson.

Perry saw, then, that Conway's face had gone bone white.

'Conway,' Dawson said suddenly, 'I wonder if you'd like to make a statement.'

'A statement,' Conway said, rolling the word around in

his mouth. 'A statement. A statement. A statement. Is that a statement – saying, "a statement"?' He smiled thinly. He looked almost asleep.

'We're going to have to detain you, Conway. Suspicion of murder. I think if I can prove it, the judge will rule for insanity, if that's any comfort.'

'Insanity is no comfort to anyone,' said Conway. His manner of speaking had changed. He'd shed his boyish, country phrasing, his uncertainty. 'Sanity is another matter: it is a thing of crystalline perfection.'

Dawson's jaw dropped.

Conway went on. 'But not everyone can recognize sanity. They don't know it when they see it, unless it's the action of a government. If a government sends out an army to kill the enemy, no one calls that insane. Or few do. But if one man kills an enemy – ' He shrugged. 'Yes, I'll make a statement.'

And he twisted around, swiveling like a basketball player. His fist darted out, jabbed Lancer hard in the belly. Lancer doubled over, gasping.

What happened next was all broken up in Perry's perception. He saw things jerkily, as if he were watching a badly edited film or a scene under a strobe light.

Perry saw Conway's hand on the butt of Lancer's gun. Then he saw Aunt June standing beside her chair – he somehow hadn't seen her rise – and driving her shoulder into Conway's ribs. Conway sprawled, the gun clattering to the floor, Dawson standing over Conway, gun in hand, shouting.

Conway on his knees. His head raised, looking at the light fixture. His eyes glazed over.

A splash of red, at Conway's left eye. When Perry had been a small boy, he'd had a water-propelled rocket he'd shoot off from under water in his wading pool; once, he'd added red dye to the propellant chemical to make it look as if its tail end were spitting rocket flame. That's what came to his mind when he saw the eruption at Conway's left eye, that small plastic rocket flying up out of wetness and leaving a brief trail of red on the air.

The thing that shot out of Conway's eye was a blur, trailing blood droplets, until it reached the ceiling. And then, an inch before impact, it stopped – and opened out, expanding like a parachute, in one second becoming eight times larger.

It performed a complicated midair stunt, turning upside down, then moved impossibly, defying gravity, to slap on to the ceiling; it clung there, between the light fixture and the wall, something roughly fly-shaped but big as a pigeon, fanning itself furiously with its wings.

Perry, Aunt June, and Dawson stared. Squatting, Lancer clasped his stomach with one hand, the other shakily feeling for the gun on the floor. He wouldn't take his eyes off the living gray-black blot on the ceiling.

Perry looked down at Conway. He lay on his stomach, arms askew beneath him, like a scarecrow dropped from its post. His left eye was missing; in its place was a welling pool of blood. His lips were faintly smiling. He twitched, twice, and then didn't move.

The buzzing. The room resounded with it; it seemed to growl out of the walls and floor; the sound grew, until it was loud as the buzz saw in the lumber mill.

And then the window shattered.

They heard it burst outward, tinkling on the parking lot outside; the blinds were flung down, rattling, so that the room blazed abruptly with sunlight. There was a creaking, grinding sound.

'It's bending that wire!' Perry blurted. Something had broken loose in him. He could talk about the insect things. 'I wanted to tell you but I couldn't – one of those things came at me last night! They can move small things without touching them! It's going to bend that wire and go out the window, Sheriff, you'd better – '

He was interrupted by a detonation, so loud his ears rang. He smelled gunpowder; there was a hole in the ceiling and the insect thing was buzzing, flying, whipping around Dawson's head in angry ellipses. Dawson fired again, and again missed; pale blue gunsmoke stung Perry's nostrils; plaster filtered down from the ceiling. He was aware that Lancer and Dawson were both shouting, and had been shouting for a full minute, but what they said didn't register on him; he couldn't quite make out anything over the buzzing, the noise that was growing to be more than a buzzing, a kind of roar.

The office door slammed. Aunt June had shut it from the inside to keep the Gray Pilot from getting out that way.

The gray-black blur dove at Dawson; he ducked, flailing, and slipped. He fell heavily behind the desk.

The gray blur dropped like a stone. For a full second, the sheriff and the flying thing were hidden behind the desk. Then the flying thing was in the air again. It shot toward the window. The metal mesh creaked, bending outward.

A double thud, too close to Perry's ear, a flash on his left: Lancer firing his Colt .45 at the thing clinging to the mesh.

There was a long, attenuated squeal, like high-pitched feedback from a big PA speaker – viciously loud, painfully shrill. Afterward, no one was sure if it had been a sound or something they'd heard *mentally*. It hurt. It made them clap their hands to their ears and cry out. It was a squeal of primeval frustration, and it resonated brutally with a chord buried in each of them.

And then the thing was dead.

It stuck to the mesh, as a smashed fly will stick to the wall. But the last bullet had caught it in the center of its thorax and split it open; it dripped something like spinal fluid. Its head was twisted around to look over its miniature shoulder, past its stilled, translucent wings. Its eyes were black obsidian; its face was a stylized miniature of Conway's. As they watched, it began to crumble into oozing fragments. What was left of it fell on the floor, a puddle, shapeless. It might have been anything.

'Oh Christ,' Lancer said, sobbing. 'I hope that thing is really dead.'

'What happened to the sheriff?' Aunt June stood behind the desk, leaning on it heavily. Her shoulders were shaking; her voice sounded very old. 'He's out cold. I guess he hit his head when he fell.'

'Oh man, oh shit, are you sure that thing's dead?' Lancer asked, turning to Perry. He stood in the door, the gun still raised, pointed toward the window, his hand trembling.

'Put that gun down, man,' Perry said. He felt a strange calmness. He knew they had a respite, now. But only a respite.

Lancer looked at the gun, then lowered it. 'Goddammit, I hope there ain't no more of them.' His voice breaking, high-pitched.

Perry looked at him and took a deep breath. 'More? Oh – ' He laughed bitterly. 'There are a lot more. A lot more where that one came from.'

'You mean' – he gestured at Conway – 'from him?'

'No. No, I mean from everyone.'

For a while after that, no one said anything.

10

It was a relief, really, what had happened in the sheriff's office. Perry had lived through the premature burial of his conscience. The eruption of the Gray Pilot had pried off the lid. Now he could talk about it.

Except that he was so tired. He sat in the open back doorway, on the back-porch stoop, with his feet on the dead grass, wondering if it were any safer inside. Feeling the heat of the day radiating from the ground as the sunset sucked the desert light away. It was getting dark outside, gradually but visibly, and it was the kind of dusk that was like the coming of unconsciousness; as if the darkness was coming from faltering eyesight and not the going of the sun. Like it was coming from inside.

It's because I'm tired, Perry thought. You feel this way, it colors how things look. Like you're hollow and the world is sucking down into the hollowness.

'Perry?'

He heard the scrape of Aunt June's shoes on the wood of the porch. 'Yeah?'

'You'd better come inside.' She stood just behind him, looking out at the gathering darkness, webs of shadows in the trees. He couldn't see her but he knew that's what she was looking at.

'I don't think they "only come out at night," do they?'

'No. But you can't see them coming so well at night.'

'I know when they're around.' He stood up and turned toward her.

She reacted to that with just a trace of fear, a flicker around the eyes.

He asked, 'Did you get a report on the sheriff?'

'He's in the hospital. Resting well. Under observation, they said.'

'I certainly hope so.'

She followed him into the kitchen. On the kitchen table was a brown, academic-looking book, titled, *Apocrypha of the Brain Sciences*. She sat down in front of it and, without looking at it, put a hand on the book. She was staring into space, and he saw that she was pale, and her eyes were smudged with the gloomy mascara of sleeplessness.

'Looks like you didn't get that nap,' Perry said, looking for the instant coffee. He pushed bottles aside in the cabinet, pushed them back into their original place again, and pushed them aside once more, until at last he realized the coffee was on the counter directly in front of him. 'Christ. I'm spaced.'

'I couldn't sleep,' she said. 'I was thinking . . . you're so vulnerable when . . .'

Something in her tone made him look at her. Her eyes were wide. 'God,' she said. 'One of my patients said that to me. A classic paranoid. This guy wore sheets of thin lead under his clothing to protect him from The Rays. Said he didn't like to sleep because you're so vulnerable when you – when you sleep.' She shook her head, and looked at the book. 'This thing is making paranoids of us all. And justifiably. Or maybe there's some kind of group hallucination going on. Something in the water.'

'You don't believe that. You have some of that kid's blood on your clothing.'

Her shoulders twitched and she smoothed out her dress, though she'd changed her clothing since the boy's blood had arced and sprayed from his eye socket, from the contrail of the insect launched from his eye.

Perry's stomach lurched, and he dropped the spoon he was using to try to get coffee from the little jar. The spoon rang on the floor, and Aunt June's head jerked around to look at it. Perry picked up the spoon and ran it under some water at the sink. A cockroach scurried from under a dish toward the drain, and, hand shaking, he crushed it under the spoon with a satisfying crunch. 'Little insect bastard,' he muttered. 'Little fucker.' He tossed the spoon aside and took the coffee jar over to the table with two cups. He dumped the brown crystals directly from the jar into the cups. 'What's with the book?' he asked.

'It contains a couple of papers by a Dr Horescu.'

'Why's it called *Apocrypha of the –* '

'Oh, it's a sort of entertainment for academics. And a what-not-to-do. Examples of wildly jumping to conclusions, making out-of-left-field inferences, some of them quite funny. Like the one that attempts to prove that people who use "electrical" light become hypnotized by the constant glow and turn into zombies of some kind.'

'I'll buy that. I'll buy anything now,' Perry said, putting the teapot on.

Aunt June didn't say anything for a few minutes. Her response came so late it was almost a non sequitur. 'I know what you mean. Everything I thought was true, a lot of it looks pretty shaky now. I mean, they're ridiculing Horescu, but he was writing about the Gray Pilots – he calls them the Waiting Ones – and he sounds like a lunatic, but everything he said about them jibes with what you experienced, with what we saw in the sheriff's office.'

'Aunt June . . .' Perry felt the panic rise in harmony with the rising pitch of the teapot's whistle as it went from a trill to a scream. He jerked the pot off the stove, and hot water splashed from the spout on to his hand. It burned him, and it hurt, but he was so preoccupied he hardly noticed the pain. 'Aunt June, let's get the hell out of town. You see people in movies, they're in some kind of scary situation, there's a monster on their tail, it's sucking the spinal fluid from people or something, and they just keep hanging around.' He turned to look at her. 'Aunt June, let's not act like jerks in a movie. Let's get the hell out of town.'

She opened her mouth – and then closed it like a snapping turtle. After a moment of staring at his hand, she said, 'You'd better run your hand under some cold water.'

'Aunt June –'

'I can't, Perry. I'm a doctor, I'm a professional, and people here need me, Sandra needs me. You can go.'

'I would, if I could get Lois to.'

'But *don't* go, Perry, Jesus, don't leave me with this.'

He was amazed to see tears in her eyes. He turned away. He went to fill the coffee cups. He knew he should hug her, give her that kind of support, but he couldn't. He was too coiled up inside to make the effort. Selfish prick, he told himself.

He put the teapot back on the stove, went to the table, sat down and stared at his cup. Undissolved lumps of brown crystal floated in it, each with its little oily corona. He picked up the cup and swirled the coffee in it. 'What does Horescu say?' He heard the resignation in his own voice and realized he was going to stay.

She opened the book, and thumbed through it. 'He says the body of the Gray Pilot is mostly brain. Made of a highly compressed, ephemeral plasma. Composition unknown. He cites the severe instinctive inhibition against talking about them. He describes the stage we saw.' She let out a long slow breath and sipped her coffee. She made a face, and in the tension of the moment they both laughed at her sour expression. 'God. Tomorrow I'm going to the supermarket to get some decent coffee . . . Uh, the stage of the "externalized" Gray Pilot, its insect form, during which – after "interbreeding via stinger with a number of people" – they burrow into a final subject and dissolve into their tissues. When killed before this stage they simply dissolve and he says, "Hence, no fossil evidence has been found." Uh, he says the sort of Gray Pilot that actually emerges from the body is very rare and "have almost been eliminated by nature as they are prone to the augmentation of extreme sociopathy in those with whom they interbreed. Indeed, they bring out and cultivate even the slightest native propensity for sadistic violence. Sometimes they subdue themselves for strategic reasons." He theorizes they have telepathic and telekinetic powers. They manifest in outbreaks after a carrier –' Her voice had begun to go hoarse. She paused to sip the acrid coffee. 'Um, after a carrier – like Tetty, I guess, one of the rare people who can produce a Breeder –'

'A Sub-B3,' Perry said tonelessly.

'I suppose so. Evidently the carrier gravitates to the key set of social pressures that' – she read out of the book, tracing the line with a finger – '"galvanize the release of the Breeder. However . . ."' She hesitated. She cleared her throat and picked up the coffee cup, then put it down without drinking. 'This stuff is killing my stomach. Don't we have any milk?'

'Nope. "However" you said. However what?'

'Social stresses may not be enough to account for the appearance of the originating carrier in an outbreak. There might be something else, some other originating factor, an outside agency. He says, well, it's not something to take seriously.'

She shrugged and turned a page in the book. 'Once the pilots destroy a community, they turn against one another, killing until there are only one or two left, who separate and go on to other communities, and then, for a time, the Waiting Ones go dormant. Go back to waiting.'

'But even if there's an inhibition against talking about them, we'd have heard something.'

'There were a number of recorded disappearances of small communities. The Croatoan incident, a whole town disappearing in the early days of the American settlement, little towns in Germany and France where everyone was found killed in the Middle Ages. Robber gangs were blamed, but one of those towns was empty except for a dozen corpses, each missing the right eye.'

'So if the altered are the essence of, like, selfishness, how come they bother breeding at all? Producing some kind of offspring.'

'It's not offspring really, it's just a medium for spreading their DNA around, presumably, through the stings. But it is an instinctive reproductive urge of some kind, despite the fact that this makes competition. I guess it's a compulsion.'

'So maybe this is where the stories about possession come from.'

'Probably. But these people aren't possessed. The pilots – well, according to Horescu, anyway, they act biochemically to simply bring out the worst in people. The very worst. The rock-bottom worst. It's just another level of their own selves.'

'Look, why don't you call up your colleagues and the newspapers and the TV – you're reputable, maybe you could get someone out here to witness this thing so the government, uh – '

She shook her head. 'I can't. I tried. I have the inhibition. I can talk to you, because you know. Maybe Sandra, a few others who know enough. But . . .' She shook her head helplessly. 'Even if I could, it would be hell getting anyone to believe me. What've we got to show them?' She snorted and slapped her hand down on the book. '*This?*'

'Yeah. He sounds like a lunatic. No wonder no one took the guy seriously.'

'The capper was his conclusion. That's where they really started laughing.'

'What was that?'

'He said . . .' She licked her lips, and Perry saw they were dry and cracked. She seemed to have difficulty saying it. 'He theorized about the cause of the first carrier; he said the pilots are the "seeds of the Invisible Predators." When he described these invisible predators . . .' She shrugged as if apologizing. 'It sounded like demonic spirits. Or some one spirit. Like they're little offshoots of this one dark spirit. He refers to a text written by a Franciscan monk describing "The One Who Hungers Always."'

'Sounds like . . .' The nervous joke died on his lips. *Sounds like a guy I used to sit next to in high school cafeteria.*

He'd heard a sound . . .

A buzzing. Getting closer, behind him.

He stood up, convulsively, upsetting his chair, and spun around, flung his coffee cup at the buzzing thing.

The cup smashed on the kitchen wall, and porcelain spun away from the brown splash of coffee. The mosquito spiraled toward the ceiling and affixed itself there, upside down.

'Just a mosquito, honey,' Aunt June said, coming up behind him. She stood close behind him and squeezed his upper arms.

'How are we going to sleep?' he said, staring at the mosquito.

After a moment she said, 'In shifts, I guess.'

Perry put the phone down. Lois still wasn't home. No one home at all there. He pictured her guardian, with an insect gleam in his eye, stalking through the house, shotgun in hand; he pictured walking through Lois's house and looking at one smashed-open body after another, till at last he found her.

The phone rang, and he almost treated it the way he had the coffee cup. But he took a deep breath and answered it. 'Yes?'

A voice with a twang said. 'Howdy, is this the residence of Sandra –'

'Yes, it is, who's this?' Perry broke in.

'Deputy Lancer, sheriff's department. We're trying to locate the sheriff, he wouldn't be over there, would he?'

'Why should he be?'

'We tried almost everywhere else. We thought he might be there talking to your aunt about the, uh, bug problem.'

Ice water trickled down Perry's back as he asked, 'I thought the sheriff was in the hospital.'

'He was. But he left there an hour ago, they tell me. Just walked out. His uniform's gone from the hospital closet and he took off without telling anyone where –'

'His uniform? Was his gun with it?'

'His gun? I guess it musta been. Hell, I forgot I was

supposed to pick it up, it musta been with it. Well that's good; he might need it. Look, if you hear from him – '

'Yeah, okay.' Perry hung up. He stared at the wall, thinking.

Well, that's good, Lancer had said. *He might need it.*

Joanie couldn't stand any more of it.

But she kept staring at the TV, because Rofocale had asked her to.

The TV showed a washed-out, oddly angled image of Joanie sitting in a chair, her feet drawn up, hugging her knees to her chest. Sobbing. Her hands wringing the hem of her blouse. The tape was twenty minutes of this sort of thing.

'What are you afraid of, Joanie?' Rofocale's voice, from the TV, off-camera. 'Why are you hiding like that, behind your knees, eh?'

'I can't help it,' said the TV Joanie.

God, how whiny and scratchy and stupid her own voice sounded to her on TV. Her knees, visible as her lollipop-patterned cotton skirt rode up, looked knobbier than ever. The dress looked childish. How could she wear it in front of Dr Rofocale? Her white canvas tennis shoes were all dirty. And looking at the picture, seeing how she'd squeezed her legs together, she remembered she'd almost peed her pants during that session. Oh God, if that had happened in front of Dr Rofocale, in front of Arthur . . .

'Look at yourself, Joanie.' Rofocale was talking to the Joanie he knew would be watching the videotape. 'Is that you?' The camera awkwardly zoomed in on her red, sob-swollen face. 'Is that you? Is that you? Is that you?'

'Yes,' the watching Joanie said, under her breath. 'I'm sorry, doctor.' Adding after a moment, tenderly. 'I'm sorry . . . Arthur.'

197

'No, it's not!' said Rofocale's voice-over. 'That's the blind Joanie. The Joanie with her eyes wide open looks like this!' A ragged edit to a shot of Joanie smiling, laughing, shouting, 'I am everything I want to be!' Joanie looked at it and thought: I was putting that on for the doctor. I wasn't feeling it. It's a lie.

The tape edited back to the red-faced Joanie with her quivering lower lip, a bubble of mucus expanding at one nostril.

Joanie's stomach contracted, and her gorge rose. She looked away.

'Is that you?' Rofocale's voice. 'It's not really you.' Someone else chiming in. That cunt, Lola. That perfume-drippy makeup-pasty paragon of perfection, Lola Turnette, chiming in, 'Is that you?'

'Bitch!' Joanie hissed, punching the on-off button with the heel of her hand.

The picture collapsed on itself, cutting off Lola's voice. 'Don't let that be y – '

Joanie sat for a moment in the welcome silence. The room came back. Part of it had been gone when the TV was there, or so it seemed to her. There was the light blue leatherette sofa, the twenty-four-inch TV console on a stand equipped with plastic rollers. There was the pressboard, imitation redwood walls; the four-tone poster on one wall, printed in dim quarter tones like a *Parade* magazine cover, showing a man standing on a cliff overlooking the sea under the calligraphied quote: *Who am I? I am Self! And Self is what I want it to be!*

And under that, the attribution: *Arthur Rofocale*.

He's a great man, Joanie told herself. He has his name on posters. I should be honored to be here.

She thought about the day he had touched her.

They'd been doing some one-on-one in his office, Dr

Rofocale, Arthur, sitting with his chair pulled up to hers, their knees almost touching. Arthur was looking her in the eyes, telling her, 'Tell me the rest of it and don't avert your eyes. Tell it to me proudly. They made you look like a fool, you said.'

She'd shaken her head, unable to go on, pinching inside at the shame of disappointing him, and she'd dropped her eyes.

He'd bent nearer, taken her chin in his hand, lifted her face to his, and she could feel the heat of him, smell cigarettes and coffee on him, felt the fatherly compassion in his face draw her close.

And then Lola had come in. She'd *banged* the door open so Arthur, who'd been about to kiss her, sprang up, startled and stammering. 'Ah, Lola, um, is it time for group al-uh-ready?'

He had been about to kiss me, Joanie thought. He feels it too. He looks beyond the outside of a person. He sees the person underneath. The full self under the broken self.

And he *had* been about to kiss her. She was *sure* of it.

She knew what the bitch Lola would say, all infuriatingly reasonable. *You're losing yourself in the fantasy about the doctor because your sense of true Self is so badly developed. It's just another symptom, Joanie.*

Joanie shook her head. It wasn't true. There was something really special between her and the doctor. He looked at her differently than he looked at the others.

She couldn't stay here anymore unless he showed her he cared. The pressure was too much. This place was scaring her too much.

Things had changed since they'd moved out here. They'd come to this big, split-level house, on the opposite side of Jasper from the center because Worldley, Inc. had leased it specially for Dr Rofocale . . . and because Arthur was being 'persecuted, like all great men,' as Lola put it. The police had been looking for him for a while. And then the police just sort of gave up. Too many other things happening.

But Rofocale didn't move them back to the center. They stayed here and made it over into another center; except it wasn't the same, because the men from Axis were all around. And there were so many secret meetings now. People talking in whispers in the hall, and when they saw you they stopped talking. The noises from the attic. The back bedroom they kept locked all the time. The girl's voice Joanie'd heard when she'd walked by that locked door, once; a voice that said, 'If you come in, I'll put you out of your misery.' She hadn't slept the rest of that night.

If you asked the doctor's assistants about the locked bedroom, they said, 'Oh, you know, there's no two therapies alike. Some people need privacy so they can kind of get crazy for a while. You need the freedom to be an asshole sometimes.' That's all they'd say. There was weeping from that room too.

And there were the men in the dark suits. Crisp young men with perfect haircuts and dark glasses and clipboards. She'd been in his office for a one-on-one and Lola had come in and said, 'Mr Gant and Mr Forester are here from Axis Industries, doctor.' And then those men had come in and looked at her like, *Why are you staying?* So she'd got up to leave, even before Dr Rofocale cleared his throat and said, 'Uh, Joanie, maybe you'd better – '

She'd thought the men looked like the Secret Service agents she'd seen on TV. Maybe they were some kind of G-men.

But today she'd gone out for her morning walk, and as

she went by the white Axis Industries limousine, she heard one of them talking on his car phone. 'The bottom line is, identity printing will maximize efficiency and that means maximized profits, sir. I'm convinced of it.' That sounded like corporate business, all right. Not G-men. But why had he come out to the car to use the phone?

She felt like she was the only one who didn't know what was going on at the center. And therapy was harder every day. Yesterday when Tommy tried to kill himself again . . .

She'd envied him.

She couldn't stay. Unless Dr Rofocale asked her to, personally. Unless he admitted his feelings to her. Then she'd have the strength.

She felt a weight slide off her. It felt good to have made up her mind.

She had moved up from the slough of depression and into one of those giddy, fast-driving moods that came on her sometimes. Not very often – but sometimes. Sometimes Arthur could bring them out in her, the kind of feeling that made her want to do things.

As if carried on a wave that came from within, she stood up and went to Dr Rofocale's office. The office door was open and he wasn't there. He wasn't in the group room. She went downstairs. No one in the living room, or – she heard a shout from the back bedroom. Shouts were ordinary at the center. Shouting was a part of therapy, and you didn't pay much attention after a while. But this was Dr Rofocale's voice. 'Arthur,' Joanie said, aloud, to enjoy the sound of his name on her lips. 'You're a marvel. Always working.'

She went down the hall to the back bedroom. Wondering where the other patients were – probably out to 'tell the outdoors.' They were supposed to go to the canyon and shout their therapy Repeats at the woods. Joanie didn't like that one. It was embarrassing when the tourists saw you.

She paused at the door to the back bedroom. It was quiet inside now, except for a rustling sound, and a mutter she couldn't make out.

She almost lost her nerve. Maybe she shouldn't be bothering him now. He might be doing something really important with someone.

You're the most important person in the world, he always told them. *Remember that*.

If she didn't go in now and assert herself, all her therapy would be for nothing.

The door would be locked, though.

She should knock. But she didn't have the nerve to pound on the door. There was whispering on the other side.

Maybe since there was more than one person in there, the door would be unlocked. She could just open it a bit and look in and decide if . . .

Joanie turned the knob. It was unlocked. The door opened. She looked through.

The windows were shuttered; the room was dimly lit by a little table lamp with a light green scarf over it, to dim it further; everything was cast in a subaquatic light. And on the bed . . .

She misinterpreted the scene at first. She thought she saw a woman in labor on a bed. Dr Rofocale and Lola and the big red-haired guy Charlie delivering. The woman arched her back and groaned. But that wasn't what it was. What it was, what it really was . . .

Four people. On the bed was a girl who'd come in a couple of days earlier. Her name was Wendy something. She'd come in with Charlie, who'd said, 'Right through here, Wendy.' The look on Wendy's face had scared Joanie. They'd taken her . . . here? Joanie hadn't realized till now that this girl had been the one in here all this time. The one who'd said, *Come in and I'll put you out of your misery*.

This Wendy was lying on the bed, on her back. Strapped down. Big leather restraints. Wearing only a hospital gown. They had earphones on her, big stereo earphones. Charlie had a metal rod in his hands. There was a wire running from the rubber handle of the rod down to a socket beside the bed. On the other side, Rofocale was speaking into a microphone that fed into a small black box; the earphones were connected to the black box. Lola was standing nearby with a videocamera.

They had their back to Joanie. They were looking at the girl. Focused on her completely.

There was a spiderweb over the girl.

No, it was some kind of net. Like mosquito netting, but it looked stronger. In the dim green light it looked like a sheer membrane of algae. It was warped over an armature of wires, enclosing the girl's upper half in an irregular bubble. But Joanie could see her clearly through it, could hear her cursing without words, spitting so the phlegm caught on the net and dripped down from it inside.

As Rofocale yelled into the microphone, '*You're dead unless you escape you're dead unless you escape you're dead unless you escape!*' and with each word the girl wrenched her head, her face contorting, Joanie could hear the words leaking from the earphones as a sort of fizzy bark. *You're dead unless* . . .

And the girl's legs twitched like things apart from her when Charlie put the rod on them.

That's a cattle prod, Joanie realized. She felt like she'd inhaled a double lungful of frigid air, though the room was warm. 'Oh God, Arthur,' she breathed. They didn't hear her. They were fixated on the writhing girl.

'It's not responding,' Rofocale said.

But it looked like he hadn't said this to Charlie or Lola. It looked like he'd turned toward a dark corner, on the opposite side of the bed from the lamp . . . the darkest corner in the room. Like he'd said it to the corner . . .

'Okay,' Rofocale said, as if he were answering someone, though no one had spoken. Charlie looked at Lola. She shrugged. They didn't understand it either.

Joanie wanted to slam the door and run. But she was frozen. Her eyes kept returning to the prod. If they catch me here they'll use that on me, she thought. Oh God, Arthur, how could you be this person too?

Rofocale had taken something from his pocket. At first she thought it was a scalpel. But she looked closer.

It was a corkscrew.

He bent over the girl.

Then he turned toward the dark corner again. (Joanie wanted to run. She was rooted. She felt a trickle of warmth at her crotch. Her bladder was letting go. It did that when she was panicked sometimes. She was near . . .) Rofocale asking the dark corner, 'Maybe if we use some – ' He cut off, as if someone had interrupted him. But no one had spoken. 'Okay.' Resignation. He bent over the girl and Joanie couldn't see what he did with the corkscrew, but the girl screamed and the scream was like a glass needle that went right into Joanie's bladder. She felt the piss run down her leg.

'Don't!' Joanie heard herself yell. 'You're so . . . it's not . . . Don't, hey, let her . . .'

She broke off as they turned to look at her. The corkscrew in Rofocale's hand had a red cork of torn flesh stuck on to it, dripping. (A buzzing noise somewhere

. . .) Lola looked disgusted. Charlie, big, broad, green-eyed, shaggy-headed, bearded Charlie, took a step toward her. (There was a buzzing like a thousand flies, growing, furious, shivering her eardrum.)

And then the girl on the bed convulsed, the spasm going through her like a whiplash, starting in her feet, rippling her body till it got to her head, her head snapping up and back and – her left eye splashed out of her head and stuck to the green net, pasted there, and the thing that had pushed it out from inside was fluttering in the net, pushing the net outward, deforming it angrily, like a tennis ball pushing into a tennis net and then not giving up, the ball coming alive and fighting the net . . . but it was a gray, blood-spattered thing, a blur of wings.

Joanie was gagging, almost vomiting; Rofocale was yelling about the camera and for Charlie to get the net. 'We need to control this one!' Lola shrieked as the camera jumped from her hands, threw itself against the wall. The windows rattled; the buzzing grew. The lamp flew from its table.

They'd forgotten about Joanie, and when her legs realized that, they turned her, flew with her down the hall; in seconds she was running under the stars, feeling the wind dry tears on her cheeks.

Running into the trees, into the wilderness, running blind into the part of the world where savagery declared itself openly.

11

'No, uh-uh,' Aunt June said, looking coldly at Sandra. 'No hallucinogenic gas, no drugs in our coffee. We saw what we saw. The Stiggins boy is dead, and dead the way Tetty died. Whatever killed him killed Tetty.'

They were in the kitchen, sitting around the table. Sandra, Lois, Perry, Aunt June. Outside, the night rustled to itself; small dark chitinous things, like little organic computers, called out to one another, operating on instinct the way computers operate on programming, Perry thought. Crickets, and other insects, singing out.

Were they louder than they had been the night before? Perry wondered. Was that his imagination? Were the insect things, the things that erupted from skulls, were they in some way in league with the insects outside the house and within the walls of the house? Would Perry wake one night to find a rustling blanket of chitinous black and brown covering him? Did they bore into the brain somehow? Maybe they were insects that deposited eggs into the skin; perhaps the larvae worked their way into the veins, drifted to the brain, and hatched.

Maybe the Horescu/Rofocale scenario was all wrong. Maybe they weren't a side effect of the human instinct for self-preservation, a forgotten X-factor of human evolution guided by some demonic spirit. Perhaps, instead, they were simply mutated insects of some kind.

But they had spoken to him.

He hadn't fantasized that. They had spoken to him,

and tainted him spiritually in that contact, and he'd had a glimpse into them.

They were human. Horribly human. All the worst of what was human. Disfigured, demented, perversely redesigned to mock insects. But quintessentially human.

'I saw something else too,' Perry said. 'I couldn't really think about it till now.'

'Something when?' Sandra snapped impatiently. She poured gin from a pint bottle into a coffee cup and knocked back enough to make Perry falling down drunk. She didn't even shudder.

'In the sheriff's office?' Lois asked. She sat next to Perry, her hand dry and pliant in his under the table. She wore an old army-surplus shirt, four sizes too big, as a dress, with a black snakeskin belt and black tights.

Perry shook his head. 'Before that. When I saw one of them – when it came at me on the back porch.'

'Good God, what perfect tripe,' Sandra muttered into her cup. It made her voice sound lugubrious. 'Bloody adolescent fantasies. Attention-seeking – '

'Cunt,' Perry said. A hot wet wax-melting feeling in his head as he let it all go. 'You fucking cunt. You are so incredibly full of shit.' The words clacking out of his mouth as if on a ticker tape, following some inner mechanism he couldn't control. The mechanism of anger releasing. He felt his face burning with it.

Aunt June was looking at him in what he assumed was shock. But when he looked at her, the expression on her face was simple fear. As he watched, she got it under control; it almost vanished under a veneer of adult reproach.

Perry realized: She thought for a moment that one of the pilots had got to me. That I'd been stung and changed.

'Why you foulmouthed little wanker,' Sandra said,

looking at him with her head cocked to one side. But she seemed more bemused than angry.

Lois had realized Perry's outburst of obscenity was just anger. She rolled her eyes at him.

Perry shrugged. 'I'm sorry. I'm just – I saw what I saw.'

'I yam what I yam,' Sandra said, mimicking his voice. 'He's Popeye the Sailor man.'

Perry wanted to smash the cup into her face. Grind its fragments in . . .

Maybe they did get to me, he thought, catching himself. Not with their stingers; not physically. But they tainted me somehow.

He took a deep breath and said, 'There was something more when they spoke to me. Something in the background. Just a feeling that . . .' Struggling to find a way to explain, he squeezed Lois's hand. Her touch had gone damp. 'A feeling that something else was watching. Calling the shots.'

He looked at Lois, and she looked down at the table, avoiding his eyes. 'In town there's a lot of talk,' she began. She hesitated, and then went on. 'There's been a lot of weird things happening around town. Reverend Martindale and those people in that fire, that old man cutting off his wife's head and disappearing. Rumors about rabies turning people crazy. And some people tried to contact the state cops and the state cops said they'd talked to the sheriff and he'd told them not to come, that everything was under control. And the town council went to the sheriff and he said, "Forget it! It's under control!" They talked to him in the hospital – and then he disappeared.'

'So what's the point of all this gibbering?' Sandra asked, arching her eyebrows as she looked at Lois. 'Hm, little girl?'

'You can throw me out,' Perry said. 'But if you talk to her like that again I'll – '

'Perry!' Aunt June broke in, a hand raised. 'Let me, okay?' She turned to Sandra. 'Sandra, shut up, or talk civilly to people. You asked me to stay so we could figure out exactly what happened to your daughter. I'm doing that. I won't stay without Perry, though.'

Sandra turned away. She began to quiver, and for a moment Perry thought she was shaking with laughter. But as she turned back, tears coursed from the corners of her eyes, and when she spoke, her voice was broken. 'I'm sorry.' Her shoulders shook. Her makeup became watercolors. 'I'm sorry. But Tetty . . . and then you tell me this story . . .'

Aunt June picked up her chair and moved it close to Sandra's. She sat beside her, hugging her. There was something in the earnestness of Aunt June's hug that said she was getting as much comfort as she was giving.

Perry got up and led Lois into the next room. All the lights were blazing, including a Coleman electric lantern on the floor.

They sat on the sofa, clasping both hands, and Lois said, 'I'm trying to believe what you guys told me. But it's like something a cult would believe or – '

'I know. Don't blame you. But those things are out there.'

'You knew about it before but you couldn't talk about it?'

'Uh-huh. Aunt June had trouble talking about it at first, but she's less susceptible, I guess, to whatever it is that holds people back. Maybe because she's a scientist, more, uh, left-brained. I don't know. She finally was able to . . .' He shrugged.

'Who did you talk to about it? I mean – '

'I know what you mean. She made some calls. She had trouble getting it out, but she did it, and a lot of people hung up on her. We haven't got any evidence. The one we killed just sort of melted away into slush. Tomorrow we're going into Portland, talk to the state cops, health department, whoever. I can't get her to go tonight. She won't say why. But I think it's because' – his mouth was dry – 'because she doesn't think it'd be safe out there. On the road.'

'Maybe we should try to evacuate the town. Talk to the town council, or – '

'Uh-uh. We just can't. How many people have been infected by those things? If they go with the ones who've evacuated, they could spread it into the big cities.'

'Oh Lord. You're right. Jesus fucking Christ. Perry, I'm scared. I hereby freely admit it.'

He smiled wearily. 'So you believe us.'

'Well, something weird is spreading through town. Oh, shit, the Indian rights rally is tonight. My uncle's there. If any of this stuff is true, if some of those people are there, Perry – ' She shook her head. 'I just picture myself trying to tell him to call it off and explaining why.'

'Don't worry about it. Tomorrow we'll talk him into going with us. It's only one night. What could happen in one night?'

Albright had just come back from vacation and found everything changed.

He'd only been gone two weeks. Two weeks fishing in Canada with Alma. They'd hardly argued at all. Once or twice, at first. But then as the sweet green days relaxed them and the pure cold mountain air brought them together in bed, they hadn't felt the need to talk, let alone argue. Happy and quiet as clams.

Still he'd almost been looking forward to coming back to his job. He liked being deputy sheriff in Jasper. Dawson was a grouchy old bigot, sometimes, but he was a good guy, and a good cop. Anyway, that's what Albright had been thinking, driving the RV home, the day before.

But now . . . Now, Dawson and Lancer were acting like a couple of prime assholes. Kind of like a couple of yokel James Bonds, scheming and sneaking around and talking about using explosives.

Albright thought, Did I hear him right? Is he really talking about blowing the phone lines?

They were in Dawson's cruiser, all three of them, Albright riding shotgun, Lancer prattling in the back, driving down Salt Springs Road, almost in sight of the lake. It was dark out, and it was a gravel fire road; they were the only car in sight, a little moving island of sleek metal design and electric light in the rolling landscape of trees and clumps of thorn-bound rock. Sometimes the land flattened enough he could make out the horizon as they swept by; trees etched jet black against an indigo sky.

The car was moving at almost sixty, fast for a road like this; it fishtailed slightly when Dawson took a curve. Nervously, Albright tightened his seat belt. It was a little loose. That was one good thing anyway. He'd lost some of that paunch, on the trip.

Albright was a broad-shouldered man, six-one and almost two hundred pounds but used to feeling trim, athletic. Former high school quarterback, former army ranger. Still kept himself austerely clean shaven and his blond hair crewcut, though it was twelve years since that eight-year stint in the army.

Dawson wasn't wearing his seat belt, Albright noticed. Not usual for him.

'What we do here is,' Dawson was saying, his eyes fixed on the road, 'we find that seventy-eight line. We set a charge under those poles.'

Albright turned to stare at the sheriff. It was dark in the car; the blunt lines of the sheriff's face were lit eerily by the sickly green light of the dashboard. 'You're serious,' Albright said. 'For a while I figured you guys were putting me on. Maybe you are.' He turned in his seat to look at Lancer. Wondering again why Lancer was here anyway. He'd been his replacement while he was out of town, but he was supposed to be laid off now. Was Dawson going to replace him with Lancer? It seemed hard to believe. Lancer had always annoyed Dawson. He was just a glorified security guard.

'No joke,' Lancer said, chuckling.

'Then what're you laughing for?' Albright asked.

'Why should we be jokin'?' Dawson asked suddenly. He hadn't taken his eyes off the road for a second. Which was good, because he was driving too damn fast for Albright's liking. That was unusual for Dawson too. Normally Dawson would let a perpetrator get away rather than take wild chances on driving.

They screeched around a curve, and Dawson went on: 'It's very simple. The fucking red niggers are having their fucking war dance tonight. We're going to see it doesn't happen again. But we got to see to it there's no interference from the other kind of red element, if you know what I mean.'

Lancer snickered.

'Communist bastards crawling like cockroaches over the whole fucking state,' Lancer said. Echoing something Dawson had said earlier.

'That'll take out the phones for all of Jasper,' Albright pointed out. Thinking, More important, it'll get us all busted and tossed in the state pen. But for reasons he couldn't put his finger on, he was scared to say it aloud.

'Will it *do* that?' Dawson said, making a gag of pretending he hadn't known. 'No shit?'

Albright looked at Dawson and thought, The man's had a stroke or something. On drugs. Something. 'I still think you fellas are kidding me 'cause you know how I feel about that stuff.' *That stuff* meaning racism.

'You're what they call the Aryan type,' Lancer pointed out. 'Time you came home to your people.'

'That's a moving speech, Lancer,' Albright said sarcastically. 'You should go into politics. You can run on the Klan ticket.' Lancer was rumored to be a Klansman.

'Politics, that's what we're doin',' Dawson said. 'You know I always wanted to do something about the red niggers throwin' their weight around. Fucking aborigines. Drunks. Rapists.'

'Only one of them raped a girl – how many white men raped – ' Albright began.

Dawson steamrolled on through. 'Rapist drunk whinin' red niggers. But every time I wanted to do something, Ol' Marv Nigger Lover and his liberal pals put the pressure on the town council.' He paused, grunting as the car jumped in a rut, giving them all a brutal rattling. 'Organizing the Indian vote. You think they're going to reelect ol' Sheriff Dawson, all them drunk Indians? This fucking rally is to see to it I don't get reelected, that's what it's about. See to it the radicals take over.'

'The rally, what I heard, is about land rights. They don't want to be moved to another reservation or something,' Albright objected.

'If you believe that, then you'd lick Gorbachev's ass if he told you it was candy,' Lancer said.

213

'It's me they're after,' Sheriff Dawson said. 'But we'll see who gets who first.'

Albright didn't say anything for a while. He sat there, feeling funny, and after a while he realized it was something he hadn't felt since 1971, in Nam. It was deep, bone-deep scared.

Her name was Betty Prakesh. And lately she'd been waking up scared.

Tonight she sat bolt upright on the couch, her blouse stuck to her back with perspiration, her hands cold, her scalp contracting, skin crawling, and what made it worse was the way Hassan was looking at her. 'That what happens,' he said, his Iranian accent rolling like syrup through the syllables, 'when you sleep in the middle of the day, Betty.' He said her name like *Bitty*. 'You have bad dreams. That what happens.'

He was sitting there in his La-Z-Boy recliner, the Persian slippers his mother had sent him from Teheran on his feet, his eyes large and dark as the petroleum seepage at the LaBrea tar pits. She always thought of that because they'd met in the park by the tar pits, in Los Angeles, both of them out on their lunch hour. She'd stood by the railing, looking at the statue of the mammoth half sunk in the tar pits – the mammoth straining upward against the sucking swamp, the glue of the tar, perpetually desperate. It was an ugly sight, and the tar pits were ugly, but it had matched her mood that day. She was thinking, the mammoth's weight is pulling it down. And me, my weight is dragging me under too.

Eight diets in eight months, every one a failure.

And then Hassan had leaned up against the rail next to her and said, 'It stinks, this water, eh?' Not exactly a romantic first line. But five minutes later he'd asked her to have a drink after work. Her mother hadn't liked him, her friends hadn't liked him, and he was a foreigner with a thick accent and a smell of funny spiced foods and gallons of cheap after-shave on him. But he had dark good looks, and he petted her as if she was a cat, and she was afraid of dying without a husband, so . . .

'I *didn't* sleep during the day,' she pointed out, now. 'It wasn't *day*, it was evening and I took a little nap. I was tired from being on my feet all day. Waitress work wears you out.'

'You are have a bad dream, eh?' He was still looking at her like that. Hardly even blinking.

She swallowed. The bad taste of the dream was still in her mouth. Blood in her mouth. She must have bitten her tongue. She did that when she got scared. She felt cold, remembering the dream.

'You don't like being waitress, okay. Seven-Eleven, that's not so easy either.' Restrained anger in his tone.

What was he mad about?

She didn't think, anyway, that operating the 7-Eleven was as hard as waitressing. The 7-Eleven was why they'd moved to Jasper, so he could quit his cashier job and go into partnership with his uncle Behrooz on the 7-Eleven franchise outside the tract housing spread by the lake. But there was no explaining to Hassan that her life might be as hard as his. She was a woman. Persians regarded women as second-class citizens. She'd learned that only a few hours after they were married. And just the day before Uncle Behrooz had come over for dinner and they'd spent the whole time talking in Persian, leaving her out completely, rude as you can be.

'And anyway, that how you lose some of that heaviness,' he said.

Betty winced. They'd been married a year. He'd been

nice about her weight the first few months. Pretended he liked it. And then the comments started.

The dream. The rancid smell of –

'What you dream about?' he asked. Still staring at her. Sitting in the chair in his pajamas and slippers. His arms limp on the armrests, ringed fingers hanging over the edges. Gold chain on his furry chest gleaming dully in the light of the floor lamp. Sweating. Why? It wasn't particularly hot tonight. But there was a bead of sweat on each tip of his oily black mustache. And it was funny he didn't put the TV on. Whether or not she was asleep, he tended to watch TV when he wasn't working. Even when he was working. He'd watch anything. Julia Child, Bugs Bunny, anything.

He reached up, as if in slow motion, and rubbed at his neck, under his left ear.

'I dreamed . . .' Betty shook her head. 'I don't want to talk about it.'

But she remembered it. Dreams were supposed to fade by now; they usually did. But this one hung on, clung like a bat in her hair, gnawing.

The dream starts at the bathroom door. She's coming out of the bathroom, trying to get her pants snapped up. Realizing she must have gained back what she lost because they're harder to do up than they should be. Then she stops, seeing the man in the black ski mask, holes where his eyes should be. Just empty holes. The room goes dark around him, like someone is turning down a stage light; the dark corners thicken with shadow. She thinks she glimpses something moving in one of those corners, but she can't look to see what it is because she can't take her eyes off this man, the sight of him is like a slug dropped down her blouse.

He's wearing . . . she was fuzzy on that. But she was

sure he's got the ski mask, the black gloves, and he pads toward her, talking in nonsense syllables. 'Gee balsh,' he says. Artificially low, rumbly voice. 'Gush-nish fargin bastiches kah-loo-uh,' he says. Backing her up toward the bathroom.

She's scared to get caught in the bathroom, so she turns and, holding up her pants with one hand, bolts for the kitchen. She can go out the back door. She feels so heavy, so slow, and he moves behind her so effortlessly, confident he'll catch her, hardly trying.

Then she's in the kitchen, running toward the back door . . . but it gets smaller, shrinking like an *Alice in Wonderland* thing, till it's too small for a midget, it's a doll-house door, and she can't get through it.

As she stares at the tiny door, wanting to scream with frustration, the room gets darker around her, as if stage lights are turned down, and she knows he's coming into the kitchen, coming closer to her.

'If you weren't so fat,' says the man behind her, 'maybe you could get through the door.'

She turns and looks for weapons, but he grabs her from behind, by the wrists, and with an inexorable strength bends her toward the kitchen sink, bends her over it. She struggles but she's weak as an infant in his arms. She can feel her unbuttoned pants coming down, his breath on the back of her neck. She looks up and sees the ceiling has gone shadowy; there's one spot where the shadow is deepest, and she can't understand why her eyes are drawn to it when this man to trying to kill her. He forces her wrist down against the cold metal of the sink and then begins to slide her hand across toward the drain . . . toward the garbage disposal.

Oh, no. She can smell the rancid flecks of garbage clinging to the disposal blades.

She gives a terrific wrench, trying to escape, and her left arm comes free of his grip, but he clubs a fist into her mouth, battering her head back into his chest; she can feel her lips pop open with the blow like those little plastic packets of ketchup she gives people at work, spraying red, she tastes blood and claws at his fist as it closes on her throat.

But his other hand (her heart is the tiny heart of a frightened rabbit thumping so fast you couldn't make out the beats separately, overworked as it struggles to maintain a heavy human body) is tightening on her wrist (her lungs are squeezing frantically, her throat closing off) pushing her hand (her back rigid with terror) toward the disposal (her bowels threatening to give way) and forcing it in, down . . . as his hand leaves her throat and hits the switch and the disposal grinds and she feels her fingers catch and –

'What's matter?' Hassan asked her. With not even a shred of genuine concern in his tone.

'I was remembering the dream. God. I have to – ' Her bowels were screaming at her. She got up and hurried to the bathroom, locked the door, hurried through the bowel movement. She wanted to get out of the house. Just get away, go and have a daiquiri and maybe a hamburger somewhere, like that restaurant-bar on the highway to Bend.

She wiped, flushed the toilet, turned on the overhead fan, tried to button her pants. She thought she had it buttoned, but as she opened the door the button came undone. Must have gained back that –

And then she realized.

She was standing in the bathroom door with her pants undone. She looked up – and exhaled in relief. No man in a ski mask.

Just Hassan. Coming toward her. Talking in Persian.

One hand clenched at his side. The other one up rubbing something she hadn't seen before, looked like a bee sting on his neck . . . coming toward her. Each of his eyes was a dark corner. Talking in Iranian . . . coming toward her.

'Oh. Hassan.' The words all gummy in her dry mouth as she turned and bolted for the kitchen, to go out the back door, forgetting the dream in her terror till she tried to open the back door.

There was a chain on the outside of the door. It was Hassan's bicycle chain, around the knob and then running to a bolt of some kind that he had put in . . . when? While she was asleep. He had been planning this, sitting in the chair thinking about it as she slept. The door opened about a foot.

'If you weren't so fat,' Hassan says, chuckling, 'maybe you could get through the door.'

She gave a wail of despair and turned – but he was on her from behind, clamping her wrists, his cloying cheap after-shave choking her; he was bending her over the sink, pressing her hand to the disposal, and her despair made her feel so weak . . . some part of her mind aware of the deep shadow overhead, that slice of deep blackness where the wall and ceiling came together, where something was watching . . . as, between her sobs, she heard him say, 'All of you is going in, starting with your hand. I use the butcher knife to help soon. With fat pig like you, it take all night.'

He shoved her hand deep into the disposal and reached up to flick the switch.

'You must be joking, Sandra.' Aunt June was staring at her, mouth a little open, frankly astonished.

Sandra was standing by the phone in the living room, across from Perry and Lois. She'd just put down the phone, and now she turned sloppily toward Aunt June, just the faintest slurring in her enunciation as she said, 'Only in the sense that everything is a joke now, June. I re-iter-ate' – she paused, pleased that she'd said *reiterate* without screwing up – 'that I am going to the party.'

'A party. Tonight.' Aunt June shook her head in disbelief.

'*He* will be there. Mr Right. Or, anyhow, he's Mr Available. Besides, it couldn't be as awful as you think, around town, or people wouldn't be throwing a party.'

Perry said, slowly, 'Unless it's one of them. Someone changed. With their own reasons.'

With a drunken flourish, Sandra turned to him, her eyes piggish red from drinking. 'I have been commanded by Mistress June not to speak sharply to you. Hence . . .' She repeated it again, as if savoring the sound of it. '*Hence*, I will not tell you what I think of that moronic idea.' She turned and made for her bedroom, only weaving slightly. 'I am going to change for the party. If you will excuse me.'

'*San*-dra,' Aunt June began.

'Useless to try to talk me out of it!' Sandra called over her shoulder. 'I've made up my mind!' She slammed the bedroom door behind her.

'I can't believe it,' Lois said. 'Someone's having a party tonight. That feels so weird.'

Aunt June nodded slowly. 'But I don't think it's what Perry suggested. Most people are still unaware of what's happening. Actually . . .' She looked thoughtful. 'It might be interesting to observe the people at the party. In the context of the situation I might be able to learn if – '

'Now *you've* got to be kidding!' Perry burst out. 'I mean you're not really going to go *with* her are you?'

Aunt June sat down on the armrest of the sofa and smiled distantly. 'I am, yes. I have to. I know her; there's no talking her out of going out when she's set on it. I really think it would come to blows. And I have to keep an eye on her. Baby-sit. And it could be interesting if – '

'I can't believe you're going to a party tonight,' Perry said, again.

'Neither can I,' Aunt June said. 'I feel like Nero. All I need's the violin.'

When Joanie had been a little girl, her daddy had given her a pretty, sky-blue silk scarf. She loved the tender feel of it around her neck. One windy day it had been blown off her head into a patch of blackberry brambles. There were little paths into the brambles made by people who'd gone hunting for berries, and she hurried into one of these to try to reach her scarf. But just before she got it, it was tugged from its snag by another gust of wind and blown a little farther on – and torn a bit in the going. She pursued it again, and again it was blown away. Some minutes later she caught up to it – and found it tattered by thorns and wind, and flecked red with berry juice.

She felt like that scarf tonight. Blown through the desert, tattered, bloodied, torn away bit by bit.

Panting, leaning on a boulder (afraid to sit down, something might crawl up her dress), Joanie didn't yet have a definite sense of place. She knew she'd run through the trees and into the stunted trees and desert foliage and volcanic rock that ringed Jasper; she knew that the only illumination came from the light of the stars. She knew that she'd cut herself many times, running through the brush in only her canvas shoes and skirt and blouse.

But she didn't really understand where she was until the first wave of panic began to die away, till the panting subsided and a warm breeze dried the sweat to sticky patches of salt on her skin; salt that burned in the contusions on her legs and arms and ankles. She looked around and began to realize that she was lost.

The starlight made Japanese-fan silhouettes of yucca leaves; it picked out knobs of rock and socked a deeper darkness into stony pores and concavities. Foliage shadows sawed at the night-purpled sand in the sluggish wind. One of the shadows detached from the others and moved jerkily toward her.

She kicked sand at it and the lizard scurried away.

A cactus owl made a low ratcheting sound, somewhere; an insect repeated a complex rasping pattern with inane persistence. A night hawk said, *Pur-EEE*. Something rustled in the rocks behind her; something else made a click-click sound, off to her left.

She squinted through the banks of shadow, trying to make out the lights of houses, somewhere. She saw nothing. Stupid, she told herself. You should have run to another house, not into the woods. Idiot.

But she'd fled in disgust as much as in panic; she'd wanted to get away from *people*.

'You've done that all right,' she said softly.

All she saw were humps of rock, each with its surround of bristling vegetation. It was like looking at an archipelago in the sea of sand. Some peculiarity of the area's geology; the almost garden-regular outcroppings of rock, a maze in the desert.

A maze. She'd run headlong into it and had no idea how to find her way out. She tried to see her tracks in the starlight, to follow them back . . .

But the ground was a lace work of shadow. She had no

matches, nothing. She could make out, here and there, traces of tracks. They were not her own.

If your car runs out of gas when you're driving through the desert, people had told her, *don't take any shortcuts across the land, stay on the road! There are rattlers and scorpions out there, packs of wild dogs, coyotes.*

Rattlers. Scorpions. Wild dogs.

Wild dogs would smell the blood from her cuts.

Suddenly she became sharply aware of the throb of pain in her legs and arms. Cuts and bruises, itching from plant resin. She reached down and brushed at her legs, imagining insects crawling on them, and her fingertips picked up the glutinous syrup of her own blood. A mosquito whined nearby; she pictured it settling to drink from the blood on her legs like an animal at a water hole.

The thing in the net. The girl's eye. The flying camera, the flying lamp. The fountain of blood. The angry buzzing.

She clapped her hand over her mouth because she didn't want to scream. The scream might attract something.

The thing in the net. The girl's eye, pasted to –

She bent double, gagging.

She vomited – but nothing came out but bile and stomach acid, burning her throat.

After a few moments the quaking nausea in the pit of her stomach died away, and she was able to straighten up.

Maybe there was an explanation for what she'd seen.

The eye? The . . . corkscrew? In *his* hand? Dripping.

No. The only way to deal with it was not to think about it.

She had to find her way out of the desert. She tried to remember what direction she'd come from when she'd fetched up against the boulder. She decided it was the direction she was facing now. She took a deep breath, and legs throbbing, she walked off, between the islands of rock and brush, her arms clasped over her chest. Smelling the sage, menthol smells of other plants, an alien spiciness that hinted of poisonous resins and made her wounds itch.

She hurried on, stumbling over rocks, felt a toenail break, skin pared from an ankle by a flinty edge. Now and then she had to press between thickets of spiny growth where needles sharp as doctor's hypos jabbed her arm, seeming to do it capriciously.

She paused, squinting, thinking she'd seen a splinter of light at the horizon.

There: a thin stick of light like a dowser's wand sweeping out over the desert and back; the distant seashell sound of a car on a highway. The lights, the sounds of cars!

She hurried on – and stopped, ten feet further. She'd heard a sharp noise. A rattling of stones off to her right. She looked into the mass of grey and black and blue tones, the hump of purplish red that was the desert floor.

Two tiny green glimmers. Fireflies?

No. The glimmers moved in parallel. There were two more.

Shapes formed around the glimmers and held them in place. The glimmers were eyes. The shapes were the outlines of . . . coyotes. Or dogs.

She had a flash of herself flailing on the ground as a pack of dogs tore gobbets of flesh from her.

But she couldn't move. She felt her bladder let go again; smelled her own urine. The animals came closer, their outlines taking on definition, their heads low, swaying over the ground as they approached. Frozen, she stared at them, thinking, find a tree. Find a rock. But don't try to run for it or they'll pull you down.

The animals made noises that were halfway between whimpers and growls, noises of hunger and curiosity, an undertone of whining urgency.

They came snuffling toward her, at least four of them; the one in the lead stopped, went rigid, its head uplifted. Its head turned like a radar tracking scope as it watched something she couldn't see pass overhead. She heard a soft *hmmmm* that became a *bzzz* and then a *BZZZZ*.

The animals cringed, as one, and turned away from her. She could almost smell their terror.

She felt a feathery brush at the back of her neck. As if something had tasted her with a tongue made of warm mist.

She shivered and cringed like one of the wild dogs, looking up. A shadow blotted a piece of the Milky Way and she glimpsed something that might have been a small gray owl.

The thing under the net. Angry.

She began to move, slowly at first, then trotting, working up to a run.

Where are you going? she heard it say. A soft, teenage girl's voice. *Don't run off. Let's be friends. Let's hang out. Let's get drunk. Let's watch TV. Let's go driving.*

'Shut up!' Joanie rasped, running now. 'Out of my head.'

But things were cutting her; it was as if the desert itself was clawing at her with plants and sharp rocks, trying to skin her alive, render her raw for the thing that flew just behind her.

She ran almost blindly, zigzagging to try to keep it out of her hair. She was sure it would get in her hair like a bat, she'd always been scared of bats getting in her hair, and it'd bite her, sting her.

She felt the feathery touch again at her ankle, but

stronger now, and her foot was jerked out from under her, she was falling.

Squealing, bursting into sobs, chest racked with pain, she fell headlong into a patch of scree, the earth slapping up at her, slamming the breath from her, rocks scraping her arms and legs as if she were being dragged down a giant swatch of sandpaper.

She *was* being dragged. She was moving backward.

The metallic taste of her own blood in her mouth . . . she looked over her shoulder and saw her right leg was lifted into the air, was jerking as if something was tugging at it, but nothing was there – except, overhead, there was a dark blur, like an oversized hummingbird, a smudge in the darkness.

It was moving her the way it had moved the lamp and the camera. It had her in its grip. It was pulling her out from a screen of plant spears that sheltered her neck. Somehow she knew it wanted to get at her spine.

She wrenched away, felt its grip slide off her like living cotton, and the tremor of its fury. *Don't!* it said. *I want to release you. It's what Dr Rofocale wanted, Joanie. We want to let you be yourself and do exactly what you want and never deny yourself anything and renew the Self. Right? Right?*

The brush. Crawl for the brush.

Joanie wriggled on her stomach, like a soldier in no-man's-land, into the plants, hoping she wouldn't put out her eye, hoping she wasn't crawling on to a snake, a scorpion. But that would be better than if that thing got her and got into her head and then climbed out again through her eye.

She was moving through a sheath of sweat, caked in a second skin of dust and sand and blood; her sensations were rasp and itch and hurt. But all that was background to the get-away-from-it feeling, her sense that the thing was hovering over her.

I'm going to punish you for running away from me, it told her. *I'm going to burrow up your ass and sting you in there and then I'm going to play inside you.*

It sent her a sharp mental image of that happening.

She stood up as if electrified, and the cacti she'd crawled into might've been stuffed toys of soft linen for all she felt of its tearing her. She lost a shoe; she ran on through the patch, feeling the spines as distant *pops* somewhere on the exterior of her; they were nothing compared to what the flying thing would do if it caught her.

Its feather touch on the back of her neck – never mind its softness – was a sensation a thousand times uglier than the jab of a three-inch barb into her thigh.

She felt that touch, and felt herself lifted on a hurricane of her own raw fear, carried suddenly out of the brush, into a place of open air and asphalt. She saw lights, and ran toward them. She felt the flying thing near her again, tugging at her leg, but she wrenched loose and kept running, and she heard it hiss in frustration. She couldn't feel anything except the internal hurricane of terror.

Maybe it was three minutes, maybe it was twenty, before the lights flashed around her. Suddenly she was in Jasper. She saw a man, staring, his mouth dropping open, but she ignored him. Some part of her mind told her to look for a certain street, a place where someone had said they'd help her.

You don't think I'm going to let you go, do you?

12

Perry found himself wondering if Lois was safe with him.

He was in the bathroom, washing his face in cold water, trying to wake himself up, and he'd been thinking a little too much.

The thing to do, he told himself, is not think. Just *don't*. Just get through it.

He sloshed cold water on his face, then turned off the tap and leaned his head against the mirror glass to feel its coolness on his skin. He could feel the beads of water warming on his cheeks. It was stifling in the bathroom. But it felt secure.

Lois is alone out there.

Alone? Christ, there were people in the houses all around them. There was a whole town. There was a road with regular truck traffic on it. There was a bus that stopped here; there were phone lines and radios. They weren't isolated. On the other side of those phone lines was every city in the world. Newspapers and televisions and 57 varieties of cops.

So why did it feel like they were all alone with this thing?

A different kind of isolation. The isolation of a whole different consensual reality. Suddenly, Perry and Aunt June had seen into another world, something that lay alongside the familiar world, perhaps, but usually remained unseen. And seeing it changed you, made it as if you spoke a whole different language. The people who populated the world of the familiar wouldn't understand you if you tried to tell them about it. They'd call the pilots rabies, or insect infestation, or psychosis or mass hallucination. There was simply no explaining it to them. They had to see it. They needed a whole different perception of reality. It was hopeless.

He shook his head at his reflection in the mirror. The naked light on the ceiling gave his reflection a pasty, mime-face look. 'No, uh-uh,' he told himself. 'Don't give in to that.'

It was them, buzzing around the house somewhere, putting those thoughts in his head. Thoughts of the futility of trying to contact –

'Perry?' Lois's worried voice from the other side of the door. 'Are you okay?'

'Sure!' He dried his face and left the bathroom. She was standing in the middle of the living room, hugging herself. He smiled at her and said, 'What's the matter? You think I fell in, as my mother used to say?'

'No, I heard you say something.' She turned away, and he could see that she was covering up.

She'd heard him talking to himself, he realized, and she'd been afraid that the pilots had got to him, made him crazy.

She was scared of him.

For a moment he burned with anger at the thought. How could she think . . .

And then he shook the anger out of himself. It could happen to anyone. Anyone could be stung, changed. She was right to be worried, even about him. There was no one they could trust.

They had to be scared of each other.

But he crossed the room and put his arms around her. For a moment she held herself stiff, then she relaxed, nestling against him. 'I'm sorry,' she mumbled into his shoulder.

'Nothing to be sorry about.'

Maybe, he thought, she was right to be scared about him. Him in particular.

They had come so close to taking him over. He felt they had left their footprints on his soul. Maybe planted some less-than-physical seed in him.

He'd almost given in to them. The visions of killing that asshole who –

He wrenched himself away from the thought.

Don't give them grist, he told himself. Don't think about violence. That could attract them. Like flies to decay.

And if they came again, he might give in to them.

On the other hand, maybe it was crazy not to think about violence – defensively. There was no telling how many people in Jasper had been infected. They might just break into the house.

Very suddenly, he made two decisions.

First, he was going to be prepared, somehow, to fight, should one of the pilots come around. He'd find a weapon.

Second, he was leaving town, as soon as possible. He'd find Aunt June, and if she was coming, fine. If not, screw it. He'd take Lois, and they'd get the hell out.

Because he could feel them out there.

A sob from the front door. *Bang*. Another *bang*.

Lois had gone stiff again, looking toward the door. 'Perry. There's someone . . .'

'I hear it.' He heard it again. A sob, a thump. It sounded wrong. It didn't sound like the ordinary way someone knocks at a door. 'Wait,' he said. He went to the kitchen, methodically opened a kitchen drawer. When

Lois heard the knives in the drawer clink, she called, 'Perry!' from the living room, in a quavery voice.

He selected the butcher knife and carried it as casually and unthreateningly as he could manage, so as not to scare Lois, into the living room. Lois was flattened against a wall. 'Perry . . .'

'It's just in case,' he said. He opened the front door.

There was a woman – at least, he thought it was a woman – on the front porch, and she was covered in blood, and scabbed in sand, and there was a black bristling from her in patches, and her eyes were wide and there was foam on her lips and she was shaking.

One of *them*. Had to be.

Perry raised the knife.

'A party,' Aunt June muttered. 'I must be out of my mind.'

It was a nice place, though, made of redwood and red sandstone, with thick amber rugs; the living-room ceiling was two stories up; a stairway circled up to the second-floor landing, which flowed eventually onto a terrace built over the hillside. The house was isolated, surrounded by pine and Douglas fir, but it was lively with overlapping conversations and music recorded from a California 'Mellow Sounds' station: Joni Mitchell, Stephen Stills, Jim Croce, the Eagles. A dull-eyed Indian maid kept a table stocked with canapés and slivers of quiche and an expensive-looking antipasto ringed with slices of imported dry salami. The room smelled of pine wood from a spitting, hissing fireplace made of large rounded riverbed stones, of someone's clove cigarettes, and, faintly, of spilled wine and salami.

There were about thirty people in the living room,

leaning against the bookcases, sitting on the rawhide-leather sofa's cushions and arms, and in the rawhide chairs; most of them were fortyish, or older; there were a few young couples. A single small boy sat on the rug by the fire staring listlessly into it, his head jerking now and then when the logs spat sparks at the black metal screen.

Sandra was on the upper level, leaning on the railing, a glass of white wine in her hand – she'd muttered bitterly when she'd learned that wine and beer were all there was to drink – talking to a paunchy man with a receding hairline and a plaid shirt. Her prospect. Her voice cut brassily through the drone of the other conversations, and now and then someone glanced up at her.

Aunt June stood with her back to the fire, on the other side of the fireplace from the little boy, an untasted glass of wine growing warm in her fingers. She set it on the mantel, beside the awkwardly floral products of someone's pottery class, and said, 'Do you live here?' to the little boy.

Without looking up from the fire, he shook his head. 'My mom couldn't get a sitter and Mrs Bullock – that's whose house it is – she knows us, so she said it's okay.'

'She's decided you're not a troublemaker, huh?'

He shrugged. He might've been about ten. Maybe as old as twelve. His straight brown hair was cut in bangs and grew neatly to cover his ears, like a soft helmet. He had spindly arms and brown eyes, thick dark eyelashes. He wore a red 'alligator' shirt and creased cream-colored trousers and brown loafers, all very adult clothes – adult like his expression. For a moment, remembering how glib Tetty had been, she wondered.

Can't go around suspecting everyone, even little boys.

Or can you . . .

But she relaxed when he said, 'I didn't wanna come.

They finally got *Labyrinth* in at the videostore in Bend. Jim Henson made it. Mom was gonna take me to see it and she never did. She said we could get the tape. I wanted to go get it, but Mom said we had to go to this party.'

June smiled. He was an ordinary, selfish modern kid. 'You like Jim Henson?'

'He does the best puppets. He calls 'em muppets but they're just another kind of puppet. I like puppets. I made some.'

'That's unusual,' Aunt June said. 'Most modern kids aren't much into puppets. But when I was – '

'I bet lots of kids are into puppets,' he interrupted, looking sullen. She'd forgotten that among kids being called unusual is an insult.

'I meant it as a compliment.'

'My mom acts like a puppet now,' he said, glancing venomously across the room. He'd been looking at a group of five middle-aged women. One of them was more animated than the others, 'a big heifer of a woman,' June's father would've said. Her teased-out hair was dyed a lurid red, she had a grummy patina of makeup given vivid direction by fire-engine-red lipstick and luminous green eye shadow; she was wide-shouldered, bulky, unwisely wearing a soft black-leather skirt that emphasized her thick legs.

Looks like a goddamn puppet all right, Aunt June thought. But aloud she said, 'Is that your mom? How's she a puppet these days?'

He didn't say anything for a while. She looked at him and saw he was trying to keep from crying. 'She started dressing like that and . . . she acts like my dad did when he was taking cocaine.'

They didn't exactly 'keep it from the children,' Aunt

June thought. 'So you feel like your mom's not in control of herself, huh?' She modulated her voice carefully to sound interested and sympathetic but not threateningly nosy.

'It's like something's got her inside, like a hand in a puppet,' he said. 'She used to be a – my dad said – "a quiet person." And my dad . . .' His voice broke. 'He's in the hospital. We coulda gone to see my dad and then we coulda gone to the video store.' He looked at her suddenly, as if remembering he was talking to a stranger about personal things.

His anger, she thought, overrode the usual inhibitions. He's angrier than I thought. 'What happened to your dad?'

The boy tapped a fireplace poker in its rack to make it clink against the other irons. After a moment he said, 'He fell down the basement stairs.'

'Was he hurt bad?'

'I don't know. They won't tell me shit.' He glanced at her defiantly to see how she'd take his use of obscenity.

She nodded gravely. 'That sucks.'

He smiled.

'What's your name?' she asked.

'Chris Muggeridge.'

He stressed the last name. Giving last names was more adult. 'My name's June.' She looked at Mrs Muggeridge, and for the first time noticed the woman had a scarf around her neck. Thinking: Maybe she *is* one of them. But she could be manic depressive, could be hormone euphoric from menopause, any number of things to account for a change in look, behavior, loss of self-awareness. The scarf doesn't prove anything either.

But if she is . . . 'You think your mom might be – don't quote me on this – you think she might be sick, Chris?'

'Maybe. I'll bet you're a doctor.'

She looked at him in surprise. 'Good guess. How'd you know? Just because I asked if she was sick?'

'Nope. The way you looked at Mom. Like a doctor trying to make up their mind. I saw a lot of 'em looking at people in the hospital.'

'Huh. Be damned. Yeah, I'm a psychiatrist. Want me to talk to your mom?'

He nodded sharply once, a flicker of pleasure at the corners of his mouth. He was mad at his mom. Sic a doctor on her, served her right. 'But don't tell her.'

'I won't if you won't.' She picked up her glass and crossed to the group standing by the stereo.

What do I think I'm going to learn this way? she wondered. She stood by the racks of tapes and compact discs, pretending to look at their labels. From somewhere in the house she could just make out the smell of marijuana. Not such an old crowd.

She watched the faces of the group of people around Mrs Muggeridge, who was holding forth about something on 'The Colbys,' something about a sordid love triangle. Mrs Muggeridge did a parody of the scene, making the others laugh. 'I mean my *God*,' Mrs Muggeridge was saying, 'she's talking about committing suicide because her father caught her cheating on her husband with a younger man! Can you *believe* the jelly-spined wimpiness of it!'

The others laughed, and June watched them, and wondered: What do I think I'm going to find out?

Some sort of formless hunch had brought her here.

I'm watching the others, she realized. Not Mrs Muggeridge.

There was something too open, too hungry in their

faces when they looked at Mrs Muggeridge. But their eyes had the glaze of TV addicts.

They're just soaking it up, Aunt June realized. She has a sort of . . . not charisma, but grip, sheer dominance maybe.

Looking at the people Mrs Muggeridge held in her thrall, June thought she saw a discomfort in some of them, as if they were struggling. Just the faintest flicker of conflict.

But they stayed.

Did some of the ones who'd been changed have that power – sheer psychic domination? What would they lead the unchanged to? To be changed themselves? But why? It wasn't a Breeder, it couldn't sting them. It couldn't breed, per se, until it broke out of her physically. It could arrange for these others to be stung by Breeders, though. Why would something so quintessentially selfish create all that competition for itself? she wondered.

The other factor. The originating factor, Horescu had called it. The thing that had brought it out in Tetty.

Something that used the changed ones, while making them think they did as they pleased.

Something? What had put that word in her mind?

It implied an entity of some kind.

June realized that Mrs Muggeridge was staring at her.

June smiled at the woman. Mrs Muggeridge didn't smile back. She kept staring, and the others, their uncertain smiles wavering, turned to see what she was staring at. June found herself locked into Mrs Muggeridge's gaze.

The insect gleam was there. But, as with the boy in the sheriff's office, there was a seething emotion there too, behind it. Like the power behind a laser's precision.

It was insect but then again it wasn't. There was an

insect's voracity, an insect's relentless drive and methodical thoroughness when it went about destroying, but insects have no passion. And June could feel the waves of real hatred radiating from this woman.

She's one of them, June thought, her misgivings gone.

She smiled awkwardly and turned away, to find Sandra.

'That *woman*,' June heard Mrs Muggeridge say to the others in her little circle, 'was looking at me as if I was a *bug* or something!' The others laughed.

June was almost to the stairs when Chris Muggeridge popped out of the crowd. 'Hey,' he said, sotto voce. He glanced at his mother, then moved closer to June. 'What did you, um . . .'

She bent, and whispered, 'Chris, do you have any relatives who would pick you up here and not ask any questions?'

His eyes widened. 'My big sister. She moved out. She hates my dad and – '

'Okay. Go upstairs, find the telephone, and call her. You know her number?'

Mouth open, he nodded.

'Good,' June said, softly. 'Call her, ask her to pick you up. But don't tell anyone I told you this. And don't spend any more time with your mom for a while. She's sick, all right.'

She reached out and stroked his hair, and then went up the stairs.

As she went, she noticed that the party had changed key. They do that as the alcohol begins to work. But this one had raised its pitch and its volume louder than usual, especially for a predominantly middle-aged crowd.

She paused at the top of the stairs to watch a group of people beside the snack table just below. There was a young man with long, prematurely gray hair and an

Ichabod Crane face, a brilliant big-toothed smile: Garret Kuntsler. She'd met him earlier, briefly, had an impression of impish confidence.

He was talking to the younger group, a yuppy-ish bunch of couples in their late twenties, early thirties. She looked at the expressions on their faces and felt a chill. The same air of ravenous subjugation.

They were laughing loudly, nervously, at something Kuntsler was saying, some glancing around as if looking for a way out that wasn't there.

Just walk away, she thought. But she knew, somehow, that it wasn't so easy.

A little man in thick glasses perched awkwardly on the arm of a wooden chair beside Kuntsler. He was overdressed, in a frumpy suit and bow tie; he had a bland face and a sheeplike expression. He smiled when everyone laughed, but uncertainly, as if they were laughing at him. In a moment, they were.

'And here's Beadle,' Kuntsler was saying, winking at the others as he hooked a thumb toward the little man. 'The reincarnation of Wally Cox maybe.' Everyone laughed; Beadle smiled dutifully. 'And check out that bow tie!' He reached down and pulled out the bow tie, let it snap back; Beadle nearly fell off his seat, reacting. The laughter was a roar. Beadle turned red but he smiled. 'You can kill flies with that, snap 'em out of the air,' Kuntsler said. As he said this, he turned and looked up at June. She shivered, sensing that the comment was meant for her.

He turned back to Beadle and took one of his ears in his hand. 'I wonder if this snaps back.' He pulled it viciously, and Beadle slapped at his hand. But Kuntsler didn't let go. The others stared, and laughed, but June could see a sort of desperation on their faces; they didn't like this, they wanted to break away from it.

June looked around the party. Out of habit, when she'd come in, she sized up the partners, checking out their body language, verbal vocal signals, their clothing semiotics seeing someone fishing for flattery and a date over here, someone else using a sympathetic ear to vent spleen, a developer trying to one-up another businessman, boasting about a real estate killing. Sex and hubris. The usual.

But now, an electricity had gone through the room, changed the body language, the voices, and she had an impression of mob tension, knots of fear and smoldering fury behind a veneer of raucous laughter and darting glances.

The talk and laughter seemed to roar at her, as if someone had turned up an unseen volume knob, and June felt herself swaying at the edge of panic, and she thought: What's going to happen?

'You were going to kill her,' Lois said, looking at him strangely as she came out of the bathroom. She had a bloody washcloth in her hands. She looked at it and winced, turned, tossed it through the half-open bathroom door into the sink. The girl, Joanie something, was whimpering softly in the bathtub.

'No I wasn't,' Perry said, not sure if it was the truth. 'It was in case she was one of them. I just wanted to be as ready as possible.'

They sat down on the couch. Lois sat farther from him than he would've liked. He glanced at his watch. Ten-thirty. He wondered if he should go get Aunt June or if he should wait for her to come home. If he went to get her, he might miss her.

'The poor thing,' Lois said, looking toward the bathroom. 'I think I got all the spines out. I really think she could've bled to death. I hope those bandages don't come off in the water.'

'I thought she was a crazy woman.'

'She was, for a while. From being scared. God, she looked so relieved when I told her I knew what she was talking about.'

'We should take her with us. There's enough of us who know, someone will believe us.'

Lois was looking at the windows. 'Perry . . .'

'What?'

'There's something I didn't tell you.'

'What's that?'

She looked at the windows, then down at her hands. She pried some crusted blood from under a fingernail with a thumbnail. She seemed to be struggling to keep from trembling.

'I don't know if I should – '

'Lois!'

'Okay. First of all, she says she knows where Wendy is. She says she saw her dying. The way Tetty did.' Her voice broke.

He moved to put his arm around her but she put an upraised hand between them. 'Don't.'

'I'm just – '

'I know, I'm too upset to be touched, even from someone who's comforting me. Wendy was . . . like a lost kid.'

He swallowed his hurt and sat back. 'What was the other thing?'

She looked at the windows. 'She says that she thinks one followed her here. And she thinks it's still around.'

13

Rofocale was kneeling on the rough wooden boards, clutching the flashlight in both his hands, staring at the spotlight circle it made inside the triangle of wood a dozen feet away. The triangle was formed by the peak of the roof and the boards of the attic floor. A circle in a triangle: one of the signs of invocation, he thought.

God, what a mistake to take them as only symbolic.

'You promised I could stay clean,' Rofocale said. 'You promised I could stay myself.'

'I promised nothing,' the dark corner said. 'I said you could remain as you were. That's rather ambiguous, don't you think? And even if you mean only as unclean as you were, I did not say for how long. I have no need, of course, to abide by verbal contracts. But it gives me pleasure to explain to you why you must do as I tell you, for reasons that ultimately are meaninglessly arbitrary and even farcical.' The darkness chuckled. 'The details give me pleasure. I do enjoy you, Rofocale.'

The flashlight felt slippery in his hands. The fear was a vise squeezing his heart. 'I can't be as effective if I'm not myself.'

'You aren't effective anyway. That is why this is happening to you.'

'We couldn't contain it.' Whining now. 'It was simply too *strong*.'

'You didn't follow instructions. You didn't give me what I needed. I needed one of them contained, doctor. They're difficult to control unless you externalize them and trap them. I had plans for a much more efficient liberation of the populace. But you confounded me with your ineptitude, doctor. You lost Tetty's pilot; the first task I gave you, and you lost this one. What a joy it is to prepare you. Oh, I am enjoying this!'

Its exclamation of pleasure set up a viscous perturbation in the air, an ugly resonance that slipped into him, carrying visions of sadistic excess: a glimpse into suffering's deepest pit.

His stomach clenched, the imagery wafting to him like a stench, and he shook himself. 'You can talk to them,' he said. 'Make them come here, make them – '

'I released them. But I don't control them. I can only influence them if they're in the mood. You'll see how it is. It's a question of their joy and mine finding mutuality. You'll see. Go now, Rofocale: go downstairs.' A bray of impish laughter. 'Run along.'

Maybe the light, Rofocale thought. Maybe if I –

He brought the flashlight up and shone its beam into the dark corner.

A hiss of annoyance as the light scattered the shadow to other pockets around the attic. 'That won't work, doctor, you ludicrous fumbler, you funny little boy. There is always a dark corner, somewhere in a room, no matter how bright you make it. In a room or in a man. There is always a place for me.'

He let the flashlight drop from his fingers. The shadows zipped back and pooled where they'd been. It was like pressing your finger into a blob of mercury; it might splash into little droplets, but remove your finger and they'll run together, re-form seamlessly.

His knees ached, his back hurt, he wanted to run, but it all seemed so distant. Again he had the sense that he was dreaming this place. He saw all the mundane proofs of its reality. The blankets of fiberglass insulation between the rafters; the insulation was in a crinkly silvery wrapper with WARM-EVER INC. printed on it, many times over. Between the insulation and the rafters were the gray electrical wires and switch boxes and the flesh-colored TV cable. There was dust in his throat, irritating his nose; there was the smell of the wood.

But none of this helped. It seemed unreal, compared to the shell of helplessness that bound him, the bands of terror that clamped him in place. The images the Lord of Dark Corners thrust into his mind.

'You're a silly little boy,' it said. 'Remember? You were only seven. Look.'

'Don't!' he rasped.

'Remember this? Look! they tied you to the toilet and they –'

He writhed as they replayed the humiliation, the suffering.

And afterward, wrung out, thirty-six years of carefully built up self-esteem shattered, he went willingly downstairs to wait for the pilots. Any change had to be better. Anything.

Hassan was walking down Main Street, hands in his pockets, when he met the old man. He knew instantly that the old man was one of the Higher.

Partly it was the suspicion on the old man's face; it so perfectly mirrored his own. Partly it was just a feeling, a tension. Like you turned two magnets so that their positive poles faced one another, and tried to press them together. They pushed apart. Hassan wanted to avoid this man, but at the same time he was fascinated.

The old man had wind-reddened skin and a balding, sun-mottled head, and roostery jowls. His eyes were almost lost in his squint. He had two bags in his arms. One looked like it contained bottles. The other bag Hassan wasn't sure about.

The two men stopped, face-to-face on the sidewalk, staring at each other. The old man was coming out of the liquor store. 'You ain't gettin' any,' he said.

Hassan said, 'If I want liquor, I buy it myself. Or I drink wine free: we sell wine at Seven-Eleven.'

'I didn't mean liquor.' The old man looked balefully at him. Then he grinned. 'I meant the money.' He was boasting now, Hassan realized. The old man jerked his head at the store behind him. The lights were out, Hassan noticed.

'They closed early tonight,' Hassan said. But he was joking. He knew, now, that the old man had killed the proprietor and robbed the store. Hassan looked at the two bags in his arms.

'They sure did. Closed early!' the old man said, with a laugh that sounded like Uncle Beyrooz's emphysema.

Hassan made a mental note to kill Uncle Beyrooz and his family. He knew where Beyrooz kept his money. Beyrooz didn't trust banks. Perhaps a fire. Make it look like –

'Did the Talker bring you down here?' the old man asked.

The Talker? He meant the voice that came sometimes, with its promptings and suggestions. 'I don't listen to that voice unless I want to.'

The old man wheezed his amusement. He shifted to accommodate his bags. 'You think you work for yourself, huh? Boy, how many times in my life did I think I was working for myself. Left the navy and started my sheet-metal business, thought I was working for myself. No sir. Nup. What with taxes and – well, you just don't never work for yourself really, now do ya? Nup. The Talker he's always there. He sent some fellas over to that party. Well, one of them was a lady. People'll are doing what He wants.'

Hassan knew what the old man was referring to. They all listened in when the Talker talked to the others; it was like a CB radio frequency. Hassan had had a truck driver come in to the 7-Eleven sometimes who told him about the funny things he heard on the CB. Hassan made a mental note to kill the truck driver next time. He carried color televisions in his truck. 'I heard them. He told them to go to the party because they had that talent. For making people do what they want. It made sense for *them* to go. Then they have power. For me, I can't talk to people like that, I don't have that talent. I don't go to the party.' He shrugged. 'But I go where I want.'

'Sure.' Wheeze. 'Sure ya do.'

Annoyed, Hassan said, 'Am I the foolish one here? You stand with these bags and the dead man in there. If the sheriff comes . . .'

'You didn't pay attention to that one, huh. Sheriff is one of the Higher now. He's gonna block off the roads so we can finish up here. He's working on the phone lines now. And why? Because the Talker suggested it. Do what we want? Shit!'

A car passed behind them. It streaked past without headlights, a ton-and-a-half of cold metal flying through the darkness, flagrantly ignoring the speed limit. More of the Higher. The old man's wheezing laughter grated on Hassan. He felt the sweet redness come on him again.

'Don't you even think about it. I got a nice little thirty-two in my back pocket,' the old man said, his voice flat.

The other bag was filled with money.

'I'm telling you,' the old man said, about to put down the bags so he could reach for the gun. 'I've got the – '

Work with the tools at hand, the Talker said in Persian. *You can do wonders with any old thing if you use it right!*

Hassan stepped in, took a bottle from one of the old man's bags; grasping it by the neck, he smashed the bottle on the mottled forehead. Amber liquid splashed. The old man dropped the bags and yelled. Glass broke on the sidewalk. The old man fumbled for the gun. A cloud of liquor fumes rose as Hassan pressed his advantages and shoved the broken edges of the bottle into the old man's face, twisting it, working it into all those folds of flesh to get at the wrinkle-sheltered eyes. The old man screamed and clawed at his face.

Hassan drew his arm back and thrust the jagged glass into the red jowly neck, taking pleasure in destroying something so ugly.

Really, he was improving the world, bit by bit.

The old man fell, neck pumping his stinking red life, and Hassan dropped the bottle, picked up the sack of money. The bottom was wet, coming apart with the tequila splashed from the other sack, so Hassan had to hold it underneath, getting his hands wet and sticky. 'Clumsy old man!' He kicked the old man's shaking carcass.

The old man's body gave a tremor, and his single intact eye bulged.

Hassan ran. It was best not to be there when the Breeder broke free. He might remember.

And there was so much to do.

Albright stood on a hummock of sand; it held its shape with a network of ground-clinging vines. He wondered vaguely if it were an Indian grave barrow of some kind. That would be appropriate.

He was looking through the Joshuas at the flames shimmying up the wreckage of the phone pole, the fire and the blue sparks that popped now and then lit up the foliage in a shadowy-shaky circle.

That flame could spread, Albright thought. Could get way out of hand. What've we got here? Destruction of public property, arson, illegal demolition. Jasper's phone lines cut.

Dawson has the keys to the cruiser. Saw him put them in his pocket. Maybe, Albright thought, the thing to do would be to hot-wire it. Maybe he should just set off on foot, jog back down the road. This might be his last chance to –

Suddenly Dawson was there, with Lancer so close behind him that in the darkness their bodies blurred together; for a moment they looked like a two-headed man, the right side of both faces lit by the flame-red/flame-blue light from the demolition. 'You sure missed it,' Lancer said. 'Boy, you shoulda seen 'er blow.'

'I saw it. God knows I *heard* it,' Albright said. He was cold. He put his hands in his pocket, thinking: It's not a cold night. So why am I cold?

'Nice 'n' neat,' Dawson said. 'Good explosives.'

Where had he got them? Albright wondered. He didn't ask. He didn't want to hear Dawson say he'd broken in somewhere and stolen them.

'Where, uh, did you learn to do that?' Albright asked, as Dawson trudged past him toward the car. 'Demolition, I mean.'

'Korea,' Dawson said. 'Wish I'd known then what I know now. About what the world is.'

Albright turned to follow them, then paused. Looking around, wondering if he could –

'You coming?' Dawson was poised beside the cruiser. His hand wasn't on his gun, nothing like that. But Albright knew he had to forget about running.

'Hell yeah. Let's get it done!' Albright said, in his best false heartiness. He walked up to the car.

He could try to arrest them, of course. He had his .38. He could try to get the drop on them.

No, there were two of them, and they were trigger-happy, and Dawson was watching him closely.

He had to play along and wait his chance.

Albright sat up front next to Dawson. Lancer sat in the back, giggling in the darkness.

Dawson switched on the car. The dashboard glow made his face sickly green. He revved the engine but made no move, yet, to take it into the road. Albright looked at the Joshuas. The spreading, licking flames.

'Red niggers,' Lancer said, as if he simply liked the sound of it. 'Red niggers'll kill us in our fucking beds.'

'They're not that stupid,' Dawson said. 'They work with the KGB, you know it and I know it. They're too clever to do anything like that. But they'll destroy us just the same, slowly like, working with the others. Starting with the election. The assholes organizing that Indian vote, they're smug. But they got a surprise coming. Lord, they sure do. Isolate 'em, kill their leaders, they'll come around. After tonight the fucking Indians'll be scared *not* to vote for me.'

Albright looked at Dawson and then quickly looked away. Dawson and Lancer had always had that undercurrent of racism. But this was something completely different. This was . . .

They're around the goddamn bend, Albright thought.

The KGB? Is that really what he said? He thinks the KGB is in this! He thinks if he kills a few Indians, the others'll vote for him!

A blaze of light; Albright's eyes hurt, and for a moment he thought they'd turned a flashlight in his eyes.

But it was the car's interior light. Dawson had turned it on to look at a map he'd taken from the glove box. 'Got all the power lines marked on here,' Dawson muttered, bending over the map. He'd spread it on the seat between them.

The back of his neck was exposed. There was a white swelling there with a red dot in its center. Like an oversized bee sting.

On a hunch, Albright looked at Lancer, who was obligingly looking out the left-hand window. Same mark on his neck.

Albright felt a chill so deep it merged with nausea.

'There it is,' Dawson was saying. 'Sperling Road.'

He folded up the map, put it in the glove compartment, turned off the overhead light.

He started the car and drove. The gravel crunched under the tires; it spanged and rattled under the fenders. 'What we're gonna do,' Dawson said, 'is on our way to blow that power pole, we're gonna be going by Zaggy's place and after that Dixie. We pick 'em up. They're ready for this.'

How does he know they're ready for this? Dawson wondered. What happened to him and Lancer? What were the –

'Git him!' Lancer yelled, leaning his elbows on the back of the front seat. 'Run the fucker down!' Meaning the coyote in the road up ahead; the headlights lit green fires in its eyes as it stared at them, looking hypnotized, frozen in the act of crossing the road.

Dawson stomped the accelerator and the car surged forward. The coyote just stared. Dawson angled for him. At the last moment the coyote bolted into the brush.

Wait, Albright thought. Take me with you.

'She might be hysterical,' Perry said.

'You want to take the chance?' Lois stared at the bathroom door. 'She thinks one of them followed her here. Maybe we should take her somewhere. We can leave a note for your – '

'I!' Joanie shouted from the bathroom. Just that single syllable. Then: 'I don't!'

Perry wanted to get up, but his legs felt sodden. Lois stood and moved woodenly toward the bathroom. 'What's the matter, Joanie?' she called through the door.

'*I don't feel good!*' The words were mild, prosaic, like a little kid complaining of the onset of flu. But the edge in her voice said, *I'm going to die*.

Lois went in, and Perry heard water sloshing, glimpsed, through the half-open door, part of Joanie's pallid, swollen, red-pocked body cupped in the old-fashioned tub. Her leg contracted convulsively, and she whimpered.

Lois came out, closing the door behind her. She went straight for the phone, talking breathlessly. 'I think she's got a blood clot or maybe a piece of cactus spine broke off in a vein and – and she can't feel anything in her left leg and part of her arm. And she's having convulsions.' She put the phone to her ear, punched for the operator. 'I'm gonna call an ambulance.' She frowned and hit the receiver, punched operator again. 'Oh God. The phone's dead.'

Perry crossed to her and examined the wall jack. Everything was plugged in as it should be.

'It's them,' Lois said, slamming the phone down. She

hugged herself. An edge of hysteria in her voice as she said, 'They've cut the line. *They must be around the house.*'

He felt leaden with the inertia that came from being afraid to move. As if any movement at all could bring them all swarming, buzzing in on him. 'The phones for the whole area could be – '

The bathroom door slammed shut.

Perry turned to stare at it. Lois was looking past him at the bathroom. She said slowly, 'I saw her in the tub when it slammed. She can't reach the door from there. She didn't do it.'

They heard Joanie cry out. 'Aahhh.' It was a small protest, weak, like a teenage girl might make as her ear was being pierced. 'Aaaah!' Louder, more high pitched. '*Aaaaah!*'

'Perry!' Lois said. Saying it that way was asking him to do something. Anything.

Perry made himself go to the bathroom door. He put his hand on the knob, turned it, pushed. It opened a few inches.

Something pushed back, slamming the door again. And he heard – or perhaps felt, through the metal of the knob – an almost subsonic vibration, a buzzing.

June put the telephone down and told her host, 'Your phone is out.'

The woman looked at her bleary-eyed, and ran a shaky hand over her hair. 'What, dear?'

June couldn't quite hear the words over the pandemonium of the party – the music turned up full blast now, the hoots and shouts and piercing laughter and the squeals, all of it extreme – but she read her lips. 'Your phone – ' But the woman had already turned away, looking for her drink. Something crashed and shattered with an expensive-sounding tinkle from the living room below; the woman didn't seem to care. She walked off, in search of a cocktail.

June spotted Sandra on the other side of the landing, arguing with the little man, Markowitz, the supposed Mr Right, who was shaking his head furiously. He turned away; Sandra grabbed a piece of his plaid flannel shirt, and he turned back, swore at her – June couldn't hear that either but she made it out from his expression – and jerked his shirt away, stalked off. He walked duck-footed, June noticed. She crossed to Sandra, wondering: What was so wonderful about him?

She had her answer when Sandra said, mournfully, 'There goes half a million dollars.'

'We're going too. Let's blow this place, Sandra. It's getting crazy.' Something else smashed in the living room. 'And dangerous.'

Sandra said something June couldn't hear over the wave of hysterical party noise. Sandra bent nearer, shouted it in her ear. 'I'm going to have another go at him! One more! Meet you back here!'

'No, Sandra, really, this is – '

But she was gone, maneuvering through the press of frantic partiers.

The noise rose to an overwhelming peak that threatened to swamp June's control completely. The background of tension had grown impossibly taut; it felt as if the party was about to erupt into a riot.

She saw a door, and headed for it. Maybe a place to retreat to for a while . . .

A few minutes earlier, Ernst and Dolly had awakened together in that same room. It was an office belonging to the man of the house. They'd come here, like June, to escape from the party, but for different reasons. They'd closed the office door, and stoned on Ernst's hashish, they'd lain down on the little office's daybed to make love.

Ernst was a fortyish Swiss who'd come out to Jasper to investigate some property for his father's resort firm; he had long, beauty-shop sculpted brown hair streaked with gray and a rather austere, sharply boned face that didn't go with the hair; it almost looked as if he were wearing a wig. Dolly was a plump raven-haired divorcee given to dangly bead earrings and bead-worked leather skirts; this faint echo of 1960s hip had attracted Ernst, who was nostalgic for the American Summer of Love. He hadn't been here, but he'd seen *Woodstock* six times.

Both having declared the mutuality of their desires – through a variety of euphemisms, like an advocacy of Free Love – they'd made out in a corner of the kitchen for a while, snugly swirled in hashish smoke, and then, looking for privacy, found this little haven for a spot of quick sex.

They'd laid down, wriggling, giggling, pawing at buckles and brassiere hooks – and then they'd both heard the loud buzzing.

A flash of pain and a red-edged darkness. And forty minutes later they'd awakened to find themselves transformed. Still locked in an embrace, but seething with repugnance for one another. They each saw in the other what they despised in themselves: a weary fraud looking for a pathetically cheap escape into sex and trumped-up romance.

But the sexual hormones that had been flowing when they'd lost consciousness – when the thing that clung to the ceiling had stung them – were still in them, and they woke up horny. Aroused and furious; attracted and repelled: somehow, biochemically, the two emotions worked to intensify one another.

'I'm going to have you, you ugly creature,' Ernst hissed, saying something worse in Swiss as he forced his member into her. She squealed and hit him in the face with her small, soft fist.

'You disgusting foreign bastard, fuck me right fucking *now*!' as she dug her nails into his eyes.

He screamed and thrust deeper into her and closed his fingers around her throat.

She gagged and bit hard into his cheek, felt the blood spurt into her mouth. He brought his fist down hard on her nose, breaking it, at the same time thrusting his angry masculinity into her. She reached behind her and found a large, irregular chunk of quartz someone used as a book end, brought its sharp crystal down hard on the top of his head, again and again, as his fingers tightened around her throat so he could barely hear her insisting in a strangled croak, 'Fuck me, you moron!' And they fucked in a welter of blood, each pounding, digging into the flesh of the other, each trying to get at the living core under the sexual sheath.

While the dark corners grew darker in appreciation . . .

June opened the door to the office and heard a scream. High-pitched – she thought it was a woman's scream but then she saw it was the man on the couch screaming as the woman he was driving his genitals into drove a spike of crystal into his skull and blood spurted.

June gagged and looked away.

Felt a psychic pressure from above. Something was up there.

She looked up, saw that the ceiling was a welter of

shifting darkness, like a turbulent pool of oil defying gravity. A Gray Pilot clung to the wall, just beneath it. But it was the shifting pool of darkness that exerted the real power here.

When they die this way, she thought, it gets them. They go to this thing.

She knew it instantly, and she couldn't have explained where the knowledge came from. Somehow it was there, the very air of the room was pregnant with the knowledge: the Lord of Dark Corners is waiting to feed.

'*Hello, June,*' it said. '*Let's talk.*'

When they heard the gurgling, gagging sounds, Perry and Lois decided to break the door down.

There was no thought of going around to the bathroom window. They must have got in that way. They'll be there.

So they pushed on the door, together. They felt it give way, bit by bit, felt the spongy pressure of the thing on the other side pushing back with its will, with its presence. They could feel its essence vibrating to them through the wood, and they wanted to draw back in repugnance. But Joanie was thrashing in the tub.

(What are they *doing* to her? Why is it *taking* so long?)

Until, when Lois was sobbing with exhaustion, the door gave in a little, and Perry could see through the six-inch gap.

One of them was on the ceiling over the tub. Joanie's head was underwater, but she was alive, thrashing. There was a claw-shaped depression in the dingy water, a place where the water wasn't; something invisible displacing it; and the claw-shaped place was pressing her down.

She was reaching up blindly to the edge of the tub, trying to get a grip. Her hand stiffened and a red mark appeared on it – and her hand turned around the wrong way with a nasty *crick*: broken. He could almost hear her silent screaming as her sudden, despairing exhalation made the water bubble.

They don't want to seed her, he thought. They know she was going to die. And there's more than one of them in there.

The door was beginning to give way.

Perry stepped back, pulling Lois with him. The door slammed. She wrenched away from him, staring openmouthed. 'Perry, what are you – '

'She's dead. Gone.' Desperately hoping she'd accept the lie. 'Come on.' He took her by the wrist and led her to the door. 'We can't wait for them anymore.'

'We're going to have to run. They'll follow us.'

He thought: No, they're busy with Joanie. We'll have a minute or so while they finish her, maybe long enough to get away from the house.

He just hoped Lois didn't realize Joanie was, for the moment, still alive.

I left her in there to die, he thought, feeling shame twisting in his gut. And then told himself furiously: Had to. For real. For Lois. Totally, honestly, really had to!

They stepped out on the porch.

A guy with a shotgun was standing there.

'Evan!' Lois blurted.

He was in his early twenties. Stringy blond hair, bulbous nose, thin lips; skinny but with the beginning of a paunch; held one of his pale blue eyes most of the time in a squint; eyebrows so light they were hard to see. He wore a shapeless army jacket and a John Deere cap. Jeans and green rubber hunter's boots.

Remington 12-gauge in his hands. 'I ain't goin' out there alone,' Evan said. 'Wendy was your friend, Lois.'

'Wendy Marsteller?' Perry asked.

Evan's eyes flicked at him. 'Yeah. Who the hell are you?'

'Friend of Lois. I met Wendy once. Listen, uh – ' Got to get the fuck out of here *fast*. But he was afraid of the shotgun.

'She's dead,' Lois told him. 'Someone saw her at Rofocale's new place.'

'I know about her being out there and she ain't dead,' Evan said, all in a rush. 'Just talked to someone who saw her tied up out there. There's a dead girl there too; your friend got 'em mixed up, is all. I can't fuckin' get nobody to go out there with me.' His voice was almost toneless, his expression quizzical, annoyed.

'Forget it, man,' Perry said. 'We got to get out of here. I don't know how much you know of what's going down – '

'I know about the bugs. I seen things.'

'A couple of 'em are here. Understand? We're getting out.' Hard to make his tone easy and reasonable now.

He felt the subsonic vibration in the bones of his feet, his temple, in his teeth. Coming from behind, growing. The buzzing . . .

'They're coming,' Lois said, looking over her shoulder.

'You're coming with me!' Evan barked, pointing the shotgun at them. He backed toward his jeep in the street behind him.

'Okay, sure, anything you say.'

They hurried past him to the car. (Buzzing. Growing.)

'Got to grab his shotgun,' Perry whispered. 'We can't – '

'Perry, you don't have to go. But I'm going out there.'

They stood by the jeep. Evan got in the driver's seat, which didn't make much sense if he was taking them by force. This was their chance to run. But Lois wanted to go with him.

Perry looked at her. 'You got to be kidding.'

'Wendy's out there. He says she's still alive. Who else is going to go?' She was crying now.

'Shit.' He took a deep breath. This wasn't wise. 'Okay. Let's go.'

14

'I don't know if I can make you understand this,' June told the woman. 'But everyone here is in the worst kind of danger. If you'll just look in your office – '

'I had some of that hash too,' the party's host said. 'It *will* make a person paranoid. Have a drink, honey, you'll feel better.'

June turned back to the little bar, and seething with frustration and trembling on the verge of panic, she hurried off to look for Sandra. Giving the office door a wide berth.

The darkness had tried to talk to her. It knew her. It had singled her out. She'd run from there, but it was here too, more diffusely, but here all the same.

The party was rollicking at the edge of her vision; someone slapped someone else with the sharp, distinctive sound of a palm on cheekbone; someone fell, laughing; a glimpse of a glossy red pump jabbing its high heel into a thigh; a bust of John Kennedy knocked from a shelf, smashing; laughter, a blur of leering faces. She had a nightmarish impression that the faces in the crowd were deliberately not looking at her, and yet were watching her with sidelong glances, flicks of their eyes, sniggering as she passed.

She tried the bathroom door, shouting 'Sandra!' through it. A man's voice yelled back, 'She's not in here!' and broke into cackles; someone else inside moaned, 'Please, help me, they're – they won't let me – *wait*!' She made herself move away from the door, found a bedroom;

she'd tried that door before and found it locked. She tried it again – still locked.

But suddenly it opened, and Sandra stepped out, opening the door only a little and pressing herself through, closing it behind her, grinning, her eyes weirdly distant; clutching her imitation-alligator purse to her chest.

'Let's blow this wretched dive,' she said, to June's relief.

Sandra led the way, plowing through the crowd with rude determination. The throb of party noise, yelling, curses, laughter – all of it was given a kind of framework by the music blasting from the stereo. A lugubrious masculine voice singing, 'There's a killer on the road, his brain is squirming like a toad.'

They passed a mirror on the wall of the landing, a small, purely decorative thing above a shelf holding another homemade, exaggeratedly expressive earthtone vase. A buzzing. Buzzing –

The mirror shattered, and the vase split in two. Aunt June leapt back from the flurry of broken glass, almost fell over the railing; felt someone behind her, thought they were trying to help her, but then she felt them pushing – oh God they wanted to push her over the railing.

Sandra grabbed her wrist and pulled her back, along behind her to the stairs. 'Don't dawdle, June.'

June's heart was rebounding in her chest; she had an absurd image of it bouncing off her ribs, hitting her spine, her ribs, her spine.

Down the stairs, between the people on either side, her knees weak, the noise of the party louder yet, laughter and hoarse voices almost drowning the background buzzing. It was hot, hot from bodies and her own fear, sweat tickling her as she edged between them, down the stairs one step at a time.

The lights went out.

Darkness. The voice on the stereo slowed, dropped in pitch, dragged its words syrupy slow. *Riders . . . on the . . . storrrrrrmmm* faded out. The power had been cut. People cheered, whooped. 'Awright!' someone yelled gleefully.

June's bowels contracted. She heard, somewhere in her head, an exclamation of pleasure. The voice of the roiling darkness in the office.

The house was pitch black. And it was as if, with the going of the light, the constraints were thrown off the crowd. What had been seething bubbled over.

A woman screamed. Sandra lit her cigarette lighter to guide them down the stairs. In its gelatinous bowl of light June saw a face on the stairs – and old woman fallen on her side, in a torn velvet dress, her face bloody, her eyes staring, mouthing soundlessly.

June forced herself to ignore her. *Keep going.*

Someone thrust a foot under hers, deliberately tripping her; she managed to keep her footing, cursing them under her breath; someone else poured a drink down the back of her dress; she stiffened for a second, then kept on. Hysterical giggling from somewhere. A flash of thin metal; someone jabbed a brooch pin into her arm: hot pinching pain. She yelped and jerked away, pressed after Sandra, found herself at the bottom of the stairs, in the hall now. Buzzing was louder . . . *crash* as a window broke. More people up ahead. *Smash* as someone broke a bottle. Someone screamed in pain. She glimpsed someone pushing someone else into a hall closet as she passed, several men pressing the door shut on at least four people, giggling wildly as one of them lit a book of matches and tossed it in.

Someone behind her threw a paperback or a shoe – she never knew what it was – that hit her hard in the back of her head, a blaze of pain, flickers danced in her eyes, but she kept to her feet.

Thinking: Stupid, June, stupid, should never have come.

The black pool roiling in the ceiling. Not seen but felt . . .

She heard someone say, calmly, 'Maybe we shouldn't let them leave.'

Oh God. 'Sandra!' June screamed.

And then Sandra had pulled her through the front door and they were hurrying down the steps, running for the car.

Sandra got there first, piled in, and started it, just as June came running up. 'Sorry dear!' Sandra yelled, cheerfully malicious. 'Changed my mind! I've got plans that don't include you!'

June shouted hoarsely after her as Sandra floored the accelerator and the car lunged into the darkness. Not even bothering to turn on her headlights.

June stared after her, amazed, and feeling as lost as any little kid abandoned on a country road at night.

She thought she heard something buzzing.

The transformers hissed blue fire and broken power lines leapt like frantic electric eels, crackling and sparking when they slapped into the twisted grids of the fallen tower. Little pockets of flame leapt up in the sage. Sizzling, spitting, hissing, crackling: the sounds of this new electric beast that had exploded into life in the midst of the desert. It smelled of ozone and ionizing metal and burning brush.

Albright made himself say, 'That oughta keep the bastards guessin',' and glanced at Dawson to see if he believed it, to see if he believed that Albright was one of them. Dawson snorted, and Albright's heart sank.

He knew.

And then a thought crept into his head on tiny legs of ice: He's saving me for something.

Dawson was looking at the shattered power pole, smiling crookedly. Lancer stood behind them, talking excitedly to his Klan buddies, Dixie of the forked beard and tufted eyebrows and deep-set eyes; and what's-his-name, a roosterish little guy with a drooping mouth and freckles and a *USS Nimitz* tattoo on his wiry biceps.

Albright kept his face turned toward the dynamited tower. But his eyes roved through the shadowy brush, wondering which way to run. Because surely the time had come. He couldn't go along to the rally. He'd end up indicted for complicity in murder. Or shot down by an Indian.

Christ, he thought. Dawson's screwed us out of a century of progress. We're on our way to massacre Indians.

'Trouble is,' he ventured, 'the power and the phones going out – maybe it'll make 'em suspicious.'

'Who?' Dawson said, looking at him.

The question surprised Albright.

'The Indians.'

'Oh.' He chuckled. 'Them.' He turned back toward the car. 'Don't worry about it.'

'But – ' Albright called after him. 'They're gonna outnumber us! Don't you think we oughta, uh, head into Jasper, maybe get up a posse of some kind?'

'We ain't gonna go up against 'em like a couple of armies!' Dawson said, pausing to explain to him. But with his back to him. 'We're gonna get a few of them, and get the hell out of there, and then see what else needs doin'.'

Albright realized, then, that Dawson wasn't really trying to cut off the 'red niggers,' not particularly. Not just them.

It was the whole town. It was Jasper. It was Lake Chemeka, the reservation, everything around it. Cut their phone lines so they can't call out.

Why the power lines too? Albright wondered, not for the first time. Why do they want everything . . . dark?

Dawson paused beyond the ring of light and said, a voice from the darkness: 'Albright. Lancer. Let's go.'

To Albright's surprise, Lancer turned toward Dawson and snarled: 'Fuck off, man! Don't be barkin' orders like I'm a fuckin' gook coolie.'

Just like that, Lancer had gone from tagging after Dawson like a happy puppy to a rabid dog snapping at him.

Dawson said, coolly but with just as much authority, 'You get your butt up here or you're gonna be walkin'. I got the keys.'

Lancer stared after him. 'Sure, Sheriff.' His voice said, *We do it your way now but don't fuck with me again.*

Christ, Albright thought. What *happened* to these guys?

Albright felt Lancer's grip on his arm, squeezing hard. 'Come on, "Deputy Albright,"' Lancer said, almost sniggering. 'Let's go git them red niggers.'

Albright jerked his arm loose. Then warned himself: Don't lose your temper. You're outnumbered and these guys are out of their gourds.

'Sure,' he said. 'I was just waitin' for you guys.'

They picked their way through the brush back toward the road; starlight traced clumps of rocks and made sharp silhouettes of yuccas and cacti.

Suddenly Lancer had his sidearm out. He tracked the pistol and fired. The gunshot lit up the little area like a flashbulb and its abbreviated thunder clapped from the stands of rock and twisted trees, and faded. Something in the brush gave a squeak.

Lancer holstered his gun and loped ahead of them. He reached into a clump of tumbleweed, pulled out a jackrabbit, still kicking and squealing. He tossed it on the ground in front of Albright. A good-size jack, its rump a bloody mess, making running motions with its front paws, twitches with its back feet, arching its back in pain.

Lancer and the Klansmen hooted and laughed; the one called Dixie lolled his tongue out when he laughed, clowning it up. Lancer poked at the rabbit's wound with a stick, making it spasm. That set them into an uproar of giggling.

Lancer said, 'Hey, my old lady got this cat, you ever see what they do with a squirrel they get 'em? Lookee here.'

Albright gaped in amazement as Lancer got down on his hands and knees and clamped the back of the panting, dying animal's neck in his teeth, picked it up so that blood dripped on his knees, shook it in his jaws, growling, making it squeal.

'Lancer, goddammit!' Dawson stalked up and snatched the rabbit from his mouth, tossed it into the bushes. 'The fuckin' rally's gonna be over! Let's go!'

Lancer got to his feet, hand straying to his gunbutt.

'I don't like the way you're talkin' to me, Sheriff. Things're changed now. You know that. So don't go. . .'

'Hey,' Albright said. 'I'll wait for you guys at the car. I got to take a pee.'

He stepped into the brush. They were still arguing back

there. Good. He kept going, moving toward the car, thinking, Can I hot-wire it?

No. Dawson had locked it up. No time to break into it and hot-wire it. He'd have to duck into the desert and hope he didn't step on a rattler.

He veered off left, the direction he thought Jasper was.

After about three minutes he stopped, listening. He couldn't hear them arguing anymore. It was so quiet, no animal sounds.

Then he heard it. The sound of several men moving through the underbrush, coming his way.

They knew. They were coming after him.

Everyone cheered when the lights came back on in the barn. They could hear the cheerful rumble of the generator from out back. John Sunwalker came through the barn door, smiling. 'Generator's on,' he said, knowing it was unnecessary. A ripple of laughter from the rally crowd. Someone yelled, 'Your barn door is open, John!' More gentle laughter. He grinned and closed the door behind him.

Lois's Uncle, Marv Rutherford, sat on a hay bale at the back on the flatbed truck they were using as a speaker's platform. There were about sixty people in the barn, most of them Indian men, a few Indian women, a handful of the local liberal politicos – of which only a handful existed anyway – plus Marv Rutherford and his two sons. Rutherford glanced at his watch. Late. Where was Lois? Said she was coming.

Carl Stetson was speaking into the feedback-squawky microphone. Rutherford and John Sunwalker sat behind him, waiting their turn. The others stood or sat on the floor or on the hay bales scattered around the horse barn. It smelled good in there, of horses, straw, pleasantly mildewed wood. Cobwebs on the ceiling were coated in grain dust. Indian children watched and listened from the loft. A few harnesses hung from the rafters, rusty.

It was the barn of Chief Sticky Berries' horse ranch. He sat against the wall, a white-haired man with a leathery face, a perpetual expression of benevolent amusement, his right hand on his grand-daughter's shoulder. He had lived on government compensation for years, and had given up horse breeding in disgust with the government's taxing it.

Sunwalker was full Indian, but he wore suits and kept his hair cropped short and neatly parted. He scrupulously avoided wearing Indian trappings, except for the turquoise and silver string tie he sported at tribal functions; it had been made by the tribal artisans. He was young, college-educated, grim, angry about Indian rights.

Carl 'Little Bear' Stetson, a professional Amerind activist, was really only half Indian, with his lighter skin and green eyes; he nevertheless played up the Indian side, wearing braids and beaded belts. Tonight he wore full tribal costume. He was in his late thirties, had been married four times, was notorious for making flamboyant statements to the press and setting up publicity-hot demonstrations. He wasn't of this tribe; he was a Cherokee, but he spent most of his time traveling on grants from one Indian cause to another. He was not as highly regarded, here, as Sunwalker; he was thought of as a grandstander who might be useful.

His tones rolling with urgency and comradeship, his hand slashing to emphasize each exclamation point, Stetson boomed, 'They're rolling back the Indian rights reforms, one by one! A conservative administration is taking full advantage of the widespread public apathy! Well, my friends, apathy arises from ignorance! If we make sure people are aware of the issues, they'll back us up! To that end, I would like to announce plans for a demonstration at the state capital building in Salem.'

Rutherford let him go on, but he exchanged weary glances with Sunwalker. Rutherford had arranged a meeting with the governor for him and Sunwalker, and a demonstration now might be regarded as an act of bad faith in the governor's office.

When Stetson paused to draw a breath, Sunwalker stood and clapped his hands. The audience clapped enthusiastically, knowing this was the best way to bring the speech to an end, and Sunwalker commandeered the mike.

'A demonstration is a good idea, but at the right time!' he declared. 'Brother Stetson's gifts for organizing are appreciated, and when the time is ripe we'd be grateful if he set up a demonstration for us. My feeling, though, is that it's best we wait till after our conference with the governor. Our mandate tonight is to decide exactly what issues we're going to bring up during that conference. First, of course, there's the main issue, reapportionment of tribal land.'

'There just might be more pressing issues!' Stetson cut in, standing up. 'Issues of life and death! I've heard you have a Ku Klux Klan hereabouts that harasses Amerinds, and that the local sheriff is involved in it! Obviously that man should be removed from office! Violence against Amerinds cannot be tolerated for a single day.'

Sunwalker broke in, 'Racism is part and parcel of all our issues and you can be sure every aspect of it will be brought up at the conference. But at the moment we have no real problem with violence.'

He broke off, staring at the barn door as it swung open.

It creaked slowly outward, as if blown by some mischievous wind, revealing an apparition in the doorway.

A figure of crackling flame stood there, shaking, framed by the night's darkness: a man set on fire, burning from head to toe. And now he screamed, tearing a great ragged rent in the silence, and pandemonium exploded through the barn.

Rutherford stood and moved as if in a dream toward the door as the barn echoed with cries of horror and disgust and fear and shouts for water, fire extinguishers. Rutherford thought: I know this man.

He could just make out his face through the flame; through the bubbling, blackening of his flesh. It was Albright. A local sheriff's deputy, sheathed in fire, staggering, waving his arms, shrieking as his eyes melted.

Chief Sticky Berries ran up to him with the barn's fire extinguisher as Albright fell to the ground in front of them writhing, crackling, stinking of gasoline and the smell of burning fat. Other men ran outside to see who had done this thing. Rutherford shouted, 'Come back in here, dammit, we don't know who – '

Gunshots. Two, maybe three of them. There was a ring of people around Albright, laying a blanket over him and arguing about how to help him. But at the sound of the gunshots they looked up at the door, then scattered to get away from it. Rutherford ran to the door and pulled it shut. He heard someone groaning in pain outside.

Albright was lying facedown, twitching. He wasn't going to make it. Poor bastard. Rutherford hoped he died soon.

He looked up and saw Sunwalker pulling his shotgun from the cab of his truck, checking the load, heading for the back window.

'John!' Rutherford shouted. 'Hold up, now!'

More bloodshed! Rutherford thought, pushing through the crowd of arguing Indians, trying to catch up with Sunwalker. 'Wait, dammit! We don't know how many of them they are, they could have us surrounded!'

But Sunwalker was already lifting the window, angrily brushing spiderwebs aside, climbing through, shotgun in hand.

'The barn's on fire!' someone shouted.

Shouts of fear. Sobs from one of the women. 'Back here!' the old chief bellowed. 'Follow me! Side door heads into the brush! They can't have too many men back there, terrain's too rough! Come on!'

Stetson was the first one to follow him.

Rutherford saw the flames licking up outside the windows. The bastards were trying to burn them alive in here.

The kids were climbing down from the loft, running to follow the crowd out through the back.

Suddenly Rutherford's sons were following John Sunwalker out the window, the eldest shouting over his shoulder. 'Come on, Dad, let's – '

Boom. Boom. Two shotgun blasts, from out front. 'Goddammit it!' Rutherford yelled. He ran to the front door, skirting the still body of Albright, and too furious to remember his injunctions to the others for caution, pushed the door open and ran out into the night. He glanced at the two Indian men lying facedown in the dirt not far outside the door and looked up at the sound of a car.

He saw a car backing down the narrow access road, without headlights; but in the starlight and the growing light from the burning barn he could see it was the sheriff's car.

John was crouched by the wooden fence, shotgun

pushed through a gap between boards. The gun bucked against his shoulder as he fired at the retreating cruiser. A web of cracks appeared in the windshield of the car, but the car kept going, backing away.

There were two more men lying on the ground by the gate. Caucasians, looked like.

He ran, arriving there, puffing, just as someone else came with a flashlight. John Sunwalker walked up, shotgun cradled in his arms. 'I shot the white men,' he said flatly.

One of the dead white men, in a deputy's uniform, Rutherford knew. Lancer. A jerk. The other one, in the Klansman robes sans hood, he'd never seen before. Nearby was a gas can lying on its side. What they'd used on Albright, and the barn.

Lancer's head gave a jerk. Rutherford thought: He's still alive.

The flashlight beam swung on to Lancer's face. A dead face.

Lancer's right eye bulged. Sank back. Bulged again.

Exploded outward.

Rutherford jumped back, but he felt blood spatter his hands and face. His stomach lurched.

Something had flown, buzzing angrily, from Lancer's eye.

The flying thing clung to the fence post now, its wings moving in a blur as it dried itself . . . as it buzzed, a buzz that you could feel in your bones, a vibration that made you feel unclean.

Openmouthed, they stared at it. After a moment, Sunwalker turned the gun toward it.

It flashed upward, a gray streak, and melted into the night sky.

* * *

Evan switched off the jeep's lights as they drove on to the development's roads. The new streets had bogus-sounding names like Pine Vista Drive and Cactus Flower Place. All the houses were dark. Now that he thought about it, Perry realized that every house they'd passed had been dark.

They'd cut the power too.

Perry sat rigidly in his seat, hands clenched, stomach clenched, bowels clenched, jaws clenched. Quietly furious with everything. Not thinking. Too blindly furious to think. He was a mass of reflexes and trembling impatience, just waiting for this to get over.

It was as if they'd been running to get out of a forest fire; they'd seen the edge of the burning ahead, they were making for it – and suddenly someone came and dragged them by the wrists back into the fire. Sidetracked from the road out of hell.

The thing to do now was not to think about anything. Not to let anything get to him. Just do what he had to do, like it was rote. Because if you thought about those things . . .

Lois put her hand on his arm, but the tension in him made her draw it back.

'There's the place,' Evan said. He nodded toward the second-to-last house on a dead end, Pine Breeze Place. He pulled up across the street from the house and turned off the jeep. They looked at the house as the engine ticked in the darkness. There was a little light coming from the back of the house.

Volcano Rock Estates, on the far side of town – and the lake – from Chemeka Village, was designed as a resort/retirement community, with a security guard and limited public access.

But it had failed; the weather here was too variable for

the affluent, so they'd begun leasing and selling the homes to whoever would take them.

The one Evan had indicated was a big brown and white split-level house, more or less identical to the others. It was surrounded by lawn fringed with bark dust; the red bark dust was tricked out with chunks of volcanic rock and a couple of logs pulled from the river, weathered enough to be picturesque. The grass was in need of cutting. Rofocale's car was in the driveway and, beside it, a white limousine.

The house next door was dark. It had a yard of newly planted grass; at each corner were baby trees held up by splints; a plastic Go-Racer tricycle was overturned in the driveway. It seemed incredible that anything murderous could be going on next door to this house.

The grassy hill behind the houses rose to a line of trees. Beyond the house was another line of trees, and beyond those the desert. Joanie had run that way, Perry thought.

Rofocale's place showed only one light, around the back. It spilled blue white on to the side yard from the back downstairs corner.

'I should have brought a weapon,' Perry said. 'A knife or something.'

'Uh-uh,' Evan said, opening his door. 'I got us covered. Come on.'

Lois got out and followed him. Perry trailed after her, looking wistfully back at the jeep, thinking he might get a tire iron at least.

But they were crossing the bark dust, and then the lawn. The house loomed over them.

Evan went around the corner with no hesitation. Perry wanted to shout, *Go easy, dammit! Slow, quiet, on tiptoes or something!*

But he bit his lip and followed them around the corner.

On the other side was a concrete patio, which had cracked and settled some, already, and held a few pine-needle-dimpled puddles. Double glass doors led on to the patio. The doors were curtained on the inside. The light shone through the offwhite curtains.

'You guys check it out,' Evan whispered, tilting his head toward the glass. 'I'm gonna look around the corner. I think there's, like, a side door over there.'

He turned and hurried off, before Perry could object.

Perry felt a familiar tremulousness in his bones, vibrating in the roots of his teeth. What you felt when the pilots were around, before you heard the actual buzzing.

His scalp contracted on his head; the hair on the back of his neck rose. 'Lois!' he hissed. 'Wait!'

But she was moving to the curtains, peering through the slit into the room on the other side. She looked for two full seconds, then she stepped back and clapped a hand over her mouth, her eyes wide.

Perry moved toward the glass.

She reached out and gripped his shoulder painfully. 'Don't,' she said. 'Don't look.'

15

June was walking down the road under the stars. It was a walk she might have enjoyed, another time. The stars were bright and abundant; the trees lining the road gave out their own aroma and ushered others on the gentle breeze. The soft calls of nocturnal birds laced into one another like a silken fringe on the night. Bats dove and swooped after insects. She wasn't afraid of bats. When she was a little girl, her half-brother, Cornelius, ten years her senior, had told her that bats were the swallows of the night. Or, if she preferred, they were mice with wings.

Cornelius. She almost laughed, remembering him. She hadn't thought of him in years. Tall, pale, long mournful face, yellow snaggly teeth, rumpled tweed suits. A pipe he never managed to keep lit; he liked the literary aura. Her father had muttered more than once that, 'the boy has delusions of grandeur.' Cornelius had been a sort of minor celebrity, for a while, when he'd been writing. He'd written for a pulp magazine called *Weird Tales* and published a couple of dark fantasy novels. Then he'd stopped writing, taken a job teaching nineteenth-century literature, and devoted his free time to a lodge called the Order of the Golden Dawn. He'd written a letter to her mother saying, 'I'm tired of fantasies. I'm going to the heart of fantasy. To the place where magic is real.' Eye-rolling stuff. He had a smug, portentous way about him. 'Darkness has its own rules of ethics and esthetics,' he'd said (at a Christmas dinner!), 'and it is more than the occlusion of light. It is a kingdom.' He'd died at the age of thirty-eight, supposedly of tuberculosis.

He'd had his flaws. He didn't bathe often enough. He was quietly anti-Semitic, given to fits of anxiety about 'the poisoning of the race with miscegenation.' But mostly she remembered him as a charming eccentric. Gloomy but always patient with her. Sometimes willing to tell her stories of a dark world that existed in the Hollow Earth, a subterranean land lit only by phosphorescent fungi and streams of lava and occupied by lordly elves. He'd made the night seem a place of baroque fascination. Not scary, but weirdly elegant. And so she'd never been afraid of the dark.

Until tonight. Tonight she'd seen a living essence of darkness. The darkness of darkness. Or so it had seemed to her.

Now, only starlight kept the darkness at bay with the thinnest of defences. She saw blackness all around her, like the walls of water around the tribe of Moses crossing the Red Sea. But she doubted that a Jehovah held it back for her.

It pressed against the fence of trees lining the road; it tried to get through to her.

Her feet hurt. How long had she been walking, since she'd left the party? She just hoped she were going the right direction. She'd expected to see the lights of Jasper just ahead. Had expected that for some time now.

Lights. She saw them now, through the trees. But no: the lights were moving. Headlight beams, swinging around a corner, pointing her way, bearing down on her.

She stood by the side of the road, paralyzed with indecision. It would be some of them, surely. The ones who moved through the darkness like fish in water. She should run.

But to run – that would mean running into the woods. Into deeper darkness.

Did she hear a buzzing, somewhere?

Run.

Too late. A land rover with a canopy pulled up beside her. Crammed into it were two young men, and two Indians, and a man about her age, behind the wheel. Her heart sank when she saw that one of the Indians carried a shotgun and one of the teenage boys carried a rifle.

'Ma'am . . .' the man behind the wheel said.

If I run now, she thought, they'll shoot me in the back.

The man behind the wheel said, 'I'm Marv Rutherford. Lois's uncle? Unless I'm mistaken, you're Perry's Aunt June. Lois and I drove by you the opposite way when you were carrying some groceries the other morning; she pointed you out to me. She chewed my ears for not offering you a ride. Like to make up for it now if you don't mind jamming in with us. You see, it ain't safe out tonight.'

Perry had to know.

He brushed past Lois and looked through the slit for a full minute, maybe two, trying to understand what he was seeing.

Seven people, lying on the floor and on the sofa. Lying very still, in various positions. And the Gray Pilots crept over them. Seven of them . . . Two of the bodies were sprawled on the sofa, frozen in midconvulsion. The others on the floor, some facedown, some faceup, some with arms thrown over their faces. United in one thing: a puddle of blood looking purplish brown in the light. The light came from the long, silvery high-powered flashlight propped on a stack of books – paperbacks of *Ego Truth* – so it pointed at the ceiling. The light reflected down on the room more or less uniformly. The blood matted the rug, half dried in the overhead brightness. In every visible face, the right eye missing.

One of them was Rofocale. Dead.

Perry couldn't see a Gray Pilot on Rofocale – but a moment later a small, pale, triangular face, its features a miniature blur of Rofocale's, rose from the far side of his head, like a moon rising over a bloodied landscape. The insect thing crept up on to his face, making his cheek wobble with its movements; Perry could see a dimple in the man's flesh where its feet pressed.

On each body the things moved, restless, looking like flies roaming across something rotten. But each fly was at least six inches long and three across. Moving around with the alien purposefulness of flies, as if considering the corpse with their feet, thinking about it with the rooting motions of their heads. Their wings were still – then they fanned nervously. They were still again . . . they fanned . . .

The motion of the things over the dead was horrible; especially seen in total, all seven of them moving together, in patterns random but communicative. There was something primally ugly in the way they moved on the corpses: as if expressing contempt, at the same time enjoying the touch of dead flesh, communing with decay itself.

Bile squirted into Perry's throat. He gagged and his shoulders hunched as he fought to keep from throwing up. He heard them buzzing softly through the glass; the glass of the doors vibrated with it. He wanted to run before they should notice him. But made himself look again, trying to understand what had happened.

There were several people he'd seen before. Rofocale, his perky assistant – what was her name? Lola? – the Japanese boy, Tommy. All of them dead. Others he'd never seen. Wendy wasn't there. A man in a suit and tie, a briefcase fallen near him.

There was blood on a corner of the briefcase, and specks of bluish tissue. As if it had been used as a weapon. He saw, now, a shattered table lamp in the blue-white hand of the girl Lola; shards of its bulb glass were lodged in the face of the man who lay beside her. Blood crusted under fingernails.

Perry realized, then.

One, or several pilots had come, had changed them. They'd all been together in the house, transformed more or less at the same time. Their savagery released, one of them had lashed out at another, a third had become involved, and it had spread like a fire through dry tinder. Perhaps there had been others, victors, long since departed. And the pilots had erupted from the corpses of the fallen.

He was about to turn away, but hesitated, afraid to move, as a surge of buzzing and restlessness in the pilots had them hopping up, wings flurrying, making threatening half charges at one another. He had an impression that three of them were aligning, as if held together in some hidden magnetic field, their lipless mouths opening and shutting like the mouths of puppets, murmuring pieces of what they communicated telepathically. He heard it riding on the swell and ebb of the background buzzing. '. . . to kill alone is freedom . . . to kill together efficiency . . . to kill alone is safety . . . to kill in group is power . . .' As the buzzing grew louder, louder.

The light cast a shadow to one side of the sofa. Something flowed from the shadow; a dark corner spreading. Eclipsing part of the light in the room. It flowed up the wall, on to the ceiling, like dry-ice fog crossed with soot; it flowed into a sort of benedictory shape above the three insect things that moved in alignment. As if it were the medium that connected them – a slow-motion gray-edged black smoke. But it wasn't smoke. It was more like . . .

Like a sick feeling. When you have the flu and you try to imagine what the sickness made visible would look like.

Rofocale's body was one of those under the slow-motion black fog. A sudden surge of buzzing and the corpse's arm twitched, jerked by an invisible hand, and blood oozed from a place where two of the corpse's fingers had been – as the fingers, torn off, flew across the room, slapped from a wall.

As if this were the opening shot of a fusillade, the other bodies began to jerk, torsos lurching, legs drawing up and snapping out straight again, arms flapping like dying fish, the buzzing louder, louder.

The girl's face exploded. As if it were a mask with a charge set off under it, it flew off her head in twirling scraps and a spray of blood and bone . . . The buzzing louder . . .

The pilots were fighting, those aligned with the dark cloud against the others; group rage against independent rage; using telekinesis, working together sometimes for a strength they didn't have individually, shielding themselves with that same strength so that the bodies they perched on took the punishment from the diverted energies.

Rofocale's legs twisted around backward, knees popping out in blue and white bone ends through torn fabric; his face peeled away in strips, ripped methodically from his skull like peeling a fruit.

The insect thing on the guy with the business suit was caught in three prongs of invisible pressure; the body twisted around it as if trying to squirm away, and then began to rip down the middle, blood erupting – and the insect thing was caught, crushed like a thing of papier-mâché balled up in an invisible fist, glutinous clear fluid squirting.

The Japanese boy's gut puffed out like a fast-action soufflé, his shirt and pants peeling back to expose the slick skin, a taut bubble like a fully pregnant belly – bursting, blood splashing upward, entrails like strings of sausages whipping, blood and feces spattering the glass in front of Perry . . . followed a moment later by a severed tongue that stuck to the glass and began to skid slowly down it leaving a smear of red and brown.

Perry turned away, gagging.

The buzzing behind him grew to some kind of peak as he looked for Lois. Where had she –

She came running around the corner, her face contorted by sobbing, gasping, 'I saw Wendy through another window, she's dead, all crushed.'

The buzzing was intolerably loud as he grabbed her wrist. 'We got to get out now, where's Evan?'

Two men stepped around the corner. Evan and a man with long, braided red hair, a forked red beard, a limp grin.

'Charlie Myers,' Lois whispered, staring at them. Myers had a hammer in one hand and a chisel in the other. The chisel was wet.

Evan pointed the shotgun at them.

He grinned and spoke to Charlie without looking away from them, having to yell over the growing buzz, like a sawmill's grinding roar now: 'I told you it'd be simpler if I brought 'em here this way.'

'Wise guys. The wise guys,' Myers said. 'Where's Tetty's old lady and the old doctor biddy?'

'They weren't there. But if we can get them in there to change these two – '

Cold inside with an icy despair, feeling like a man in a blizzard having to force himself to move to keep from freezing to death, Perry began to edge away from them, pulling Lois after him.

The shotgun swiveled to follow him and Myers started toward them, shouting something lost over the grinding all-consuming buzz from the room to their right.

Two things happened fast. The flashlight beyond the glass doors exploded, and darkness swept over them – and then the glass doors themselves shattered outward, glass shrapnel flying, a curtain billowing, blood droplets in an aerosol haze, Evan screaming, dropping the shotgun, clutching at his eyes, Myers cursing, staggering, the buzzing all around them, gray flutterings, Perry feeling lances of pain in his right shoulder and thigh from splinters of glass.

Lois was pulling him away from there, shouting at him to come on, *come on!* as they ran around the corner. Something – maybe several somethings – darting after them in the air, clutching at them with unseen fingers, but still fighting among themselves at the same time, getting in each other's way.

Perry and Lois ignored the pain of the glass fragments and sprinted out toward the jeep. They could see it out on the road, but it didn't seem to get any closer as they ran, and they felt telekinetic fingers tugging at their ankles. Lois pitched forward, fell, skidding on her face. 'Owww!'

Perry bent and helped her, and the buzzing swarmed around them, something darted at him, and he ducked. It missed him, and he heard it cursing him through the buzz buzz buzz. In the starlight, as he slung an arm around

Lois and pulled her to her feet, Perry saw red marks appear on her face, and she screamed – the things were pummeling her with their telekinetic fists. Her nose spurted blood. As if of its own accord, a cut opened on her chin.

'Mine,' something said.

'Mine,' said something else.

There was a flurry of energy discharge overhead, a sense of unseen pressures releasing in the air, a furious buzzing. They were fighting among themselves again, and Perry used the opportunity, pulled Lois into a run.

'Come on!'

She jerked her hand away from him, her panic gone for a moment as she focused on reaching the jeep.

'I can start the jeep!' she was yelling. 'It's like my uncle's, there's a wire you – '

He couldn't hear the rest for the buzzing. They were coming again.

We're not going to make it, he thought.

'You boys are just playing,' Mrs Chilton said. 'I know that.' Her voice quavered. She tried to smile. Clement, Louis, and Terry tittered and pushed her closer to the edge of the pit.

'Snake Ranch,' Terry said to himself, loving the sound of it. 'Snake Ranch. They call it a Snake Ranch.'

'*Snake* Ranch!' Clement said, pushing the lever on the little box that operated Mrs Chilton's electric wheelchair. The chair hummed forward to the edge of the pit, and the rustling from below seemed to increase, as if they were eager for her.

'Scorpion Ranch,' Louis pointed out. Adding, 'Gila Monster Ranch. Tarantula Ranch. Dead Lady Ranch.' Sticking the hat pin into Mrs Chilton's thigh again.

She squealed with pain and tried to wrench free of the lamp wires they'd tied her with.

'She feels the needle,' Clement said. 'She ain't paralyzed.'

'Polio,' Mrs Chilton wailed. 'Ain't that enough hurt in my life you got to do this to me too?'

She was a dried-up rag of an old woman, her face seamed as sunbaked hide, her lower parts spindly, her upper shapeless; her hair thinning out, its few remaining wisps pathetically dyed red blonde, as they had been once. 'I was a beauty queen,' she'd told the boys, with a snapping nod of her head that dismissed all unbelievers. 'I was Miss Pendleton Rodeo. And Bubba, he was a rodeo star.' The boys had come up to the ranch after dark, all alone, which was strange, but they had their pockets stuffed with money, and they'd asked to be shown around the Snake Ranch. Well. Paying customers. Their parents would probably show up, were probably down the road at the store. Dirty little kids, all grubby, one of them with some blood on his shirt, must've cut himself. None of Mrs Chilton's business how their parents took care of them. Paying customers, show 'em the exhibit. Never mind the lights. Use the flashlight and the electric portalamps out in the exhibit sheds. Bubba usually did the showing but he wasn't here, and there were wooden ramps for her wheelchair out to all the exhibits. Showing almost everything advertised on the sun-faded signs out in the highway.

SEE! A HUNGRY SIX-FOOT RATTLER FED HIS LIVING DINNER!

SEE! A NEST OF BLACK SCORPIONS, KILLER OF THE DESERT!

SEE! THE INJUN SNAKE PIT!

SEE! THE COYOTE CAGE! THE TARANTULA BIN! VAMPIRE BATS! THE SNARLING PUMA!

SEE! THE DREAD GILA MONSTER! DESERT SNAKES OF ALL

KINDS! INDIAN ARTIFACTS! PROSPECTOR'S EQUIPMENT! – WE ALSO HAVE FRESH WORMS FOR BAIT –

Well. The vampire bats were actually ordinary insect-eating bats. The six-foot rattler, the puma and coyote had died of old age and ennui. But anyway you could see them stuffed.

They had all the others, alive. Smaller rattlers, sidewinders, gopher snakes, numerous scorpions, several Gila monsters, the spiders, plenty to see. Worth the four dollars admission.

The boys had paid four dollars each, and she'd taken them out to see the scorpions and snakes. They were sort of funny kids, not just being identical, but snickering and acting like they had a big secret. They went out behind the stucco ranch house, her complaining about the power going out, having to use the flashlight as she rolled along the ramps to the old gray wooden building that contained the main exhibits. She'd switched on the battery portalamps, and then rolled along the exhibit cases, pointing out the scorpion terrarium, grudgingly getting a white mouse from the mouse cage to show the boys how the stingers worked – white mice were expensive and that exhibit was usually for a bigger crowd – and then they'd asked to see the Injun Snake Pit.

'Snake Pit's closed,' she told them. 'We only do that for groups with a reservation. Fill it with snakes. Scorpions. Tell the people how the Apaches would dig 'em, fill 'em up with snakes and scorpions, throw prisoners in.' She always felt a little guilty telling about it. It was Bubba's invention, 'for a little color.' Far as she knew the Indians had never done any such thing. 'I can show you the pit but without the snakes it's just a hole in the ground with a dummy of a US cavalryman in it. Not much of a dummy.'

That's when the kids had started getting mean, and she'd noticed one of them toying with Bubba's wallet. Hand-tooled, edged with rawhide thread, made in Mexico, image of a sleepy peon leaning on a hitching rail; she'd've known it anywhere. 'That's my husband's wallet! I *thought* I heard someone in the house! Why you little sneaks, you came in the back door and stole it off the kitchen table! I told that man a thousand times he'd forget his head if it wasn't attached, went into town without his – give it to me!'

'Sure!' Louis had thrown it at her face. It had hit her smack in the cheek. Almost crying with fury, she'd picked it up off her lap and looked into it. Empty. They'd paid her with her own money. Well, with Bubba's drinking money.

'You little bastards! Where are your parents?'

'Fuck you, you old crip!' Clement had yelled. They'd howled with laughter at that.

She'd picked up one of the aluminum grabbers Bubba used for handling the snakes and swung it at them. Louis had pulled it from her, and as the others chivvied her into a corner with the pickax head from the prospector exhibit, Louis had climbed on to a wooden box, pushed the top off a terrarium, used the grabber to snatch up a couple of scorpions, come over and waved them in her face, just out of reach of those stingers.

Giggling.

What was *wrong* with these kids?

They'd used the scorpions to keep her still, found the cord, tied her up, moved her to the edge of the Injun Snake Pit, taking turns guarding her and bringing snakes and scorpions and tarantulas over and tossing them in.

The room was dark, the light had burned out here and Bubba hadn't replaced it because they never used the

Snake Pit anymore. Wooden, cobwebby walls, tin roof, dirt floor, rim around the pit, ten foot deep, twelve feet across. One of the boys had a flashlight and sometimes he went to the edge and looked in with the flashlight and whistled. The light brought a hissing, rustling from below.

She tried to keep calm, tried to think her way out of it. All she had was her brain, her voice. 'You kids think about this: Bubba, he's gonna realize he left his wallet here, right? He's gonna come back here. That's his drinkin' money. He's coming back for it for sure. He carries a gun. Big one.'

'Lying old biddy cripple,' Terry said. 'He didn't have a gun.'

Rustling, dry rustling, below. 'What?' She stared at the boy.

'He didn't have shit,' Terry said. 'Clement hit him onna head with a rock and he fell down and then we dragged him back here.'

They pushed her right to the rim, and shone the light in.

'He was alive when we dragged him in, before we went up to the house,' Louis said. 'But now since we dropped the snakes and stuff in. God, looka that, lady, he's all swollen up and blue. Pus coming out of his eyes. God. You used to kiss that guy? Yuck.'

'Make her kiss him some more,' Clement said.

'No!' Terry said. 'Wait!'

But Louis had already pushed the lever on the control and the goddamn machine that didn't work half the time chose this moment to work, to roll neatly to the edge and pitch down.

'*Bubba!*'

She fell across him. She didn't even try to crawl out. She knew it was useless. They didn't start in stinging and biting her right away. She'd scared them back, some. But after a moment they moved in, rustling, hissing, rattling, chirring, and she felt the bitter smack of their strikes in her meaty places and in a breast, her ankles.

It took her a surprisingly long time to die, and through the waves of nausea, pain, cramps, and paralysis, she had time to hear the boys arguing, one of them shouting, 'You shouldn't have pushed her in! I wanted to play with her awhile first!'

And the other one saying. 'Never mind that. Let's get the grabber things and that leather bag. The town's only a little ways away.'

Then the final wave of pain came rolling in, and the rest of the exhibits closed over her, so that at last she knew what it felt like to be a white mouse.

'I thought you said you could start that thing!' Perry said, hissing it between clenched teeth as he fought to hold the torn flaps together. He was in the backseat; she was in the front, lying across the seats, head under the dashboard. He'd pulled the jeep's convertible top over them and put up the windows, but *they* were pulling on it, tearing it with their invisible grip, unable to reach through it efficiently, it seemed, but shredding it around them.

The buzzing was so loud it made him shake. The windows began to crack; there was an engine sound, a thrumming, as she got the car started. At the same time, accompanying a voiceless howl of frustration, the roof split down the middle. The buzzing –

The car wrenched itself away from its tormentors and whipped out into the street, did a squealing U-turn, burned rubber, and roared down the road. The buzzing receded. After a moment she remembered to turn on the lights.

He leaned back in the passenger seat and put his hand on her shoulder. He felt it shaking under his fingers. She shrugged him off, and he glimpsed tears making snail tracks on her cheeks.

'I just want to get there,' she said, her voice breaking. 'I just want to fucking get there.'

'Where we've got to get is the hell away from Jasper.'

'I'm not going anywhere till I see Uncle Marv.'

'Your uncle and my aunt. God. Where is she? I can't stand the idea of going back to Sandra's but – '

'No way, Perry.'

She slung the car into a sloppy left turn, down a side road.

'Where are you – '

'That party she was going to. Those people live out here. It's near here, so we can swing by, but no way I'm going back to Sandra's.'

She slowed for a series of winding curves leading up into the hills. On one brief stretch of straightaway, a car approached in the opposite lane. Perry squinted at it. 'I don't think that car's got its lights – '

The car swerved at them. A Volvo sedan, dark except for the reflection of the jeep's lights, swerving at them like an animal taking a swipe, gouging at their fender. Metal squealed, sparks flew, tires screamed as the jeep fishtailed with the glancing impact. Perry, gripping the seat with white fingers, heart hammering, glimpsed a dark face in the other vehicle; the man looked Arab, or perhaps Iranian. And then it had swept past them, having rent the side of the jeep. Lois had kept them on the road, just barely.

Perry looked over his shoulder, afraid the car would turn and follow them, try to kill them again. But it continued on, and merged with the darkness.

'Jesus,' Lois said. 'Jesus. I don't know how much more I can – I don't think I can – ' She broke off, shaking her head.

'We have to just *get through it*,' Perry said. 'We just have to be careful and last it out and try not to feel anything at all. We can't feel anything about the stuff we're going to see.'

'Big masculine voice of calm, don't worry, ma'am, everything's under control!' She was breaking down. He could hear it in her voice. The car was unsteady in the lane.

'I'm just as scared as anybody. But I know the only thing to do is – '

'Oh, shut up. Here's the house.' She turned up a new, narrow strip of blacktop that curved through a screen of bushes.

'Shit!' Perry burst out.

A column of flame shifted ponderously into view as they drew around the curve and pulled up in front of the burning house; the house rippled in the blaze of light that was its own death, consumed in blue and golden flame. There was an overturned sports car blocking the front way out of the drive. They'd come by the back, the drive curving up from the road then back down to it. Perry saw the slashed, oozing body of a woman in the front yard. After a chilling moment, Perry realized it wasn't his Aunt June or Sandra. This was a much stouter woman than either.

Shading his eyes against the flame, Perry looked around.

'Sandra's car isn't here. God, I hope Aunt June got out with her.'

'*I'm* getting the fuck out.'

Lois put the car into reverse and, her face set grimly,

turned to look over her shoulder as she backed down the drive.

'Lois, I should look for her.'

'If she's here, she's dead.'

Perry bit off his reply. She backed down the driveway into the road and headed back the way they'd come.

'Where we going now?'

'Shut up.'

There was no real malice in her voice. He had the feeling she just couldn't deal with answering questions.

They found the main highway, and in five minutes more they reached a gravel road. They turned right on to it –

And stopped abruptly, with teeth-jarring suddenness.

Three dark men stood in the road, blinking in the blaze from the headlights, all of them with guns pointed at the jeep.

'That's Chief Sticky Berries!' Lois said with relief as she pointed at a white-haired old man in the middle. She opened the door of the jeep, leaving it idling in park.

'Lois, wait; they could be infected! They could be changed!' He grabbed at her. But she'd piled out, run up to them.

What do I do now, if they attack her? Perry thought. Got no weapons, except the jeep.

He found the seat's lever, pushed the seat forward, climbed in front and into the driver's seat. Thinking: Start the jeep, drive it into them, slowly, force them away from her.

He shifted gears, but then stomped the brake as he saw her run back to him. She got in beside him. 'He's not here. He left with his sons and some other guys to look for me and to go to the sheriff's office, try to use the sheriff's radio. He'll probably look for me over to your place. Sandra's.'

She was panting, barely getting the words out.

'Shit. Looks like we got to go back there. Aunt June'll probably head there too. But I don't want to.'

'Perry. Like I told you before, I don't want to either. But fuck. We have to. Just drive. Okay?'

He thought about the corpse in the tub. 'Shit.' He thought about the pilots, maybe still hovering around the house. 'Fuck.' He thought about Aunt June. He sighed and put the car in reverse. 'Okay.'

16

'This is where Markowitz lives,' Rutherford said. 'If it's the same guy. Markowitz Real Estate Development.'

'I just have a feeling Sandra might have come here. She was obsessed with this man,' June said as they pulled up in front of the Colonial-style house. It looked out of place here, with the split levels around it. With its white columns and eighteenth-century lines. Built recently, and not at all authentic, probably, if you looked close. But in the darkness it looked like an old southern Colonial mansion.

The place was unlit. The front door was wide open.

Come in, it said.

'Well hell,' Rutherford said reluctantly. 'Let's have a look. I guess.'

They got out of the land rover and, hearing an approaching car, looked down the street. It zigzagged down the road, driving past them. A convertible with an old man driving it and a young girl beside him. Dragging a teenage boy behind on a chain. Dragged naked, by his wrists, the boy screamed. The car went around the corner. Driving without lights. They stared after it.

There was a red streak on the street where it had gone.

'Maybe,' Joey said, 'we oughta go after 'em.'

Joey, one of Rutherford's sons, was wearing a football jersey; he looked more like a basketball player. The younger one, a sharp-eyed kid with fear in his voice and an Elvis Costello T-shirt on his chest, was Bryce. The Indians were Sunwalker and Carl Stetson.

'We can't go after 'em every time we see 'em mistreat someone,' Rutherford said sadly. 'We've seen it too much already. We'd just get ourselves killed. One thing at a time.'

'Right,' Stetson said, looking at the dark eaves of the house. 'Fact is, I've said before and I'll say again, our responsibility is to get out of the area and contact the authorities.'

'We're gonna do that, just as soon as we locate this lady's friend,' Sunwalker said. 'We agreed to do it. It was on the way to the sheriff's office. And we got to pick up Marv's niece Lois.'

'I don't think we should even bother going to the sheriff's office to radio anywhere,' Stetson said, his voice edging close to a whine. 'We should get out of town, head for Bend.'

'They'll have the roads blocked,' June said. She said it with conviction, though she wasn't sure how she knew. Perhaps it was her encounters with them, and the thing at the party. She'd had a glimpse into their thinking.

'There are ways through the desert,' Rutherford said. 'They can't cover 'em all. We try to get to that radio first, though. After this stop. Come on, let's check it out so we can get the hell outta here.'

Carrying a flashlight, Rutherford led the way. Sunwalker, June, and the boys followed. Stetson came last. Sunwalker carried a shotgun; Joey carried a deer rifle.

They paused at the porch and shone the light in. The place had been trashed. There was a shattered gilt-frame mirror lying at the foot of the steps. A torn, bloodied yellow curtain lay twisted in the entranceway to the living room.

'Sandra!' June called. 'Are you – '

Stetson clamped a hand over her mouth. 'Dammit, woman! If those things are around –'

June slapped his hand away and glared at him.

Rutherford said, 'They'll know we're here anyway, like as not. Let's look around.'

Stetson raised a hand as if to signal halt. 'I hear something. You hear that? A hissing, kind of?'

June heard it. *Sisssss*.

'Coming from in here,' Rutherford said, stepping into the living room. He stabbed the flashlight beam into the shadows.

The living-room sofa had been slashed open; the gold and green wallpaper had been torn in strips with the randomness of fury. The lamps lay in rubble. Across the room, in the door to the kitchen was a spreading puddle of water; the living-room rug was darkened black in a scallop shape with it. Sunwalker beside him, shotgun levelled at the door, Rutherford led the way to the kitchen. He stepped into the doorway and shone the light inside. June could see his shoulders slump as tension went out of them. 'Just a water faucet left running. Flooded the kitchen. Nobody in here except – oh God.'

Sunwalker pumped the shotgun and raised it to his shoulder. 'Where is it?'

'No, forget it. I thought it was one of those things, but it's a Siamese cat. In the microwave. Very dead.'

June winced. 'In the – don't tell me any more about it.'

They checked the bathroom, the pantry, the dining room, and found no one – just the wreckage. They retraced their steps to the front entrance and – Rutherford and Sunwalker leading – climbed the hall stairs, to the second-floor landing. The gloom seemed to deepen as they went. June thought: The dark thing was here. Maybe it's not here now. But it was here.

They looked in every upstairs room except one. No one around. All that was left was the bedroom.

They stopped in the door to the bedroom. Rutherford's flashlight beam spot-lit a man lying facedown on the bed, his arm thrown forward so his hand drooped over the edge. He was fully dressed, except that he was missing one shoe. A ring of brown encircled him on the rumpled bedclothes.

'I think that's Markowitz,' June said.

Rutherford shone the light around the room, at the closets, the ceilings, the windows. Nothing.

They stepped into the room. June stayed near the door, as Rutherford and Joey went to Markowitz. Rutherford touched his shoulder. 'Man's dead, feels like.' He turned him over and shone the light on him.

His face was locked into an expression of hurt disbelief. He was unscathed, except at the groin, which was matted with blood. Rutherford shone the light into it, rather too impulsively, and they let the body drop.

A deep, ragged crater had been gouged in his groin. His genitals had been entirely cut away.

'It would be crazy to stop for him. For anyone we don't know. And maybe even people we know.'

'Pull over, Perry. I don't want to be like those things.'

He pulled the jeep over, muttering, 'Could be a trap.'

They'd seen the man up ahead, waving his arms, clearly signaling that he needed help, looking desperate. He'd slowed, planning to drive around him.

Perry pulled up about ten yards past the man. He looked into the trees on either side of the road, half expecting some sort of ambush to materialize. 'Not long ago you were saying you just wanted to get there.'

'I thought about it. We've got to scrape up some dignity or we'll end up – oh shit, here he is.'

He was in his late twenties, baby-faced, short brown hair, undernourished mustache. He wore a three-piece suit, his tan jacket now slung over his shoulder, his collar opened, tie spilling from a jacket pocket. He was huffing as he ran up to them, his face blotchy with exertion, butter-colored shirt stained with sweat. 'Thanks, oh God thanks for stopping!' He opened the back door and climbed in behind Perry. 'Let's get out of here, those things could be around.'

Perry drove back on to the road and picked up speed, flooring the accelerator.

'If you're headed into town, you could drop me off at the Thunderegg Motel. My car's there.'

After a moment Lois turned to him. 'What do you know about them? How do you know we're not . . .'

'You're driving with your lights on. They don't do that. They see better in the dark. Headlights confuse their vision. Makes coronas.'

Perry looked at him in the mirror. 'How come you know so much about them?'

The man made a weary whimper and shook his head, leaning back. 'Oh God, oh shit. If you knew.'

'I want to know,' Perry said. 'Or we let you out here.'

'Perry,' Lois began.

'I mean it. I want to know about this guy, Lois.'

The man said, 'Forget it, it's okay. I'm gonna spill my guts to anyone who'll listen. I've had it. Look, my name's Barry Sandestin. I was a vice-president of the Axis Industries R&D department. A subcompany, actually, what we called Worldkey Incorporated.'

'Rofocale's backers,' Perry said.

'Yeah. Sorry to say. You know that asshole?'

'Knew him a little. He's dead.'

Sandestin snorted. 'Not surprised. They were tearing each other apart when I left. I just lit out down the road, boy. Didn't have the keys to the limo. Barker had 'em. They got him.' His voice broke. 'They almost got *me*.'

'What were you people *doing* there?' Lois asked.

Sandestin sighed. 'ESS. You got to understand, Axis was into this executive therapy stuff. Workplace psychology. You name it. Booming parasitic business, feeds off big industry, guys who go around trying to sell the big corporations on new training programs to make workers work harder, make them more efficient, more loyal, more comfortable in their jobs, reduce stress – which makes for greater efficiency in the long run – and, you know, blah-blah-blah. And Rofocale had his ESS thing except he was calling it Loyalty Stimulus because Empathy Sublimation sounded kind of, you know, fascist or something . . .

'And, uh, it wasn't working that well. Our test subjects hated the hell out of it. We were about to drop him. And he was almost broke. Had some lawsuits, a lot of debts. So then he called us up and said he had a big breakthrough, something new. And we came out and talked to this girl Tetty we met before when she started out in his therapy. And she really was different. Smarter, more articulate. Cunning too. At first, she seemed like a miracle. Some of us thought she'd been acting before. But Rofocale talked a good game, talked us into supporting his new program. You got to understand about Axis. It's a multinational, see.'

It started out like Union Carbide, he explained (almost chattering it out, talking nervously over his fear, talking to give pattern to chaos, meaning to a nightmare). And diversified, gobbling up other companies at every opportunity, making Beatrice look small beside it. But a multinational is almost too big to manage; it's unwieldy, given to bottlenecks between its various parts, and with so many employees there's always someone eager to sell out to another company, taking information and contacts with them. New employees meant costly training delays. The core of powerful motivation, Rofocale said, was self-interest. Good salaries and benefits weren't enough anymore; some ruthless competitor would always offer better.

The trick, Rofocale said, was to see to it that the employee or exec invariably viewed the best interests of the company as his own best interests. That was to be achieved with something called Identity Imprinting. Essentially a form of brainwashing combined with drug therapy, and disguised as a routine job-motivational-therapy program. After Identity Imprinting – training the employees to think of the company as an extension of themselves – the self-interest gene was activated through, Axis were told, 'a chemical stimulus.' One to be extracted from the Gray Pilots . . .

'You're wondering how we justified all this to ourselves, huh? Playing God with people's lives?' Sandestin asked. 'You don't know the half of what we have to justify, man. But the bottom line was, management ate it up, because Rofocale "absolutely guaranteed" to provide employees who'd be Axis fanatics. Worked ruthlessly and obsessively for the corporation, and only that one, you know – to death. It ain't that unthinkable, the way things are now, believe me. Things have changed in the eighties.'

In the new world of the multinational, Sandestin said, the corporation's top people have discarded patriotic values, except for lip service, and discarded cultural identity. The company is multinational – so are the employees. They no longer regard themselves as citizens of any one country. Below the surface, Sandestin insisted, that's the way it is. Their allegiances are defined by money and privilege and *only* by money and privilege. The multinational itself becomes family and country.

The multinational will no longer tolerate execs who are stricken by inexplicable changes in attitude and who depart to cooperate with environmentalists or investigative journalists. You need gritty pragmatism to accept the third-world sweat shops where Axis pays a third of minimum wage, with long hours and no benefits; to shrug off the necessity of whitewashing your low-level employees' exposures to cancer-causing toxics in chemical factories; to embrace Axis's plans to sidestep toxic-waste-disposal regulations; to approve Axis's union busting. And certainly Axis will no longer tolerate employees with even the faint potential of cooperating with IRS investigations.

Only the most ruthless, rigidly devoted employees will do for today's modern new multinationals . . .

'Funny thing is,' Sandestin said. 'At first, I wanted to take the treatment myself. 'Cause I couldn't stand myself anymore after I found out some things about the company. Subversion of the democratic process through lobbying. Working with the CIA, and with dictators who tortured people because we needed the resources from those countries at the cheap prices we were getting them. I was all screwed up with guilt when I found out. And I could see how Rofocale's treatment would shift things around, change your perspective, you'd lose your guilt. I mean, I noticed how easy biochemical things could change your attitude about what's real and what's right. Like, I used to fantasize about having an affair with my secretary. When I was horny, it seemed like a safe, harmless thing, if I could do it discreetly. So I did it. I seduced her, and the first time we did it, right after the ejaculation, everything looked different. I saw that it was a big complication, that it could screw up her life and mine. When I was horny, I couldn't see it anymore. My hormones gave me a whole different vision of reality, and of right and wrong. And when I gave up cigarettes! Shit, for a month after I gave them up, everyone I met was an asshole. I was *sure* they were an asshole. They deserved to be snapped at, screamed at, slapped if I could get away with it. It was my body, its craving for nicotine. Shifted my whole worldview. So I figured his treatment had a chance of working, and it'd be an escape into – '

'Christ, Sandestin, enough about you,' Perry said. 'What *happened*?'

'Sure, I was coming to that. See, the whole thing was scaring us, anyway,' Sandestin went on. 'When we saw the pilots, we almost blew it off right there. But management said stiff upper lip, right? We thought we could capture the pilots, extract the brain-changing stuff, separate out the parts that make people violent, keep the parts that make them ruthlessly pragmatic. Synthesize it later, right? Only the useful part and the scary part turned out to be inseparable. And every time we had someone to send up to our new extraction lab – built at a staggering cost, let me tell you – they escaped. We couldn't control the subjects. Rofocale said we'd busted open the "floodgates of the unconscious." And what came out wouldn't be controlled. So we were giving up. Wrapping things up, closing it down, and Rofocale – I guess he was desperate – tried to capture one his own way, using torture and this web he developed with some synthetics guy, and it didn't work and the damn thing got out and – '

He broke off, staring into the middle distance. 'After I saw the pilots for the first time, I tried to talk to Rofocale, in private. I said – I guess I was a little out of my gourd, I was taking uppers then – and I said, "Hey. That thing is something . . . supernatural. I mean, when they're around, you ever notice how the room kind of gets darker and all, and hey, maybe we're fucking with something really, you know . . . *evil*." That's what I said. I *told* him! He said I was paranoid from taking uppers. But let me tell you, I never believed in evil before but now – *oh God shit fuck!*'

He shrieked it, and pointed at an upper corner of the windshield. There were two little black legs and between them a tiny heart-shaped face, upside down. Perry looked up into it, from two feet away, and recognized a version of Rofocale's features. His hands became vises on the wheel.

'They're on the roof! They're coming to shut me up!' Sandestin screamed.

A buzzing. The windshield cracked, just below the pilot. The crack continued down the glass.

Lois yelled, 'Shit, Perry, *do* something!'

He swerved the car hard right, and left, so it fishtailed and he had to fight to keep from piling into the ditch. The pilot was dislodged from the roof and slid down the glass, turned, wings blurring, buzzing angrily, just in front of him. An irregularly round crack appeared in the glass around its head. Another circle cracked around that, and another, a web of cracks growing with the pilot at its center.

A truck was coming down the road the other way; a semitruck without a trailer, running with its lights blazing. Perry swerved into the oncoming lane, driving at the truck. The truck blasted its horn. Perry hit the brakes, sharply, so that Lois had to grab the dashboard and the tires squealed, the car skating . . .

The pilot was pitched forward, turning end over end,

and as Perry drove back into the right lane he saw the thing smash into the grille of the oncoming truck. Swack: It was a gray splash. The truck thundered past them.

Shaking, Perry drove on, around a long curve. On the other side of the curve, just ahead, was Jasper. Some of it was burning.

Bryce was in the metal bed behind the backseat of the land rover, sitting on a box of tools. Joey, Sunwalker, and Stetson were crammed into the backseat itself; June and Rutherford rode up front. They pulled away from the sheriff's office. 'I told you the radio would be busted,' Stetson said.

'Fire up ahead,' Rutherford noted, nodding at the blue and red tongues flickering in the smashed-out windows of the bar. The firelight played over the body of the man lying in the doorway – the back of his head shot away – and over the otherwise darkened street as they drove past.

'The other bar's burning too,' Sunwalker said. 'And the Wild West Museum.' His voice was desultory, even amused. He didn't give a damn for the bars or the Wild West Museum. 'I hope they burn the housing project.'

'Be okay with me if they get the people out first,' Bryce said.

'Big of you,' June said.

Rutherford pulled up at the corner of Sandra's street, angling to turn. 'This it?'

'Wait,' she said.

She was looking down the road, toward the slaughterhouse. She thought she'd seen, in the sweep of their headlights, a cherry-top red glint.

'Look, lady,' Stetson began. 'We can't ride around on your whim all night, we got to get the fuck out of town.'

'I think I saw the sheriff's car,' June said.

Silence. Then, his voice chilled, Sunwalker said, 'Let's check it out. But cut the lights, Marv.'

'Yeah, okay.' Rutherford cut off the lights and pulled the land rover back on to the highway, driving slowly, for minimum noise, up the road to the slaughterhouse.

The slaughterhouse was unlit; the glazed, dust-coated windows, high and rectangular, were dark. June could just make out the thick metal mesh in them, guarding against burglars. The building was in two red brick, one-story wings. In the dimness it might have been made of blocks of raw, dirty meat. On the far side a mistletoe-choked oaktree bent over the roof of the slaughterhouse, holding an armful of darkness like a diabolic benediction above the building. Brush and heavy rabbit grass grew untended on the back and nearer side. The dirt access road ran a hundred yards from the highway through a field of thistles, curving into the crotch of the two brick wings, where the ground had been beaten into an impromptu parking lot of dusty ruts and gravel-filled potholes.

Two fresh pathways, tire-wide, led in perfect parallel off the dirt road and into the rabbit grass; silvery in the starlight, the car tracks led up to the slaughterhouse and around behind it. 'Car tracks going behind the slaughterhouse,' Sunwalker said. 'Dawson's back there. I can feel the son of a bitch back there.'

Rutherford nodded. 'Chances are. Or more likely in the slaughterhouse. He's in there, up to something ugly.'

Stetson began, 'How about you fellas – '

'We keep an eye on it,' Sunwalker interrupted dryly, 'while you take the car and drive off to get help. That what you were going to suggest?'

Stetson scowled and shrugged.

Quietly, Sunwalker got out of the car. He checked the load on his shotgun. 'Never thought lawmen were pigs. Sheriff Dawson, though; he's in the right place for him.'

June nodded. 'He's a pig. He's worse, now. But if we kill him, we lose our only definite immediate opportunity to capture one of them. We're going to need help here. We've got to convince the authorities about what's going on and capturing one of those things'll be proof – '

'When they see the bodies,' Sunwalker said, 'they'll be convinced we need help. They'll come and check the situation out. *You* want him for scientific reasons. Fuck that. I'm going to kill the asshole.'

June looked at Rutherford. He shook his head. 'If Dawson was still human, I'd say don't kill him no matter what he's done. I'd say capture him. But he isn't human.'

That's debatable, she thought. Aloud she said: 'But studying them is the way we'll – '

She broke off, seeing that they were all getting out of the car, ignoring her, moving silently towards the slaughterhouse. Stetson looked regretfully back at her, as if thinking he wanted to stay, for all the wrong reasons. But his pride wouldn't let him.

I should go with them, she thought. Safety in numbers.

But she sat in the darkened land rover. It smelled of leather and vinyl and dirty socks and old beer and gasoline.

The darkness held the land in thrall. Looking in the rearview mirror, she saw miniaturized flames cavorting in the distance like tiny glowing cartoon characters.

Looking at the men walking toward the slaughterhouse, her eye was caught by an anomalous shape in the rabbit grass beside the road, about a hundred feet behind them and fifty from the car.

It was the shape of a man. The starlight lit the upper

part of the grass; below, it was dark, as if the grass blades were growing out of a pond of shadows. The grass was pressed into the outline of a reclining man, arms outflung. It might be debris, fallen tree branches, anything, changed by dimness and her imagination into the shape of a man.

Or it might be Dawson, lying there with his pistol, planning to jump up and shoot them from behind.

She didn't think so. If it was anyone human, judging by the outflung arms, the lack of tension in the positioning, it was a corpse.

Perhaps she should shout a warning just in case.

But that would warn Dawson in the slaughterhouse.

She made up her mind. She got out of the land rover and moved down the road toward the man-shadow. She would get just close enough to see if whoever it was – if it were anyone – was alive. Then she'd run to warn Rutherford and the others.

When she was almost adjacent to the man-shadow, she looked up for Rutherford – and saw him lead the others around the corner. They were out of sight. She would have to shout for them. If this were someone lying in wait, by now the ambusher had seen her, was aiming his gun at her.

But looking toward the man-shape, she saw, through a place where chance had parted the grass, a man's hand. The hand was half curled, palm upward, frozen in that posture. An arrow shape of darkness darted on to the hand, pausing in stop-action suddenness on the palm to look around: a lizard. The hand didn't twitch. A corpse.

She walked slowly across the grass toward it, wondering at somehow feeling drawn. Thinking: It could be anyone. It could be Perry.

She stood in the grass, looking down at the body. The lizard skittered away.

It was a teenage boy. Someone she'd never seen. He had fine, prettily drawn features, dark eyes – open and glassy now – dark, cupid's-bow lips, slightly parted, longish curly black hair spilling down over his shoulders, a long, perfectly chiseled nose. Her eyes traveled down his body; he'd been slashed open from sternum to groin. His exposed guts were a tangled wreckage of red and blue. Something moved in them. It wriggled and lifted its pink snout to the light, licked its wetted chops.

She made an involuntary hiss of revulsion. Frightened, the rat whipped sinuously into the grass.

'June.'

She froze. Don't raise your eyes to the boy's face.

'June!' A rasp. The voice faintly tingling her with its familiarity. '*June!*'

Don't look at his –

'*June!*' Pleading.

She looked at his face, and nothing would come out of her mouth, though she tried to shout the sight away.

The corpse had lifted its head a little. Was looking directly at her. 'June!' it said. She could smell its rotting breath.

She knew that voice.

And the features had changed. No, they hadn't changed of themselves, not fundamentally. But a new expression had altered them, given them a mature, focused intensity this boy had probably never had. Shifted into someone else's characteristic expression.

The corpse sat up, guts spilling, making a sound like the sudden squeezing of a grease-filled sponge. It was still looking at her.

'June . . .'

The voice. The expression.

They belonged to her half-brother Cornelius. Dead for almost two decades.

17

'Hi kids,' Sandra said, smiling boozily. 'Come on in.'

Remaining on the porch, Perry and Lois looked at one another. 'Uh,' Perry began, 'is Aunt June . . .'

'Haven't seen her. Said she wanted to look into something and off she went.'

'My uncle,' Lois began. 'Have you – '

'Haven't seen anyone at all,' Sandra interrupted. Still smiling, though a trifle impatient.

'Have you, um, looked in the bathtub?' Lois asked, rather guiltily. As if she'd left a dirty towel on the floor.

'Oh yes,' Sandra said cheerfully, 'I moved her out back. Who was she?'

'Um, we don't know, except she was at Rofocale's place.'

'Another of his victims,' she said, her face hardening. 'Like my poor Tetty. Poor little thing.' She shook her head sadly. 'Well. No use dwelling on it, what?'

'But – ' Perry looked up at the porch roof, then out into the shadows around the house. The Coleman light from inside was inviting. 'I don't know if we want to come in. It took some nerve to just walk up to the house like this. The pilots were here. They – shit, you've got no idea the stuff that happened.'

'Yes, I do. I know what they are,' Sandra said, nodding gravely. 'I saw some things tonight. I'm convinced. But they're gone. June said she could sense when they were around; she said they left here. They're making someone else's life hell, elsewhere in town.' She gestured past him, toward the shifting light of the fires beyond the pine trees. 'They figure we've left. So this is probably the safest place to be.'

Perry was thinking about Joanie. Sandra had put her 'out back.' What did that mean? Tossed the body in the bushes? Buried it? How could she be so casual about it?

After what had happened to Tetty, to all of them, maybe Sandra was simply inured to death.

'Come on in, then,' Sandra said, gesturing a little irritably. 'June said she'd be back here in about an hour. That was about an hour ago so . . . any time now.' She turned and went into the living room, leaving the door open behind her.

'Oh.' Perry started to go into the house.

Lois grabbed his arm, held him back. 'Perry, maybe we should head for the sheriff's office. They said he was going to try to use his radio.'

'She said Aunt June would be back any second. I've got to wait here. I don't think you should go out alone. I don't think either of us should.'

'When we dropped off that guy Sandestin, you see the way he ran to his car? You hear what he said?'

He shrugged. 'He said we were crazy if we stayed one minute more, no matter what. He laid rubber peeling out. I just hope he makes it. He's just as likely to run into – '

'Perry, we keep vacillating about leaving town. But when he did that, it really scared me. It was like he was the mouse with the sense to run when the cat came into the room. All the other mice just sit there staring in terror. And the cat – Perry, I want to find Marv *now*.'

'Look, you could head over there to the sheriff's office, but it's just as likely Marv'll be on his way here. He'll probably come here looking for you.'

She chewed her lip and nodded, once. Reluctantly, she followed him into the house.

Outside, somewhere in the little town, there was a series of gunshots. From a block or two away, moronic laughter.

The Coleman sat on the corner of a beat-up card table, set up near the dark rectangle of the door to the kitchen. Three kitchen chairs were arranged around the table. The shadows thrown by the lantern were deep and long. A deck of cards was laid out. 'I was just thinking you might be coming by,' Sandra said. 'So I set up the table for a game of cards.'

Perry and Lois stared at her. 'Cards?' Lois said.

Perry said, '*Cards?*'

She said, 'Uh-huh. You know, to break up the monotony as we wait.' She took a swig from a pint of gin, emptying it. As expertly as any Bowery drunk. She tossed it into a corner.

Then she sat down at the card table and began to shuffle the deck. The cards made zippering sounds as she shuffled them. *Zii-iip. Zii-iip.*

Perry whistled softly through his teeth in amazement. Play cards? With Aunt June gone? With a dead girl somewhere in back of the house? With killers wandering at random around town? With the pilots out there, somewhere? First a party. Now cards.

He thought, She's drunk, completely numb.

But what else *would* they do while they waited? Chew their nails? 'Yeah okay,' he said.

'Oh Jesus,' Lois muttered. 'How about Trivial Pursuit? Or charades?'

'Why not indeed,' Sandra answered breezily. 'Nothing matters, at this point. Those things out there are going to get us. So why not?'

Lois looked as if she were going to shout at Sandra, so Perry said, quickly, 'Anything to keep our minds busy, Lois. Just for a few minutes.' He sat down to Sandra's right. Lois sat across from him.

Sandra started to shuffle the cards, then frowned at the lamp and put the cards down. She picked up the lamp and carried it to the sofa, balanced it on the sofa's back. Her purse was sitting on a sofa cushion. She opened it, stared inside for a moment, then reached in and took out a cigarette and a lighter. She returned to the card table and sat down.

'It's too dim over here to play cards,' Perry said. 'Without the lamp.'

'The lamp's close enough, dear,' Sandra said, shuffling the cards, the cigarette dancing in a corner of her mouth as she spoke.

'What are we going to play?' Lois asked miserably.

Sandra beamed at her. 'Hearts,' she said.

She dealt out the cards. There was another gunshot from somewhere. Perry went through the motions of playing hearts. A car screeched by out front. He glanced at the window as it went by and saw no headlights. They heard it turn at the corner. Sandra didn't even look up. She kept playing, looking as if she had her life savings bet on the game. Four times, she got up and went to the couch for a fresh cigarette. Perry kept expecting her to bring the pack back with her, but she didn't. He watched her the fourth time. She opened the purse, stared inside for a moment, smiled, then reached in for a cigarette. She came back humming.

'I'm tired of this game,' Sandra said as they finished the first one. 'Right. How about blackjack? It's quick and exciting. It's the one I always play in Reno.'

'Sure,' Lois muttered. 'Anything.'

Three hands of blackjack, and then Sandra went for another cigarette. Perry couldn't bear it anymore. 'Why don't you bring the pack over to the table?'

She looked up from her prolonged scrutiny of the purse's interior. 'Trying to cut back,' she said, after a moment. She smiled, seemed pleased with her own reply. 'Got to keep them inconvenient.'

Forgetting the cigarette, Sandra started for the card table – and then stopped. She turned and looked toward the front window.

'What is it?' Perry asked, tensing. 'You hear something?'

Sandra shook her head. 'No,' she said dreamily. 'Just want a look.'

She went to the window and stared out at the street.

She stood there . . .

Lois looked at Perry. He shrugged. He got up and crossed to Sandra, looking past her.

'Sit down, will you!' Sandra snapped, turning to him. 'You're getting on my nerves.'

Automatically, Perry turned away from the window. But he'd seen someone out there.

Three little boys. Just standing there, at the edge of the street, looking at the house. Dirty-faced but more or less identical. One of them was carrying something.

June and the dead boy were strolling down the road together. She knew that she ought to have run away screaming. But she felt . . . drugged. Like the time she'd been given a shot of Demerol after her operation. As if anything was acceptable in the cool, flowing shadow-draped place the world had become.

A spell, she thought. There's a sort of spell or, anyway, a psychic influence on me. Perhaps to make me helpless.

Maybe any moment he's going to turn to me and begin to choke me.

But the thought didn't frighten her. It was only a small whisper of thought in a distant part of her mind, anyway. Mostly she was thinking about their conversation, and what Cornelius, through the dead boy, had just said to her.

'But if the Lord of Dark Corners owns you now, Cornelius,' she said amiably, 'why is he letting you tell me this?'

His voice was slurred, whiny because he sometimes lost control of pitch. It vacillated up and down like a bassoon in an amateur's hands. 'He can't always control us completely. Everyone he's swallowed up is his, but sometimes we can slip through the cracks.'

That distant, worried part of her mind wondered if he were lying.

She looked at him, but could read nothing. He was not Cornelius physically. Cornelius had inhabited this boy's castoff flesh and made it animate again. But she could not read its animation. His facial expressions were arch, grimly self-pitying, like her half-brother's. His decaying, reluctantly galvanized tissues functioned jerkily, like a dissected frog's legs twitched with a jolt of electricity; his expressions moved slowly and inefficiently; the dead face made a smile into a grimace and thoughtfulness into a look expressing nausea.

They strolled on. His left leg moved gamely, but his right leg was stiff, and had to be dragged ahead: she thought of the old Mummy films. He kept his right arm clasped over the great gash in his belly, now and then his shaky hands absentmindedly tucking a ragged intestine end back in. 'I'm dreadfully sorry about the way I must smell,' he said once.

They were nearing the slaughterhouse. Curious, she looked toward it.

'I sense that your friends are crouching around the back,' Cornelius said. 'And near the front door. They exchanged shots with the sheriff but no one was hit. They've got him more or less pinned down in the freezer. You mustn't let them kill him, not yet. Some of the Higher have stronger personalities than others. He can influence the others, to some extent. They're rogues and uncontrollable, as my Lord found out, but they can be influenced, seduced. They trust Dawson, as much as they can trust anyone, and they can see into his thoughts only as far as he lets them. He could trick them into coming here. You could isolate them in there, destroy them.'

'Why do you want to help me do that? Your Lord cultivated these things. Why does it – '

'The Lord is focused elsewhere. I am acting independently. I wish to put a stop to this to make up for – for having opened the door. Because I gave the summoning text to a young man who admired me, who admired me carnally, and I him . . . and he, in later years, became one of Rofocale's students. He gave it to Rofocale. I am trying to – to purge myself.'

Again she felt the tug of doubt. But she could not trace it. 'How did you come to be like this, Cornelius? I mean, to belong to that thing.'

A crude expression of woe came into his face. 'As Rofocale did. For different reasons. Rofocale was toying with Jungism, using the summoning text to get in touch with his anima. With the symbols of his subconscious. Not believing in the fullness of the Lord's reality. But it was the Lord, though he knew it not, who led Rofocale to your work, to ESS, to the Horescu manuscript. It has always been there, trifling with us where it could. The

Lord of Dark Corners had its hand in evolution, as did the Lord of Light. Do you really suppose that the biological processes are immune from interference on the higher planes? It toyed with the genes and, in some, planted the pilots. The pilots – the Higher – are its own special messenger to the dark places that each thing living contains.'

'Your Lord is a manipulator, then,' June said, trying to get at the under-truths. 'One who tugs us about, plays us and the pilots against one another. Why?'

Cornelius sobbed. 'So that it can feed off souls released in the Higher fury.' His shoulders shook. He paused, and swayed, and clutched at his monumental wound as if at last he could feel its hurt. 'How angry I was at my darling Jason when he left me. In my fury, I tried to kill him. The Lord of Dark Corners was there, hovering in the dark places of my loft – and when Jason fought back, and bore me down . . .' He turned his milky, frozen eyes toward her. His lower jaw wobbled, and yellow, corrupt spittle dripped between each word. 'When Jason killed me, smothered me with a pillow, the Lord *fed*. On *me*. Try to imagine it. What it's like. To be eaten alive forever, June. Always in its jaws, crushed, again and again – swallowed and regurgitated whole and crushed again.'

'Cornelius . . .'

She felt a tightness in her chest, a choking. The druggy feeling, the spell, whatever it was, was lifting. She realized she was talking to a walking corpse. She found herself staring into his ragged-edged wound.

In shadowy places, some of the darkness is always darker than the rest. In the wound, those darkest places coalesced, became an obsidian face grinning at her out of the stinking gap where his guts should have been.

She staggered backward and turned to run.

'June!' Cornelius's voice, begging. She turned back, snagged by some soul-skewering note in it.

The roiling darkness was seething upward like a djinn from a bottle, hissing as it encircled the corpse's head. The Lord had come to reclaim one of its toys.

The darkness arranged itself in a conical seashell shape, the large end enclosing the head, the smaller end draining off into the navel of infinity . . . and she felt a tidal pull, a sense that it was sucking, as if the boy's corpse were a bottle . . .

She saw it in the rhythmic twitches of the corpse's limbs: the essence of Cornelius drawn up through the body, sucked into the cone of darkness.

From inside that darkness, a note of despair and warning: '*June!*'

She turned and ran.

Sandra laid her cards down. She looked towards the front window. Perry found himself wondering if the three kids were out there again.

Sandra said, dreamily, 'You finish without me. I'm going to have a look at something in the kitchen. See if there's anything to eat.' She stood up. The chair made a grating sound. She went into the kitchen, and Perry heard the back door open. Sandra had gone outside.

Lois reached over to him and closed her fingers around his wrist. It wasn't a touch of affection: its white-knuckled grip conveyed urgency. 'Perry, I'm getting too scared to stay around here, even for Uncle Marv. I'm going to – '

'Why did she go outside?' Perry wondered aloud, staring at the kitchen door.

'Goddammit, you're not *listening* to me!' Lois hissed, jerking her hand away from him.

He looked at her, saw tears and anger glistening in her eyes. 'I'm sorry.'

'Forget it. I'm just so tense I feel like I'm going to bust. Maybe if I smoke a cigarette.' She got up, knocking her chair over. She ignored it and went to the sofa, opened Sandra's purse. She frowned. She lifted the purse up beside the Coleman so the light shone into it.

She screamed, so sharply and piercingly the hair rose on the back of Perry's neck and he leapt to his feet. 'What –'

She dropped the purse as if it contained a viper. It fell open, on the back of the couch, and something indeed almost snakelike lolled out, something pink and soft. More like a slug. And a hump of flesh bristling with curly black hairs that . . .

Flesh. Human flesh. A man's genitals, severed whole, like a snail in the shell of Sandra's purse.

Lois staggered back from it, gagging. Perry felt a sympathetic pain at his groin. He stared. *Sandra* . . .

The purse began to move. Sliding slowly down on to the sofa. As if crawling away.

It was only the purse's imbalance. The purse fell on to the sofa cushions, something inside it clinking. Flies buzzed upward as it fell.

As if in a dream, Perry drew nearer, and looked. A .22 pistol. A small, bloodied kitchen knife. The torn flesh lolling in revolting repose, utterly relaxed, as the flies lit on it again, began exploring its ruby-crusty edges.

'Perry!' As much a scream as a vocalization of his name.

He looked up, saw Lois pointing at the open side window.

A small boy was climbing through the window. In his hand was a forked stick, and coiling round the fork in the stick was a four-foot rattlesnake. Making a maracca sound, the snake oozed off the stick, dropped on to the floor, began to weave its way toward Perry and Lois, its slitted eyes glistening, its small, perfect, diamond-marked body exactingly etched, the light sliding on it as it moved.

Perry reached down, forced himself to take the gun – though he had a mental image of the ripped genitals somehow rearing up to sink their own improbable fangs in his hand – and backed toward Lois, thinking: Just get through it. Do what you have to and get through it.

Lois gripped his elbow. The boy in the window was laughing.

No. The boy was at the front door. Same boy, surely. Scorpion in a mechanical gripper. Waving it at them.

'Perry, dammit, come on!' Lois tugged him toward the kitchen as the laughing boy at the front of the room tossed the scorpion at them. It fell end over end and, chirring, landed on its side. It flipped over and ran in a zigzag, stinger tail poised, toward the sofa.

Perry stepped into the kitchen. There was light from the gas stove; all the burners were lit, shedding blue light on Sandra, who stood in the middle of the kitchen with a carving knife in her hands, smiling wistfully. She said brightly, 'I wanted to save you two for something special. But, oh well.'

She came at them, raising the knife.

Perry pointed the gun and pulled the trigger.

Nothing. The safety was on. He fumbled with it, didn't know anything about guns.

Sandra was there, within reach, the knife overhead. Lois was backing away but they heard the rattler behind them.

'Hey lady!'

Sandra turned toward the voice, coming from the back

door. A dirty-faced little boy with another rattler on a stick stood there, his face lit up as if he'd just seen the presents on Christmas morning.

He whipped the stick, the snake wriggled through the air and fell on to Sandra, sinking its teeth into her face. She shrieked in rage and fell heavily on to her back, slashing at the snake with the knife. Lois snatched the gun from Perry and called him an idiot and switched off the safety and fired it at the boy in the back door who was taking something else from a bag. The boy leapt back and ran into the backyard. A rattling from the front room . . .

They skirted Sandra, who writhed, cursing on the floor, and ran across the kitchen. On the back porch a bag writhed with a life of its own. They gave it a wide berth and ran out into the cool, all-encompassing night.

Behind them, in the kitchen, something was buzzing.

'This isn't going to work,' Sunwalker said.

'The woman is crazy,' Stetson said.

They stood in the doorway of the walk-in freezer, just inside; feeling the air move wetly past them as the temperature equalized with the air outside. June and Rutherford and Stetson and Sunwalker and Joey and Bryce, crowded together. Sunwalker and June in front. Dawson was farther inside the freezer, facing them. Twelve feet away.

'Let her speak,' Dawson said, clearly grateful for the delay she represented. 'What's the harm?'

He was backed into the freezer, which had gone mostly defrosted since the power loss. In the indirect light from Dawson's flashlight and the one in Rutherford's hand, the walk-in freezer's interior seemed the slimy, silvery slick dripping insides of some nightmare sea creature's guts. Sides of raw, half-frozen meat hung from hooks behind and to either side of Dawson; thawing, the meat dripped red; the gutted, skinned, headless carcasses of horses and cattle and a pig or two: the marbled, striated meat glistened with moisture; beads of pink water trembled where it marked rows of ribs. June could smell the raw meat beginning to decompose.

Dawson's face was in shadow. For no sane reason, he wore his sunglasses. Sometimes when he moved, they caught a little light and glinted, shades in shadow, alone. His pistol, emptied of rounds, lay on the floor near his booted feet, a puddle of bloody water around it dripping from the slightly swaying side of beef – or was it horse? – that hung above.

Hanging on a peg, on the slicked, icy wall to one side, was a steel hook extruding from a wooden handle: a hand-held hook used for gripping meat. Water ran down the curve of its hook and dripped with tick-tock regularity from its sharp point.

'What you ought to think about,' Dawson was saying, 'is that you guys could be wrong about me. Just think about the possibility. Because if you are – '

'I climbed the tree,' Sunwalker said. 'I looked through the broken window. I saw what you were doing to the girl's body. You can't tell me someone else left it there. I saw you do it. In that hole in her breast.'

'Didn't you ever wanta fuck a titty?' the sheriff asked, chuckling.

'Let me kill him,' Sunwalker said.

June said, 'Wait.'

A fist-sized piece of thawing ice broke off the back wall and fell with a crash to the floor. Everyone but Dawson turned to look that way. Dawson moved behind a pendulous hunk of bleeding meat and grabbed at something.

'He's got the – ' June began.

Sunwalker was stepping to one side, bringing the shotgun to bear – Dawson leapt out of the shadows with the meat hook in his hand. It came arcing down, singing with its passage through the air as it sliced into Sunwalker's shirt, ripped down his chest.

The shotgun going off in that closed place made a painfully loud, deep-voiced smashing sound that rang from the walls as Dawson bent double around the wound and screamed, falling to writhe around the post hole battered straight through him, flinders of bone showing at the gushing exit wound in his back.

His blood ran to pool with cattle blood, horse blood, ice water.

Joey said, 'Oh God, oh shit.'

A buzzing . . .

June shouted, 'Close the goddamn door!'

Stetson jumped through the doorway and closed it part way from the outside, not enough to lock it. Joey grabbed the interior handle.

Face taut, Sunwalker pulled the meat hook from where it had caught on his belt. A streak of blood traced the gash on his chest. 'How badly are you hurt?' June asked him. 'You could get a variety of infections from that hook, you know.'

'It's shallow. I'll get penicillin later. Forget it.' He was staring at Dawson.

Dawson's body went rigid, snapped over on to its back. His eye bulged. He convulsed – and the thing unfolded from his brain, shot upward, stuck itself to a red-streaked shoulder of meat that swayed from Dawson's lunge. It fanned itself and glared at them in the flashlight glow, with its miniature joke of Dawson's face.

The background darkness seemed to thicken, June thought. Was it her imagination?

Sunwalker raised the shotgun. June slapped it down.

'Uh-uh,' she said. 'No way. I'm going to talk to it. Perry said they spoke to him, in that form. They can talk.'

'Let me kill that thing,' Sunwalker said. 'It shouldn't ever be alive, something like that. Just being there, it insults us.'

'We shouldn't be making deals with it, June, for God's sake,' Rutherford said, staring at the pilot.

It buzzed. They felt a vibration ripple through the room, and more ice crashed down from the walls. The pilot looked at the door.

'Forget it,' June told it. 'You're not going anywhere.'

She felt something unseen slap her cheek, stinging hard. She staggered. Joey yelled and his gun went clattering. Sunwalker was already pumping his shotgun and firing. A hunk of meat exploded from the side of beef the pilot had perched on; the stripped carcass swung violently on its hook, as if in pain, while the Gray Pilot buzzed furiously around the ceiling, tugging at the shotgun.

Sunwalker fired again; missed. The round sent shotgun pellets ricocheting between floor and ceiling. Rutherford cursed as two of the small pellets caught him in the neck. The pilot buzzed toward the back of the freezer. 'No way you're going to get this gun away from me!' Sunwalker yelled, reloading. 'My pockets are full of shells!'

In the shadows at the back of the freezer, it buzzed once, angrily, but didn't try to attack them.

The body on the floor steamed slightly. June moved back from the sticky pool growing around it. Gunsmoke scraped at her lungs, and she coughed. She realized she was almost falling-down exhausted. Rutherford reached out to steady her. She told herself: Calm. Calm. She relaxed, leaning against Rutherford.

'I'm going back there,' Sunwalker said.

'I don't think so,' Rutherford said. 'We got it trapped in here. Let's head out, get some scientists, some health authorities – *somebody* out here.'

'No,' June said. 'My second idea is better.' She thought about Cornelius, wondered if he'd been lying. Her stomach did a flip-flop as she remembered him, the boy, the distorted, twitching face.

'It's not going to cooperate with you, lady,' Bryce said.

'Just let me talk to it.' She took a step into the freezer and spoke to the pilot: to the shadows.

'We're in command here,' she told it. 'You can't win past all of us. We will kill you. You have one chance. Bring the others here. The Lord who set you free will help you bring them. They will be suspicious. But they will come. You understand me?'

'Yes . . .' A susurrous voice, almost inaudible, followed by a nearly subsonic buzz she felt in the bones of her skull.

'Will you bring them?'

'No.'

'What do you owe them? If you don't bring them, we will kill you. If you do bring them, they will outnumber us, attack us. You'll have a greater chance to escape. And think about this: why should they survive when you don't?'

'Truth. Thissss isssss truth.'

'This is *insane*,' Joey said.

Bryce's voice cracked when he said, 'Joey's right.' June thought the boy was near breaking down. He'd seen too much. The man burning to death in front of him, Markowitz with his genitals cut away, the woman hanging from the hook in the other room, her throat cut, her breasts slashed open.

She put her hand on his arm. 'It's going to be over soon.'

He shook loose from her. 'What's to keep this thing from tellin' the others with its mind what we're doin' here, huh?' His voice was getting shrill.

'It knows that if the others surround us, attack us, show that they're aware of what we had planned, we'll realize it. And then we'd kill what's left of Dawson here before they kill us.' She looked toward the back of the freezer, and spoke to Dawson's pilot. 'You know that, don't you?'

'Yes. Yezzzzz.'

Rutherford said, 'You can't make deals with the fucking devil and come out a winner. I think we ought to kill it now.'

'No,' the pilot said. 'They are coming here now. The Higher are gathering. I have decided to summon them, because I wish to watch them kill you.'

18

It was Perry who spotted the land rover as they stepped up on to the highway, wondering where to go. 'That's your uncle's, isn't it?' he said. He'd never forget seeing Marv and his sons in the land rover the day he'd met Lois.

That seemed an age ago. Another life. The world had been redefined since then.

Lois had the pistol; she held it in her hand like a woman carrying a clutchbag. They walked up behind the land rover, looking for Marv and Joey and Bryce. Seeing no one, at first. Looking at the slaughterhouse, Perry's heart stammered in its beating. A premonition . . .

'There's a light in the slaughterhouse,' Lois said.

Perry nodded. He'd seen it too. A flicker at the window, like a flashlight beam passing over it.

They stood by the land rover, looking in, and saw Stetson. He was huddled in the backseat, snoring. Lois said, 'It's Carl.' She reached in through the open window and shook the Indian's arm.

He sat up bolt upright, as if startled from a bad dream. He shuddered, and looked at them, blinking. 'Whuh? Whusgonon?'

'You're crazy to sleep out here tonight, Carl,' Lois said. 'Where's Marv?'

'Uh . . .' He passed a hand over his eyes. 'In the slaughterhouse.'

'I was afraid of that,' Lois said, looking toward the building. 'I don't want to have to go in there. I always hated it. And tonight . . .'

'No animals in there tonight except in the freezer,' Stetson said, rubbing his eyes vigorously now. 'And we took the girl down from the hook. Covered her up.' He lowered his hands and looked at her. 'You got a key to this damn thing?'

'The rover? No.'

'Shit.'

'There a lady with them?' Perry asked. 'She's about – '

'You're the kid Perry. Yeah, she's in there.'

Lois sighed. 'Let's go.'

She and Perry turned toward the slaughterhouse, walked down the road. The slaughterhouse loomed up ahead of them. Perry just didn't want to get any closer. But his feet drew him on. It seemed to him, for a moment, as if he were standing still and the slaughterhouse were moving toward him.

Just do it, he told himself. Whatever comes, whatever you have to do, just do it. Don't think, don't look too hard at the things you see, just do what you have to and get out.

'Hi!' the old man shouted cheerily, coming around the corner of the building. Perry recognized him as the old man from the museum. He looked like someone's friendly grandfather, with his suspenders, rolled-up sleeves, smiling eyes. 'Hold up there!' He came toward them. 'Wanta have a word with ya!'

He got within ten feet, smiling, making small talk, and reached behind him.

'Maybe he's just the caretaker,' Lois said.

But looking at the old man, Perry knew what he was. He could feel it. He could hear the buzzing, even if Lois couldn't.

Perry turned and snatched the .22 from Lois's hand, turned to the old man, pointed it at his head, and pulled the trigger. The gun barked, leapt in Perry's hand. The old man's eyes crossed, as if trying to look at the hole between them, and his legs went rubbery. He fell, facedown.

'Perry, Jesus!' Lois put her hands over her mouth and took a step back from Perry.

'Look at his hand. Behind him.'

There was a big handgun in the waist of the old man's baggy pants, at the small of his back. His right hand was on the butt of the gun.

She stared and nodded. 'Do you think he's going to – that one of those things will . . .'

'Probably not.' I shot someone. 'The bullet in the head . . .' I killed someone. 'Probably blew the thing up in there.' Like it was nothing, I shot him in the head.

'Perry, what if you were wrong?'

He didn't want to tell her how he knew he wasn't wrong. That he could feel them. He didn't want her to know they'd established that much connection with him.

Why don't I feel anything? I shot a man! Why don't I –

Perry wrenched the thought away. Don't think about it. Do it. Whatever you have to. He had bent over, pulled back the man's collar. There was a swelling on the back of his neck. 'Yeah. He was stung.'

'Perry, there's more of them!' She pointed. There was a crowd coming across the grass from the road. Maybe forty-five people. Thirty, maybe forty more coming from the opposite side. Men, women, children. Carrying deer rifles, axes, knives, hammers. They came about the same time, from the same two directions, but they didn't look like a single-minded group. The way they moved, glanced at one another; they were each after something for themselves.

In the background, the buzzing. Not the kind you could

hear. But you could feel it. And glimpsed in the air, the pilots, buzzing, zipping nervously, diving in and out of the stars, moving in an unruly cloud toward the door of the slaughterhouse.

Breathlessly, Lois said, 'Perry, maybe they're real people, normal people, hunting the changed ones. Maybe they're not – '

One of the women, a stocky Indian woman in jeans, was in the way of an overweight teenage boy wearing a Bon Jovi T-shirt. The boy impatiently shoved her aside. She turned, slashing with her kitchen knife, and his throat gushed. He wailed and staggered. Someone else smashed the back of his head with a hammer and he went down. They walked over and past him, indifferent. Coming closer to Perry and Lois. Twenty yards. Perry and Lois stared, frozen with not knowing which way to run. Eighteen yards.

'Oh *fuck*!' Lois burst out. She knew, now.

One of the men popped the deer rifle to his shoulder to sight in on Perry.

Their paralysis passed: Perry and Lois turned and ran for the front of the building. A *crack* and chips of brick flew from the corner of the slaughterhouse as they ran past it, across the battered ground that served for a parking lot, up to the open double doorway, like a small barn door with a ramp leading up to it. Where they led the animals to be slaughtered . . .

They ran around the body of another boy with long curly black hair, his gut ripped open from sternum to groin, dead face staring up at the stars as if in awe. They ran up the ramp. Where they led the animals to be slaughtered, Perry thought.

Inside, four kerosene lanterns June had found in a storeroom hung in the four corners of the main room, from meat hooks on the ceiling. They cast a mucus-yellow light around the room, but the shadows were thick, and restless.

It was a wide room with a worn wooden floor, splintery in spots, worn smooth in others, and sagging. An age-grayed wooden railing ran into the room from both sides of the door, intended for shunting animals to the right, into a pen. Another 'chute' ran from the holding pen to a rusty iron harness that hung on chains from the ceiling. On a framework below the ceiling were parallel rows of rusty iron rails studded with work-shiny hooks on wheels. At the back was the big metal door to the freezer. Closed. They looked closer, and the nervous shadows solidified, and they saw they were pilots on the ceiling, crawling along the rusty rafters.

On the far left, in a mesh of shadow, was a stainless-steel meat-cutting saw. It was a thirty-inch rotary saw run by a big engine armatured under the blood-flecked cutting counter.

Beside the freezer door was another door, standing open, and Aunt June leaned in it, hugging herself, talking to Rutherford and a tall Indian with a ripped shirt. 'Perry!' she yelled, catching sight of them.

She started to cross the room, but the Indian reached out and held her back. 'He might be one of them, now. He's got a gun.'

The Indian stepped in front of her and pointed the shotgun at Perry.

'It's okay,' Perry said, raising his hands. 'You can check us over for stings.'

'Those people outside,' Lois began. 'Sunwalker, they're – '

'Lois!' Rutherford stepped up beside Sunwalker,

pushed the gun aside. 'It's all right. I can see my girl is all right. They're okay. You get a sense for 'em.'

'Come on,' June said. 'Before they come in. Out this way – everyone. Come *on*!'

Hassan stood in the center of the room, looking at the door to the corridor, beside the freezer. They were in that corridor, Dawson was telling him. The rest of the Higher, coming in behind him, heard it too.

They're in the corridor, Dawson said.

And the Lord, the One Who Hungers Always, said it too: *They're locked in there. They cannot be reached from behind. The door is weakest on this side.*

We guard the back, Dawson said. *Break into the corridor from this side.*

They are the ones who know about you, the Lord said.

Where was Dawson speaking from? Hassan wondered. From behind the building, he said. But the feel of it was more from the freezer . . .

The others, herded by their own urgent need to kill those who knew about them, poured into the room, looking for the door to the slaughterhouse's back corridor, the corridor where the boy Strandman and Rutherford and the old woman were said to be. The ones who knew . . .

The Higher saw the door and rushed to it. It was locked. A group of them began to batter it. A thick pig-eyed man, battering the door, misjudged his rush, and struck another of the Higher at the door in the small of his back so that he broke his nose on the door. The smaller man with the shattered nose turned and shoved a pistol in the bigger man's gut and pulled the trigger three times. The pig-eyed man went down clutching at the other's eyes, while more of the Higher pushed closer to the door. 'Break it down! They know us; they're in there!'

Hassan felt some of them holding back, urging the others. From somewhere outside the building. Not commanding: the Higher won't stand for that. But influencing. And a sort of vacuum, sucking them in here: the Lord of Dark Corners wanted to feed. And another fight broke out. The seductive energy of rage crackled the air. It coursed around them like a warm fountain. Building, building, charging on itself, reaching for critical mass.

Hassan turned to run back the way they'd come, but someone swung the doors shut from the outside, and Hassan heard the click as they bolted them.

'There are two or three of them out there,' Perry said, looking through the back door, out into the night. He heard a *crack* and ducked back in as a rifle bullet creased the door frame a few inches over his head. 'Fuck!'

'You can die quick or slow!' someone shouted from the brush behind the slaughterhouse. 'If you make us come in for you, you gonna wish you gave yourself up!'

Heart pounding, he pressed himself against the inner wall of the back corridor. Lois stood beside him, chewing a knuckle, her eyes glistening in the reflected glow of Rutherford's flashlight, struggling to keep her head. Beside Lois, Aunt June was hunkered down, hugging her knees, her eyes shut, looking exhausted. 'I can't do any more,' she said, her voice lifeless.

Bryce was balled up in a corner, rocking himself, sobbing. He'd broken.

Across from the half-open back door, the heavy door to the main room of the slaughterhouse was heaving, thudding, showing cracks. They'd be breaking through in a minute or so. The killers filled the room beyond the locked door behind them; and they waited outside to shoot them down.

'It's that woman from the party,' Aunt June said. 'And the man from the party. The two who were controlling people there. I saw them.' She said it matter-of-factly. 'Cornelius betrayed me. Lied to me. Trapped me here, where they'd find me. The Lord made him, of course.'

Joey and Rutherford were taking turns at the door, firing into the brush with Joey's rifle, darting back. Just before they'd been pinned down in here, Sunwalker had gone out to shut the front door behind the Higher. Maybe they'd got him.

'Where's that bastard Stetson,' Joey growled, firing, and pulling back as the return fire smacked into the door.

Someone yelped on the other side of the inner door. The round had gone through.

'Who's Cornelius?' Perry asked. His mouth was so dry it was difficult to talk. He was scared: he could taste brass.

Aunt June chuckled. Her voice was hoarse when she said, 'Maybe a hallucination, I don't know. But I took his advice. And here we are. I think the One Who Hungers wanted most of them trapped in there, turning on each other. So it could feed – and so it could snuff out the ones it wasn't in control of. It didn't want too many of them wandering about, calling attention to themselves. It wanted just a few of its Breeders to survive, to start all this again somewhere else. It set them outside here, to make sure we didn't get out.'

Perry glanced at her and shook his head. She was making no sense at all. Maybe she'd broken too.

There were three gunshots outside. But they didn't seem to come from the same place the others had come from. And they sounded like a shotgun.

They heard Stetson's voice. 'Hey! Come on out. We got them!'

Perry risked a look and saw Stetson and Sunwalker standing in the starlight, the brush boiling in shadow around them, two bodies facedown between them. Stetson had a pistol in his hand; he'd taken it from the body of the old man Perry had shot.

Perry exhaled windily in relief and stepped out into the night. Thirty feet away, Sunwalker was staring at Stetson. Accusingly. 'You? You didn't get anybody. I did the shooting, Stetson. You just stood there. You're acting kind of funny, too. Kind of different.'

'This thing'd make anybody act – '

'The door's busting!' Joey shouted. 'They're coming through!'

Sunwalker turned to look toward the slaughterhouse. Stetson raised the pistol and pointed it at Sunwalker.

Perry pointed the .22 and fired, twice, till the hammer fell on an empty chamber. Stetson staggered back. Sunwalker turned toward him and fired the shotgun. Stetson went spinning, and fell, his face shot away.

Perry ran to retrieve the gun, shouting at Sunwalker, 'I had to shoot him, he was going to shoot you!'

'Those things got to him,' Sunwalker said.

'I'm telling you they're coming through.' Joey's voice, cut off by a double gunshot. They'd shot Joey.

Perry grabbed the pistol and turned to run to the slaughterhouse. He pulled up short, staring. Aunt June was leaning on the outer wall, holding her head. Sobbing, Bryce was slamming the back door from the outside and, automatically, it locked.

He turned and ran, shouting incoherently, into the darkness.

'Where are the others?' Perry asked, walking up to Aunt June.

'Joey's dead. I think Lois ran off. Rutherford's inside.'

'You think? Goddammit, where is she?' He grabbed her shoulders and shook her. 'Where's Lois?'

Someone was pounding on the door from the inside, screaming, 'Let me out or I'm going to cut off your fucking hands and choke you with 'em!'

Aunt June pulled loose from him, looking as if she might collapse. 'I told you. I think Lois ran off. Like Bryce. Scared. They got her uncle.'

Lois had, in fact, gone out before June. June had followed, and then, dizzy from exhaustion, had slumped against the outer wall, covered her eyes. Hadn't seen Lois go back in.

Lois went back in. Not thinking, running, crying. She went back in because she saw the men who'd broken through the door grab her Uncle Marv.

She ran in and tried to pull Marv from the men who had him, and one of them let go of Marv and grabbed her instead, as a woman used a rusty tin-can lid to slash Marv's throat (*the bitch cut his throat! He was shaking, dying, they cut his* –) and then she heard the door slam behind her, she heard it lock, she felt the big man grab her from behind, his arm crooked around her neck as he pulled her inside the main room, into Bedlam, and she choked with a scream too large to let go as she realized: I'm locked in with them.

He was a big-bellied man in a grey, sweat-stained T-shirt, stinking with perspiration, his mouth round as it panted, his eyes round with lust, his cheeks flushed. He had his thick, sweaty arm locked around her neck, was pawing her with the other hand, thrusting doglike at her ass as she struggled like an animal in a net, hopeless, and the room wheeled around her, her impressions shaky, blurred, fragmented, as if taken by a palsied cameraman: knots of people struggling in and out of patches of light and shadow; shadows roiling like something alive, near the ceiling, tinting the lugubrious glow of the lanterns; Gray Pilots buzzing angrily past the hooks and railings, clinging to the harness; someone hanging a boy – one of the kids who'd attacked them with snakes – from a meat hook, lowering his jaw on to the hook like a fish, using a straight razor to gut him with a *whoosh* of blood as two others locked in combat spun past, as if dancing; the room a wall of sound, a demented wallpaper pattern of screaming, shouting, obscenity, whimpering, faces flashing by – almost a party feeling, a riotous party in hell.

One of the faces detached from a group and came at them, a lean, snarling man with a steel mallet in his hands, shrilling, 'Give me the woman, I want the woman!' and flashing the mallet down at the big man's head. The big man grabbed the other's mallet hand and let her go so he could claw at the lean man's face, and the two of them, wrestling furiously, tottered off into the melee.

She had fallen, she realized dazedly, was lying on the floor. Instinctively, she crawled toward the wall, to the nearest shelter: the meat-cutting table with its saw. She crept under the table and balled herself up there in the shadows, a pile of rotting meat shavings and bone dust between her back and the concrete wall cushioning her. Maybe they wouldn't see her here.

Lois tried not to look at what was going on out there.

But she was afraid not to look. Afraid that if she took her eyes off it, it would come in after her. She was tied to watching it with the irrational sense that watching it somehow protected her, kept it at bay.

So she looked out through a four-inch space between the metal body of the engine that ran the saw and the table's thick metal legs. At first it looked like a barroom brawl, or a riot raging out of control, several hundred of the Higher turned against one another, the pilots whirring above, crawling on the dead. But then she saw it for what it was . . . she saw . . .

A fountain of red spray. The red spurting from here, from there, but united by fields of telekinesis, the warring psychic fields projected by the pilots creating bubbles in the red spray, butting thunderheads of electro-magnetic force, their conflict shattering the spray into mist that was sculpted by the uncontrolled power of Mind, made to conform to the imagery crackling from the tortured minds of the pilots: images painted on the air in blood spray, airbrushed scarlet on nothing, given detail and secondary colors with bits of levitated bone and sinew and blue underflesh and hair and torn skin: a brief image of a woman's living head exuding toothy worms, as if Medusa's snakes had turned against her, dug into her skull, emerged from her eyes and mouth; a man with a human face on one side of his head, a gargoyle on the back, the two melding together, compressing fluidly to become one pathetic grotesquery, human inadequacy's hopeless struggle against moral dissolution; a hawk ripping a rabbit open; a rabbit devouring its own young; a fetus chewing its way out through a woman's pregnancy-swollen belly, its snaggly teeth flecked with its mother's shredded uterus; a dog reaching back to gnaw chunks of meat from its own side; Jesus Christ writhing on His nails as a pig with human hands and a giant insect's wings thrusts its snout into the wound on His side; flies, flies choking the mouths and noses of children dying in a Nazi execution pit; Nazis choking Jews and Israeli Jews hanging Nazis; a pope in full regalia strapped into an electric chair; a man's penis growing fantastically oversized till it thrust into its owner's mouth and smashed up into his brain so blood and cum squirted from the place his eyes had occupied; an old woman shaking in a nest of rattlesnakes and scorpions, her wheelchair changing shape to become a pair of steel-spoked jaws clamping her down; another sweet-faced old woman feeding on a pretty little girl's throat; a man with a cactus for a cock thrusting it into a delicate Victorian lady; a child's head lopped with the single stroke of a machete, the head spinning away to change shape, becoming rubbery, bloating, bursting open in the air to erupt a furious swarm of blood-sticky bees; leering demonic faces, vomiting happily, eyes wide with pleasure as bits of maggoty flesh gushed over their horny lips; a lamprey engorging on Marilyn Monroe's ripe bosom as her skirt blows up exposing her vagina which exudes thousand-dollar bills; the bills flow down to become the wings of vampiric moths which descend in a cloud on the singer Madonna, sucking her into a draggled bag of wizened flesh; the flesh falls away from her skeleton which embraces a nude fat lady, compressing her corpulence so tightly her skin rips and her suet-lumpy yellow fat squeezes out between the dead-white bones like dough, flows like human lava into the hardening shape of a soldier thrusting a bayonet into the belly of a soldier who thrusts another bayonet back into the first, both thrusting in, out, in and out, each thrusting wildly in the other but showing no pain, their faces imbecilically happy until they reach some kind of climax and explode into fragments which twist and re-form into children burning with napalm, running down a road sizzling and screaming and becoming a group of Nicaraguan children hit by anti-personnel shells fired by the Contras, the children torn limb from limb by the fléchettes and tiny razors so that their blood runs down an invisible screen and paints itself into the shape of a man stepping into his children's bedroom with a shotgun, blowing heads and headlines into the air . . .

And beneath this canopy of swimming shapes, writhing images, Lois glimpsed the people who were really there, people she'd known for years in Jasper: she saw Old Burt who ran the fishing and hunting-goods store, slashing at Charlie Myers with a hunting knife; Charlie swinging an ax that connected with Burt's head as Wendy's husband Evan, blind now but seeing with rage, straddled Mrs Garibaldi, banging her head on the floor: Mrs Garibaldi, who had taught Lois how to read in the first grade, and who had a small, broken-necked infant in her arms, busily crushing what remained of it; Buck Henson who'd dated Lois for a year was sodomizing the corpse of his sister Emmy as his brother Slim hung a woman alive from a meat hook . . . Dozens more, people up to their shins in bodies, a sewage of dismembered human bodies; parts that were never meant to mix were mixed; blood and shit uniting everything. The sewer of torn flesh below, the sewer of trapped spirit above: the Lord of Dark Corners overhead, feeding, rippling with excitement like a black silk canopy in a high wind.

All the time the pilots struggling, buzzing furiously, a backdrop of distilled and living rage using telekinetic hands to tear limbs from the dead and skin the living alive . . . their energies making a storm of the insides of the living and dying: blood and shit and fragments of bone raining, caking everything, flowing in a foamy red and brown surf under the meat cutter, carrying a sickening flotsam of entrails, a tongue, an eye, a pair of faces ripped whole from their skulls; of hair and bone ends and a lady's perfectly manicured red-nailed finger . . .

Long past vomiting, long past feeling, Lois saw it all, and knew murder and death as an environment, a storm, with rage the clouds and murder the lightning and death the driving red rain.

The rage, the screaming, the buzzing, the sounds of killing merged into one great black noise.

Her mind simply closed up shop.

Feeling as if his insides were made of broken crockery, Perry wandered listlessly back to the slaughterhouse. Aunt June was still slumped outside, hunkered down against the wall, hugging herself, her face pressed into her knees.

'Lois come back here?' Perry asked.

'No.'

'You okay?' Perry asked her.

She nodded into her knees. Then she shook her head. 'No, I'm not all right.'

He nodded.

Sunwalker was at the back door of the slaughterhouse, working on the latch with a tire iron, the shotgun ready in his free hand.

'Hey,' Perry said, walking up to him. 'You seen Lois?'

Sunwalker looked at him distractedly and shook his head. He looked back at his work. 'It's quiet in there now.'

Perry looked at the slaughterhouse. 'How long's it been quiet?'

'Ten, fifteen minutes.'

'You going in?'

'Yeah. To finish off whoever's left.' The lock popped open. The door swung outward a few inches.

'Watch it,' Aunt June said, without looking up. 'The pilots could fly out over your head, if there're any left.'

Blood flowed over the door stoop and discolored the ground. It kept coming for a while.

Looking at it, Perry felt nothing.

Sunwalker squinted at the blood, as if trying to bring it into focus. His mouth twitched. His voice raspy, he said, 'Close the door quick, after me.' He shook his head, took a deep breath, let it out, and stepped into the building, looking up. Perry shut the door after him.

A buzzing –

Perry opened his mouth to shout a warning. But then he heard the shotgun go off, and the buzzing ended, abruptly.

Perry waited outside. He had no desire to go in. The shotgun went off, again. Again. Again.

A charnel breeze rolled hot and sticky out of the building, carrying a smell that would have instantly curdled fresh cream, coming like the yawn of a dragon who's just fed on a small town. The smell made him gag, and he was glad. Glad he could feel that much.

Aunt June looked up, frowning. 'I don't know why I didn't think of it.'

Perry looked at her. 'What?'

'Lois might have got locked inside.'

Perry stared at her.

Inside the building, the shotgun went off again.

They were wretches, really. Lois saw that now. They'd been captivated by what they were, what their lives had made them. The dark spot in them had grown like botulism in badly kept food, and poisoned them.

The real horror of it, of course, was the recognition she'd felt, watching them tear each other apart. As if she remembered when she'd done things like this herself, in some dream.

And the real horror of it was that each of them seemed utterly convinced that they'd been violated in some way: she'd seen it in their faces, even in the height of the frenzy, their conviction that they were vindicated, perfectly right to splash their neighbour's brains with an ax, slice their mother's heart out with a kitchen knife. They were all of them certain they were doing what was just: redressing the injustices the world had stamped into their lives.

She thought this the way a machine ticker-tapes stock statistics, or a computer compiles the names of accident victims. Completely dispassionate. Staring at the Red Pond – which lapped around her buttocks, her thighs and feet, swirling bits of people and scraps of smashed Gray Pilots around her – she stared at it the way a TV camera stares, recording, knowing. Remembering the horror but not *feeling* it, now.

Feeling nothing at all.

Not even fear. She wasn't afraid of the thing crawling toward her, twenty feet away, or the man with the shotgun on the other side of the room. She knew the thing crawling toward her was one of Them, one of the corrupted ones. She thought that it might have been somebody she'd known once. It was hard to tell, because his features had been pretty much pulled away. His face was a mask of red and yellow ooze. One eye socket a collapsed welter of blood; the other showing the exposed orb of an eye, a large, glossy, lidless eye with a brown-black pupil, fixed on her, never blinking – it had nothing to blink with – and never shifting away from her as the thing, the once-man, crawled toward her through the human sludge, the literal gene pool, making stinking ripples as it pulled itself closer with its one arm and the three-fingered hand . . . the pilot in it perhaps wanting one more kill before it emerged . . . the one-arm crawler trailing its intestines as it came, pulling itself closer, with that one arm . . . the stump of the other waving a little as if it tried to use the missing arm. Then the good arm slapping down into the Red Pond, gripping the floor, pulling its body closer with excruciating effort, wheezing, blood bubbling through the exposed teeth, a bubble of phlegm forming there, popping . . . wheezing liquidly, pulling a little closer, almost in reach of her ankle . . .

It might die before it got to her, of course. But she didn't think so. She thought it would reach her and use those teeth on her. It was anyone's guess where on her it would begin to chew.

And she really didn't care.

The man with the shotgun killed another of the dying ones. The man hadn't seen her, or the one-armed thing; they were both behind the heap of bodies in front of the meat-saw table. The one-armed thing was crawling up to her, between the wall and the meat saw. She was under the meat saw. The man with the shotgun would find her.

The thing had her ankle in its three fingers. Fingers slimed with blood, shit, and phlegm. It pulled her closer to it, dragging her from her perch. She didn't resist. It didn't occur to her to go to it and get it over. She was indifferent to getting it over, or surviving it. She didn't want anything.

The one-arm made a bubbling moan and fastened its jaws on her thigh.

Then there was a shrill grating sound and some light in her face as the man with the shotgun, grunting, pulled the table away from them. Looked at them, looking sick. He raised the shotgun and pointed it at the thing at her ankle and pulled the trigger. There was a *boom* and the top of the thing's head disappeared.

Lois waited for the man to shoot her.

He pointed the shotgun at her – and then he fell down; someone had their arms around his waist, tackling him into the Red Pond. Ugly splash . . . cursing . . .

She heard a voice she knew was Perry's, and then tones she knew were arguing.

'Sorry I had to tackle you into the – the . . .' Perry began.

'Forget it,' Sunwalker snapped. 'I just hope for your sake you're right about that girl.' He glowered at her. He was sticky brown, head to toe, with blood. Perry had it on him mostly from the waist down.

'She isn't changed,' Aunt June said. 'Except she's had a breakdown of some kind. She doesn't behave the way they do, even when they're being careful.'

They were standing by the land rover, talking. Lois was sitting in the back of the land rover, smiling vacantly. She was almost mummified in blood.

'We're going to have to get her a gamma globulin shot,' Aunt June said. 'Against hepatitis.'

Perry heard a whoosh and turned to look at the slaughterhouse. Flame bellydanced in the windows. The men that Sunwalker had rounded up from the reservation were burning the slaughterhouse. 'Took a lot of gasoline,' Sunwalker said. 'It won't burn easy.'

'You sure you didn't see anything else inside?' Aunt June asked him.

'I'm sure,' he said. 'No black clouds, no . . . no nothing but dead people, dead "bugs." A few half dead.' He looked at her. 'You think we got them all?'

'They all seemed compulsively drawn. Like sharks or piranha,' she said tonelessly, looking at the burning slaughterhouse. 'I think so. They could have broken out, of course, if they'd concerted their efforts on the door. But they can't cooperate, they reek suspicion. And there was some kind of . . . something that caught them up in it. Carried them away. The rage was infectious. They forgot about escaping, when it was all around them like that. So yeah. I think so.'

'What about Dawson's pilot?' Perry said.

'I went in the freezer,' Sunwalker said, with some satisfaction. 'I got the bastard.'

Perry bent to look in the open back door of the land rover. He smiled experimentally at Lois. 'Hey, Lois,' he said softly. No response. Not even a flicker. She gazed vacantly into nowhere.

'It's going to be a while before she responds,' Aunt June said. She looked half dead, numbed herself. The way Perry felt inside. 'We're going to get into the jeep and drive to Portland and take her to a motel and clean her up. Then we'll take her to a hospital for a shot. And then we go to the airport. And we get as far away as we can.'

'I wonder,' Sunwalker said, walking toward the slaughterhouse, 'if we got all of them.'

Epilogue

'There was really no need for you to come, Sandestin,' Aunt June said.

The sunlight poured through the big picture window above the blue dyed-leather couch. No one sat on the couch. Aunt June sat in her rocker, looking out the window at the brown, suburban hills of La Mesa, the pale blue San Diego sky. Sandestin stood near the front door. No one had asked him to sit. He was dressed in a steel-blue suit with a turquoise shirt, matching silk tie. He stood there awkwardly, hands in his pockets, chewing his lower lip and looking to Perry for support.

Perry shrugged. He was sitting in the easy chair between the couch and Aunt June. Behind him on the wall was her collection of jade figurines. 'She's right,' he said. 'The authorities passed the whole thing off as a rabies epidemic. And mass hysteria. We decided not to take a chance on saving one of them to show to people. We didn't want any of them to survive, in case they escaped. Which means we had no proof and no one believes us. So why does Axis bother to threaten us?'

'I don't know,' Sandestin said. His voice and expression told them he felt helpless, that he was making this visit under duress and wanted them to know it. 'I guess they're afraid if you're persistent, the Axis connection will come out.'

'If I thought I could prove their connection, I would,' Aunt June said. She smoothed out a wrinkle in her housedress and then pushed a hair back into place. Her hair had thinned, Perry noticed. Her face was more sunken. She was so much older now, just four months after.

'It's been four months,' Perry pointed out, 'and Axis hasn't come up. The whole thing's been dropped. Everyone just moved away from Jasper; the town was sort of ashamed.' He made a dismissive gesture with his hand. 'Tell them to forget it. Tell the cold-blooded jack boots at Axis if they weren't such assholes they wouldn't get caught up in this kind of shit.'

'I'd better not tell them that,' Sandestin said, nervously jingling the change in his pocket. 'You don't want them mad at you. Believe me. I'm lucky to be alive. Lucky they didn't . . .' He let it trail off. 'It's because my dad's a big shot in the company, if you want to know. That's probably the only reason they didn't, you know . . .'

'Fuck 'em,' Perry said savagely. Feeling the anger boil up in him again.

'Perry,' Aunt June said, 'take your medication.'

'I did already. Hey, Sandestin, I thought you were going to have nothing to do with Axis after . . .'

Sandestin winced. 'I was scared to run off. You don't know them.'

'Fucking glad I don't.'

'How's the girl?' Sandestin asked.

'Lois? She's . . . okay. She started talking last month. Aunt June's been working with her.'

Perry looked at the door to the hall. Just down the hall was the bedroom where Lois was taking her nap. The medication made her sleepy in the afternoon.

'Well, if you folks are agreed,' Sandestin began.

Perry looked sharply at him. 'Get the fuck out.'

'Perry. Cool off,' Aunt June said.

Sandestin muttered something Perry couldn't make out

and turned, opened the front door, went through, closed it behind him.

Perry got up and watched through the window as Sandestin went out to the white limo. He got in and sat there a moment, spoke to someone Perry couldn't see. Then the limo drove away.

Perry turned and went to the hall door.

'Don't wake her up, Perry,' Aunt June said. Her eyes shut now.

'I won't.'

He went through the door and down the hall, softly opened the bedroom door. The overhead light and both table lamps were on. She always slept with the lights on.

Aunt June had done the same thing, for a while. Because of the Lord of Dark Corners. But she'd made herself get used to darkness again.

No matter how brightly lit the room was, Aunt June said, there was always a dark place in it somewhere. It's useless to try to escape from the One Who Hungers, that way. You have to go into the places in your brain you've never visited before, and check the locks on the doors you'll find there. Make sure they're all locked . . .

Lois was lying on her side, on the nearer of the twin beds, in her nightgown; she was on top of the covers, snoring softly. He sat down on the other bed and looked at her. He wanted to touch her hip. Just touch it.

But if he touched her, she'd wake instantly, and she'd be angry. She wouldn't let anyone touch her yet. They'd moved in with Aunt June so they could work out what had happened. All of them had to work it out; Aunt June too. Reach some kind of reconciliation with it. Lois and Perry slept in this room together. But they didn't make love. They didn't touch at all . . .

Aunt June was pretty certain that would pass. Perry

wondered, though, if Lois would ever let him touch her. A few days ago Lois had told him she wished she didn't have to see anyone who was out there that day, ever. But at the same time, she was afraid to be around people who didn't understand, who didn't *know*. So she stayed.

She'll warm up to me, Perry told himself. None of us are thawed yet, really.

Perry thought about Sandestin. God damn, the little prig made him angry. He'd like to strangle him with his pretty silk tie. Tie him up in the trunk of that limo and run it off a –

He wrenched his thoughts from those things. The carnage that haunted him. The rage that came sometimes . . .

He hadn't been stung, of course. But he'd been exposed to them a lot. He wasn't like other people. Aunt June thought he was a Sub-B3, like Tetty. And the exposure might've awakened the gene in him.

Or maybe it was all psychological. Maybe he was just imagining he could feel the pilot growing in him.

But if it *was* a pilot . . .

He tried to control himself. He tried to think positively about people. He tried to look for constructive options so he didn't get frustrated and angry and self-centered. Hoping he could keep the thing from growing much.

But just in case, there was the gun he kept in the shoe box under his bed. The gun had one bullet in it.

He looked at Lois. She was peacefully asleep. Utterly vulnerable. He hoped he'd know, when the time came, who to use the bullet on.